The Beauty Shop

Suzy Henderson

Cover design by JD Smith Design

www.suzyhendersonauthor.com

ISBN 978-0-9956456-0-8

This book is dedicated to my beloved grandmother, Joan Charlton, and to everyone else who belonged to that extraordinary generation who, without hesitation, volunteered to 'do their bit' for King and country back in 1939. Lest we forget.

For Alan, who always encouraged my writing and longed to read the book, but sadly left us before he could. The story is also for you, and I know the words will have reached you by now. (1934-2016)

1

Ward III, Queen Victoria Hospital, East Grinstead, November 1942

The boy lay swathed in bandages that masked third-degree burns to the face, neck, chest, arms, and legs; the aftermath of a skirmish with the Luftwaffe. It was a miracle he'd been able to bail out of his flaming Spitfire and pull the cord on his parachute, with hands of molten wax, skin that hung in shards like ripped silk, and fingers melded together by the heat of the furnace. Archibald McIndoe inhaled as he hovered in the doorway of the side room and wrinkled his nose against the cloying stench of charred flesh that assaulted his nostrils. It was a nauseating odour he was used to and usually ignored, but tonight was different. Tonight it was especially malodorous and reached into the back of his throat, and he cupped his nose with his hand as he tried not to gag.

He sauntered out into the ward. Music flowed from the gramophone further down, and the upbeat, familiar Glenn Miller sound swung out, a delightful blend of saxophones, trumpets, and strings. 'American Patrol.' The volume was unusually low; he sensed that was purposefully done out of respect and his heart contracted. A haze of stale cigarette smoke and the sweet aroma of beer blended in the air to mask any clinical odours or otherwise. With the blackout curtains drawn, the bedside lighting cast a subdued glow around the ward. He stopped in front of the coke stove and held his hands in the wave of heat that streamed from the door. They were still numb from the frosty evening air, even though he had been back inside for a while.

He glanced around. The place looked more like a barracks than a hospital. One airman lay stretched out on top of his bed, reading a newspaper, a smouldering cigarette resting between the first two fingers of his right hand. He glanced up.

'Evening, Maestro.' The voice was flat.

Archie nodded a greeting. Three others sat huddled around the table in the middle of the ward, playing cards. Suddenly, an airman in RAF blues sprang up from his chair and grabbed the blonde VAD nurse with the ruby lips and twirled her around, dancing to the tune, which promptly changed to a slower number. Then he drew her close as they waltzed to notes that quivered in the air. He glanced at Archie and grinned. 'Hello, Maestro. Fancy a beer?'

'No thanks, Dickie, not tonight.'

His upturned mouth sagged into a straight line, and he nodded, his hand slipping from the nurse's waist as he moved away – thirty seconds of frivolity anaesthetised by the gathering dark clouds. As Archie ambled back towards the side room, the boys gazed at him with sombre faces, their eyes glazed. Amidst the clink of beer glasses, the chain-smoking, and the banter, they all knew.

Back in the side room, another sound filtered in, a desperate, chilling rasp, and the hairs at the nape of Archie's neck prickled. He sighed. He had told the boy exactly what he said to all of them when they first arrived. 'Don't worry. We'll fix you up.' His stomach sank. He'd tried his best, truly he had.

He strode over to the bed. David's breathing had changed since this morning. He was in the period of transition; the final phase. Archie swallowed. *Dear God, why had it come to this?* David lay quite still, rattling breaths cutting through the hush, a thatch of golden blond hair just visible above his bandages. *Did he have a girl and did she ever thread her fingers through his hair?* It was a random thought, plucked from nowhere, silly really, but then this whole event was bizarre and surreal. It shouldn't be happening – just like this bloody war. The words of his cousin Harold Gillies sprung into his mind: *This war will bring injuries never seen before.* Archie nodded. 'Right again, as usual,' he muttered.

Why couldn't he have saved him? Yes, the boy had severe injuries, albeit injuries he *could* have survived. However, the infection that had taken a serious hold several days ago had changed the course of David's life, bending its flow in another direction. Sepsis had spread, his organs were failing, and there was nothing to be done. Nothing at all, except sit here and wait. The boy sucked in breaths through an open mouth. Archie glanced around and spotted the kidney dish on the bedside table with a mouth swab and water. He gently dabbed David's dry lips and tongue. At least he could do that.

Archie was not familiar with death. Most of the time, his patients lived, so it was a dreadful blow when death came calling. This boy had suffered enough, and now in a cruel twist, he would die after all, and he'd put up such a splendid fight. Archie heard Richard Hillary's words loud and clear as if the young fighter pilot were standing next to him: *Tell me, Archie. Does a chap ever sense that death is waiting?*

'I don't know,' Archie murmured. 'But *I* sense it.' He sank down on the chair next to the bed and glanced at his watch. Eleven o'clock. He pinched the bridge of his nose and closed his eyes, stifling a yawn as fatigue closed around him like a warm, fuzzy blanket. He'd spent twelve hours in surgery and longed to return home, but he would wait. The boy was an American with the RAF; a stranger on foreign soil. No one should be alone at the end.

Sister Jamieson bustled into the room carrying a steaming, white enamel mug, her rubber-soled shoes squelching across the linoleum floor. 'I saw you come in, and I thought you might like a cup of tea,' she said in a hushed tone.

'Thanks.' He was in need of something a little stronger, in all honesty, but that would have to wait. He took a sip. At least it was warm.

'I can ask one of the nurses to sit with him if you need to go. There's no telling how long it will be.' Her thin, pale lips flickered to form a faint compassionate smile, revealing a dimple on her left cheek he'd never noticed before, although the woman rarely ever smiled.

'It's all right. I'll stay a while. Besides, there's no one to rush home for.' Home was but a mere shell now that his wife and daughters were in America, but at least they were safe, thank God.

'Such bad luck he came down behind enemy lines. If only they could have repatriated him sooner.'

'Yes, well I suppose he's lucky they sent him back at all.' Archie sipped the tea and Sister Jamieson retreated. He liked to think that even German doctors would obey the

Hippocratic Oath and do their best for their patients. *The enemy.* His elder brother's face slipped into his mind. Jack had been captured in Crete in 1941 and was now in a camp somewhere in Germany. Two birthdays spent in captivity. Archie prayed he was well and wondered if he'd received the Red Cross parcel as yet. Why in heaven had Jack joined up? He'd even had to lie about his age, given that he was forty-one at the time. Archie shook his head. Jack had inherited Mother's artistic ability and had studied art, but he'd gone on to run the family printing business after Father passed away. It was as if war had sought him out, with the lure of one final fling.

The music from the ward suddenly ceased, and a hush descended. Out in the corridor, the sluice door protested as it swung shut with its usual creaky groan and water gushed as someone turned on a tap. The night nurse rattled past the door with a tray of steaming mugs, and he caught the comforting aroma of malt as it drifted in the air on a ribbon of steam. He glanced at the rise and fall of David's chest as the boy sucked in shallow breaths, followed by the release of excruciating rasps that snarled over his lips.

He placed the cup down on the table and sat back, his eyes closing as thoughts hurtled around in his head. David was nineteen years old. Such a waste of a young life. Not even old enough to vote or drink alcohol in his own country – yet old enough to die for it. Archie sighed. He usually found the late nights to be a tranquil haven as the hospital's beating heart slowed, but tonight there was no comfort to be found here amidst the rattling gasps and the persistent frustration burrowing deep into his soul. Dear God, he was trying to rehabilitate these boys, not stand back as they slipped away. He pursed his lips and swallowed, balling his hands into fists, his nails digging sharply into his palms. Failure cut deep and he ruminated over the futility of war. A chill crept in through the half-open door and clung to his shoulders.

He dragged his glasses off and rubbed his weary eyes, then shuffled his chair closer to the bed. David's chest rose and fell with a rattle and a gurgle of breath. Archie reached out and took the boy's bandaged hand in his. 'It's all right, David. It's Archie here. Don't worry, my boy.' The hearing was always the last to go.

David's laboured breaths alternated between raspy and quiet as the hours ticked away, and Archie lost all sense of time as he waited in the dimness of night. Finally, the boy released a gentle hiss of breath, like a retreating tidal wave shushed back to the sea. Archie sat still, partially relieved, partially stunned, and then he leaned forward and pressed his fingertips to David's neck, locating the carotid artery. He reached for the stethoscope and listened to David's heart. Nothing. Already his skin was draining to a sallow yellow in the wake of the body's shutdown, rapidly cooling.

Ten past two. Archie placed his hand gently on the boy's chest. 'Rest now, my boy, and God bless you.' His eyes suddenly welled up, and he took a deep breath as he dragged the cold, crisp sheet up over David's head, then exhaled some of the tension away. At least it had been a peaceful end.

In a matter of days, a telegram would arrive at David's home, and the boy's parents would be distraught. Archie would write to them and assure them he'd sat with their son up until the end. It was vital they knew their son had not been alone. It was important to know *something*, no matter how small. *Damn this bloody war.*

He hovered in the doorway for a moment before closing it, grasping the handle while he stood quietly in the shadows, surveying the ward. These boys were lucky to have a second chance, although not many of them felt that way in the beginning. It's not easy to count your blessings when you've had your entire face burned away or lost the use of your hands. Archie had seen outcasts and what had become of them, and he was determined that was not going to happen to these boys.

He glanced at the door once more as sadness wrapped itself around his chest and squeezed, and he wrenched his grip from the handle. The boy should have lived – could have, perhaps, if he'd been brought here sooner. If. Always an if.

Archie strolled along London's Bond Street beneath the cover of black, dense clouds, his breath escaping before him as white vapour. He pulled his coat tighter around him, glad of the scarf he had wrapped around his neck as the icy air nipped at his cheeks. His hands tingled, and numbness crept into his aching fingers. He thrust them into his pockets. The thick, acrid smell of smoke hung all around, smouldering from some bomb site after last night's raid, lining his nostrils. London still breathed as she always did and retained an air of regal elegance as ladies picked their way through rubble-strewn streets, well-dressed in heels with coiffed hair and made-up faces, smiles painted on to boost morale, heads held high, defiant.

He crossed the road and as he glanced left, a familiar face emerged from among the bustling crowd, his air-force blue prominent within a wave of khaki. Richard Hillary, one of his first patients from the Battle of Britain. Archie grinned and stood stock-still as he waited to catch his eye.

'Richard, of all the people to run into, it had to be you.' Archie laughed and shook his hand, Richard's brown leather glove ice-cold in his palm, a sheen of blond hair visible at the side of his blue cap. 'You're meant to be up in Scotland.'

'A spot of leave, Archie. How about you?'

'Oh, just killing time before I head back to the ward. I had some business here this morning. How about a drink?' Archie clapped him on the back and led the way. The lad was rather subdued, and there was no bravado – something he'd used as a shield on the ward. It was as if his spark had finally waned.

The mood in the Embassy Club was uplifting as swing music flowed out, and people danced and laughed. The stifling air inside blended with stale smoke and beer. Archie ordered drinks, and they found seats at a table near the door. Richard opened his silver cigarette case and offered it to Archie. He plucked one and leaned in for a light, flicking a gaze at Richard's eyes. They were dull and bloodshot as if he had not slept properly in days. 'Been working you hard up there?'

Richard drew on his cigarette and exhaled a white plume of smoke. 'You know how it is. These Blenheims aren't Spits and night-flying is tougher than I'd imagined.' He reached out to grab his glass, and his hand trembled. 'My left eye is troubling me now as well, which makes matters worse.' He gulped a mouthful of whisky.

Archie honed his gaze on the lad's eye, where scar tissue tightened and contracted. Clearly, the issue was now urgent.

'When I'm up there, I can't see properly.' Richard pointed skyward with his gloved index finger. 'How the bloody hell do they think I'm going to be able to bomb accurately like this?'

A boisterous group barged in, laughing and shouting, and Richard jumped. Archie downed his whisky in one fiery gulp. 'You'll have to tell the MO. Perhaps he can put you on sick leave until we get you sorted out. I'll take a look at it and get you booked in for surgery.' An extra spot of leave would be beneficial too, by the look of him.

'It's not as simple as that.' Richard downed the last of his whisky and sighed. 'Besides, I'm not crying off at the first sign of trouble.' He shifted his gaze to the couples dancing, a faraway look in his eyes.

And there it was. That underlying current that flowed through all these boys, crackling each time they wavered to remind them of their duty; to remind them they were in the spotlight. Well, to hell with expectations. What good is that when you're dead? The boy was asking for help and by the look of him, he was desperate.

'It's the night-flying, you see. Daylight would be easier. To be honest, I'm not sure I can carry on for much longer.' Richard's tone was ominous, his gaze intense and screaming. He ran his tongue over his lips, then cast a nervous smile.

Archie drew on his cigarette as an uneasy feeling settled within him. Richard had hoped to return to flying Spitfires but had instead been assigned to a squadron in Scotland, flying Blenheims, a light bomber aircraft. Archie couldn't fathom the RAF mentality that had decided the boy was fit to fly bombers.

'I'll write to your MO, let him know I've seen you, and that I expect you back here as soon as possible for further surgery.'

As they parted company, Richard shook Archie's hand, grasping it firmly. 'Thanks for everything, Archie. You've been a marvel. Take care of yourself.' The corners of his mouth twitched to form a sombre smile.

Archie's chest tightened as he watched him walk away, his blue-grey form melting into the ripple of people. He wished that Richard had contacted him sooner rather than struggling on.

The lead-grey sky deepened as dusk approached and the first spots of rain began to fall, speckling the pavement as a veil of mist stole in from the east and draped over London. A faint rumble filtered in and he turned his face towards the sky as a dark shape neared from the east. It was an American bomber, with a white star prominent on the fuselage. They were becoming a familiar sight now the Americans had arrived. The cruciform shape slipped overhead and droned into the distance.

Archie shivered and drew his scarf up closer to his chin. Flying aircraft was dangerous – they were so high risk – but bombers? He shook his head as he hurried back to his car before the light faded.

2

Saint-Nazaire, November, 1942

What do ten men sound like when they're burning?
Nothing, unless you listen in on the group radio. That's
when you hear it, etched into their yells and cries. Terror.

Lieutenant John 'Mac' Mackenzie glanced at the B-17 Flying Fortress on his port side. That had been Bill's slot a couple of weeks back, waving Mac a thumbs up from the co-pilot's window. Seconds later, flames had leapt from the engines, danced across the wings, licked the cockpit and engulfed the fuselage. A whole Fort powdered. Their luck ran out when that Focke-Wulf sneaked in from out of the sun's glare, rolled over and came in head-on, gun ports blinking silver flashes. Then, in an instant, a bright glow and a bloody wound opened as chunks of flaming, twisted metal and tears of flame fell from the sky along with men blown to bits, caught in the slipstream.

Bill had lost his cross and chain that morning before take-off. He'd always worn it when flying missions. Mac's gloved fingers reached for the St. Christopher around his neck. *There.* He sucked in a breath, exhaling slowly into his mask. The muffled thunderous roar of the four Cyclone engines cut in, the background thrum of four propellers spinning, constant and reassuring. He glanced again at the B-17 on his left. A rookie crew had that slot today. He didn't know their names. He didn't want to. They had taken off from Bassingbourn at dawn, soaring into a veil of cumulus. Mist draped across the Channel, but above the cloud at twenty thousand feet, the blood-orange sun peeked over the horizon, bleeding hues of amber into a cornflower sky. *Sure is beautiful,* Mac thought. As they approached the French coast at Longues-sur-Mer, the blue void gave way to brown-black puffs of smoke which hung in the air like shrouds. He pulled the oxygen mask off his face for a few seconds and embraced the rush of the cockpit's icy chill over his nose and mouth. He wondered if he'd ever adjust to the stench of rubber as he wiped beads of sweat from his brow. The mission, their tenth, bombing the U-boat pens at Saint-Nazaire, was hotting up fast. 'Looks like they're throwing everything they've got at us today.' Mac glanced at his co-pilot, Dennis Wilson.

'Can't see a darn thing down there. It's all closed in,' Wilson said as he gazed out of the side window.

A flash of red caught Mac's eye and their B-17, the *Texas Rose*, shook as a hail of flak peppered the fuselage. That was just the warm-up. They'd get the full greeting soon enough. He wrestled with the control wheel as he struggled to stay in formation, keeping his eyes focused on the bomber in front. He rapidly sucked in oxygen, and his pulse pounded as the *Texas Rose* bobbed around like a sailboat on a rough sea, but he held her tight, maintaining their place in the formation. 'Pilot to crew. Keep sharp out there and remember to check your masks for ice. Spit freezes.' Anoxia was a silent killer and up here at twenty-seven thousand feet, oxygen was the crew's lifeline.

As they neared Saint-Nazaire, the brown-black puffs sprung up once more.

'Pilot to navigator. How long to the IP?' Mac pictured William Stewart, hunched over his desk down in the nose behind the bombardier, plotting their course.

'Navigator to pilot. Bomb run in five minutes.'

'Bogey, nine o'clock!' Bud, the waist gunner, yelled into the interphone.

The staccato sound of machine-gun fire from Tex, the flight engineer in the top turret, drilled through the cockpit. The flash of a black swastika flicked past their port side, and Mac's stomach lurched as the Messerschmitt scythed through the group.

'Tail, you got him?' Bud's voice, high with excitement.

'I got him.' Birdie's smooth, laid-back tone.

More machine-gun fire arced across the sky and with a flash of yellow and silver-grey, the Messerschmitt peeled away swift as a minnow, diving through the formation. As they approached the target, a blend of hazy yellow, brown and black smoke stretched out across the sky. Anti-aircraft shells exploded all around, some of it mighty close with a glow of orange. Red flak.

'Here comes the coffin run.' Wilson eased back on the throttles as they approached the bomb run, and the engines slowed in response. 'Flak bursts ahead, heavy.'

'Yeah, it's flak city all right.' Mac gripped onto the control wheel. The rookie pilot on his port side drifted a little too close for comfort and was bobbing all over the place, probably riding through prop wash. 'Get on the ball, rookie. You've got to stay in there.' He gestured to the co-pilot peering back at him and got the thumbs up. Within a minute, the rookies had hauled their Fortress into line and Mac puffed out a breath.

'Bombardier to pilot – bomb bay doors open,' Danny drawled.

Mac switched on the autopilot. 'She's all yours, Danny.' Five minutes of flying straight and slow to the target. Easy meat. But as Mac leaned back slightly, flexing his gloved fingers, he noticed a flash of red from the side of the *Texas Rose*. From the cockpit, he had a bird's-eye view as one of the B-17s in formation juddered and bucked as flak rained down. He crossed his chest.

'They got one.' Bud's voice. 'Come on guys, jump.'

As the stricken ship spiralled towards the ground, Mac glimpsed white silk billowing between shrouds of black. He waited, breath paused, craning his neck to see as one chute after another blossomed into uncertainty. 'Six,' he murmured. He didn't have time to dwell as there was a sudden flash followed by the sound of hailstones peppering the *Texas Rose*.

'What the hell was that?' Beside him, Wilson spun around, looking frantically at the instruments on the control panel.

Mac glanced at the wings. Both intact, all four props spinning, not smoking. He peered at the formation below and the breath caught in his throat.

'Christ, a fighter just flew into Jackson's ship. It's a goddamn fireball!' Wilson stared, his eyes wide.

Mac shook his head as he glanced at the space where Jackson's B-17 had been; flaming chunks of aircraft and debris fell from the sky. Men plummeted towards the ground, helpless, limbs flailing as they tumbled. His stomach tightened, and his breaths became rapid and shallow as the dead weight of his flak suit bore down on his shoulders. He rubbed the back of his neck.

'They weren't wearing chutes.' Wilson shook his head, and his eyes glazed over.

'Pilot to crew. Make sure you've got your chutes on.' Jesus. There was nothing they could do for them, and he had to block it out. As the group tightened up, Mac kept a close watch as Hutchinson sidled his B-17 across to fill the gap below. 'The Colonel always said, keep 'em tucked in tight and you'll come home,' Mac muttered. The rookie co-pilot on his left put his hand up and Mac gestured with a nod. They were doing all right, so far.

'Here they come again!' Tex bellowed into the interphone. 'Fighter, six o'clock!'

The guns opened up and short bursts of machine-gun fire hailed from all around the ship. The pungent waft of burned cordite drifted into the cockpit while the *Texas Rose* trembled from the recoil of the machine guns.

A flash of silver-grey and a swastika streaked by Mac's window and dived beneath the belly of the ship in front. As the *Texas Rose* flew on, flak pounded her aluminium body. A few pieces pierced her skin and from inside, it sounded like a hail of spanners was showering the ship. She lurched, the right wing bucked, and black smoke belched out from an engine. *Christ, what now?* 'Number three's smoking.' Mac checked the engine dials. 'Cut the fuel. Feather the prop. Shut it down,' he ordered.

Wilson pulled the mixture lever back and hit the fire extinguisher button.

'Pilot to crew. Check in.' The fighters had fled, but reinforcements would be buzzing around them soon enough, and maybe they'd be the prime target. Mac's heart pounded in his chest as he suddenly longed for home.

'Radio operator checking in,' Virg said over the interphone. 'Are we on fire?'

'No, we're not on fire.' Mac gritted his teeth.

'Tail gunner checking in. Smoke means fire. I can't see what's happening back here.'

'There's no goddamn fire.' Mac flicked a gaze at Wilson. 'What the hell's going on back there?'

Angry voices filtered through the interphone, one of them Bud's. Mac glanced out at the dead engine; the spinning disc of a prop now feathered into a still, upright Y, a trail of pencil-lead smoke streaming behind them. *Swell. Might as well be towing a stars and stripes banner.*

'Christ! That almost took my fucking head off.' Bud's voice.

'It wouldn't have made much difference if it had.' Irv's voice.

'Say that again and I'll knock yours clean off!'

'Pilot to waist. Cut the crap, guys – that's an order. You know the rules for using the interphone.'

'There's a hole the size of a football in the waist, but nobody's hurt,' Bud said.

Mac tried to quell the irritation rising inside him. *Fighting like kids when they ought to be pulling together.* Through a break in the undercast, he glimpsed a streak of red eclipsed by billowing plumes of smoke, which shrouded the harbour town and obscured the mouth of the Loire River and the submarine base. The B-17s in the lead group had just released their bombs. Mac recalled their last visit, two weeks ago. He'd flown in the high formation, similar altitude, but the low formation flew in at ten thousand feet. Anti-aircraft gunners had a field day with those boys. Three flamers and twenty-three more had limped home on a wing and a prayer.

As they neared the target, the familiar tendrils of doubt that gnawed away at him at this point during a mission twisted around him and squeezed. Most of the guys laughed it off once the bourbon got flowing. How did Carleton put it the other day? 'Who gives a shit? They're all Nazis anyway, so it's a few less to worry about.' *But they're people, women, and children*, Mac thought.

'Pilot to bombardier. How's that target looking, Danny?' Hunched over the Norden bombsight like a priest at an altar, Danny's hand would be poised on the bomb release trigger, waiting. Mac sucked in a breath.

'Almost there,' Danny drawled. 'Can't see much through this smoke and cloud.'

Gripped by a familiar sickly feeling, Mac couldn't shake the image of the people caught up in the midst of this hell. He wasn't releasing the bombs, but he *was* flying the ship, and somehow this war made less sense with every mission he flew. How the hell was he even alive? The clock was ticking louder than ever before.

'I see it. Bombs gone.' Danny's words rang out. 'Bomb bay doors closing. Pilot, she's all yours.'

Mac felt the *Texas Rose* lift, free at last. He switched off the autopilot and applied more throttle to increase their speed. It was too early for relief, but he sensed it flowing through the ship like an undercurrent. Teeth gritted in determination, he banked the *Texas Rose* in a sweeping turn out over the Atlantic Ocean and back around to the land. He flicked a gaze at the water where sunlight splintered on crested waves, sparkling like diamonds. As he pointed her nose towards the line of blue up ahead, a sudden flash on their port side caught his eye.

'They got *Smokin' Sue*,' Wilson yelled as he watched the stricken Fortress. 'Poor bastards.'

Smokin' Sue took another hit, and Mac watched as a large hole blossomed in the wing and flames erupted, lashing the airframe. She hovered for a moment as if suspended in the air. Then, with a graceful, slow half-roll, she flipped onto her back and fell away towards the icy waters of the Atlantic. Mac forced himself to focus as his heart raced. With one engine down, the last thing they needed was to fall behind the group. *Just hold on, please God*, he prayed. In an instant, he pictured his father and heard his calm words. *Keep her steady. You could fly her blindfolded.* Mac gritted his teeth, took a deep breath and exhaled slowly, as he pictured England, his heart easing to a steady beat.

'Jump. Come on, you guys, get outta there.' Wilson crossed his chest, his eyes wide. 'Hell, why don't they jump?'

'The centrifugal force is too great. They'll be pinned against the side.' There was no getting out of a tight spin like that. Mac gripped the control wheel tight, but in his mind, he pictured the base. Ten beds stripped, made ready for a new crew. He forced himself to concentrate – there was no room for errors on the home run, and he steeled himself as they ploughed through the blue, slipping through all the lost souls.

As they headed north to the Channel, a surge of adrenaline flooded his veins. 'Pilot to crew. Keep a look out for Jerry – he's just waiting, so we'd better be ready.' He gazed around at the Flying Fortresses that flecked the sky. An armada winging its way home to England, except for three lost ships and thirty men. His eyes flicked over the dials on the instrument panel. The oil pressure was holding. A lone Fortress was easy prey.

At twenty-one thousand feet the sky was dotted with cumulus clouds stacked up like cotton wool balls. As they flew over Loudeac, more flak spotted the sky, but it was light and didn't seem able to reach them. Mac cast his eye over the fuel gauges. Halfway home – so close.

Then, what began as a tiny, dark smudge on the horizon, multiplied and swelled into several larger specks, darting across the void like a pack of wolves. 'Here they come again.' Mac stared, transfixed, as the wolves separated up ahead, veering off left and right – flashes of yellow noses and black crosses on silver-grey. 'Bandits, twelve o'clock high. Don't fire until they're in range.' He clutched at breaths, and the reek of rubber clung to his throat and nostrils. They had to make it. He had nine crew to fly home, and he was damned if he was going to fail. He focused and offered up a silent prayer to God.

'Man, the sky's swarming with those bastards. I'm gonna get one if it kills me.' Bud's voice, edged with determination.

'Yeah? You keep telling yourself that,' Irv said.

A pair of Messerschmitt Bf 109s targeted a Fortress head-on, peppering it with cannon fire before moving on to the *Texas Rose*. Above the thrum of the engines and machine-gun fire, a terror-filled scream howled in Mac's ear.

'Jesus, I'm hit!'

'Waist to pilot, Bud's hurt. Send someone back here with the medical kit.' Irv paused. 'Hang in there, buddy.'

'Okay, Irv, man your gun. Pilot to bombardier. Waist gunner's hit. Get back there and help him.' *Shit. That's all we need.*

'Tail to waist. Fighter, six o'clock, coming around.'

'I got him, Birdie. Come on, closer, closer,' Irv said in a sing-song voice.

Mac pictured him, poised with his gun, waiting for the precise moment before spitting orange tracer fire into the belly of the enemy. As the fighter soared past their starboard side, Mac watched as the skilled hunter turned and headed back, weaving in and out of the bombers behind them.

'Bombardier to pilot.'

'Go ahead, Danny.'

'Bud's hit in the leg, but he's okay. He's damn lucky it missed the artery. I've bandaged him up and given him morphine.'

'Okay. Thanks, Danny.' Mac heaved a sigh of relief. It could have been so much worse. He pictured Bud sprawled out there in the waist with his rosary in his hand, praying. He carried it on every mission, but then they all carried something they treasured. Some of the guys had several lucky charms from a favourite jumper to a teddy or their bible – armour-plated, of course, and kept in your breast pocket just in case. He glanced across at the rookies. They were doing okay. He blew out a breath.

The rhythmic staccato of machine-gun fire punctuated the constant roar of the engines, and gunners on the surrounding ships spat tracer fire across the sky at a pair of marauding Messerschmitts. The fighters soon peeled away, heading off into the blue. 'I think the wolves are low on fuel, boys.' Mac blew out a breath.

'About time. Let's hope that's the last,' Wilson said.

'Waist to pilot.' Irv's voice.

'Pilot here. How's Bud doing?'

'He's okay. Are we gonna make it home?'

'Just hang in there. We'll make it.' *Home.* Montana and the ranch in the summer. His mom at the stove making meatloaf, dad outside, breaking in a new horse beneath the amber sun. Mac felt the soothing warmth of the sun's fingers on his cold skin. The sweet scent of the pine trees that stagnated in the still air and flowed with the prairie breeze, and the drift of the horse's sweat after a long ride. Suddenly, a frantic cry cut in over the radio and wrenched him back to the present, and the sharp, icy chill returned with the stench of rubber, oil, and cordite.

'It's *Last Orders*, from the low formation,' Virg said over the interphone.

The breathless words of the pilot from *Last Orders* crackled through the radio, high-pitched and frantic. 'We gotta go down. Oxygen's almost gone. My bombardier's shot to hell. I don't think he's gonna make it.'

Mac felt a chill creep over him. From the cockpit, he looked on as *Last Orders* peeled away from the formation, heading down into occupied France. As the desperate voice screamed in Mac's ears, his stomach tightened. A bombardier was stretchered off a Fort last week, and he was so shot up that his lungs were exposed. His heart had pumped the life right out of him by the time they'd landed, and his body was so slick with blood, the medics dropped him twice. Mac heaved in a breath and tried to block out the image. Rivulets of sweat trickled down his back, and his mouth and throat ran dry.

'He's still going on about his bombardier dying. What good's that gonna do?' Wilson cussed under his breath.

Mac's heart hammered against his ribs and the blood pounded in his ears. He trembled and fought to suppress the swell of nausea in his gut as Bill's face reared in his mind

– that final glimpse. His wild eyes had said it all as he paused for a second to look over at Mac, seconds before he became a fireball in the sky.

'Wilson, take over for me.' Mac reached for his canteen and gulped the water down. He rested his head back and screwed his eyes shut. He was tired. They all were. It spread like a disease, drifting first to your mind and then to your limbs and nerves, and moving was like wading through treacle.

He pictured the girl he'd met at the dance a few weeks ago. Slim, hair the colour of platinum. She'd refused to dance with him because she was with some other guy, but her moment's hesitation and that flicker in her emerald-green eyes had instilled hope and soothed the dent in his pride. *So, she's loyal* and *beautiful.* Those eyes bore depth and soul, and as he'd leant in close to speak to her, a scent like sweet prairie flowers soared to meet him. A voice in his head whispered that beautiful girl was his guiding light, and he harnessed the memory.

The Channel shimmered up ahead and light flak sprang up but failed to reach them as the bombers punched their way through cotton wool cumulus. As they left the French coast behind, Mac gazed at the sheet-metal surface of lead-grey, icy water. His toes were almost numb, and he wriggled them in his fur-lined overboots.

They'd almost done it. Another mission down, fifteen to go. They were old hands, the old men of the 324.th Squadron. A well-oiled machine, so in tune with one another. 'Pilot to crew. We're at ten thousand feet. You can come off oxygen.' It was a relief to tear the mask from his face, which was sore from where it chafed his skin, and he nudged his cheek with his gloved hand.

'Hey, smell that sea air, boys,' Danny said over the interphone.

'Pilot to crew. We're landing at Exeter to refuel.' A chorus of groans erupted over the interphone. 'It's not all bad. We might get a cup of coffee.'

'Pilot, with respect, Limeys don't know how to make good coffee,' Irv said. 'But if it's served up by a good-looking dame then I'll drink it – and more besides.' Laughter and whistles flowed.

Mac craved something stronger than coffee and was looking forward to the evening back at Bassingbourn. Drinks, cards, catch up on the mail... but first, they had to go through debriefing with a slug of bourbon thrown in as a sweetener. A tiny black dot up ahead caught his eye, or was it a smudge on the windshield? A smudge that moved, divided and grew into several larger specks. His heart quickened, but with a closing speed of over four hundred miles an hour, the specks merged into P-47 fighters within seconds and he exhaled. 'Look, boys. Our little friends have arrived.' Mid-afternoon sun glinted on silver as the fighter aircraft zipped through the sky to shepherd the bombers home.

'Gee, now that's one beautiful sight.' Wilson whistled.

'More beautiful than any girl on her wedding day,' Danny drawled.

With a greeting waggle of wings, the P-47s flew by, turned, and escorted them back to England. Before long, the horizon surrendered the terracotta sandstone cliffs of the Jurassic Coast. Beyond draped the English tapestry stretched taut across the undulating land – a ripple of greens and browns. Home.

3

AF Station 121, Bassingbourn
December 31st, 1942

Glen Miller's 'In the Mood' drifted through the hangar doors, across the moonlit airfield, and bubbled out into the night. The passion wagons and American jeeps in olive-green glistened beneath a thin film of frost. Stella shivered, her cheeks smarting from the cold. She smoothed out her WAAF service dress tunic and skirt and tried to ignore the throbbing in her toes from the icy chill. Travelling for twenty minutes in an American Army truck, which only had a flimsy canvas canopy for cover, was no match for the winter's eve.

Vera nudged her arm. 'Here. Put some of this on, love.' She held out her treasured lipstick. 'Regimental red. Now remember, beauty is your duty.' She smirked, casting Stella a knowing look, her eyebrows raised and one hand resting on her hip.

Stella dabbed a streak of red on her lips as Vera cast an approving look. 'I hope Alex doesn't find out.' She gazed around as GIs helped girls down from the truck. A faint breeze teased out a platinum blonde curl, and she hastily tucked it back into place.

'Come on. We'll have a wizard time, and you can forget about Alex for the rest of the night, seeing as he's forgotten you.' Vera linked arms with her. 'Besides, it beats spending the night in with your landlady, Miss Prim and Proper.'

'Give over. She's lovely.' Stella took a deep breath, and muttered, 'Oh well, in for a penny...'

The music grew louder as they made their way across the frosted ground towards the hangar, their footsteps falling into time to the big-band music swinging out into the night. In the distance, the silhouettes of B-17s loomed all around the airfield, bathed in moonlight. Vera sang under her breath, releasing wispy, white vapour into the evening air.

As they passed through the hangar doors, the trumpet solo swung out, and the springy beat drew a crowd of eager dancers into a bouncing foxtrot. Bunting bearing the American flag decorated the vast space and adorned every wall. Wooden trestle tables stood in a procession along one side, laden with bowls of punch, bottles of Coca-Cola, and food. Plates of towering sandwiches sat next to jellies that wobbled and cakes and pastries that made Stella's mouth water. Large platters of meat stood proud; such a feast they had not seen since the rationing began. Stella stared, open-mouthed. On the opposite side of the hangar, a B-17 Flying Fortress stood to attention, and in front of its mighty wings, on a raised platform, the band played.

'Come on. I'm famished.' Stella made a beeline for the food. 'Did you ever see such a spread?'

Vera handed her a plate. 'Go on then, get stuck in. See, I said you'd enjoy yourself.'

'Yes, well, anything's better than beetroot sandwiches and carrot pie.' Stella wrinkled her nose, then looked on as the other young women they had arrived with made a beeline for the GIs. *Stockings, chocolate, and plenty of money to take you out.*

Vera popped the last piece of cake in her mouth and put her plate to one side. 'I'm going in search of a real drink. Not be a tick, love.'

'Looks as if there might be a bar on the other side.' Stella looked on as her friend ploughed through a group of American servicemen, parting them like the Red Sea.

'Oh, I love this tune,' Vera said, snapping her fingers in rhythm to the music, pouting at the GIs as she sashayed by. Men always noticed Vera. She was a slender brunette of medium height with blue eyes and plump lips. She really stood out.

Stella stayed where she was, nursing her plate as she devoured the most delicious, sweet donut. The sweet, gritty sugar coated her tongue and tantalised her taste buds and for a moment, she forgot all about mundane life as the vibrant atmosphere bustled and fizzed throughout the hangar. The local girls gazed starry-eyed at their American partners, giggling at their smooth banter. They certainly had a way with words. No wonder girls swooned when they were so handsome – and they knew it. Overpaid, oversexed and over here.

As she glanced around, a tall American pilot caught her eye. He stood out among the crowd, a smouldering cigarette dangling from his lips. As he looked around, he met her gaze and paused, a warm smile tugging at the corners of his mouth. Stella was captivated by his striking blue eyes, and his dimpled chin. There was something familiar about him, but she couldn't think why. Shrieks of laughter erupted behind her, and she spun around to look, but when she turned back, the pilot had vanished, eclipsed by the crowd.

Her mother's warning rang shrill and sharp in her ears. Whatever happens, stay away from those Americans. It's not decent all this carrying on you hear about nowadays. You'll end up getting into trouble, my girl. One of them called the vicar's wife "honey" the other day. Oh, the nerve.

But Stella recalled the girls and their excitement that zipped through the town like an electric current. She sighed and turned to watch the band. Resplendent in their Army Air Force uniforms, the trumpeters stood to play their piece, swaying to 'Sing, Sing, Sing.' Brass instruments sparkled beneath the lights, and her skin tingled.

The floor bustled with dancers, with people packed in as tight as sardines. A GI dancing with a blonde threw her up over his shoulders and her ruby dress billowed up, flashing pink cami-knickers. Stella gazed in awe. She'd never danced like that, and it looked like such fun. As she stared into the crowd looking for Vera, someone lunged at her, and she staggered forward, dropping her bag on the floor.

A man's voice slurred close to her ear. 'Hey, baby, wanna have a drink?'

Stella came face-to-face with two GIs wielding bottles of beer. The shorter man lit a cigarette, took a drag, and blew smoke in her face, leering at her with bloodshot eyes.

She coughed. 'No, thank you.' She turned to walk away, but the tall one grabbed her by the arm and the breath hitched in her throat.

'Just one drink, that's all, baby,' he said, draping his thick arm around her, pinning her to his side. He stank of beer, cigarettes, and sweat, and wore a menacing two-inch scar on his left cheek.

His grimy hand gripped her hard; her throat tightened, and she told herself to stay calm. 'No thank you,' she said in a quavering voice. The man increased his grip and her shoulder throbbed. 'Please, let go, you're hurting me.' Stella struggled and broke free, and as she spun around, she slammed into another man whose muscular arms engulfed her. Out of instinct she reached out and touched silver wings on his left olive-green breast pocket. *It's him.*

'You heard the lady, now beat it!' The officer glared at them, his eyes narrow and piercing. He released Stella from his arms and stepped between her and the drunken, disorderly men.

'Sorry, lieutenant, we were just...'

'I saw what you were doing, private. Now beat it, unless you want to be on KP duty for the next two weeks.'

His olive skin was flawless, and as he turned his gaze on Stella, she was drawn into deep sapphire depths. *The eyes are the window to the soul.* He cut a dashing figure in his dress uniform and at that moment, a kaleidoscope of butterflies took flight within her.

'Thank you.'

He dragged a hand through wavy ebony hair which bore a note of defiance as it refused to lie flat, navigating its own direction.

'Sorry about that, ma'am. I believe this belongs to you.' He picked up her bag. 'First Lieutenant John Mackenzie.' He held out his hand.

'Thank you, lieutenant.' She said it in the American way. 'Stella Charlton.' His hand was firm and warm in hers, his touch electric, and the heat bloomed beneath her skin.

'My friends call me Mac.' With a hint of mischief in his smouldering eyes, he smirked, studying her for a moment. 'Well, now, if I didn't know any better I'd say you've fallen for me, throwing yourself into my arms like that.' His face creased into a wide smile, flashing straight, white teeth while his velvet voice was a southern drawl as she'd heard in Western films and newsreels.

Stella blushed. He was tall and broad-shouldered with a crooked half-smile that made his eyes crinkle at the corners. She chided herself for not knowing what to say, and a silence stretched out between them, a river of opportunity and uncertainty. She bit her lower lip as she gazed around for signs of Vera.

'Looking for someone?'

'Yes, my friend, Vera. Here she is now.'

A determined Vera, with a drink in each hand, pushed through the throng of people. Triumphant, she shimmied her way across to Stella, through accompanying wolf whistles, admiring stares, and propositions, with a confident smile and no hint of a blush.

'Here you go,' Vera said in a sing-song voice, passing Stella a glass of fruit punch as she studied her with narrowed eyes. 'Someone's been a busy bee.' She glanced at Mac. 'Nice to meet you.' She flashed him a warm smile.

'This is Lieutenant John Mackenzie.' Stella sipped her drink, savouring the fruity tang on her tongue, but the silken scarlet liquid had fiery depths which seared her throat.

'Go steady with that stuff.' Mac pointed to the fruit punch. 'I saw a corporal tip a gallon of bourbon in there earlier.'

Vera laughed. 'Stella, you're a dark horse.' She raised her eyebrows, lips pursed, and scanned the room, eyes like radar, honing in on a young airman taking to the dance floor with a land girl. 'Didn't I say we'd have a great night? That one over there's mine.' Vera winked, and Stella laughed when she saw the steely look in her eye.

'Stella, would you like to dance?' Mac held out his hand. Her heart lifted with an unexpected buoyancy, only to fall like a bomb when she remembered Alex. 'I can't.' Mac looked crestfallen for a moment, and her chest tightened. She sighed. Not a single letter for weeks, no whisperings of love, no promises made. Her heart squeezed as she recalled Alex's last words: 'I'd be lost without you.' It was almost two months since he'd been posted to Lincoln.

'Can't or won't?' Mac's gentle voice broke her reverie, and he gazed at her with one eyebrow raised.

'Is there a difference?'

'Sure. The former implies that something or someone is stopping you, whereas the latter means you don't want to dance *with me*.' His eyes flickered.

Stella's heartbeat pounded in her ears. Lord help her, he was so handsome – the epitome of sophistication – and there was something about him that drew her close. As his intense eyes searched hers, the blood pulsed through her veins.

'Go on.' Vera laughed and gave her a gentle shove.

He held his hand out again. 'Stella, I promise to take good care of you.'

It was now or never. 'Okay.' Her name on his lips was a sweet melody, and the notes ricocheted down her spine. 'I'm afraid I'm a little out of practice.' She took his hand, and a spark ran through her.

'Well, the trick is to pretend you know what you're doing.' Mac's gaze held hers, and he grinned as he led her to the dance floor.

The band struck up the next tune, 'Moonlight Serenade', and a female singer in a flowing white evening gown approached the microphone. Then, in a single fluid movement, Mac slipped his arm around Stella's waist and she tingled, catching her breath as his hand settled on the small of her back, his fingers outstretched as he guided her across the floor. The clarinet and saxophones resonated in harmony.

'You don't remember me, do you?'

She raised her chin and gazed into his eyes.

'It was at the dance in Meldreth last month.'

The penny dropped. He'd asked her to dance, but she was there with Alex, so she'd turned him down. 'I remember now.' The singer's voice, soft as silk, flowed throughout the hangar. Mac's firm body pressed close to hers as they danced, and she welcomed his warmth as the throng of people around them faded into the distance. She glided like silk in his arms and for the first time in a while, she felt alive and joyous, and the war faded into the background. The clarinettist rose to play a solo, and soft, velvety notes punctuated the air.

Stella raised her chin, and her eyes met Mac's, and as the band played the final bars, musical notes soared to dizzy heights then melted away as she lost herself in his gaze. Mac lifted her hand and pressed it to his lips before leading her from the floor. No one had ever done that before, or looked at her in that way, and all her nerve endings fizzed.

Stella sank onto a chair and took a small sip of fruit punch, aware that Mac was watching her. She took a deep breath as she fought to steady her racing heart.

'So, Stella, where are you based?' He dragged his chair closer.

'RAF Bourn, it's about seven miles north of here.'

'Oh, yeah. I know it. So what do you do when you're not on duty?' He leaned forward, and his eyes twinkled as they caught the light.

'Nothing much, apart from shopping or walking, Lieutenant.'

'Call me Mac,' he said with a smile to soften his southern drawl, before draining his glass. 'Sometimes I go walking or take a trip to the village here, but I still manage to get lost. It doesn't help that there aren't any signs.' He laughed. 'Maybe you could show me around sometime?'

Stella, caught unaware, paused. She longed to say yes, but then Alex's grieving face flashed in her mind. The last time they met had filled her with dread, and she hoped he hadn't done anything stupid. She swallowed as a hollowness opened up within her. *The rumours.* Vera was always right and had told her all about Alex's little indiscretions months ago, but Stella couldn't leave him. Not yet. He needed her.

'I'm afraid there's not much to see.' As she spoke, Mac's eyes never left hers, and she felt the heat rise in her cheeks. She swirled the drink in her glass and sipped the last of the punch, aware of him hanging on her every word.

His face lit up, and a wicked smile played on his lips. 'I wouldn't mind being lost with you.'

The air whooshed from her lungs as she desperately thought of what to say. To her relief, Mac took a silver cigarette case from his breast pocket and offered it to her. 'Thanks.' She leant in close for a light, their hands brushing against each other. His skin was soft and warm, and a spark soared through her veins.

'Now, I've just realised – you talk differently.' He shot her an amused glance.

His gentle voice jolted her from her reverie. 'So do you.' She blew a cloud of smoke into the air.

'What I mean is, you don't sound like the locals.'

'No, I live in the north of England.' Stella was proud of her accent. Even when her parents had insisted on sending her to Durham High School for Girls, she had excelled in education but failed in elocution, much to her mother's dismay. Her accent, perhaps subtle now, retained a gentle north-east lilt. 'Whereabouts in America do you live?'

'Montana. My folks have a cattle ranch, but I guess you'd call it a farm.'

'It makes me think of cowboy films and John Wayne.' It all sounded so far away, and yet so exciting. She turned to face him more and crossed her legs in his direction.

Mac laughed. 'Well, now, I don't know any movie stars, but cowboys, that's different.' He drew on his cigarette. 'My mother calls it God's own country, and the mountains when they're snow-capped, oh man, they're beautiful. And vast, green plains all around.' He leant back in his chair and stretched out his long legs. 'There's a river winds through our land. My grandfather taught me to fish there when I was a boy. I swear he could catch anything.' As Stella hung on every word, she glimpsed the emerging cowboy beneath the warrior and forgot all about her mother's warning as his voice melted away her reservations.

'Now, how about you tell me more about you?' His piercing eyes held her gaze, asking, prompting.

'There's nothing much to say. I live in a rural town, no siblings. After dad passed away, my mother bought a shop, and I worked there before I joined up.' She stubbed out her cigarette. In truth, there was a lot more to say, such as her mother hoping to hear wedding bells imminently as she pushed Stella closer to Alex.

'Well, I'm mighty glad you came here tonight.' Mac leaned forward and rested his elbow on the table. 'I hoped I'd run into you again.' A soft smile tugged at his mouth.

A warm glow rose from Stella's neck to her cheeks. The brief silence that ensued made her feel even more self-conscious. 'Do you enjoy flying, Mac?'

His face lit up, and his eyes twinkled. 'Well, now, I've loved it from the first time my father flew me up into the blue.' He took a swig of his beer. 'Dad was one of the first American pilots to see combat in the last war. When you consider the aircraft they had back then, he's darn lucky to be alive.' Mac gazed around the room with a faraway look in his eyes. 'Yeah, real fortunate. Hey, listen to me yakking away.'

'No, it's fascinating, really. How old were you when you learned to fly?' Stella sipped her punch.

'Nine, and I remember it as if it was yesterday. Dad keeps a Curtiss Jenny out in one of the barns. It's a light trainer aircraft and man can she fly. There's nothing like it. My younger brother's learning right now. He's all set on joining the Air Force, but he's only fifteen. I'd like to think this crazy war's over before then.' He stubbed his cigarette out in the ashtray and began fidgeting with the brown watch strap on his wrist. 'You should see it up there, the land shrinking as you climb, endless blue all around and at the right time, the sunrise or sunset dancing on the horizon. It sure is one vast ocean.'

'It sounds lovely, but I'm afraid of heights. I don't think I could do it.' Stella shook her head. 'I'd be terrified.'

'You can't say until you try. Fluffy white clouds, just floating in the blue, like cotton candy.' He grinned. 'I'll take you flying and prove it, once this war's over.' He gave her a tentative glance. 'And I promise you'll love it. You'll be safe with me.' He winked.

He wasn't going to take her anywhere. It was all talk, and after tonight she'd probably never see him again, but a part of her ached for it to be true while another part chided her for daring to want more.

'How about another dance?' Mac stood up and held out his hand.

The band struck up the first notes of 'We'll Meet Again.' Stella took his hand as he slipped his arm around her, guiding her towards him, his piercing blue eyes on hers as they fell into step once more. Her hand rested on his firm shoulder, and as they danced, her chin brushed his olive-green jacket, which was soft against her skin. The singer's dulcet tones pierced all conversation, lulling them into silence.

Stella gazed up at Mac and lost herself for a moment, sinking into pools of blue. Only the present mattered as they moved to the music, close and swaying, their bodies utterly in tune.

His hold tightened, and she nestled her head against him, drinking in undertones of beer and cedar wood cologne. As the song ended and the final notes ebbed away, they stood, caught in the moment, as all around them couples began to leave the floor. Her skin prickled and her heart fluttered as Mac took her hand and led her back to their table.

'How about I get us another drink?' His face broke into that killer smile as he touched her arm.

Stella nodded as a fresh tingle coursed through her, as she watched him walk away. Everything was happening so fast, and her mind was in a whirl. It was wrong, and yet so right.

'Room for one more?' Vera sank into a chair, her cheeks as red as her lipstick, gasping for breath. 'Penny for them.'

Stella sighed. 'Sorry, I was miles away.'

'Reckon he's a keeper.'

Stella looked over at Mac, who met her gaze and winked. It was a certain smile, and she felt little flips in her tummy. 'Vera, what am I going to do? What about Alex?' She couldn't lie to Mac.

'It'll be all right, Stell, you'll see. Just go along with it for now. Have some fun for a change. Besides, Alex isn't right for you.'

'I know, you're right. But he's going through a difficult time.'

'You already said, and I told you that Jenkins ran into him last week in a pub in Cambridge. It doesn't matter how you dress it up, he doesn't treat you right, and you know it.'

Vera's words stung true. Why shouldn't she have some fun? It was one night, after all, who knew what tomorrow would bring? Her tummy flipped again as Mac strode towards her.

'Here you go.' He passed her a glass of punch.

'Thank you.' She took a small sip, the glass cool against her palm.

'Say, Stella, would you like to take a walk?'

She paused. 'All right.' She took his outstretched hand, which enveloped hers in warmth.

Outside, their breath hung in the crisp, icy air. A light covering of snow had fallen, and a sparse sprinkling dusted the ground and the trucks. The creamy moon loomed large and clouds were silhouetted against the glowing beacon as they sailed through the star-filled sky. Mac offered her a cigarette, and she leaned in for a light, raising her eyes to his. The music ceased, and a man's voice carried out over the microphone as he shushed the crowd and began the countdown. 'Ten, nine, eight... Happy New Year!' A cheer erupted, and 'Auld Lang Syne' bubbled out into the night.

'Happy New Year, Stella.'

Mac's eyes captured the soft glow of the moon as he took her hands and drew her towards him. Tentatively, he kissed her brow, and even though she knew it was wrong, it felt right.

'You're so beautiful,' he murmured before kissing her on the lips, a soft lingering kiss as he held her in his arms, and when their lips finally parted, he brushed her cheek with his fingertips. 'I've been waiting to do that all evening.' He took her hands in his. 'There's something special about you, Stella.'

Was there? Alex never said so. A wave of tingling warmth coursed through her, and she longed to stay in his arms. But, Alex. 'We shouldn't. I can't.' She stepped away, her hands slipping from his hold.

'There's that word again.' Mac sighed. 'We're not doing any harm.' He took a drag on his cigarette. 'Don't you like me? I sure like you – I knew it from the first moment I saw you.'

'It's not that. There's someone else. He's in the RAF.' She watched as Mac's face fell and the sparkle in his eyes dimmed.

'Oh, I get it. He's the guy you were with at the other dance.'

'Yes, Alex.' Stella's heart sank.

Since his friend's bomber had crashed, Alex hadn't been the same, and when she'd tried to persuade him to visit David at the burns unit, Alex had yelled at her and told her to mind her own business. It was as if he couldn't deal with it. Then David died, and Alex begged her to stay with him. What sort of person would she be to give up on him so easily? Alex's hands shook now when he tried to light a cigarette, and his eyes were like those of a hunted fox – wild and frantic. A forlorn tide swept through her. She was trapped, lost in a spiralling darkness.

'Is it serious?' Mac looked down at his feet. 'From where I was standing, it didn't look like anything much, seeing how he left you alone for most the night.'

Stella stiffened. 'You know nothing about it.'

Mac took a step towards her, his eyes widening. Those beguiling eyes she could get lost in forever. An ache gripped her chest as she tore her gaze away.

'I should get back. It's late.'

Mac threw his cigarette like a dart to the ground, grinding it beneath his shoe, but on the snow-covered ground, faint orange continued to glow.

Once they were back inside, Vera came rushing towards them through a sea of coloured balloons and a smoky haze. 'I'm worn out. Any chance of a lift home, Mac? I don't think I could bear the passion wagons a second time.' She giggled.

'I'd be happy to take you home.' He glanced at Stella with a look that sought approval.

'Vera, aren't we supposed to go back with the others?' Stella cast her friend a wide-eyed stare, but Vera took no notice.

'I'll take care of it. It's not a problem.' Mac met Stella's glance, his lips pressed tight.

Stella felt the heat prick her cheeks. If only the ground could open up now and swallow her whole.

Outside, Mac turned his face to the midnight sky. 'It's a beautiful night for stargazing. You can see the Milky Way up there.' He pointed to a hazy, large cluster of glowing, tiny white specks that flowed through the night sky. 'When I was a kid, I spent night after night laying out on the grass, waiting for a glimpse of a shooting star.'

'A stargazer?' Vera arched an eyebrow and clambered into the front seat. 'The only stars that interest me are on the screen. Lord, it's freezing.' She shivered, pulled her coat tighter and stamped her feet in the footwell. 'Bloomin' winter, I hate it.'

'I sure hope you ladies are good navigators. I make it a rule never to travel without one.'

'Oh, you'll be all right with us, won't he, Stell?' Vera winked at him.

Mac held his seat forward as Stella clambered into the back then sprang into the driver's seat. The jeep inched along the inky-black tree-lined lane. The dipped headlights, with their slotted covers and narrow beams of light, made little difference in visibility. 'Jeez, I can hardly tell where the road is.' Patches of silvery-white flecked the hedgerows and verges and shimmered in the moonlight.

'Some nights it's so dark you're bumping into people. Mind you, that's not always a bad thing, all depends on who you bump into.' Vera flashed a wicked grin.

Mac laughed, his breath escaping as silver vapour.

'This is my stop here.' Vera pointed to a row of cottages on the left. 'Ta for the lift.' She paused and glanced at Stella.

'See you tomorrow, love.' She winked at Mac. 'And don't do anything I wouldn't do, kid.' She shimmied away.

'What?' Mac laughed. 'You Brits sure talk funny. Say, Stella, hop in the front, and you can show me the way to your place.'

He held the passenger seat forward as she clambered out and then, tentatively, she climbed into the front.

'Carry on along here, it's just a little further.' Stella looked straight ahead, trying to avoid Mac's gaze, but she sensed his sideways glances. When she caught a whisper of cedar wood on the night breeze, she drank it in hungrily, desire flaring through her veins like a flame.

They crawled along the winding road, the wheels skidding on patches of ice when Mac took a corner too fast. 'Lord knows how anyone can drive safe in this ink. Give me night-flying any day.'

When they reached the village of Bourn, Stella pointed to a row of houses on the left. 'It's just here. Lilac Cottage.'

'Quaint name.' He pulled up outside a small, detached, whitewashed house with a thatched roof.

Stella faced him. 'Thanks for the lift.' She tried to avoid his smouldering eyes as he edged closer. She shifted further away, her heart beating fast.

'I had a good time tonight.' Mac rested his arm on the back of her seat, his eyes meeting hers. The moon slipped behind the clouds, casting a shadow. 'I sure wish things were different.' He took her hand and brushed it with his lips. 'Life's what we make it.'

His touch was soft, with a rush of warm breath, and his thigh nudged Stella's as he edged closer, setting her nerve endings aglow. She longed for his lips pressed against hers – those soft, parted lips she now realised were closer as he leaned in towards her and her breaths became more rapid – but she had to do what was right. She stiffened and turned away. 'I should go. Thanks again for the lift, and drive safe.' She jumped out of the jeep and hurried up the path, aware of his eyes watching her. As she reached the front door, she turned. He was waiting, casually resting his arms on the steering wheel.

With his charismatic smile and a wave, he called out, 'Don't forget you said you'd take me sightseeing. I'm holding you to it.'

'Wait. I never actually said... '

'I'll swing by two weeks today, say around eleven o'clock.'

The moon peeked out from behind the clouds as Stella met his gaze, her mouth open, poised to speak, but the breath caught in her throat as she fought for words.

'See you next week, beautiful.' With a mock salute and a broad grin, Mac drove away and olive green melted into the darkness.

'Sightseeing?' Stella muttered. She closed the door and turned the black wrought-iron key in the lock. If only she hadn't rushed off, then he would have kissed her. His soft lips on hers. She groaned as her stomach fluttered and her mouth curved up into a smile. There was nothing wrong with being friends. What harm could it do? The grandfather clock stood at the end of the hall, its brass pendulum swinging in rhythm like a metronome.

A doubting voice niggled at the back of her mind. It whispered she was dancing with temptation. Her mother had a saying for that. *If you play with fire, you'll get burned.* Yet Mac had awoken something inside her. It existed as constant as the moon and the stars. As constant as the thin strip of blood-red ribbon on the briefing map that stretched from Cambridge to somewhere in occupied Europe.

4

Ward III, January 1943

The doors to the ward burst open, and two male orderlies swept through, wheeling a patient on a trolley. The trolley jolted, and the occupant groaned. From beds and chairs, curious faces peered at the scene, startled by the fuss and disruption. Archie glanced up from the notes he was reading in the confines of Sister's office. He glimpsed a dark, charred face that resembled nothing living and he tried to quell the anger that flared inside him. This war had a knack of creating injuries that could shock even the likes of him. He dropped the medical notes onto the desk and fell into step behind Sister Jamieson, who had already risen from her throne and marched out to greet their new arrival.

'Follow me, gentlemen.' She passed them by and came to an abrupt halt at the end of the ward. 'You must be Jack. We've been expecting you.' She cast a warm smile at the young airman while holding open the door to the saline bathroom.

'Be careful as you lift him.' Sister Jamieson stood by as one orderly supported Jack's upper body while the other grabbed his legs. Between them, they lowered him like a babe into the bath, uniform and all, as the young man groaned. Then, as he lay back with the water lapping at his clavicle, a calm descended over him like a mighty exhalation of breath, his shoulders dropped, and his eyelids flickered and closed.

Briny steam drenched the air, lining Archie's nostrils, and beads of sweat tickled his brow. He removed his brown tweed jacket and draped it over a nearby stool. 'Hello,' he said, crouching by the side of the bath. His eyes raked over Jack from top to bottom. The blue-grey fabric of the boy's RAF uniform had melted into the skin of his arms, chest and thighs, creating a weave of tissue and charred cloth. Sister unravelled the bandage on Jack's left hand beneath the water. The appendage was swollen, the skin blackened and leather-like around the edges, the fingers blackened crisps. Beyond the wrist, the forearm was red and raw. Jack glanced down, and even the horrific burns to his face could not mask the look of horror now etched upon it, his eyes wide, darting in every direction.

'It's all right. We'll soon fix you up. Just rest and let the water do its work,' Archie said. Jack was gaunt, with skin so fried the nerve endings would be damaged and numb in places. Years of surgery awaited him with multiple grafts. Archie sighed and stretched up, chin raised to address Sister Jamieson. 'When did he last have morphine?'

She flicked through the notes, her long, bony fingers tracing sentences as she scanned the words with hawk-like eyes. 'Two hours ago.'

'Right. Well, by the time he's had a soak for an hour or so, you could administer another dose. Let's keep him as comfortable as we can.' Archie glanced at Jack's decaying form in the bath. Another bad burner. Why was it that some of these lads fared so much better in the flames than others?

He shook his head and ran his hand through his greying hair, smoothing it down. Piano music flowed from the ward – 'I'll never smile again'.

Suddenly, Jack tried to heave himself up, but the sheer effort proved too strenuous, and he cried out like a wounded animal. The water, which almost filled the bath, began to swirl and slosh and overflowed, spilling onto the linoleum floor. 'I gotta get out!'

'Steady on.' Archie placed his hand on the boy's shoulder and looked into his eyes, which locked onto his – obsidian beads peering from a blackened, skull-like face. *Strewth, he was in a state.* 'Was it a Hurricane or a Spitfire?'

'Hurricane.'

'Header tank?'

'Yeah. Direct hit. Exploded instantly. I almost didn't make it out.' Jack's voice was barely more than a whisper.

Archie formed a mental picture of him wrestling with the ripcord of his chute with burned hands that barely functioned. 'Jack, you have to stay in the bath. We need to get you cleaned up and dress these wounds, but first, this uniform has to come off.'

'I don't have time for all that, doc. My girl, she's having my baby. We're supposed to be getting married.'

So fragile and yet determined. The boy was exhausted and in great pain, and he was obviously a fighter – which was reassuring, because he was going to need that resilience. 'So, you're going to be a father, eh? Congratulations. Well, we'll get you fixed up as soon as we can. Don't worry, we won't keep you any longer than necessary.' Archie cast a smile to reassure him.

Jack remained unsettled and tried to heave himself up again, but his body failed him and he sank back. 'I'm getting married... next week.'

'Not in this state, I'm afraid. It's not possible. Maybe in a month or two, we'll have to see.' Archie flicked a gaze at Sister Jamieson, her eyebrows knitted together in a frown. He shook his head. These boys were all the same – always running, always fighting. Getting married, indeed. People often said Archie performed miracles – utter nonsense, of course – and this was one miracle too far.

Jack lifted his arm and looked at his hand, his mouth open wide, lips dark and swollen. He cried out again. 'Lord, help me.' He glanced up at Archie with beseeching eyes. 'Help me, please.'

Archie crouched down and rested his outstretched hand on the side of the bath and adjusted his black horn-rimmed spectacles. 'Okay, here's the plan. You agree to a soak in the tub while Pete and Jimmy there remove all this cloth. Then we can get you out and dress those burns.'

'But Doc, I haven't got time for that. My girl... '

'Will wait for you, I'm sure.' Although they didn't all wait. He'd seen it happen. Wives or girlfriends, desperate to see their husbands or lovers again, only to recoil in horror when they were reunited. For some, it was a very brief reunion.

'You don't understand. No child of mine is gonna be born a bastard!' Jack's chest heaved and determination flared in the young man's eyes.

'Okay. We'll see what we can arrange.' Archie turned to Sister Jamieson. 'Do the best you can. I'll be back later, and we'll take things from there.'

'Yes, Mr McIndoe.'

As he stepped out of the bathroom, Archie savoured the cooler air while he strolled through the ward. He glanced at his watch. Ten o'clock. He noticed some of the men who had headed out to the pub last night were still in bed, no doubt sleeping it off. Archie suppressed a chuckle as he glimpsed pictures of scantily-clad women and pin-ups which adorned walls above beds. Then there were pictures of babies, wives, and squadrons. A merry tune flowed from the radio. Music soothed the mind, healed the heart and comforted the soul while also drowning out groans and cries.

'Morning, Maestro.'

Archie turned in the direction of the voice, the Aussie's colonial accent evoking memories of his own native New Zealand. 'Morning, Tom,' he said, nodding as he carried on through the ward.

A nurse with auburn hair tied in a neat bun emerged from the sluice room, pushing a trolley filled with vases of daffodils and snowdrops. As she sailed by, Archie drank in the sweet floral scent. Silken yellow and white blooms nodded from green stalks and added a touch of home to the drab, clinical surroundings.

Thank the Lord for the ladies of East Grinstead, who had come up trumps when he'd told them how making the ward bright and cheerful was vital to the recovery of his patients. Fresh blooms arrived every few days, and a warm glow flared in his chest when he saw how the town had pulled together.

'Good morning, Archie,' the nurse said in her soft Irish accent.

'Morning, Bea. I see you're doing the honours today.' He grinned. 'The old homestead looks better already.' Of course, there was an ulterior motive for the flowers – the sweet fragrance helped mask the foul odour of burned flesh, which reeked and could be overwhelming.

When Archie reached his office, there was a letter resting on his desk, stamped RAF Charterhall. *About time.* He wondered if the MO had taken Richard Hillary off active duties. Archie recalled Richard's words. *I don't think I can go on for much longer.* Richard had been so determined to return to flying duties. Archie recalled the relentless badgering and his own reply. *You haven't a hope in hell of getting back. The Air Force won't let it happen.* Maybe he should have been more forthright, only in the end, he'd thrown up his hands and told him to get on with it. *If you're determined to kill yourself, go ahead, but don't blame me.* As his own words rang in his head, an icy chill draped over his shoulders.

He glanced up as sunlight streamed into the room, trapping dancing, shimmering dust motes in the golden haze. What a time for Jack to be thinking about marriage, although he was simply taking care of his girl the best way he could. Of course, not all girls were loyal. Women swarmed around fighter pilots, the Brylcreem Boys, and now, while at their lowest ebb and burned to a crisp, some of the wives and girlfriends buggered off. A knock on the door shattered his reverie.

'Morning, Boss.'

'Ah, Blackie. Come in.' Edward Blacksell, Archie's RAF Welfare Officer, was invaluable in keeping the airmen in line.

'I'll not stay, just checking you've remembered the committee meeting later.' Blackie dropped a stack of medical notes onto the desk.

'Yes, how can I forget? I stand accused of lowering the tone.' Archie raised his eyebrows. 'Again.'

Blackie sighed. 'Yes, well, watch out for Sister Hall today. She's barking at everyone. One of our boys came back in the early hours, drunk as a lord, and I'm afraid he lost his way.'

'Oh no, he didn't end up in the wrong bed, did he?'

'No. The daft beggar barged in on an emergency operation. Caused a bit of a stir.' Blackie smirked. 'Sent a tray of instruments flying when he staggered into a trolley. The surgeon was Mr Edwards, and he's furious.'

'Marvellous. That's me in the dog house.' Archie pictured Edwards' rounded, ruddy face and couldn't resist smirking to himself. 'Okay, thanks, Blackie.' *Boys will be boys.*

As the door closed, Archie wondered what the ladies on the committee would throw at him this time. Last time they'd been outraged over the beer barrels on his ward, the flowers, and the uniforms. Well, hydration had won the argument over the free availability of beer. Burns patients required lots of fluid. He chuckled to himself. As for the uniforms, he'd been outraged to learn that complaints had been made about his boys wearing their service uniforms. Ridiculous. The situation was simple. He disliked the convalescent uniforms – they made the men look more like convicts, and so he'd burned the lot one day in a fit of rage. His boys were serving their country and needed to feel that they still were. They needed normality.

Thank God he didn't take that RAF Commission and didn't have to follow orders. If he had to ruffle a few feathers to get what he needed for his boys, then so be it. He grabbed the silver letter opener and slit open the envelope with surgical precision. 'Now then, let's see what you've been up to, Richard.'

His eyes flicked over the words and as he read he sighed and shook his head, picturing Richard, his scarred, disfigured, claw-like hands – fingers that struggled to hold cutlery, which fumbled with buttons and gripped a pint glass as if wrapped in woollen mittens. Why hadn't the MO intervened as he had requested in his letter? That left eye of his hadn't been up to the strain of night-flying. 'What the devil was the RAF thinking?'

He wondered what made a man so desperate to return to a fight that almost killed him the first time. Perhaps they felt that flying instilled a sense of normality? They could climb through cumulus and cast aside their imperfections and scars beneath the dispassionate gaze of the sun. But flying aircraft required full hand control, something Richard had lost.

After Richard's propaganda mission to America last year, word had spread of the good work being done at East Grinstead and that along with the success of his memoir, *The Last Enemy*, had brought unexpected attention and aid to the Guinea Pig Club. Letters with cheques, money orders, and notes offering hospitality and jobs along with gifts for the injured servicemen had been arriving ever since. Blackie had been a godsend and helped set up a charitable fund to manage the donations, which Archie realised would be needed to help some of the lads start new lives after the war. That had been the only good to come of the trip.

The icy reception Richard had received from US officials had caused him to see red. Apparently, they were rather concerned about how the American people would react to Richard's disfigurement and of any adverse effects that might have on their own military recruitment, and so Richard had been shielded from the limelight. And then the eye operation he'd had over there hadn't exactly been successful. He ought to have stayed here, had surgery, and then, just perhaps, it would have been a different outcome.

Archie looked again at the letter as the words slipped in and out of focus, and he thought of the irony of fixing the injured merely to send them back for more. He strained his eyes, and read out loud:

He and his observer were killed in an accident at 0137 hours on the 8th January 1943.

It had been a night training exercise. Further details explained how Richard and his radio operator had taken off in their Blenheim bomber and climbed into the icy night sky before losing control and crashing into a nearby field. Richard's words resonated in his mind – *I don't think I can go on for much longer.* Archie clamped his eyes tight and bowed his head. The clock on the wall ticked away the seconds; a metronome slicing through the silence. Does a chap ever sense that death is waiting? Richard must have in his final seconds as he wrestled with the controls of the Blenheim.

Archie stared out into the grounds as he remembered the merry band as they had been in the summer of 1941. Richard, Geoff Page, and the others had lounged on the grass beneath the sun as they thrashed out the finer details of their newly formed drinking club. The treasurer, wheelchair-bound with both legs in plaster, had been chosen because he was the least likely to abscond to the pub with the funds. The secretary had both hands wrapped in bandages and was unable to hold a pen, never mind take notes and finally, Archie, elected as president. Youthful spirits shining through older, tougher skins. He saw their smiles and twinkling eyes and heard their raucous laughter and tales of daring air battles. 'Godspeed, Richard,' he whispered.

In the distance, a rumble escalated into a roar as a Spitfire sliced through the sky with grace and a greeting waggle of its wings to the obvious delight of the town's folk. People stopped and stared, and a small boy with straw-coloured curly hair strained at his mother's hand and waved. 'We all need to find our wings sometime or another,' Archie muttered. 'All the boys yearn to fly, and all the girls love a flyer.'

5

Milk Run To First Base, January 1943

When Major Lewis had drawn back the curtain and revealed the map with its blood-red ribbon that delved into the Third Reich, Wilhelmshaven, a hushed chorus of groans erupted around the room. They'd never been to Germany before. It was a stroke of luck when the news came through. The mission was scrubbed at the last minute. The padre had just given a blessing to the crew. He was always out on the flight line before every mission. Maybe he'd had a word with God earlier, because that weather sure changed fast.

Mac wished he hadn't drunk the extra coffee at breakfast as it now mingled with the eggs and sausages, leaving a foul taste. He drew in a sharp breath and released it slowly as he made his way along the perimeter track towards the old farmstead. The folks there didn't mind when he dropped by. He might be thousands of miles away from home, but there, in a quiet corner of rural Cambridgeshire, was a little piece of Montana.

He gazed out across green fields, where the sheep grazed upon the hard, frosted ground. Mac lifted his face to the lead-grey shroud that covered the bloodied heavens. The bitter breeze stung his cheeks, and his eyes watered. Usually, he came here to ask for forgiveness – except today they hadn't dropped a single bomb. He asked for it anyway. Afterwards, birdsong drifted over him, sweet and high-pitched – the only reply.

He leaned on the old farm gate, gazing out across the airfield and at the B-17s spread out, waiting. A gust of wind hit him, the gate shuddered, and Bill's face flashed before him. Mac swallowed. It had been a momentary glance across the narrow stretch between them in the sky that transcended words when Bill realised all was lost. A fleeting glance that was the last farewell between friends before the explosion pummelled the air with shock waves and Mac had fought to keep the ship steady. His vision swam as reality hit home. A sharp sting zipped through his palm, and he glanced at his hand, the knuckles white from gripping the splintered fence. His legs trembled.

He took a slow walk back to the base, his breath hanging in the air before him like white contrails. The missions and the losses were stacking up. Before, time had been running out. He'd been so close, sitting on a thinning ledge, drifting, and then Stella came along and rekindled his hunger for life. His name on her lips had struck more than a chord the other night. The sticking point was Alex, but he figured he stood a chance. He'd seen the flicker in her eyes.

The clouds persisted, holding the rain at bay as Mac drove along the winding lane. Since the beginning of the war, the British had removed all road signs in case of an invasion, and it sure was confusing trying to find your way around. As he drew up on the left side of the road, he flicked a gaze at the wooden plaque on the wall of the white thatched cottage – *Lilac Cottage*. He cut the engine, wondering if Stella was still mad at him, and jumped out. Before he'd reached the gate, the front door creaked open, and Stella stepped out, all ready to go. 'Hi there.' Mac pushed his cap up with his finger. Boy, she sure was a picture, and at least she didn't look mad.

'Hello.' Stella grinned and headed towards him. Her hair seemed different, longer, and she wore a slim-fitting pair of slacks which showed off the contours of her legs, a sweater, and a short jacket.

Mac smiled, waiting until she'd climbed in. A restlessness crept over him as he longed to hold her again, to taste those lips. 'I wasn't sure if you'd be home.'

'Well, you didn't give me much choice.' She placed her khaki canvas gas mask bag down in the footwell.

Mac hopped into the driver's seat. 'Where shall we go first?' He gazed into her green eyes.

'I'm not sure. Why don't we drive along here and we can have a quick tour of the village?' She pointed to the road straight ahead.

'Sure thing. Whatever you say.' He fumbled through his jacket pocket and produced a packet of gum. 'Here, try some.'

Stella took a piece. The silver paper slipped off with ease, and she folded the thin strip into her mouth, closing her eyes for a moment as if savouring the taste.

They headed out to RAF Bourn on the outskirts of the village, where several Lancaster Bombers idled on their dispersals around the airfield. From there they drove along the scenic lanes before heading back into the centre of Bourn. 'This is a Roman road,' Stella said, as the wind gusted through her hair and golden curls oscillated in its grip.

'Well, how about that? I guess I should have known, seeing how it's so straight. I'm walking in the footsteps of Roman soldiers.' Mac laughed and flicked a gaze at her, taking in her beauty.

'Driving,' Stella corrected him with a smile. 'Bourn's a medieval village and the old church of St Helena and St Mary up ahead dates back to the twelfth century.'

Mac swung into Church Lane and pulled up close to the metal gates. He reached into the back of the jeep and pulled out a compact black box. 'I brought my camera, thought I might get a few good pictures while I have the chance,' he said with a grin. As they strolled through the churchyard side by side, Mac stopped to gaze at the magnificent building. The light-coloured stone and the leaded windows along with the twisted spire intrigued him. It sure was beautiful.

Stella pointed to the belfry. 'It has eight bells, but all bell-ringing was banned when the war began. If we do hear them, we'll know the Germans have invaded.' She spoke so matter-of-factly, without a trace of fear or worry in her voice. The war had brought great change, and he guessed that such things had become a part of normal everyday life.

As they strolled towards the church, Mac stopped to read the inscriptions on some of the ancient gravestones and took a few pictures. Stella sat on a nearby bench as the breeze shook the leaves of the trees overhead and beat a rosy tinge into her cheeks. Her nose was real cute, with a hint of rouge. She pulled up the collar of her jacket and thrust her hands into her pockets. He had to admit the air was a little icy, even in the sun. 'Say, are you cold? We can go grab a bite to eat someplace.'

'I'm okay if you want to take more pictures.'

Mac smiled, removed his brown leather flight jacket, and draped it over her shoulders. It was forbidden to do so, but he figured the military police wouldn't catch him here. Besides, he was a gentleman. 'It sure is pretty here and peaceful.' The dark weathered boughs above creaked and groaned in the breeze. 'It's strange to think there's a war raging on across the Channel, and yet here we are, miles from Hell.'

He took a picture of the church and the grounds, then glanced at Stella, who was looking the other way. He pointed the camera and pressed the shutter button. That picture could go in the cockpit. She turned to look at him, and he gestured with the camera. With her head tipped down like that, looking at him from beneath those dark, long lashes, she sure was cute. Then, just as she broke into a huge smile, he clicked again. *That one's definitely just for me.*

Mac draped his arm around her and rubbed her other arm to warm her up as she nestled against his side. Being so close was tempting, with her body warm against his, the swell of her hip against his side, and the wind teasing the lavender from her hair. My God, it was going to take every last ounce of reserve he had to stop himself from drawing her into his arms. His thoughts turned back to the kiss they'd shared on New Year's Eve before guilt had snatched her away. Remembering his western upbringing, he checked himself, and sighed. He wanted to ask her about Alex, but there'd be plenty of time for that later.

'Hey, let's have a quick look inside before we go. That is, of course, if you don't mind.' He stood up and took her hand in his, leading the way. Once inside, Mac closed the door, and they walked slowly towards the altar and sat at the front. The pew was ice-cold and slippery from polish, and a faint scent of incense hung in the air.

He marvelled at the architecture and the stained glass windows. 'It's always so peaceful in church.' He flicked a gaze at the depiction of Jesus on the cross. 'Thou shalt not kill. The sixth commandment.' He sighed and looked down at the ground. 'What are we doing in the midst of another war? It's never-ending madness.' He shook his head. 'It's not right, what they're doing. What *we're* doing.'

It wasn't right how men, young men, left their base here fresh and full of life and returned as a corpse, or didn't return at all. He swallowed. *Christ, Bill and the others.* His heart raced, then Stella reached for his hand, and her warm, soft touch soothed, drawing him back, drawing him to her. He was inches away, and as he gazed into her eyes, he marvelled at tiny flecks of gold that encircled her pupils, swimming in emerald green. Her brow furrowed and a glimmer of a smile toyed with her lips as he placed his other hand on hers.

He sat for a few minutes more, thinking, praying silently for those who'd already given their lives, praying for his own friends, praying for Bill. Friendships that had been so naturally formed only to be so brutally severed, now mere ripples in the water. He'd almost lost hope. Stella was becoming a shining beacon in a dark sky; his one guiding light in this hell within which he was caught. The only problem was Alex, but Stella was here with him today, and the way she'd looked at him earlier... well, she'd felt something, and so he'd hold on to that.

Back home, Mac went to church every Sunday with his family, but now it didn't seem right sitting here. Not with what he was doing. Killing people one day, acting all normal the next. The church held no place for him now, and it was beginning to feel mighty close. 'Stella, shall we go get something to eat?'

'All right.'

He led her outside, to where the trees whispered overhead as boughs danced and murmured in the breeze, and he drew her towards him. Her natural, pink lips so close – too close. Her soft, wide eyes twinkled and fixed onto his, and when her lips parted, his composure vanished in an instant. He took her in his arms and kissed her, her skin cool against his. When they came up for air, Stella gazed into his eyes before resting her head against his chest. Her green eyes reflected the silhouette of a sunflower; a yellow, swirling floret like a spinning prop, and as a sunflower craved the sun, she was all the light he needed.

6

RAF Bourn

As Stella cycled along the perimeter track, she spotted two ground crew on a scaffold outside the hangar, working on the engine of a Lancaster Bomber. In the distance, a honeyed glow stretched across the horizon. RAF Bourn looked so unappealing and had been built in haste at the beginning of the war. There were numerous Nissen huts, grouped together with a series of cinder paths leading from one place to another. When it rained, the ground became sodden, transformed into a squelchy, mud bath with water pooling everywhere. The brick-built control tower formed the heart of Bourn and housed Flying Control on the upper floor. The Meteorological Office, Signals Office, and the telephone exchange resided on the ground floor along with Intelligence. Stella didn't often get the chance to go in there.

She reported for duty at seven o'clock and made a beeline for the single coke stove in the hut where she worked. The two-mile bicycle ride had done little to warm her from the frosty air, and her face and fingers stung. She wondered how many bombers had returned from last night's sortie as she brooded over Alex. If only he'd write to her. It was the not knowing that was difficult to cope with.

The office was barely warmer than outside, and the stove did little to thaw the chill that hung like an icy blanket, making her skin prickle. Stella's hut was dull with rows of brown, wooden desks, side by side. WAAFs typed in harmony, working through the stack of papers that grew within their in-trays. There was little chatter, the main noise being the relentless tapping of keys ricocheting through the smoky smell of burning coke that mingled with the musty odour of the hut.

She sat down at her desk. A huge stack of paperwork leaned precariously on one side and inwardly she groaned, wishing she could hurl the lot out of the window. Her thoughts drifted to the night of the dance. Swaying in Mac's arms, carried away by the tone of his soft, velvet voice, but then the sound of a sudden thud shook her from her reverie, and she jumped.

Vera had dropped a massive stack of papers onto the desk with a mischievous twinkle in her eyes. 'Wakey, wakey!'

'Shh! What if the CO hears you?'

'Needn't worry about her, she's in with top brass so go on, tell me what happened with your Yank then.'

'He's not my Yank, and nothing happened. I showed him around, he took me home, and I said goodbye.' Stella didn't want Vera to know about the kiss. She felt guilty enough without having to suffer a barrage of questions.

'That's all?' Vera sank down on her chair and put a sheet of paper into position in her typewriter. 'Ooh, so disappointing. I'll have to take you in hand.' She pursed her lips and glanced at the letter on her desk. 'Well, he might be at the pub with Sam later.' She began to type, hitting the keys with gusto.

'Who's Sam?'

Vera stopped typing and with one eye on the CO's door leant towards Stella. 'That handsome GI who danced with me all night. He's taking me out tonight.' She raised her dark-pencilled eyebrows provocatively, displaying her pleased-with-herself look. The CO's door swung open, and Vera resumed her serious face as she promptly returned to her own desk.

Later, as they cycled home together, Vera told her all about Sam.

'Well, he's from Texas. His family has a store out there and Sam says when he goes back, he'll be running it.'

Stella smiled, delighted that her friend was happy, but she sensed there was more to it than that, which for Vera was unusual. So far in the past two months, she'd had numerous dates, mainly British, some very attractive, though none who had tempted her.

'He's a real gent you know, treated me like a lady all night – and he can't half dance. Did you see him? He's terrific. Oh, and he's gorgeous.'

Stella forced a smile. Tired and confused, all she wanted was to get home, close the door and have a warm drink. There was still no word from Alex and try as she might, she couldn't stop thinking about Mac. Of course, her mother wouldn't approve, but for now, that didn't matter. Of course, he was all talk. All that nonsense about taking her flying. GIs had the gift of charming the birds out from the trees. The thing was, she wanted it to be true – for him to be true. He exuded mystery and an exotic air which had stirred her curiosity and instilled a longing that could only be quenched by the touch of his skin on hers. A tingle zipped through her like electricity as she thought of their kisses.

When she reached her billet, Stella bid her friend goodbye and slipped inside, pausing for a moment as she wondered if she was alone. Mrs Brown usually called out when she heard the door, but tonight all was quiet. Stella's body ached, and she longed to change out of her uniform, so she headed straight up to her room.

She removed her tunic jacket and threw it over the back of the small, mahogany chair, and kicked off her regulation black shoes, wiggled her aching feet, and stretched out her legs. She thought about having a wash, but the icy chill in the air warned her otherwise. Her room was sparsely furnished, although she did have an open fire which she could light on cold evenings providing they had enough coal. *They'll ration the air next.* A red floral-patterned rug covered most of the scrubbed and polished wooden floor. Next time she went home for a visit, she would bring a few of her things back with her to make it homelier. Stella closed the blackout curtains, lit the hurricane lamp, then settled down to read her book for a while until evening tea was ready. *Pride and Prejudice* was one of her favourites, and she had read it several times already. Who could resist Mr Darcy?

A short while later, the front door slammed, and she ambled out onto the landing and peered downstairs.

'How are you, dear?' Barely drawing breath, Mrs Brown continued. 'Mrs Stewart's nephew is missing. His parents received the telegram this morning. He's missing in action somewhere in Italy. Oh, it's a terrible business. She's in a dreadful state, so you can imagine what his poor parents are going through.'

Her usual rosy cheeks were scarlet, and she bustled away to the kitchen, where she placed her basket down upon the scrubbed, wooden farmhouse table. She removed her WI hat and hung it with her coat on a wall hook in the rear porch, taking a moment to glance admiringly at the regimented rows of potatoes, leeks and swede growing in the former bed of the green velvet lawn. The garden was her pride and joy. 'Shall I make us some tea, dear? Oh, and I've got a nice bit of cake I put back yesterday – a jam sponge made with real eggs. Oh, it's a blessing, keeping hens.' She put a hand up to her dark brown, greying hair, to check the curls were still pinned, no doubt.

'Thanks, Mrs B.' Stella sat down at the table, thinking of the surreal times they were living through. It was strange how quickly one could empathise for families of the missing and of the dead, and yet in the blink of an eye, set it all aside and carry on regardless. Of course, they'd sink if they didn't.

Mrs. Brown tied her white lace-frilled apron around her thick waist. 'I made this years ago when lace was easily acquired. Now it's all rationing, queues, and squabbles, and barely any lace to be had – and that butcher's up to no good.'

Stella bit her lip to suppress a laugh. 'How do you mean?'

'I saw him hand over cuts of meat he shouldn't have had in the shop. He thought I wasn't looking, but now I know exactly what he's up to – black market I shouldn't wonder. Well, he'd better be on his best behaviour from now on, and he can think twice about tricking me out of my ration, or I shall report him, make no mistake.' She turned her hand to buttering bread, scraping on a thin, sparing layer, and then she filled the kettle, placing it on the range to boil. 'Tea won't be long, and then we can have a nice little catch-up, dear, and you can tell me all about your day.'

Stella wandered into the living room, and as she gazed around, her eyes fixed upon an old grainy picture of a young man in army uniform on the mantelpiece. There was another photo of the same man, standing next to a young woman, and there was something familiar about the woman's eyes and that mouth. Mrs Brown set the tea tray down on the table by her armchair. She'd used her best china and made some sandwiches. Stella sank down in the armchair by the fire.

As Mrs Brown poured the tea, Stella studied her face. Those eyes and mouth... no, it couldn't be, could it? The fire crackled and spat sparks of brightest orange into the mouth of the chimney, and Stella gazed at the forked flames that roared. As she sat, mesmerised by the blaze, Mac slipped into her mind, while Mrs Brown chatted about the WI and what Mrs Bradshaw had been up to three doors down.

Mac had been so confident and charming at the dance, but the other day at the church he'd revealed his vulnerable side, as if he'd been laid bare before God. He was far from home, fighting a war, and, like Alex, he was struggling too. No doubt he was lonely, adrift in a strange country. The way he'd looked into her eyes before he kissed her had sent her heart soaring, and she smiled to herself.

The droning sound of engines filtered into earshot and grew into a roar. 'Merlin engines,' Stella muttered, excusing herself and slipping out into the garden. She looked up to see a group of Lancaster Bombers against the backdrop of a half moon, heading out towards the Channel.

'Good luck, keep safe,' she whispered, gentle words etched in silvery white, carried by the light breeze, dissipating into the night.

The next day, Stella awoke with a start. Rolling over, she glanced at the clock – half past nine. She'd missed breakfast. Oh, Lord, she'd overslept, and Mac was calling at eleven. She jumped up, staggered across to the window, and drew back the curtains to reveal a milky blue sky. Buds and branches glistened beneath a cloak of silver. She dressed casually, pulling on trousers, a blouse, and jumper. Mrs Brown would have gone shopping by now, which was a relief, as Stella had no wish for awkward questions.

After breakfast, she gathered her things – gas mask, money, coat, scarf, and gloves. That ought to do. A nagging doubt resurfaced, but she pushed it to one side. She was having a day out with a friend, and she meant to enjoy herself. At eleven o'clock sharp, Stella stood waiting by the living room window, and a flash of olive green sailed by. She glanced out and saw the white star on the side of the vehicle and her heart raced. She grabbed her things and opened the front door. Mac flashed that cute grin and Stella's stomach fluttered as warmth speckled her cheeks. She walked down the front path towards his intense gaze until dark beads gave way to sapphire blue.

'Morning, ma'am.' He cast a mischievous grin as he waited by the passenger door.

'It's a lovely day.' She climbed in and the hairs prickled at the nape of her neck as she met his gaze. They drove towards Bassingbourn, and as they neared Mac's base, he appeared distracted and kept glancing up at the sky. Without warning, he swung across the road and bumped the jeep up onto the grass verge, and they stopped with a hard jolt.

'What's wrong?' She glanced at him as he sprung out and squinted up into the sky.

'Not sure, yet. That's one of our boys coming in over there. Fort doesn't sound right.'

Stella turned her face to the sky, straining to focus on the black shape in the distance. The faint hum of engines grew louder, and as it neared, two red flares sailed up into the pewter sky from the upper turret of the Flying Fortress. She gripped the seat tight. 'They've only got one wheel down.'

Mac headed over to the boundary fence. Stella joined him, watching, waiting in silence. The descending aircraft shrouded them for a moment as its silhouette slipped overhead, the thunderous roar of the engines vibrating right through Stella as her hair blew back, fluttering in the slipstream. She looked up, noting its dented, silver belly, its skin ripped open in places, wounded, yet still she glided with grace. With clammy hands, Stella gripped the rough wooden fence, and held her breath, waiting.

She recalled that day at Bourn some months ago when a Wellington bomber had crash-landed and burst into flames. Thick, black, acrid smoke had billowed out, engulfing the aircraft, and she'd watched while the firemen tried to douse the flames. Those poor boys, trapped inside. Tears pricked her eyes, and she took a deep breath.

As the Fortress touched down, the lowered wheel struck the runway with a bounce and then landed with a squeal of rubber, staying level for a moment, running on one wheel, before tilting to the other side. The aircraft veered off onto the grass and came to rest at the far side of the airfield. Smoke billowed out from one of the engines, but there were no flames. The fire and ambulance trucks wailed their way to the scene as the breeze blew a waft of acrid smoke in her direction.

As she turned away, her gaze flicked over the vivid green of the surrounding fields, the white nodding snowdrops, and the trees gently bending in the breeze. It was surreal how life flowed while young men died in the skies, or died trying to reach home, and people all around simply carried on. Stella released her grip on the fence, then a sharp sting in her finger caused her to wince. 'Ouch.' She peered at it as a pin-prick spot of blood emerged and swelled into a ruby droplet.

'What's the matter?'

'Oh, it's nothing, really. I think I have a splinter.'

'Let me see.' Mac reached for her hand and lifted it close to his face. 'I see it.' With nimble fingers, he withdrew the splinter and put her finger to his mouth and kissed it.

Stella gasped as a tidal force of blood surged through her body. 'Thank you.'

'Are you all right?' Mac put his hand on her shoulder. 'You look a little pale.'

'Yes, I thought, well, I'm glad they landed safely.' She swallowed, sensing the lump swell in her throat.

'Yeah, they're not called Flying Fortresses for nothing. They take quite a beating and still bring you home.' He took her arm in his as they walked back to the jeep. 'Made a safe landing, all things considered.'

His flight jacket was soft and supple beneath her hand. A memory suddenly bobbed to the surface. In the queue at Mr Thomas's butcher's shop weeks ago, she'd overheard two of the women speaking about a crash at Bassingbourn. The B-17 had belly landed, with the ball turret gunner trapped inside, and the poor boy was crushed. They hosed his life right out of that mess of mangled metal. Not a bit of him left to bury. An icy chill seeped through her body and she shivered. *Why did she have to remember that?* It was so awful. Dreadful things were happening all over – and for what? All because of a tyrannical little man across the Channel, insistent upon ruling Europe and the world, if he could capture her. She sucked in a breath.

'Hey, we'll go grab a cup of coffee. No, wait, it's tea, right? You Brits drink tea,' Mac said, grinning. He started up the jeep and headed off to Bassingbourn village.

Stella nodded, managing a weak smile, her mind still on that ball turret.

The tea shop was empty except for an elderly couple sitting at the rear. The friendly waitress brought tea and cake and Stella soon warmed up.

Mac poked his tea with the spoon. 'Looks kinda weak.' He took a mouthful and grimaced, prompting her to laugh. 'Now tasting that was worth it just to see you smile.'

Her cheeks blazed with heat as he grinned. 'Mac, do you ever get scared when you're flying?'

'Scared? No, I don't think so, maybe sometimes.' He looked down at the floor. 'It gets a little crazy up there with all those fighters milling around. Man, they can cut it all right, but you don't have time to be scared. We're too busy trying to stay in the air.' He took out a cigarette case from his tunic pocket and offered it to her. She shook her head. 'I always wanted to fly fighters, only the powers-that-be decided I had to fly bombers.' He lit a cigarette, took a drag, and leant back in his chair. 'I'll say one thing, though. As much as it's an abomination, if it weren't for this war I'd have missed out on the greatest opportunity in my life so far.'

'What's that?'

'You.' Mac's eyes twinkled, and his face creased into that relaxed, broad grin he had.

Stella's heart quickened, and she cast a brief smile and sipped her tea. A warm glow thawed her inside, and it was nothing to do with the tea. She was like a small child on Christmas morning: expectant – of what, she was not quite certain, but for something wonderful and exciting. She turned her gaze to the window and the street beyond. Patches of sky shone in puddles left by last night's rain and GIs strolled by, stepping around the glossy sky, with their girls in tow.

Later, when Mac took her home, he turned to face her. 'What are you up to tomorrow?'

'Oh, I'm going home for two days to see my mam.'

His smile slipped away. 'Oh, right. Well, I'll sure miss you, Stella. Today's been great.' He took her hand and brushed it with a kiss, holding on to her while their eyes met.

She saw the hunger burning within his gaze and butterflies fluttered in her stomach. But Alex was always there, in her mind, in the midst of everything and, like a sword, he severed the moment. 'I'm sorry, but I must go.' She pulled her hand from Mac's and noted the disappointment on his face as she turned to get out of the jeep. 'Thank you for today. I've had a lovely time.'

Mac sprung up and dashed around to her side, offering her his hand as she clambered out. 'Maybe when you get back we can meet up for a drink?'

'Well, yes, all right.'

She felt his gaze upon her, and she dared not meet it, but then he reached for her hand again. The warm ruggedness enveloped her in a rush filled with longing, and a voice in her head screamed 'No,' while the blood coursed through her veins as she lifted her eyes to his. Transfixed by sparkling blue, she opened her mouth to speak, but Mac leaned in and put his mouth on hers. His lips were soft, beguiling, and stirred up a swelling tide stronger than ever before. As he wrapped his arms around her waist, she revelled in undertones of shaving soap and cologne, his face soft and smooth against hers.

He nuzzled her ear as he whispered 'Stella, honey, promise me you'll hurry back. I'm sure gonna miss you.'

'It's for two days. I'll be back Friday afternoon, and I'm not back on duty until Sunday.' She smiled as he brushed her cheek with his fingertips. 'I'm sure you can cope,' she said, raising her eyebrows and casting him a conciliatory smile. 'Bye, Mac. Look after yourself.' She pulled away and walked steadily up the garden path and turned to wave. He was watching, waiting for her to reach the front door, and then with a wave and a smile, he drove away. The insatiable rush of adrenaline flashed through Stella's body and mingled with the bitter taste of guilt. Once inside, she hung up her coat on the stand in the hall, while the roar of the jeep's engine faded into the distance.

She had been planning this leave for weeks, eager to see her mother, yet now she was torn. Ashamedly she would rather stay with Mac – this stranger whom she was beginning to feel she had known all her life, even though it was disloyal to Alex. Oh, Lord, her mother would be so ashamed. She pressed her fingertips to her lips, the taste of him lingered, his scent swam around her and her senses reeled.

7

Humour Is the Best Medicine

Archie peered around Ward III as the early morning sun flooded in through the windows, then he flicked his gaze back to the medical notes. As he thumbed through the pages, his hand fumbled, and he struggled to grasp the corner of the paper. Probably exhaustion, given all the hours he'd been working. Raised voices out on the ward diverted his attention, and he glanced up.

'You cheeky bastard, Tom,' Pete Watson said.

'Well, at least my nose stayed where it was put.' Tom glared.

'Certainly did, old chap – slung over your shoulder!' Pete said in a mocking tone.

'What's going on so early in the day?' Bea marched across to the breakfast table. 'Sister will be along any minute, and if she hears any of this nonsense, you'll both be in bother.' She glanced at Pete and her face dropped. 'Oh, Lord help us. Jenny, get me some swabs, and you'd best hurry.' She stared at the nose which sat in a pool of blood on the table right next to Pete's mug of tea.

'I just sneezed.' A look of boyish innocence swept over his face as his cheeks glowed scarlet. 'I had a feeling the graft wasn't taking. Something didn't feel right.' Pete sucked in a breath and slowly exhaled. 'I feel a bit sick.'

'Rotten luck. Archie will fix you up again in no time.' Tom scraped his chair back and slapped the other man on the back. 'At least it's just your face that's buggered and not your tea.' He grinned.

'Well now, Pete, that's all we need. Rest back and take some deep breaths through your mouth. Lord knows what we're going to do with you.' Bea placed her hand on his shoulder.

'Never mind me, what about my ruddy nose? I've only had it for a week.' Pete stared down at it with the look of a small child who had dropped his ice cream on the ground.

'Not to worry. Archie will re-graft it, and you'll be as good as new again.'

Archie looked on with a mix of amusement and frustration. Pete was the second person this week to have a problem with a graft. And aside from the nose, he was also waiting for skin grafts to his face and hands. As a Spitfire pilot, he'd bailed out from his blazing cockpit and landed in the Channel. His hands were severely burned, and he'd struggled to unclip his chute, which had almost dragged him beneath the water. He undid it in the nick of time, having swallowed a fair amount of the Channel in the process, then managed to inflate his Mae West. Fortunately, another pilot in his squadron had seen his plight and radioed ahead. It had been a godsend that lifeboat rescue had found Pete so promptly and plucked him from the sea before hypothermia claimed him.

'I waited long enough for that nose.'

'Not to worry, we'll soon have you shipshape again,' Bea said cheerfully with a conciliatory smile. 'I'll let Archie know.'

Jenny, the VAD nurse, returned with a pile of swabs. Bea took a couple and carefully picked up the nose. She took a few more and placed them over his face. 'There now, hold them there while I go and get some dressing tape.'

Someone started up the gramophone in the middle of the ward and Glen Miller's 'In the Mood' swung out to a sea of amused faces.

'Pilots indeed. Who entrusted them with expensive things like Spitfires? They're barely out of short trousers,' Bea muttered, doing her best to look fierce, but she couldn't prevent the smile that blossomed.

'Who indeed, Bea?' Archie chuckled, noticing how she blushed a vibrant shade of scarlet. Clearly, she hadn't realised he was standing behind her. 'A sense of humour is vital if you're to work and survive in this ward. Don't worry, I'll take a look now.'

Archie charged into his office and slammed the door behind him. His cheeks burned as the blood surged through his veins. 'Damn narrow-minded people.' He thumped his fist on the desk, winced, and quickly regretted it. There was a knock on the door, and he drew in a sharp breath. 'Come in.'

'Just wanted a quick word, Boss.' Blackie stood hovering in the doorway. 'Something wrong?'

Archie sank into his chair and clenched and unclenched his hand a few times beneath the desk, trying in vain to dispel the numbness that was spreading from his wrist to his fingertips. 'Matron has received another complaint. This time one of our VAD nurses has made an accusation against one of the men. Never mind, I'll sort it out. What was it you wanted?' He poured himself a glass of water and gulped it down, feeling the heat in his face fade.

'Well, it's our latest arrival, Boss. This American chap. He's in bad shape, isn't he?'

'Indeed. Some bugger went and doused him with tannic acid. What's it going to take to get that blasted stuff eradicated? I thought everyone had stopped using it by now.'

'Well, we have, but I believe the message is taking a little longer to reach Europe. Aside from that, he's going on about getting married.'

'Ah, yes. I meant to tell you about that.' Archie lit a cigarette, drew on it, and puffed out a plume of smoke.

'He can't get married in that state.' Blackie dropped the files down on the desk with a thump and sat perched on the edge of the seat. 'More papers for you to go through, I'm afraid.'

Archie flicked a gaze at the pile and nodded. 'His girlfriend's pregnant. Doesn't want the child being born out of wedlock.' He ran both hands through his hair, mindful of his centre parting as he smoothed it down.

Blackie leant back in his chair. 'I can understand that, I suppose. He's just a little off with his timing.'

Archie sighed and rolled his eyes. 'Very honourable of him. He's an American, from Iowa as I recall. Nineteen years old, a mere boy.'

'He's got Sister in a pickle because he's refusing treatment. Being most uncooperative by all accounts. Says he wants to see you – now.' Blackie held his hands up when

Archie glared at him. 'His words, not mine, Boss. He's very distressed, and you know how Sister gets.'

Archie sighed. 'Quite.' He retrieved the burning cigarette from the ashtray and took a drag before stubbing it out. 'I tell you, Blackie, these boys will be the death of me.' He stood up. 'Best go and see him then. Lead on.'

Piano music flowed out of the ward and men's voices sang along to the tune of 'Roll out the Barrel', although a little off-key. Archie smirked as he strolled through the open doors, with Blackie following behind. He headed straight for bed one, which was shrouded with pale-green curtained screens. Groans and shouts came from within, along with the strained voice of Sister Jamieson, who shrunk back when Archie swept in with Blackie in tow.

'Now then, young fellow, what's all this about refusing treatment?' Archie sank down on the side of the bed.

'Doc, as I told you, I gotta get married. My girl, I can't let her think she's all alone.'

Sister passed the young pilot's medical notes to Archie, who pushed his spectacles further up the bridge of his nose and flicked through the file. He studied Jack for a moment. 'I had another young fellow recently, the same situation as yours. Header tank exploded right in front of him. The tanks were self-sealing, but some clod forgot to treat the tank in front of the pilot. Made a bit of a mess of him, too.'

Archie pursed his lips and paused for a moment. 'Sister, bring some morphine. Let's get him more comfortable before we look at these wounds.' He pulled out a pen from his breast pocket and scribbled something down in the notes. 'Now, I can see you were wearing your goggles. Just as well. You'd be surprised how many take them off.' He shook his head and looked down at the heavily bandaged hands, which were showing signs of wound exudate through fresh dressings already. 'As for your hands, I'd guess you weren't wearing your gloves.'

Jack shook his head. 'Too bulky, especially when you're in a jam.'

'Hmm, well, we need to take the bandages off and have a look. Don't worry, we'll give you something for the pain first. Now, your hands are black and crispy because someone coated them in tannic acid – it hardens and forms a protective shell, only we don't use it here anymore. Still, not to worry. I'll be able to remove it with surgery and then we can see how bad the hands are and take it from there. You're going to need a few skin grafts, including some for your face.'

'But Doc, what about my girl? I can't just lie here, waiting, for weeks on end. The baby's due in around four months. I gotta marry her.' Jack struggled to raise himself up on his arms and sank back down onto the pillows, breathing hard.

Archie placed his hand on the young man's shoulder. 'Just rest there, young fellow. You're in one hell of a mess.' He couldn't help but be impressed by how strong-willed his young patient was. It really was incredible. 'Jack, we want the best for you, and we want you to be content, so if getting spliced will keep you happy then we'll arrange it. Maybe afterwards I can do some work on you.' Archie grinned. 'For the time being, you have to allow us to treat you, or you won't have a hope in hell of making it to the altar.'

Jack's twinkling eyes signified agreement. 'You got it, Doc,' he said in a more sedate tone.

'We'll fix you up, and we'll see what we can arrange.' Archie flicked a gaze at Blackie, who made a note in his diary.

'Thanks. That's a weight off my mind.' Jack's head sank further into his pillow and as his face eased, it was as if the stress melted away, taking some of the pain with it.

Archie strolled back to his office as thoughts steamed through his mind. How on earth was he supposed to organise a wedding in a hospital? The boy wasn't up to getting married, and the whole idea was ludicrous, but he'd seen the fear in his eyes, and it wasn't unfounded. He couldn't say for certain what the boy's prognosis would be, although he was confident he would survive, providing sepsis didn't set in. Other than that, Jack's RAF career was over.

There was so much to do, and these boys added more and more each day. As he stepped out into the bright sunshine with Blackie, he savoured the cool, fresh air that washed over him like a breath of mist. 'Blackie, how the devil do we sort this out? Does his girlfriend even know he's here?'

'I doubt it. I'll get the contact details and send a telegram. In the meantime, why don't I have a word with our hospital chaplain?'

Archie clapped him on the back. 'Sounds like a plan. Perhaps the sooner she's here, the faster he'll cooperate.' Thank the Lord he could rely on Blackie. 'Looks like we might be going to a wedding. Better give Sister enough notice and tell her to wear her best hat.' They both started to laugh.

The following week, Archie was relieved to hear that the registrar was happy to carry out the ceremony at the hospital chapel. It was to take place in ten days' time and Blackie had managed to contact Jack's girlfriend and make all the necessary arrangements.

'Hey, I don't even have a ring yet – no engagement ring, no wedding ring. Can you help with that?' Jack's eyes pleaded.

He looked much brighter and while some of his wounds were healing, his hands and fingers remained bound in a solid, black, crispy shell. The tannic acid had to come off. Lord knew what was brewing underneath, and Archie was concerned about infection. The fingers were contracted and would worsen steadily until the fingertips were drawn into the palms of each hand, severely compromising Jack's hand function.

'I don't suppose you'd take me up to London to a jewellery store?' Jack stared, wide-eyed.

Blackie looked surprised and glanced at Archie for an answer. 'I could buy them for you, it's no trouble.'

The boy was near half-fried, for pity's sake, and Archie blew out a breath, but then he saw the disappointment that flashed in Jack's eyes.

'No thanks, this is something I have to do myself.' Jack lay back and flicked a gaze from Archie to Blackie.

'We'll see.' That was as much as Archie was prepared to commit to for the time being, although Jack was persistent, and over the coming days, each time he saw Archie or Blackie he would ask if any arrangements had been made. Eventually, recognising the need to settle things, Archie came to see him. 'You're looking a little stronger.'

'Sure am, though I'm not up to walking yet.'

'Yes, well, it's going to take time, but you'll get there.'

'Say, Maestro. I can't get married without the rings now, can I? Are you gonna take me out so I can buy them or do I have to break outta here?'

Archie studied him for a moment. Couldn't the boy improvise or something? He still looked a bit of a mess. With a skull-like face, he would be a dreadful fright to the public, however, Archie's primary concern was Jack. He had no wish for the boy to be gawked at or subjected to looks of horror, nor to be wounded by words. While the locals here were becoming used to these men, it was very different in London. As long as he was adequately dressed and bandaged, of course, he might get away with it. After to-ing and fro-ing with himself over the dilemma, Archie gave in. 'Blackie can take you to one store only – nowhere else – then straight back here.'

Archie set his cutlery down upon the empty china plate and reached for his glass.

'Excellent dinner, as always.' Blackie leant back in his chair and picked up his smouldering pipe from the ashtray. Tobacco smoke lingered in the air.

'Yes, not bad at all. Thank goodness for Mrs. Thomas. I'd be lost without my housekeeper.' Archie poured brandies for them both. 'Now then, what exactly happened today?'

Blackie sipped his brandy. 'Well, firstly, Jack insisted that only the best jewellers would do for his girl, so I decided to take him to Mappin and Webb, in Regent Street. Well, a cheerful gentleman came out to serve us, however, he took one look at Jack's face, his smile faded sharpish, and his face drained of all colour, poor chap.' Blackie chuckled.

'Anyway, Jack told him that he wanted to buy an engagement ring and a wedding ring. So, without a word the assistant stared down at him, then glanced at me. I don't think he could believe his eyes. Nevertheless, he lifted out a tray of rings from beneath the counter. Jack leant forward, but he needed a little help so I held the rings up for him.'

'Poor man. Didn't you tell him he was still in hospital?' Archie drew on his cigarette.

'No, I never got the chance. So, Jack picked a plain gold wedding band and a sapphire engagement ring. The assistant looked most relieved by this point. Then he says, "A worthy choice, sir. Now all we need to know is the size of the lady's finger." He glanced at me and by now I'm thinking we're sunk. We'll never get the size right.' Blackie chuckled and dragged a hand through his wavy brown hair.

'Well, yes. It's something I hadn't considered.'

'Well, Jack looked at me, then at the assistant, and he says, "Well, that's easy. It's the same size as my little finger." So he pulled his right hand out of his pocket and rested it on the counter.'

Archie tried hard to suppress his laughter. 'The poor chap must have been traumatised being confronted with black, crispy fingers.'

'His face dropped like a stone when he glanced down, then he turned grey and fainted. He didn't half hit the floor with some force.'

Archie roared with laughter as his sides ached and his eyes grew moist, but a memory resurfaced and began to gnaw away at him and he ceased. When he had first arrived in London, he'd encountered Great War veterans begging and selling matchsticks or anything they could just to get by. Many of them were disabled – shunned by a government which had sent them to war and shunned by the society they returned to, all because of their disabilities and disfigurements. A lump rose in his throat. One of those beggars had met his gaze with dark, weary eyes, sunken into a grimy engrained face; the same tired and tortured face he saw in Jack. Archie swallowed.

He couldn't let the same fate befall his boys, that much was certain. Every one of them should have a future to look forward to. The Guinea Pig Club might prove its worth after the war with any luck. Sometimes a helping hand was all it took for a man to stand on his own two feet and to assist with his recovery and right now, the helping hand Jack needed was to get married.

'Blackie, it was a damn fine thing you did for that young man. Something you can be proud of, and I'm sure he's very grateful to you.' Archie rose from his chair and strode over to the open fire, stretching out his tingling fingers in front of the flames. He wasn't that cold; the intermittent symptoms in his hands weren't showing any signs of going away. He sighed, just as the air raid siren ruptured the peace with its rise and fall like the groans of some infernal animal in pain. 'Bloody Jerry.' He shook his head.

'What's it to be? The shelter or another brandy?' Blackie sat poised on the edge of his chair.

'To hell with them. Brandy it is.'

8

Willington, County Durham

Crash! Something heavy rumbled and rolled along the pavement outside, then came a clatter followed by another crash. The sound of beer kegs being delivered to the pub further down the road was a daily ritual. Between the rumbles and crashes, birdsong sang out. The ring of a bicycle bell from the main street below and a replying shout, "Morning, our Geoff," and then silence. It would only last for a minute or two now the old country town had stirred into life, but Stella welcomed it.

She lay in her old bed, feeling out of place in her childhood home, which now seemed so strange. For a time after leaving, she had suffered the worst homesickness and hankered for letters from home. In the beginning, the post had seemed to take forever, then after a while, it took no time at all. She smiled as she pictured the Valentine's card Mac had sent last week. He'd turned up unexpectedly and presented her with a beautiful box of candy tied with a red silk bow. She'd never tasted anything so delicious in her whole life.

Next door's hens clucked out in the yard. Stella glanced at the clock. 'Half past seven,' she muttered. In an hour, her mother would be opening the shop downstairs. She cast off the blankets, tumbled out of bed, and dressed quickly because of the chilled air and then drew back the curtains. The recent snow had long since thawed, though the rows of houses opposite stood shimmering in hats of silver-frosted slate. Once downstairs, she busied herself in the kitchen, made a pot of tea and carried a cup through to her mother, who was in the shop counting out the cash float for the till.

Later that morning, Stella decided to take a walk through the churchyard. It was a chance to visit her father's grave and pay her respects. St Stephen's Church always looked so peaceful and beautiful, with its stone walls and ornate stained glass windows. She gazed at the bare cherry blossom trees that would soon flower, and later cast their silken blooms across the tombstones, shrouding the fallen. Golden rays trickled through the branches and danced liked jewels upon the frosted ground.

Stella crouched in front of her father's grave, the fresh flowers in the urn evidence of her mother's latest visit. After the Great War, he'd ventured into business and following the depression, during the hard times of the 1920s, he'd paid for the poorest children in the town to have shoes on their feet. The church had overflowed with mourners. Stella blinked the tears away.

She found a bench and sat down, glad to be alone with her thoughts for a moment. She remembered sitting next to Mac in the churchyard at Bourn, and as she shivered in the bracing breeze, she longed for him to be by her side. She felt empty and yearned for the press of his thigh against hers, to drink in his smell, to fall into those strong arms because he'd made her feel safe and wanted. She sighed.

Grey clouds eclipsed the sun, and the icy wind nipped her cheeks and nose.

When she returned home, she found her mother putting stock away in the store room while it was quiet. Since the rationing, many sweets had become scarce, and Mrs Charlton had diversified, offering other items for sale when she could – biscuits, tinned food, even soap, shoe laces, and boot polish.

The bell rang ding-a-ling and the door swung open. A young boy plodded in across the wooden floor, dressed in dark grey shorts, red wellingtons, and a black coat. He gazed up at the shelves behind the counter, his wide blue eyes sailing across the bright-coloured jars of sweets, his mouth wide open. The rationing bit hard, restricting each person to twelve ounces of sweets each month, although a lot of adults handed in their coupons to local stores and Woolworths who then distributed extra to the children.

'Stella, love, I almost forgot.' Her mother carried on working as she spoke, her cheeks rosy red. She was always on the go; no wonder she was so slim. She reached for a floral-patterned apron, slipped it over her head, securing the ties at the waist, then tucked a stray grey curl behind her ear.

'A letter came for you this morning. I've put it on the mantelpiece in the living room.' She smiled as she swept past her daughter to serve the small boy, who was now slowly counting his money, placing coins on the counter.

'Thanks, mam.' Stella wondered who it was from. No one knew where she was except for Mac and Mrs. Brown, and Mac didn't have her address. She retreated to the living room at the back of the house and found the letter. The envelope was stamped RAF Coningsby. 'Alex,' she murmured, ripping it open as the smell of burning coke from the fire hung in the air.

Dearest Stella,

I'm so sorry for taking so long in writing to you. Things have been frantic here, and I'm afraid I've lost your billet address. What luck you gave me your home address that time otherwise I'd never have found you. My squadron's rather busy. Lots of flying and training, but other than that, there's nothing else to report from Lincolnshire. Hope everything's going well for you. I miss Bourn, though most of all I miss you, my darling. I had a few days leave recently and went home as mother hasn't been well. She's much better now of course. I wanted you to meet my parents so they've invited you for the weekend next time we have leave together. What do you think?

I had some bad news a few weeks ago. My cousin, Peter, was shot down while on a sortie over France. There's no trace of him, no chute seen. Damn this war. Sometimes it feels as if one can't go on, and then I picture you and I know I must.

When I went home, it wasn't the same. Even mother's struggling. As for his parents, well, they're bearing up, but Aunt Charlotte is lost without him. He was like a brother to me. Darling, please say you'll come for a weekend soon – everyone's dying to meet you. I need you. If I get the chance, I'll come down and see you, although it will probably be a last-minute thing and a flying visit. Write back when you get this.

All my love,
Alex. xxx

Stella glanced at the letter once more. His cousin was dead. Peter might have been his best friend, yet he'd made no attempt to hide his disdain of Alex's relationship with her. He'd often cast her sneering looks, and while she never liked him, she would never have wished this on him. She was sorry for Alex's loss and knowing he was grieving again made her feel even more wretched. Thoughts whizzed through her mind, thick and fast, as a dark, stormy fog settled in her head.

'Stella, I've closed the shop for lunch so I'll make the tea, shall I?' Mrs Charlton looked at the letter in her lap. 'Anything wrong, love?'

'No. I'll come and help.' There was no point in elaborating right now, although her mother had a crafty way of weeding out the information regardless. Stella followed her out to the small kitchen and watched as she filled the kettle and set it on the stove to boil.

'Well, was the letter from Alex?'

'Yes. He's settling in at his new base.' Stella arranged the tea cups and milk jug on a tray.

'Oh, that's good. He's such a nice boy. He must have said more than that.'

Here we go. Stella sighed. 'His cousin was killed in action recently, shot down over France.'

'Oh, dear. The poor boy.' Mrs Charlton's face fell and filled with compassion.

'And he's invited me to stay at his for the weekend. He wants me to meet his parents.'

'Does he indeed?' She pursed her lips.

Stella could tell she was thinking about it. 'I'm not sure when I'll next get leave, and his family lives near Exeter. I don't know why he seems so keen for me to go. It's all rather out of the blue.'

'Don't you? Well, it sounds clear enough to me.'

'How do you mean?'

'There's only one reason a young man takes his young lady home to meet his parents.'

'You don't mean?' Stella stood wide-eyed, mouth open.

'Yes, love, I do. He's going to ask you to marry him.' The kettle whistled, and Mrs Charlton removed it from the hot plate. She measured out the tea, dropped it in the teapot, and poured the boiled water. 'Take it to the living room, pet, and we'll sit in there. It's warmer than this draughty old kitchen.'

Stella did as she was told. Maybe she should never have gone to that dance at Bassingbourn, yet the thought of not knowing Mac filled her with a heavy ache. Alex had used all his charms on her in the beginning. Soon afterwards, the rumours began, and she had witnessed his roving eye for herself, but his charm and persistence paid off, despite the niggling voice at the back of her mind.

'Oh, your father would be so proud of you, love.' Mrs Charlton beamed as she set the tray down on a small table and sank into the chair by the fire. Next, she balanced the strainer on top of the china cup and poured the tea. 'And with that beautiful country estate. You'll be lady of the manor.'

The words sliced through Stella with a jolt. She'd known Alex the longest, and yet it was like she barely knew him at all. One evening spent at The Red Lion in Bassingbourn had joined them together seven months ago. She'd been enjoying a quiet drink with Vera, although Vera was rarely ever quiet. Stella smiled to herself. It was August 1942, the day had been long and hot, and locals and RAF had filled the pub, spilling out onto the pavement to enjoy a drink while watching the setting sun. While Vera chatted to a pilot from their base, Stella noticed a tall young man in RAF blues watching her, a cigar in one hand, a pint in the other. He drew on his cigar and exhaled, his eyes smiling, fixed on her. She'd been twisting a stray curl around her finger and judging by the amused look on his face, he'd enjoyed the show. The pub was stale, sweaty, and humid, adding to her discomfort, so she stepped outside for a breath of fresh air. A man's voice called out her name and she turned to face him, his dark brown eyes twinkling beneath a thatch of blonde hair.

When she asked how he knew her name, he said he'd asked her friend in the pub. And that was that. His relaxed manner, his charm, and his wit had teased her from her shell and over the weeks that followed, whenever he could, he took her dancing or for a quiet drink somewhere. But then he took leave and went away with his cousin, and there had been other dates when he simply didn't show up and made some excuse days later. When he left for his new posting to Coningsby in Lincolnshire, she'd been upset at first, and then hurt and worried when he didn't write. Once, she'd thought she was in love with him, yet now, having spent time with Mac, things had changed. As she pictured Mac, the blood pulsed through her veins, and she quivered inside.

Her heart sank. How could she abandon Alex at a time like this? He'd been close to Peter – they'd almost been inseparable, apart from the fact one was in Fighter Command, the other Bomber Command. She was trapped, and the idea of breaking it off with him raked her with guilt, while the thought of never seeing Mac again brought a crushing blow to her chest. Why did Alex want her to meet his parents? He'd never once said he loved her.

Of course, her mother was thrilled and had pushed her towards him – towards a *better life*, as she so often said. If she ended things now, her mother would be bitterly disappointed. If only her father were still alive. Her heart ached, and a lump rose in her throat. She swallowed. Her mother simply wanted the best for her, but her pushing and meddling had saddled her with an increasingly oppressive burden, and Stella was now obligated to make her proud. Would it be so bad if she shunned high society for an American? As soon as she drew Mac into her head with his smile and those deep blue eyes, a warmth flowed through her like silk. That way he had of doing everything, from sitting, to walking, to being with her. His American charm. She smiled as a warm, fuzzy haze settled within her.

9

Faint Heart Never Won Fair Lady

Mac lay in the darkness, waiting for dawn. He'd lain awake half the night, listening as the wind howled at the gable end of the brick-built barracks, and then a group of Lancaster Bombers had grumbled and groaned their way home from some raid across the Channel. It was almost six o'clock, an hour away from daylight. He reached over and drew back the curtain. A light film of silver frost speckled the inside of the glass window. England sure was cold.

He got dressed and went in search of breakfast. The mess hall was almost empty. A few of the guys looked rough – they probably hadn't slept much either. The further into the tour you got, the more you seemed to lose yourself. Your service number became your identity and you – the real you – ceased to exist. They were here for King, country, and Roosevelt. The rich aroma of coffee made his mouth water, and he grabbed a cup then asked for eggs and toast. After breakfast, he strolled back to his room to freshen up properly. He decided to hang out at the officer's club for a while and maybe write those letters home he'd been putting off.

Stella's train was due in at three o'clock. Meldreth Station was deserted except for the guard in the ticket office. Mac wondered what to say. Of course, he knew what he wanted to say, but he didn't wish to push her away. Stella was the kind of girl you took home to meet your folks. She was the real deal, forever. He'd known it from the moment he saw her across the dance hall. Yesterday, he'd checked the timetable so he could meet her when she returned. It sure would be a surprise, though would she be happy to see him? Maybe she'd think he was pushy and be mad as hell. He couldn't stand the thought of her being with another guy, especially one like Alex.

In the distance, a whistle rang out clear and shrill, and the sound of the steam engine filtered into earshot, gradually growing louder. As the black train huffed into the station, it exhaled a bilious smog of white vapour and screeched to a halt.

A grey-haired woman stepped down from one carriage, grasping a walking stick in her hand, and a porter came to her aid, gathering her bags. Mac waited, but no one else emerged. Then the door of the rear carriage swung open, and his heart lifted when he saw the slender, toned calf beneath the door as Stella stepped down. He strode over, flashing a wide grin.

'Mac, what are you doing here?' Stella's voice almost sang with surprise, and her green eyes widened and sparkled.

'I figured you might appreciate a lift home.' He grabbed her brown leather case, his hand brushing hers as he gazed into her eyes. She didn't object; in fact, she seemed pleased, and his arms twitched to hold her. A piercing screech screamed as the guard blew his whistle, and the train chuffed out of the station. Mac held out his arm, and she linked hers in his as they strode across to the jeep.

'You shouldn't have gone to all this trouble for me.'

'What trouble? I've got the whole day off, tomorrow too, so it's no problem at all.' He just loved the way her cheeks took on that rosy glow. Man, she was cute. 'Besides, you're worth it.' What he so desperately wanted to say was how much he'd missed her, but it didn't seem right somehow, not yet.

Mac put the case on the back seat then jumped into the driver's seat and gazed at her, drinking in her beauty as if for the first time.

'Did you miss me?' Stella's mouth curved upward into that tantalising smile of hers, her words catching him off-guard.

'You bet I did, honey.' He reached over and brushed her cheek with his fingertips, light and soft. As she gazed into his eyes, he lost himself in sparkling emeralds, leaning ever closer, her naked lips full and tempting.

'Oh, Mac, I...'

He heard her sharp intake of air. Her sighs and breaths exuded a power over him he couldn't resist, and he took her in his arms and kissed her. A hint of prairie flowers rose from her supple skin; she was intoxicating, and he was falling deeper and deeper under her spell. 'I guess I'd best get you home.' Reluctantly, he released her and started up the engine.

'I'd love a cup of tea,' she said, stifling a yawn. 'Come on driver, homeward bound.'

'Yes, ma'am.'

The drive to Bourn didn't take long as the jeep whipped along the tree-lined lanes. When they pulled up outside Lilac

Cottage, Mac cut the engine. 'How about coming for a drink with me tonight? We could find a quiet pub somewhere away from the base.'

'All right. Pick me up around seven.' She squeezed his hand and leant towards him, brushing his cheek with her lips.

As she did so, he turned, his mouth finding hers. She was too damn tempting, and he couldn't resist. He slipped his hand inside her great coat and placed it on her thigh, gently caressing the softness beneath. As he slid it towards her waist, she placed her hand on his, guiding it back down.

'I have to go.' Stella glanced out at the small cottage, suddenly sounding brisk.

'Is that your landlady at the window?'

'Oh no. She's looking right at us.'

'Come on then.' As Mac grabbed the case from the back seat, the front door of the cottage creaked open. Mac glanced up to find a plump middle-aged lady at the entrance.

'There you are, dear. Did you have a good trip?' She smiled as she viewed him over Stella's head with questioning eyes.

'Oh, yes, thanks.' Stella's face flushed scarlet.

'And I see you have a gallant escort today.' Mrs Brown glanced between Mac and Stella, her eyebrows raised.

'Oh, this is Lieutenant John Mackenzie. He's stationed at Bassingbourn.'

Mac stepped forward. 'It's a pleasure to meet you, ma'am.' He held out his hand.

Mrs Brown's face softened and broke into a girlish smile, and she giggled. 'Oh, I'm very pleased to meet you, Lieutenant.' She shook his hand. 'Well now, where are my manners? Come in, come in. I'll make us all a lovely cup of tea.' She turned and bustled away through the hall.

'That was easier than I expected,' Stella said with a puzzled look.

Half an hour later, they were all sitting in the living room with a tray of tea and sandwiches. Mac sat on the sofa next to Stella, and Mrs Brown sat in an armchair by the fire. She seemed intent on finding out everything about him, but he didn't mind, answering all her questions with all the patience and politeness that had been bred into him from the day he was born. 'These sandwiches are lovely, ma'am. I hope I'm not depriving you of food now.'

'Oh no, not at all, Lieutenant. You're welcome here any time.'

'Thank you, ma'am. I appreciate your hospitality.' Mac drained the last of his tea. He didn't care for it much, but it would be improper to have declined it. He flicked a gaze at the clock on the mantelpiece. Five thirty. 'Well, ladies, I think it's time I was getting along. It's been a pleasure meeting you, ma'am.' He held out his hand to Mrs Brown.

'Oh, and you, Lieutenant,' she said, remaining seated as she shook his hand.

Stella sprung up. 'I'll see you out.'

As they walked to the door, Mac couldn't stop grinning. 'See you at seven.'

'All right.' She smiled, as he reached for her hand.

He leant in and kissed her, feeling her warmth against him as he drew her close, a rush of desire rising within him. 'Hey, I'd better go,' he murmured, nuzzling her hair. He opened the door and turned his face to the salmon-pink sky, watching the sun as she slipped towards the horizon. 'Till later, then.' He zipped up his leather flight jacket.

'Bye, Mac.' Stella gazed up at him, a smile tugging on those velvet lips.

The door closed behind him with a creak as he ambled down the garden path. He sprung into the jeep and turned the key, wondering what was happening here. Did he imagine it or did she really like him? He smiled, yet he couldn't help thinking about what lay ahead. The other guys lived for today, while he was busy making plans. Without them, there was no future, but what he really wanted to know was whether he figured in hers.

A quiet drink. That's what he'd hoped for so he could ask her about Alex, only he hadn't counted on running into Vera. She was at the pub with Sam, and so far, had kept them chatting for over an hour. Boy, could she talk? At long last, he had Stella to himself, and he drew her close, the heat of her body against his as they swayed across the floor, and the soft dulcet tones of Vera Lynn eclipsed all thoughts of Alex. Holding Stella in his arms was like coming home, but then she stiffened and he felt a tap on his shoulder. He spun around to face a man a few inches shorter than himself, dressed in RAF blues.

'Alex!' Stella stepped back.

'Do you mind if I cut in?' Alex glowered at Mac, and his eyes narrowed, while the corners of his mouth twitched to form the glimmer of a smirk.

So, he'd turned up, just like that. The proverbial bad penny. Mac drew himself up to his full height of five feet eleven just as Stella stepped forward.

'Alex, I had no idea you were coming.'

'Evidently, dear girl.' Alex placed his hand on her arm and leaned in to kiss her cheek.

Mac tightened his jaw. Goddamn it. Conflict burned in Stella's eyes, his last glimmer of hope as Alex steered her away, leaving him standing there, alone.

'Cheer up. It won't last. Alex is a lying, cheating, no-good swine. Stella feels sorry for him, that's all.' Vera took his arm and steered him over to a table tucked away in a corner of the bar.

Later, as Mac cast sideways glances at Stella, he caught her eye occasionally and the look that nestled there reassured him. Ten feet of floor space separated them, though it may as well have been the Channel, the gulf was so vast. He puffed out a breath, slamming the beer bottle down on the table. When Alex slipped his arm around Stella, Mac clenched his teeth. The guy was a fake and something stirred and swelled in his gut, surging up like a volcanic eruption, but he swallowed it down.

'Hey, come on, Mac. Time to make a move, buddy.' Sam cast him a sympathetic look.

He didn't want to go, not just yet. He was keeping his eye firmly on that sleaze. Mac glanced at Stella again, only this time Alex caught him out and his mouth set in a tight line. Mac sprung up, keeping his eyes on Alex.

Sam placed his hand on Mac's arm. 'Leave it, Mac. We don't need any trouble.'

Mac shook him off and strode across to Stella. 'We're going now. It sure was nice seeing you again.' He tipped his cap and cast a half-smile.

'Yes, yes, run along now. The lady is with me, and I'd appreciate it if you'd leave her alone.' Alex drew her nearer, but she stiffened.

'Well, you've done a swell job of treating her like a lady so far.' Mac's face hardened.

Alex took a slow, deep drag of his cigarette and exhaled smoke in Mac's face. 'Like I said, the lady is with me.'

Mac's face burned and he clenched his fist by his side. The guy was trying to be cool, but he'd touched a nerve. 'Good night, Stella. Hope to see you again.' He couldn't help himself. He turned to walk away and followed Vera and Sam outside, halting at the sound of gravel crunching behind him. He spun around. Alex strode towards him with a couple of guys for backup. Just then, Stella appeared in the doorway.

'Bloody Yanks. Moving in while we're away fighting.'

'In case you hadn't noticed, we're fighting too.' Mac took a step nearer.

'Alex, please don't.' Stella came closer. 'Please.' Her voice was thin and pleading.

'Not until I've made my point,' Alex snarled. 'Get back inside.'

'Don't talk to her like that.' Mac squared up to him. 'She's not your property, pal.'

'I am not your pal.' Alex cracked his knuckles and took a swing, but Mac dodged out of the way.

'Please, both of you. Stop!' Stella's voice quavered and rang out several octaves higher. Mac turned. Panic flashed in her eyes and her face visibly paled. 'Mac, look out.'

He didn't see it coming, and the force hit him like a brick in the jaw and spun him round, his knees buckling as he sank to the ground. His head swam, and his eyes filled with white sparkling floaters. Sam was by his side in an instant. Mac looked up to see the smirk on Alex's face while he kneaded his fist.

Stella rushed towards him, but Alex grabbed her arm. 'Leave it. Go inside, now.'

'Mac, are you all right?' She turned those wide green eyes on him.

'Yeah. I'm okay. You go on.' He nodded to her and winked.

'Come on, Mac, let's get outta here before the landlord calls the MPs. That's all we need.'

Mac rubbed his face, heaved in a deep breath of fresh air, and Sam hauled him to his feet. Jeez, that was one hell of a sock to the jaw. His heart ached, and a shallow dent punched his pride. She was under his skin all right, and he couldn't get her out of his head. He had to have her, to hold her in his arms and love her forever. Stella made him feel again after this war had almost ravaged him. She eclipsed the darkness, and he couldn't lose her, not now.

10

In Sickness & In Health

The afternoon's surgery had been challenging, and Archie ached from his neck to his shoulders and all the way down to his hands. He strained to focus through weary eyes. The patient, nineteen-year-old Canadian radio operator Tony Smithson, had suffered third-degree burns when his Lancaster Bomber crash-landed. Having lost his eyelids, he was now sporting a new set and would hopefully feel more comfortable within a couple of days.

Archie sighed. The boy's girlfriend had dumped him most unceremoniously by letter, and Tony had been distraught before his surgery. Why couldn't these girls realise their husbands and boyfriends needed them, particularly at a time like this when they were most vulnerable? Talk about kicking a fellow when he's down. On that point, Archie was most resolute. Being rejected by loved ones was such a cruel blow and some of the lads withdrew from life altogether and became lost in the darkness.

He had to show them there was still hope and that not all women would turn away. That was why he had sought out the prettiest of nurses for his own ward. An air of flirting couldn't do any harm here in the hospital. The sensual drift of perfume in the air was one way of rousing interest and glancing up from a hospital bed to see a pretty face with ruby lips was another. He needed women to show his boys their disfigurements didn't matter. Why couldn't people look beyond the physical form?

Leaving home to march away to war only to return virtually unrecognisable was emotionally challenging, and Archie pondered the consequences. The mind was an enigma, and he was no psychiatrist, although he knew there was a need to address the psyche if he was to successfully reintegrate his lads into society.

Friends and colleagues were forever telling him he was too involved. *Just do your job and operate on them.* He sighed. These young men had agreed to serve their country; it was the war that had altered them, and it would be their own countries that deserted them.

It was almost seven o'clock. Time for one last ward round before he retired home for the night. As he strolled through the hospital grounds, he gazed up at the sapphire sky, a myriad of silver stars sparkling around a full creamy moon. In the distance, long beams of light reached up into the darkness, crossing paths as they swept across the night sky. The drift of chimney smoke lingered in the still air while a cacophony of noise drifted out from the closed doors of the ward.

'Evening, Maestro,' the boys called out, one by one, an ongoing chorus as he strode along by their beds.

Evans, with his leg in plaster, raced up and down the length of the ward in his wheelchair, propelling himself as if training for the next Olympics. The boy could barely sit stationary for a minute. For the time being, it would be the nearest rush he would experience after his Spitfire. The chap at the piano belted out the national anthem, and everyone who could stand to attention did so, some by their beds, while others huddled around the piano. They stood tall, stiff, chests puffed out, solemn faces held high. Sister Jamieson appeared from her office, her face a picture of calm. Evans whizzed by once more, narrowly missing Sister, who anticipated a collision and stepped out of the way just in time without so much as a flicker of her expression.

'Good evening, Mr McIndoe. Here for your rounds?'

'Yes, Sister. Before I forget, a young man will be joining us in the next week or so – an artist. Freddy someone or other.' He shrugged his shoulders, unable to recall the surname. 'He's with the War Artists Advisory Committee. They've commissioned him to produce some paintings so I expect he'll choose his own muse.'

She raised an eyebrow. 'Well, thank you for telling me. I'll make sure the men know what to expect.'

'Any problems tonight I need to know about?' Archie surveyed his domain.

'None you don't already know of. Pilot Officer Smithson is settled following his surgery. He's just had more morphine so he's a little groggy.' Sister Jamieson stood with her hands clasped in front of her, her chin raised, her back straight and rigid; she was the epitome of deportment, dressed in her navy-blue uniform and pristine, starched white apron. It was plain from the look on her face that she didn't think patients should be so unruly and boisterous, though she never challenged Archie on the matter. He could sense she didn't wish to rock the boat.

Archie glanced at the young Canadian. Tony had almost walked away from the crashed aircraft without a scratch, but he went back into the flames to save a friend. Tony staggered out like a human candle, dragging his friend with him, who died shortly afterwards in hospital. Not expected to live himself, the lad had lain for five weeks encased in bandages at a hospital in Sussex before Archie found him. He hoped he would be happy with the surgery. Of course, he had a long way to go, but it was a start.

One of the boys opened a bottle of beer and poured it into a glass. The liquid plopped, fizzed and frothed with a delicious, refreshing tone. Archie found Jack sitting up in bed along with a few others for company, a thick smoky haze rising and swirling around as they all drew on cigars.

'Hey, Maestro. Thanks for everything – you all did a swell job, and Becky's thrilled with the way the wedding turned out.'

'Well, perhaps now you'll let me do my job and fix that face of yours.'

'Yeah, sure will. I'm all set for tomorrow, although it sure is a pity we couldn't have gone away. I guess there's plenty of time for that later.'

'Bit late for all that now, don't you think? Baby's already on the way,' Tom said with a glint in his eye. 'You Yanks certainly are different.' Everyone laughed. 'Besides, she can have her honeymoon when you take her back to America with you.'

'Man, I'm just thankful to be alive, and to have married the prettiest girl I ever saw.'

'Hear, hear,' Archie said.

'Maestro, how about giving us a tune?' Pete slapped him on the back, taking a swig of beer from the half-pint glass he was holding.

Archie checked his watch. He was expecting Blackie for a late supper around eight-thirty and had to get home. 'Just the one then.' He grinned as he sauntered across to the piano. A group gathered around and cheered as he took his seat.

'Tom, a pint for the Maestro, please.' Pete thrust a glass into Tom's hands, who filled it from the keg that rested on a table in the ward and set it down with a dull thud on top of the piano.

'Thanks, Tom. Now then, what do you rabble wish to hear tonight?' Archie gulped down a third of the beer, the malted aroma drifting in the air.

'Oh, you decide. Careful how you go with that pint, you've got to drive home yet.' Tom raised his eyebrows, and everyone laughed.

'Don't worry about that, you lousy rabble. I can drink all of you under the table any day.' Archie flexed his fingers, grimacing slightly at the sharp pain that snapped through them. He must have been working too hard, although he'd never experienced pain quite like that before. Another cheer erupted as beer glasses clinked and cigarette smoke thickened.

'I know – "Kiss Me Goodnight, Sergeant Major" – liven up the old place a little.'

Archie nodded, taking another gulp of his beer. As the notes swung out into the ward, the boys and the nurses sang along with smiling faces and twinkling eyes as they bonded over a pint and a merry tune.

'Your housekeeper's outdone herself tonight. First rate.' Blackie settled back in his chair, waiting for Archie to finish eating. With the blackout curtains drawn, and the fires lit, the warm, cosy cottage held back the winter's chill.

'We'll go into the other room. It's warmer in there in the evenings.' Archie scraped his chair back as he stood up. He poured a generous measure of whisky into two crystal glasses. 'How's your wife, Blackie?' The fire roared and crackled as flames caught the logs.

'Oh, she's very well. Looking forward to my next leave.'

'Yes, I expect she is. Can't be easy you being posted here while she's left behind in Devon. Still, we're not the only ones separated because of this damn war.' Archie sat back in his armchair, drink in one hand and a cigarette in the other. 'It's a miracle we're getting all this help for the boys, isn't it?'

'Who'd have thought it? What with the war and the rationing, it's mounting up.'

'Well, at least now we've formed a charity, the Guinea Pig Club has a good chance of prospering and helping those boys who need it.' Archie removed his spectacles and rubbed his eyes. 'These men have endured hell – and worse – fighting for their country, and I feel it's up to us to ensure they don't become outcasts once this mess is finally over.'

He drew on his cigarette. The boys lost limbs, faces, wives, lovers, lives. They were wiped out and had to forge new lives. 'Over my dead body will any of them be homeless or begging for the next meal. This club of ours will help them find homes or start a business venture if need be.'

Archie drained his whisky and set the glass down on the table with a clunk. 'And what about all those men who were disfigured in the last war? Some of them simply disappeared. Left their families, friends, just walked away from the lives they had. It's unthinkable. If our boys need anything, anything at all, then they shall have it. I mean that, Blackie. They're to have a life when all of this is over. It doesn't matter how disfigured they are or what people think of them, they must live their lives. Besides, society needs to get used to them, and we can't do that without getting them out there among the people.'

And this he'd started to do already in East Grinstead, along with occasional trips to see a show in London. As for the rest of the country, well, that would be up to the boys themselves. Hopefully, they would gain the confidence at home first. 'They're not the first to suffer, you know, and they won't be the last.'

'I hear what you're saying, and you're right, but we can't be there for them all the time, Archie. Even *you* can't play God. What about your own life and family?'

'Oh, don't you worry about me.' Archie sat back and thought for a moment. Since the Battle of Britain had begun, pilots and bomber crew had kept both him and the staff at the hospital rather busy, and life as he'd known it had ceased to exist. His days brimmed with surgical operations, patient assessments, and travels to other hospitals in his quest to discover the most severely burned servicemen who required his expertise. Even if his wife and children had never left, he doubted whether there would be much time for them, as he barely had any for himself. 'Right now my family is safely tucked away in America, and that's where I hope they'll stay. Adonia isn't happy – she can't settle, though at least she and the girls are safe. As for life, well, once the war's over, we'll all be able to breathe easier.'

He stubbed out his cigarette, while his wife's latest letter preyed on his mind. Adonia had insisted on returning home. Of course, he'd written a reply telling her she must stay put; after all, it was far too dangerous to risk a voyage across the ocean in the midst of this bloody mess. Lord knows the German navy had sunk many a ship. Hunting like wolves above and below the waves of the Atlantic, their prey being any Allied convoy bearing passengers, food or military supplies. No, it would be sheer madness, and he couldn't allow them to set sail. Besides, he had enough to worry about here. 'Did I ever tell you about a fellow by the name of Leonardo Fioravanti?' Archie strode over to the drinks cabinet and poured himself another whisky, gesturing to Blackie, who shook his head.

'Fior who?'

'Ah, now, there's a story.' Archie lit his pipe and took a few puffs to get it going. Smoke swirled and rose. 'The chap was an Italian surgeon and an early pioneer of plastic surgery. He witnessed a duel in Africa in 1551 where one of the poor fellows lost his nose. It was sliced off and fell into the sand. Well, Fioravanti said that he picked up the nose, urinated on it to cleanse it,' Archie's lips flickered into a suppressed grin, 'and then sewed it back into position. After applying medicated balsam, he bandaged it.'

'Oh, dear Lord. Nowt like a bit of innovation.' Blackie chuckled.

'Now, you might laugh, but when they removed the bandage after eight days, that damn nose was attached, healing and healthy.' Archie puffed his pipe. 'If only it were as simple as that today, eh?'

'Aye, then you'd be out on your ear.' Blackie leant forward to tap his cigarette on the side of an ashtray, and grey smouldering ash tumbled into amber glass. 'Roll on summer,' he blurted out. 'This blackout and these dark winter days are all gloomy. It's about time we had a little warmth and sunshine.'

'Oh, absolutely. Well, it's almost April.' Archie pictured his beloved New Zealand. He missed the Dunedin sun and had never become accustomed to the damp, British climate – it made his bones ache. A few years ago, before the whisperings of war were in the air, it had been his dream to buy a villa in the South of France and spend some time in the sun. Back then, he'd enjoyed performing surgery on young children the most, repairing cleft palates and harelips, which he'd found to be incredibly rewarding. Now the world had turned itself upside down, scattering his plans to the wind, shattering everyone's dreams.

Blackie took out a packet of John Player's and Archie sucked his pipe. 'Jack's lucky his young lady didn't desert him.'

And then it cut in, scything through the rural peace, drowning out the spitting fire, the wail that gradually built up like a wave; eerie and haunting. 'Shit!' Blackie glanced at Archie, who was unmoving.

'Bugger Jerry. It's been one hell of a day, and I'm not going anywhere except to my bed.'

11

A Whirlwind Romance

'Stella, love. There's a letter for you,' Mrs Brown bellowed upstairs, her voice quavering into a falsetto. 'I'll leave it on the kitchen table, dear. I'm off out to my WI meeting.'

Stella swung open her bedroom door, 'Thanks, Mrs B.' She had a whole day off and nothing arranged. Vera was working – her shifts had been changed at the last minute and she was fuming, yet she'd conceded, 'There's a bleeding war on, you know.' The front door slammed shut just as Stella reached the foot of the stairs.

A rumbling outside drew her attention, and she peered out of the living room window. Seconds later, a convoy of military trucks roared past the cottage, tearing through the rural peace. She looked on as the last of khaki green slipped around the corner. The early morning frost had thawed beneath the sun, and the cloudless, milk-blue sky promised a beautiful day ahead.

With a sigh, she sauntered through to the kitchen. Two fresh eggs sat in a bowl on the table with a note: *Help yourself, dear. Would you believe it – Matilda finally laid.*

Stella giggled. 'I can have an omelette with those,' she muttered.

The letter lay upon the scrubbed farmhouse table, propped up against the small vase filled with late-blooming daffodils. Stella glanced at the handwriting and her heart sank. She sank down onto a chair and ripped it open.

My darling girl,

It was wonderful seeing you again last week. I hope you've forgiven me – I couldn't bear it if I lost you now. Life here is just the same. One minute we're flying, then we're training. It's relentless. Anyway, I have some leave next month, and you said you were free, so I thought we could nip down to Devon for a couple of days. Mother's looking forward to it. I'll meet you there. All you have to do is take the train to Exeter on Saturday morning, and I'll pick you up at the station. I can't wait to see you. You will be there, won't you? I need you, Stella. Well, I must dash. We're on ops tonight, so Jerry best watch out. Write back as soon as.

Love,
Alex xxx

Stella dropped the letter onto the table, gazing down at the kisses after his name. Kisses he seemed to give more readily in ink. She sighed, remembering how safe she'd once felt in his arms, although she'd never felt sure about the depth of his feelings. Alex's kisses were wet and clumsy on her lips whereas Mac's left a sensual taste and set all her nerve endings ablaze. She recalled something Alex's cousin, Peter, had said the last time they met. *I'm afraid you're simply a passing phase. His family won't allow it – a shop girl, you'll never be good enough.* His mocking voice echoed in her ears, now the voice of a dead man. Things between her and Alex had cooled afterwards.

She knew what forgiveness Alex was asking for, and it had nothing to do with punching Mac, only to do with not getting in touch and letting her know he was safe. Typical. Alex turning up out of the blue was a shock, but his jealousy was alarming. She'd never seen that side of him before, and after everything, all his little indiscretions. She stiffened, fighting the urge to scream and shout. And Mac had borne the brunt of it. Her lips trembled.

She wished she hadn't told Alex about her leave next weekend. Since the Bassingbourn dance, Mac had become her friend, companion and far more. He occupied her mind when she awoke each morning and before she fell asleep each night. And at dawn, when the B-17s roared up into the first light, her heart lurched as she agonised whether Mac was up there with them.

The flagstone floor was cold beneath her stocking feet as she padded across to the range to make a cup of tea. She hadn't heard from Mac since the night of the fight. Vera had told her he was fine, a message passed on from Sam. It was a busy week for the Eighth Air Force and even Sam hadn't been able to get away. She sighed. Alex was grieving, but even so, it didn't excuse his behaviour. Stella knew he was in a dark place right now, though, and definitely not in the right frame of mind.

An inner turmoil brewed and gripped her gut. She couldn't abandon him when he needed her most. Not after Peter. Alex's words in the letter replayed in her head: *I couldn't bear it if I lost you now.* The kettle whistled impatiently, and she lifted it from the hot plate. She fetched her cup from the dresser, stepping over the resident black cat who lay sprawled in a triangular sliver of sunlight flooding in through the rear window, his eyes half closed.

'I suppose I'll have to go, won't I, cat?'

There was nothing for it. She would have to tell Mac next time she saw him.

Her mother was so thrilled about Alex. Money and class had always seemed important to her. Not for Stella, though. She would marry for love and wouldn't settle for anything less. She sipped her tea as she watched the cat flick his tail to and fro, his slit-like turquoise eyes catching the glint of golden sun. The problem was how to avoid disappointing her mother, whose words now rang out. *If your father were here, he'd be so proud.* Stella swallowed, and tears pricked her eyes. She was trapped, slowly suffocating, unable to break free, and she wanted to yell and run. But where would she run? Her heart screeched one direction while her muzzy head floundered in the darkness.

A weekend away was daunting, although perhaps she ought to go. Staying loyal to Alex as a friend was the right thing to do, and yet her heart protested. A loud knock at the front door broke her reverie. She paused as her hand hovered over the handle before wrenching it open. Mac stood with the sunshine behind him, his cap in his hand and the warmest smile on his face and her heart leapt. The evidence of his scuffle with Alex remained, a fading yellowish-brown bruise on his chin.

'Hi there, beautiful.' He stepped forward and kissed her on the mouth.

'Oh, Mac.' She reached out to trail her finger across his cheek when he took her hand in his, drawing it away. His tunic jacket brushed against her bare arm, sending a frisson of desire coursing through her. 'I'm so sorry you got hurt.'

'Don't worry about it. It's just my pride. I'll get over it.' His blue eyes twinkled.

She stepped back. 'You'd best come in. How did you know I'd be home today?'

'I figured I'd take a chance and here you are.' The corners of his eyes crinkled as his face creased into a crooked half-smile.

He closed the door behind him, and Stella caught his clean, fresh scent on the slight breeze that flowed and she longed to be in his arms. Her beating heart wooshed in her ears, but a pang of guilt sliced through her as she remembered the letter. As she led the way through the hall, he pulled her back towards him, wrapping his strong arms around her.

'Hey, not so fast.' He nuzzled the top of her head as she buried her face in his chest, drinking in undertones of cedar wood. Here, she felt safe and cherished. Here, a sense of belonging wrapped around her like a familiar friend. She couldn't look up because then she would be tempted. She'd already gone too far, and now his hands had lowered to her waist and were slipping further still, resting on her hips. Tingles sparked up her spine, and she lifted her chin to intense blue.

'Jeez, Stella, you're so damn beautiful, you know that?' He kissed her, softly at first and then with more passion, his lips on hers, asking, wanting, his tongue urgent. His right hand caressed her hip before moving upward to cup her breast. She gasped, and he drew her closer, their bodies moulded as she tasted shaving soap on his lips.

'Mac, we can't... '

He stepped back, releasing her. 'I know.' He sighed and flashed an apologetic smile. 'I'm sorry, I shouldn't have, it's just you're so darn irresistible, and I've missed you.'

Stella took his hand. 'Come on. I'll make some tea.' She had to do something to distract him. For a moment there, she almost lost control.

'I take it Alex went back to Lincoln?' He followed her into the kitchen, placing his crush cap on the table.

'Yes.' She placed the kettle on the stove, aware of his eyes following her every move. Once she'd filled the teapot, she set it on the pine table and sat opposite him. It was probably best to put a little distance between them. 'I'll be mother.' She placed a china cup on the saucer, poured a little milk out, and then reached for the teapot.

'What?' His mouth stretched into a wide grin.

'Mother – oh that's what we say when we decide who's pouring the tea.'

Mac laughed as he poked at the dark brown vortex of liquid with a spoon.

She noticed his eyes, tinged with dark circles, and when he yawned, he seemed even more tired. 'Did you fly yesterday?'

'Yeah. One hell of a trip.' He glanced down at the swirling vortex of tea. 'Can't say I'd recommend it.' His gaze lifted to hers. 'I sure am glad to be here with you, though.' He took out his cigarette case and offered it to her, but she shook her head. He plucked one and lit up, taking a long drag.

Stella sensed it must have been a rough mission. Sometimes there were things you just couldn't talk about. Afterwards, they stepped out into the garden to sit in the spring sunshine. Mac slouched on the wooden bench beneath the trees and yawned, his long legs outstretched. Weathered boughs swayed overhead as leaves rustled in the light breeze.

His thigh pressed against hers, firm and warm, and her heart fluttered. 'Have you heard from your family?'

'Yeah. A letter came the other day. They're all fine. My folks asked when I might be coming home.' He blew a cloud of smoke into the air. 'It's funny, but it seems as if I left years ago, and yet it's only been five months. I tick off the missions each time we come back, always counting.' He gazed at Stella. 'Hey, don't worry. Nothing's going to happen to me. In fact, I was thinking of maybe signing on for a second tour.' He placed his arm around her.

'No, don't do that.'

'What, can't I hold you now?' He sat upright, flashing that half-smile.

'No, I mean don't do another tour, please, Mac.'

His smile faded, and his eyes grew intense. He bent his head to kiss her; a soft, unhurried yet passionate embrace that filled her with a desire she could no longer fight. Stella slipped her arms around him, revelling in the firmness of his body. When he finally lifted his lips from hers, he held her close. If anything happened to him, she didn't know what she'd do. *Oh, God.* She couldn't go on like this. It was tearing her in two. The Americans had to fly twenty-five missions before they were sent back home unless they signed on again. She didn't want him to go anywhere and the realisation of losing him, whether it was to his own country or worse, suddenly dawned on her and a hard lump knotted in her stomach.

'It's mighty peaceful here, and beautiful,' Mac said.

The sun blazed and rays danced between the branches, dappling the lawn gold as she clung to his arms, the swell of his biceps prominent beneath her hand.

'Stella, what happened last week was unfortunate, and I didn't fight back because I didn't want to hurt you.' He took her hand in his and gazed into her eyes. 'Truth is, I fell for you the moment I saw you at that dance in Meldreth, and then when we met again at the base, well I couldn't believe my luck. Now I'd say that was fate, and I just knew we were meant to be. I love you, Stella.'

The breath caught in her throat. Should she say it back? Words she longed to whisper formed on her lips, only to be repressed by thoughts of Alex. She was a hypocrite, and inside everything shrivelled. 'Mac, you hardly know me. It's madness.'

'It feels right. Besides, the whole world is upside down right now.' He smiled, and his dark blue eyes twinkled with mischief. 'And just so we're clear'—he pulled her firmly towards him—'it's not madness, honey, it's love.' He kissed the arch of her brow and held her close.

He loved her. Her entire body glowed, and desire flowed through her veins, but the memory of divided loyalties halted the rush in its tracks. 'Alex.'

'Yeah, what about him?' Mac's body stiffened next to hers.

She swallowed. 'He's written asking me to visit him at home next weekend while I'm on leave.'

Mac sighed. 'I thought that maybe you might have told him about us.' His voice had a crisp edge, chilling the air between them.

'No, I just haven't found the right time.'

'Are you going?'

She couldn't lie, and she hated the thought of hurting him. 'I think so.'

He stood up, dropped his cigarette, and ground it into the grass. 'Gee, Stella. We never did get to talk about him, but after everything that's happened, I can't believe you're going.' Mac gazed at her, his eyes flashed and his brow furrowed. 'The guy doesn't deserve you, that's for sure.'

'Mac, I'm sorry, but I can't let him down. I don't want to hurt him.' She glanced down at a mound of wet, decaying leaves, as barren boughs swayed overhead.

'Why not? Hasn't he hurt you enough times?'

What did he know about it? Unless Vera had said something. She saw the pain in his eyes and her stomach tightened. 'He's not in a good place right now. He's just lost his best friend and now his cousin. He's changed, and he's, well, he's... '

'He's what? He's suddenly decided that he wants you now? Is that it?' His eyes were cold and dark.

She looked away, aware of the heat stinging her neck and cheeks, as tears misted her eyes. She gritted her teeth and took a deep breath, knowing she had no right to expect any understanding.

'What's really going on here? Do you just feel sorry for the guy or are you obligated in some way? Do you even love him?'

Bang! Like a gunshot, his words stung and shook her to her core. Love and Alex. She loved him, but as a friend. When Alex touched her, there was no spark, no afterthought. She peered up at Mac, biting her lower lip, shaking her head.

He threw his hands up in the air and began pacing the lawn. 'No to what? You're not obligated, or you don't love him?'

'I'm not in love with him, though I'd be lying if I said I didn't care.'

He stopped pacing and shot her a confused look.

'My mother is expecting me to marry him. She wants this, she's always saying how my dad would be so proud.' A single tear slipped down Stella's cheek. She wiped it away and met Mac's gaze, only his eyes now flashed with disappointment. Another tear hovered on the crest of her upper lip and she tasted salt. 'Mac, I'm sorry. I can't abandon him yet while he's so low. You don't let your friends down.'

'No, and you don't lead them on either.'

He was angry, but that hurt all the same. She closed her eyes briefly. She had to fix it the only way she knew how. 'I'm sorry, but I have to go next weekend, and if you can't accept that then perhaps you should leave.' She heard her own voice, cold, almost detached, and her heart squeezed when she saw the crestfallen look on his face.

He stormed off without even a backwards glance. Tears pricked her eyes, and a wretchedness gripped her chest tight as she sobbed. He'd just professed his love for her, yet it seemed hopeless. No matter what she'd done, she would have been hurting someone. She choked back the tears, dabbing at her eyes with a handkerchief. And now she'd pushed him away, the kindest, gentlest man she had ever known. She puffed out a breath, telling herself it would never have worked – so why did she feel so hurt? The late daffodils wilted in the flood of warm sunlight beneath the tree. She cast her gaze over the vegetables, where a relentless army of weeds weaved a route through the neat rows.

She had to go to Devon to see Alex, if only to make sure he was all right. She was bereft, and a part of her felt let down. Why hadn't Mac understood? She was trying to do the right thing, and at least she'd been honest about it. She sighed. He'd looked exhausted; his face was so pale, and his eyes dark and bloodshot. That look claimed so many men, eventually. Ice flowed into her stomach, and seeped into her soul, and she shivered. A shadow flicked over her, and she raised her chin and squinted up into the blue. A raven soared overhead, its sleek sooty wings fanned out as it croaked a raspy, deep, gurgling call. 'Oh, Lord, please keep Mac safe next time he flies.'

12

Bremen, Saturday 17ᵗʰ April 1943

'I've got a bad feeling about this run, and I don't like it one bit.' Wilson glanced at Mac, his face pale, his eyes tired.

Mac had noticed Wilson had started drinking more than usual. When they ran through the pre-flight checks earlier, he'd made a few mistakes, but then Mac figured they were all tired. 'I hear you. Don't think about it. It's just another run, and we do everything the same.'

Bremen, a heavily defended city, was anything but another run. A deep sense of foreboding engulfed him, descending like a black, dense cloud. Fatigue had reached a whole new level. As they flew out across the Channel, Mac surveyed the armada of bombers around them – one hundred and fifteen Flying Fortresses stretched out above and below.

The thunderous roar of the engines throbbed beneath his feet and flowed up through his body, and his head pounded with the vibration, then a sudden thought had him reaching up to his neck and grappling with his dog tags. Where was it? *Damn!* His heart sank. He'd left his St Christopher on his bedside table. His heart kicked his ribcage as Bill's face slipped into his mind. Bill and his crew. Burning. He had to block it out; he had to focus.

He fixed his gaze on Stella's picture as he rapidly sucked in oxygen. The warmth of her silken hand in his, the fall of her wavy hair on her shoulders. The softness of her body in his arms, the curve of her hips, and the ache of wanting inside him that had taken every ounce of restraint he'd had to hold himself back. And then after he'd bared his soul, she pushed him away, hitting him right in the gut. And she'd be with that asshole today. What if he'd lost her? He shouldn't have walked out like that.

'We're gonna hit them with one hell of a surprise today, each Fort dropping five thousand pounds of bombs on that Focke-Wulf Factory. I sure am glad I'll be up in the clouds and not boots on the ground,' Wilson said, adjusting his throat mic.

Mac tore his gaze from Stella, and his heart ached. He needed her now more than ever.

'Yeah, a few more Krauts out of the way and a blow to Hitler's war machine,' Wilson said. 'We get to see the fourth of July a little early.'

They headed further east towards the island of Juist at the northern tip of Germany, where the flak was moderate, with black smoky wisps that barely reached them.

'Navigator to pilot. We're over the West Frisian Islands.'

'Thanks, Will. Pilot to crew. Check in. Make sure your oxygen's working.' Mac turned to Wilson. 'See anything down there?'

'Nope. Ten-tenths cloud.' Wilson looked straight ahead as something caught his eye. 'What the hell is that goon doing? *Lucky Star's* weaving around all over the place. Rookies.' He rolled his eyes.

As they reached Juist Island, they banked, heading south, and crossed the German coast, straight for Bremen. Below, ragged breaks in the cloud revealed sparkling sunlight on the Weser River which cut through the land, a shimmering snake luring them all the way to the target. The flak here was more intense, and Mac strained his eyes at black specks up ahead, closing in fast.

'Fighters, twelve o'clock high!' Tex fired short bursts from the top turret.

'I see them, Tex. Jeez, there must be about twenty of 'em.' Bud's voice.

Two Messerschmitt Bf 109s hurtled towards them with a flash of yellow noses and gun ports glinting silver before they veered off left and right.

'Keep her in tight, dammit!' Mac yelled. 'You're drifting out.' He watched as Wilson wrestled with the control wheel, easing the throttles to move her back in, sweat slipping down his forehead, rolling over his oxygen mask, his eyes wide. 'Easy on the throttle.' Mac glanced out at the low formation below. 'I'll take her for a while.' He grabbed the control wheel. They were taking a beating out there as the wolves picked them off, one by one. One ship took a direct hit on both right engines and now trailed smoke. They soon fell back, God help them. Mac gritted his teeth and narrowed his eyes at the sight of the gathering swarm ahead. 'Jesus Christ.' Icy claws dug into his shoulders and pinned him against his seat. 'Fighters, twelve o'clock high!'

The anti-aircraft fire intensified and the *Texas Rose* took a few direct hits as pieces of red-hot metal ripped her skin wide open. The air inside the cockpit filled with the haze of smoke from the guns.

'Fighters one o'clock high.' Tex's voice.

Bud and Irv fired while yelling obscenities. No doubt they'd be an inch deep in spent shell cases by now, skating on marbles in the waist. The German fighters kept on coming, and fresh swarms arrived to replace those low on fuel. It seemed the Mighty Eighth was to be plagued all the way in and all the way out.

'Coming about, three o'clock high.' Bud's voice.

The Luftwaffe flew and circled like hornets, returning for more, thinking nothing of flying through their own flak to rip the armada apart. Another ship in the low formation trailed smoke after a direct hit from a Focke-Wulf. Mac watched as flames erupted from one engine. There was no time to dwell on the fate of those ten men as up ahead, wave after wave of enemy fighters kept on coming. He focused on the bomber in front while watching those above and below in case they strayed a little too close.

'Pilot to navigator. How long to the IP?'

'Navigator to pilot. Four minutes.'

'Bombardier, how's it looking down there?'

'Fair visibility, so far.'

Mac checked his watch. Twelve fifty-five. Almost there. Up ahead, a fresh swarm of enemy fighters headed straight for them. At twenty-five thousand feet, the sky was a stormy sea as flak shells exploded all around every few seconds. Up ahead, the lead squadron, the 323rd. released their bombs.

'Pilot to bombardier, she's all yours, Danny.'

'Roger.'

Mac stiffened. Danny had the ship, and their fate was in God's hands as the engines slowed and they sailed and rocked over brown-black waves through a grim, smoky haze.

'Jeez, there goes another.' Wilson craned his neck to follow the path of the flaming Fortress nosediving below them. 'Goddam, flak's so thick because they're spitting it out so fast. It's the luck of the draw which one of us makes it through.'

Mac flicked a gaze at him, and determination flowed through his veins like steel. 'Hey, we're gonna make it if I have to haul this ship back with my bare hands. We'll make it.' He took a deep breath and exhaled. His heart pounded, and beads of sweat slipped down his temples like mercury, skirting round his oxygen mask; irritating. He swiped them away.

A fighter headed straight for the *Texas Rose* and for a split-second, Mac froze, clenching his buttocks as the black nose was almost upon them like a bullet. Then he ducked, but the fighter veered off to their port side at the last moment, peppering the fuselage with cannon fire. The staccato sound of machine-gun fire from the gunners vibrated through the cockpit and blended with the thrum of the engines and drilled through his body.

'I got him, hot damn!' Irv yelled from the waist. 'That'll teach you, you bastard.' The Focke-Wulf 190 trailed smoke and nosedived. The Perspex canopy popped open, and the pilot bailed, white plumes of silk blossoming above. 'Jeez, would you look at that?'

'Must be the fuel dump.' Bud's voice.

Mac glanced down as a massive fireball mushroomed upward.

'Bombs gone.' Danny's voice.

The *Texas Rose* lifted, freed once more from her deathly cargo.

'Bomb bay doors closing. Ship's all yours, Mac.'

'Got it, Danny.' Job done. Now for the hard part. Mac followed the bombers in front and steered the ship in a sweeping turn north, heading towards the Frisian Islands.

'Those fighters aren't about to leave any time soon,' Mac said. 'Keep sharp back there.'

'Here they come again.' Danny's voice.

Mac watched, transfixed, as a Focke-Wulf approached from twelve o'clock high. Short bursts of tracer fire hailed from the nose below him, but the swift fighter darted away beneath them. Another Fortress sailed down in flames while others were under heavy attack from the relentless swarm in the air. They were still within range of the anti-aircraft gunners below as they flew back through the barrage of flak, fighters, and cannon fire. The *Texas Rose* shuddered, and Mac lurched forward in his seat as an audible clunk reverberated from the waist section.

Wilson swivelled around, his eyes wide. 'Are we hit?'

'Not me,' Mac said. 'Here they come again.'

'Two more cutting in at three o'clock high.' Tex's voice.

'Come to papa.' Irv's voice. 'Come on in, you bastards.'

As the gunners fired short bursts, orange tracer fire lashed the sky. Two of the fighters peeled away while another belched out black smoke before exploding into flames. 'Pilot to crew, check in.'

One by one they called in, except for Birdie. 'Pilot to tail, you okay?' Still nothing. 'Irv, go aft and check on tail gun.'

'Sure thing.'

Mac had a bad feeling. Space was real tight back there, and he knew Irv would struggle to squeeze past everything, especially with that huge metal toolbox in the way.

'What's happening, Irv?'

'He's out cold, slumped over his guns. Jesus Christ, the tail's riddled with holes, and there's a huge chunk ripped out the side. There's a tornado in here. I can't wake him.'

Mac clenched his teeth. His throat mike dug in, crushing his windpipe and he tugged at it.

'He just opened his eyes and tried to speak, only he ain't making no sense. His head's hit real bad. There's a pool of blood on the floor.'

'Okay, Irv. Danny, go aft with the medical kit and help with tail gun.' Mac swallowed hard. Another flak shell exploded close by, and the *Texas Rose* lurched and shuddered as she rode out the storm.

A few more minutes passed. 'Mac, Birdie's not with it. I've given him a shot of morphine, but his pulse is real weak. Irv's dressing the head wound.'

'Thanks, Danny. Stay with him and send Irv back.'

'Jimmy, Birdie can you hear me?' Irv's voice from the tail. 'You're gonna be okay. We'll be home soon, and you'll be chasing those girls from the bakery in no time. You remember the blonde? She's kinda sweet on you.'

The *Texas Rose* lurched once more beneath a hail of cannon fire along her aluminium body. A chunk of flak ripped through the cockpit on her port side with a loud clunk, and Mac jumped, aware of the punch as it pierced its way out the starboard side. He glanced to his left, where an icy wind howled through a gaping, jagged hole in the ship's skin, and his arms ached as he tried to keep her steady. 'Number one engine's hit. It's smoking,' he yelled. 'Extinguishers. Feather prop one.'

Wilson wiped sweat from his eyes and quickly followed the order. As he hit the number one extinguisher button, the blades of the propeller ceased to spin. 'Don't worry, that bullet didn't have your name on it.'

'No, but it said "To whom it may concern".' Mac gritted his teeth.

'They got *The Lucky Lass.*' Virg's voice on the interphone, tense.

That made six from the 401.st Squadron. Sixty men plus ships from the rest of the group. Mac sure wished he had his St Christopher. It had been a gift from his mother to keep him safe. A siren screeched in his brain and his heart as they slipped through the dead sky. All he could do now was pray.

The padre's voice from the base rang in his ears. 'Son, in war, in the skies, there are no atheists.' Amen.

The Channel shimmered up ahead, and he could almost taste the sea air. Almost home. The fighters had finally given up, and as they pushed on, the sunlight glinted like diamonds on the grey waters beneath them. In a gradual descent, they dipped down to eleven thousand feet as they approached the English coast, heading for Great Yarmouth. From there it was a stone's throw to Bassingbourn. 'Pilot to crew. You can come off oxygen now.' Mac pulled his mask free of his face, relishing the naked freedom. They cut in across the land and sailed over weathered houses and cobbled streets.

Wilson hit the switch for the landing gear. 'That don't sound right. I think one of the wheels is stuck.' He blew out a breath and pursed his lips.

'Bring it back up and try again.' Mac glanced at him. That was all they needed.

'Nope. It won't budge. Can't get it to retract.'

'Tex, you'd better take a look,' Mac said.

Tex sprang into action, but no matter how hard he tried, the landing gear was jammed solid. 'Reckon the electronics are all shot out. I'll do it by hand.' He turned off the electronic switch for the landing gear and headed to the bomb bay. He'd have to manually crank the wheels in there. Within a few minutes, he returned. 'It won't budge.'

'Shit!' Wilson looked at Mac. 'Can't land on one wheel, number one's still smoking.'

'Well, what do you want me to do? We got no other choice. Pilot to crew, prepare for a crash landing and get in the radio room. We're going down.' One way or another. 'Ernie, get outta that ball.'

'I'm out.'

Silence prevailed over the interphone for about thirty seconds and then Irv cut in. 'Hey, Ernie. That flak suit you're always sitting on to protect your family jewels, well you've been wastin' time. Might as well kiss your ass goodbye – and your jewels.'

'Up yours, Irv, besides, you ain't got much to boast about.'

'Okay, guys. Can I have silence now until we land unless it's real urgent?' Mac needed to concentrate. He'd never had a situation like this before. Sure, he'd belly landed once, and that had been hair-raising enough. If you go down too fast and too hard, you risk starting a fire. That same risk went with a one-wheel landing. He tried to remember everything he knew about emergency landings.

While he fought to clear his mind, images of Stella and his family slipped in, and he recalled flying over the Montana plains, and how the old Curtiss 'Jenny' handled in his control – light, responsive, almost like a part of him. His father's words before every flight. *Make her sing, boy.* It was Mac's mantra, his good luck charm.

'Make her sing,' he muttered as he focused on the movement of the ship and the feel of her in his hands; a sensation that flowed through his body and mind as if she were whispering in his ear.

As they descended, acres of green, yellow and brown interspersed by hedgerows and grey winding lanes flashed beneath them, and his heart swelled as he glimpsed the spires of King's College Chapel stretching up into the sky.

He sucked in a breath, the rush stretching his chest as he sucked in cold air. He was still wearing his flak suit, and he sure regretted it now as it bore down on him, making his shoulders and neck ache with a relentless persistence. No doubt Bud would be hanging on to his rosary, whispering a prayer.

Wilson peered out of the cockpit window. 'Runway coming up.' He glanced over at Tex. 'Signal ahead.'

Tex grabbed the flare gun and fired from the upper turret; two streaks of red sailed into the blue. Mac gripped the control wheel so determinedly that his hands slid inside his flight gloves. He flicked a gaze at Stella's picture and heaved in a breath as the blood pulsed through his body. He was going to see her just as sure as he was going to land this ship, and then he'd apologise, and hope for forgiveness. 'Here we go, hold on tight.' Below them, the dark silhouette of the *Texas Rose* raced across English soil, keeping pace as the gap between the two closed.

'Our Father, which art in heaven. Hallowed be thy name.' Bud's voice filtered through the interphone.

Lower, lower they came as the concrete runway rushed up beneath them.

'But deliver us from evil. For thine is the kingdom.'

The control wheel now shuddered so violently, the vibrations juddering through Mac's arms and torso as he bounced in his seat, and they jolted as they touched down hard with a squeal of rubber. The ship immediately bounced back up before coming down hard with the single wheel now firmly on the ground, screeching in delight. Mac kept the *Texas Rose* upright for several seconds before she gracefully tilted over to the other side, her wingtip gouging concrete, orange sparks fizzing into the air like hundreds of fireflies glowing at dusk. He applied the brakes, but nothing happened. As the runway ran out, they rode across the bumpy grassed field at speed. Mac glimpsed the meat wagon in pursuit, the blood-red cross on its olive-green roof. Still travelling at around fifty miles per hour, Mac stared ahead as the end of the airfield approached, the boundary hedgerows rushing forward to greet them, and then the wing clipped a concrete building, sending Mac lurching forward as they spun around in an arc and finally came to a standstill. The number one engine belched out black smoke, and the sharp smell of high octane fuel reeked in the air.

For a few seconds, Mac sat stunned, and then a flicker of orange flashed from the corner of his eye. He glanced at the engine where flames now leapt, lashing the wing. 'Fire! Everybody out!' He unclipped his belt. Wilson rushed ahead of him and jumped through the nose hatch, closely followed by Tex. Mac charged through the ship. The radio room was empty. Just as he entered the waist, a loud explosion knocked him off his feet and everything went silent. His face stung, and something wet slipped down his cheek and neck, but the fire was spreading fast, and he had to reach the tail. He jumped out of the waist door and ran to the rear of the ship. The tail door was still shut. He opened it and found Danny unconscious on the floor. 'Hey, Tex. Give me a hand. Danny's out cold.' Mac jumped inside, despite the stifling intensity of the flames. Tongues of orange-red lashed the waist, sweeping towards them. Tex climbed in and between the two of them they half dragged, half carried Danny to the awaiting medics, while the flames licked at their heels.

'Come on, Mac. The whole ship's burning. There's nothing more you can do.'

'I'm not leaving Birdie in there to burn, goddammit.' He darted back inside. The smoke, thick and black, caught in his throat and he coughed, gasping for breath. One side of his face prickled as the searing heat intensified. Every breath was a fight, and his nose and throat seared as the flames devoured the oxygen. He grabbed Birdie by his arms and dragged him towards the door, but another explosion rocked him and his knees buckled as he dropped to the floor. The portable oxygen cylinders in the tail must have gone up. This was it. He was burning to death. He swallowed and closed his eyes for a second, as his family and Stella flashed through his mind. Then, a surge of adrenaline flooded his body like a raging torrent, and he hauled himself up and cried out as the fire reached him, lashing his lower legs as he dragged Birdie to the exit.

'Jesus Christ, Mac! You're burning.' Wilson, standing waiting by the door, pulled the injured gunner out and let his body drop to the ground, where he rolled him and threw his jacket over him to beat out the flames. Mac staggered out and fell onto the grass, which was now soaked with water from the fire hoses. A medic threw a blanket over his legs to smother the flames, and the wet ground soaked into him. Intense pain radiated through his legs, his hands, and face, and a wave of nausea swelled in his gut. As he lay sprawled on the ground, his limbs began to shake and his teeth chattered, but he fixed his gaze on the medic now attending to Birdie.

'Get back, clear the area.' The firemen stepped back, still pointing hoses at the B-17, as the greedy flames raged, blackening her skin, tearing it from her frame, devouring her whole.

A second medic draped a blanket over Birdie's body, and dragged it up over his face. Mac glanced at his crew who looked on, stunned, and Virg stood, wide-eyed, wiping his eyes with gloved hands.

Mac's heart lurched, and his chest heaved. 'No!' He twisted to one side and retched. Then, like lightning, sharp, stabbing pain seared through both hands. He held one out in front of him. The flight glove was crispy, blackened and partially melted. He tried to remove it, then a searing pain plunged through his hand, throbbing and stabbing, and he cried out.

'Don't do that, Lieutenant, I'll see to those for you.' The medic shouted to his colleague. 'I need another stretcher over here.' They carried Mac to the awaiting field ambulance.

'He can't be dead.' Mac's voice quavered. The acrid smell of smoke drifted in the air, but a stranger, nauseating odour filtered in, pungent, foul, like burned meat. He swallowed.

'He's gone, the poor kid. You did everything you could.' Wilson took out a cigarette and lit it, his hands trembling. 'Looks like he got hit pretty bad. Nothing anyone could have done, Mac.'

Mac lay back on the stretcher and gazed at the sky. Milky blue with white cloud, the perfect day for flying in the old Curtiss. Maybe dad was up there right now putting her through her paces. His heart suddenly ached for home.

'I'm just going to give you a shot of morphine, Lieutenant.'

There was a sharp sting in his right arm and within a few minutes, Mac relaxed and floated on a warm, hazy cloud. 'So tired,' he mumbled, as he sailed into the fog. 'So goddamn tired.' His eyes closed as the pain subsided, embracing the darkness which somehow seemed reassuring.

13

Longthorn Manor, April 17th 1943

The sleek, black locomotive steamed into Exeter station at half past three in the afternoon. The journey had been long and the conditions cramped, with soldiers and kitbags spilling out into the corridor. Stella couldn't stop thinking about Mac, and she longed to see him – to explain. She picked up her leather suitcase, and made her way across the platform, as a sickly hollow feeling seeped into her stomach. Never before had she felt so torn. She sighed, wishing she wasn't here at all.

'Stella!'

Alex strode towards her, resplendent as ever in his RAF uniform and his mouth creased into a smile, making him even more handsome, his blonde hair smoothed back, glinting gold in the afternoon sun. Seeing him again, so close, she realised why she fell for him all those months ago. But would it ever be enough? He fixed his dark chestnut eyes on her, took her in his arms and planted a kiss on her mouth. 'Oh, darling, I've missed you. I'd almost forgotten just how beautiful you are.'

Despite his warm smile, his dim eyes gave him away, along with the new lines etched around them and the freshly carved furrows on his brow. They hadn't had the chance to talk properly before now, and he still hadn't said anything about his cousin. 'I'm so sorry about Peter.' Stella met his gaze, but he looked away.

He coughed to clear his throat. 'Yes, jolly bad luck.' He grabbed the suitcase from her and strode across to the car, a Triumph Dolomite Roadster in ice blue. 'He kept saying his time was running out.' His face twisted into a semblance of a half-smile but then sagged, replaced by a drawn, downcast expression of grief.

'He expected it?' As soon as she said the words, she regretted them.

'Don't we all? Oh, let's not talk about it.' Alex's voice was cold and brusque. He turned the key, the engine roared to life, and he sped out of the station.

The journey to his home took about ten minutes, and he barely spoke except to answer her questions. He was beyond reach and had obviously taken Peter's death hard. He braked suddenly, and Stella lurched forward as they turned into a narrow lane flanked by large black iron gates.

Alex's face brightened. 'Well, here we are. The old homestead.' He smiled as he drove along the rough, rutted tree-lined road. A grey-stone Georgian house loomed ahead, shrouded by a cloak of creeping ivy which clung to its skin.

'It's lovely, Alex,' Stella lied. An icy prickle snaked around her shoulders as she turned her face to the roof, where demonic stone gargoyles leered at her. Established hydrangea and rhododendron bushes with blooms of pink and red flanked the well-tended lawns.

Alex drove up to the front door and cut the engine. 'Come on.' He patted her knee and cast a smile before clambering out.

She stepped onto the gravelled drive and stones rolled and crunched beneath her feet. A black Labrador bounded towards them, ears flapping in the gentle breeze, barking and wagging its tail with vigour. A tall, middle-aged woman, elegant in dress and poise, stood at the dark oak front door, her mouth a tight red line.

'Ben, old boy.' Alex knelt to greet the dog, who furiously licked his face. 'Have you missed me?' Ben barked and trotted around, his tail held high.

'Mother, this is Stella. I told you she was adorable.' Alex beamed and slipped his arm around Stella's waist.

'It's lovely to meet you, Mrs Russell.' Stella smiled politely.

'I trust you had a pleasant journey.' Her cold, clipped, tone belied the smile she wore – if you could call it a smile. She closed the door behind them, blocking out the light.

Stella followed behind as Mrs. Russell led the way through an oak-panelled hallway into a library, with walls filled from top to bottom with books. The Labrador slipped past and retreated to a wicker basket near the fire. The smell of burning logs failed to mask the stale, musty odour which hung in the air. Pictures crammed the remaining walls, which Alex pointed out were portraits of his ancestors. He seemed pleased to be home and hadn't stopped smiling, but it was almost a forced smile. Perhaps this was just what he needed – a weekend away from the war.

'Alex, I'll ask Mrs Briars to bring you some tea.' Mrs. Russell's smile faded as she breezed out of the room.

Stella sensed the icy unease drift away, and she smiled as Alex drew her close and kissed her. 'I'm so glad you're here.' He exhaled a deep sigh. 'I'd almost forgotten how it feels to be at home.'

She leaned against him on the sofa, his arm around her shoulders. He hadn't been this affectionate in ages. Perhaps she could believe in his love for her, but the moment's thought brought with it a fresh wave of pain and loss, and then Alex released her abruptly when the door opened.

'Ah, hello, Mrs Briars.'

A grey-haired woman bustled in carrying a large tray laden with tea and sandwiches and set it down on a nearby table. 'Will that be all, Master Alex?' she said, her rounded, ruddy face breaking into a warming smile.

'Yes, thanks, this looks wonderful.'

Stella was famished after her journey and in desperate need of sustenance. Alex poured the tea, and they helped themselves to food. The fire crackled and spat as they ate and chatted, and the war might have been a million miles away, but she couldn't shake the image of Mac from her head.

Alex glanced at his watch. 'Goodness, it's half past five already. I'd better show you to your room so you can get unpacked. Dinner's at seven thirty sharp.' He took her hands and pulled her towards him, taking her in his arms. His uniform was rough and scratchy against her cheek, and the memory of Mac's soft touch and his smell sailed into her head and pinched her heart.

'I've missed you, darling, you know that, don't you?'

She raised her chin to speak and found his lips, waiting. His kiss was soft at first, but then a hunger set in and his tongue, urgent and searching, surprised her. He'd never kissed her like that before. 'Oh Stella,' he whispered, kissing the length of her neck, drawing her body to his. She was so close to him – too close. It wasn't the same, and the intuitive voice in her head yelled as much. Since the moment she arrived, she'd been making comparisons.

'Come on.' Alex led her to a sweeping staircase and to the first floor, where more ancestry portraits hung. She followed him along a dusky hallway, her eyes sweeping over every picture, a swirl of faces adding to the confusion in her mind. The dark-red carpet was threadbare in places, and abruptly ended where Alex stopped, its edge frayed as if it had been severed. Beyond stretched dark, stained floorboards running to the end of the corridor. A musty odour drifted in the air.

'Here we are.' Inside, the bedroom was large, with windows overlooking the rear gardens. He placed her suitcase on the double bed, which was flanked by two mahogany bedside tables with matching cream lamps. 'I wish I didn't have to dash, but there's something I have to do before dinner. I'll leave you to unpack, and I'll come for you at seven.' He cast a brief smile before closing the door behind him.

A chill slid down her neck. The room seemed unused and unloved. Stella sank down onto the bed. She was alone in a strange old house; an intruder, or was it that she was an outsider? A gentle breeze flowed into the room through the open sash window, carrying a sweet floral scent. She peered out. Blobs of blue flecked the grey sky, and light rain drizzled. From below, roses clung to the stone walls with flowers of red and white, their heads nodding in the shower. Cherry blossom trees graced the garden, with soft, pink flowers casting their skins adrift in the gentle breeze, blanketing the carpet of velvet green below.

The clip-clop of hooves grew nearer, and she glimpsed the gravelled yard over to the right where a rider approached on a sleek black horse headed towards the house; towards Alex. He was waiting in the arched entrance to the stable yard. The rider dismounted and removed her hat, revealing a sheen of blonde hair scraped back into a hairnet. Dressed in riding breeches and a tweed jacket, she hugged Alex tightly, and he greeted her with a kiss on the cheek. Who was she? Whoever she was, he was inviting her inside. A stable boy appeared and led the horse away. She half expected Alex to come and get her so that the two women might be introduced, but there was no knock on her door, no sound at all.

After about ten minutes, she could bear it no longer, so she tiptoed out into the hall where she caught the sound of laughter drifting upstairs. She peered over the oak bannister into the entrance hall. It was a woman's laugh. Alex didn't have a sister. Perhaps she was his cousin or a family friend. No doubt he'd tell her about it later. Footsteps clattered across the tiles below, and the woman slipped into view, leading Alex by the hand towards the front door. She whispered something in his ear and Alex laughed, then she kissed him on the lips. That wasn't the touch of a friend. Stella's vision clouded with swarms of red, and she trembled as a rush of adrenaline surged through her veins.

She stormed back to her room and locked the door behind her. How could she have been so stupid? When Alex had professed love, she'd almost believed him. She sank down on the bed as a wave of nausea struck her and her eyes swam with tears. She'd been a fool – the biggest fool –

and pushed Mac away for this. Why? Because she'd felt it was right to support a friend in need. Clearly, Alex didn't need her at all.

The image of Mac's hurt face perched in her mind. How dare Alex treat her this way? He'd betrayed and used her once too often. What if Mac had given up on her? For all she knew, he could be meeting someone else right now, and it was all of her own making; all because of her misplaced loyalty. Why had Alex pleaded with her to come here when he clearly had someone else sheltering in the wings? Nothing made sense as she sank down on the bed. Her mother had pushed too far this time and read it all wrong, yet she was glad. Now she was free, or at least she would be as soon as she could leave. However, what would she find when she returned?

Tears stung her eyes. She cast a gaze outside at the sky. 'Please be safe, Mac. Please come home,' she whispered. She might be stuck here for tonight, but tomorrow she would return home. She only had to make it through dinner and afterwards, she would confront him. Adopting a steel resolve, she flicked a gaze at the long, black cocktail dress hanging up – a dress she had no appetite to wear.

At seven o'clock, Alex knocked on her door and came into the room. 'Oh, Stella, you look beautiful.' He kissed her cheek and took her hand in his and led her downstairs to the dining room.

Stella walked into a chilled atmosphere, despite the log fire. Alex pulled out the chair for her, waiting for her to be seated. His parents glanced up then exchanged a look between them. Stella gazed around at the red painted walls, which were adorned with pictures of hunting scenes. The conversation seemed a little awkward, yet Stella bore their questions with grace. They asked her all about her family, her background, and her aspirations. It was almost as if they were interviewing her for a position in the household. Whatever it was, she was not in the mood for it.

Alex's mother set her cutlery down. 'Alex, darling, how is Elizabeth? It's such a pity I missed her earlier.'

His gaze darted across to Stella, and a pink flush tinged his cheeks. He shuffled in his seat. 'Oh, well, she's very well. She wanted to know how it was all going, service life and all that.'

'I hear she might volunteer with the Red Cross – good girl, she'll do a grand job no doubt.' Alex's father smiled. 'And you, young lady, how do you find life in the WAAF?'

Stella swallowed a mouthful of potato and peered along the stretch of polished mahogany towards Mr Russell, who raised his crystal glass to his mouth and drained the last of his red wine, swallowing deeply. 'I enjoy it. Well, we all have to do what we can for the war effort.' *At least, some of us do.* She eyed Mrs Russell, who didn't appear to be the sort who did anything useful.

'Elizabeth is the daughter of Earl Hamilton-Jones. They own quite a large estate just north of here. Such dear friends. She's an only child now, so sad. Her brother joined the RAF in 1939 and was shot down in his Spitfire over the Channel. They never found him, poor boy.' Mr Russell sighed.

'Oh, I'm so sorry.' Stella cast an empathetic look. A loud bang emanated from the fire as the logs burned, and as a flurry of sparks billowed upwards, the clock cast its piercing chimes, which echoed around the room. The hair at the nape of Stella's neck bristled and icy fingers traversed her shoulders and kneaded her back.

'Yes, well, Stewart was heir to the estate, but now it will pass to Elizabeth, so she's about to become a wealthy young lady.' Alex's mother smirked, glancing at her son.

Stella caught the steely glare Alex shot back. God, they were comparing her to Elizabeth. If they wanted to make her feel even more unwelcome, then mission accomplished. She swallowed, and her appetite ebbed away. An air raid would be better than being trapped here. She sighed, chiding herself for being so selfish.

How was she going to get through this? Her room at Mrs Brown's was waiting for her, warm and homely. Mrs. Brown would be sat by the fire right now nursing her cup of Horlicks, listening to the BBC Home Service on the radio and Mac, well, perhaps he was at the pub. She clenched her hands beneath the table as Bourn tugged at the bonds of her heart.

After dinner, Stella and Alex retreated to the library, alone. He brought along a bottle of sherry and two crystal glasses, and they sat in front of the fire.

'I wish you didn't have to leave tomorrow.'

'Well, I have something I need to do before I'm back on duty.' Stella sipped her sherry and looked away.

'Come back to my room tonight,' he whispered as he leant forward to kiss her.

She turned her head so his lips brushed her cheek instead. 'I don't think that would be right.' She leant back in her chair. 'Besides, your parents are here.' She wasn't sure what to say, but she wasn't about to keep up a pretence either.

'They won't know a thing. They sleep in the north wing at the far side of the house. Well, I'll come to you instead.'

Just then there was a knock on the door and his father stood there and coughed as if to announce his presence.

'Alex, can I have a quick word, please?'

He glanced at her. 'Back in a tick.'

'Come to my room if you dare, but I'll not let you in,' Stella muttered. She sipped her sherry as she wandered over to the books, her fingers trailing the shelves, raking dust into fluff as she cast her eyes over their spines. To think her mother had thought all this could have been hers. Relief burrowed through her. She had no wish to be part of his family; his parents were cold and interested in one thing only – money. She could kick herself for being so gullible and for hurting Mac in the process. God, Alex had punched him. None of it made any sense.

Time passed, and she wondered what was keeping Alex so long. She overheard raised voices and peered out into the hall, glimpsing the thin sliver of light that spilled from the dining room doorway.

'Alex, keep your voice down, please. All I'm saying is that you understand our situation and what is expected of you.' His mother's voice sounded almost pleading.

'I know, but really, Mother, you expect me to marry for money. Peter's gone, and all you care about is this crumbling old pit. I won't do it. I'd rather take a chance with Stella.' Alex's voice was strained.

'Well, we can't last here forever, my boy. The place will have to be sold, piece by piece. Is that what you want?' Mr Russell's voice. 'It's your inheritance, and it comes with great responsibility.'

Stella had heard enough. And what did Alex mean by taking a chance? She closed the library door and drained the last of her sherry in one gulp which burned her throat, and water rushed to her eyes. Alex returned, looking as if he'd just lost his wings.

'Is everything all right?' She knew it wasn't, and now she knew why.

He grabbed his glass and gulped down the sherry before sinking into an armchair. 'Yes, perfectly fine,' he snapped.

He was flustered and on edge, and somehow it didn't feel like the right time to talk about things. 'Alex, I'm sorry, but I have an awful headache. I think I'll have an early night.'

He glanced at her, a preoccupied look in his eyes. 'Oh, well, okay. If you need anything, just say. Goodnight.' He looked away and stared into the fire.

Later, as she rested in bed, raised voices drifted up towards her room so she tiptoed across to the door and opened it slightly. Alex's voice, followed by his mother's, drifted upstairs, but their words were unclear and muffled. Holding her breath, Stella caught the odd word – 'marry Elizabeth' and 'disinherited.' Stella soon gave up as the voices appeared to fade away. His parents didn't approve of her because she wasn't an heiress to a fortune, and right now that was a good thing. Mac loved her for who she was. *Oh God, please don't let me have ruined something so special.*

Alex's behaviour with another woman had given her the perfect excuse for leaving. There was no question of guilt or of letting him down or even causing upset, and there was something about the way he'd shouted 'take a chance with Stella' that had unsettled her.

Mac's image sailed into her head, and her heart quickened as she looked forward to returning home. Sleep would be impossible now. She longed to be in his arms, but then out of the blue an oppressive darkness draped over her, pressing down, burying into her bones. The sooner she returned, the better.

The following morning, Stella had breakfast alone with Alex. The one good thing about this weekend was that she knew who she wanted in her life.

'I wish you didn't have to leave yet.' He reached across the table and caressed her hand.

Stella pulled away. 'I saw you yesterday.'

'What do you mean?'

'In the afternoon, outside with that girl. You were kissing.' She stared into his eyes, and his pupils swelled then he turned away.

'Oh, I see.' He took out a battered silver cigarette case, plucked a cigarette, and lit up. He took a drag then exhaled a plume of smoke. 'It's not what you think, darling.'

He suddenly struck her as being so calm and collected. 'You could have fooled me. I'll guess that's Elizabeth.' Alex stared at her without a word. He didn't even deny it. 'Well, don't I at least deserve an explanation?'

'It's not my decision, it's my parents. I either marry Elizabeth, or we'll lose the estate. Stella, please understand.' His pleading eyes were pathetic; his weak voice droned on, and he no longer resembled the strong, independent, dashing young pilot she'd met all those months ago.

'It's all right, Alex. You don't need to explain. I understand.' She sighed.

'Oh, darling. You really are the best.' He reached for her hand again. 'I knew you would.'

Oh God. She saw the hunger in his eyes, she saw desperation.

'I'm not *that* understanding. In fact, I don't know what I'm doing here at all. Why did you ask me to come?'

'I suppose I thought that if my parents met you, they'd see how happy you make me.' He sighed heavily. 'Perhaps then they'd let me decide my own future. I do love you.'

'Are you sure about that? Because I think your affections lie elsewhere.' Her cheeks burned with heat and her voice trembled. Alex had strung her along for months, and now he was asking her to be his mistress.

'This is something to do with that Yank, isn't it? If he's laid a finger on you, I'll kill him.' Alex's eyes bulged, and his face reddened.

'This has nothing to do with him at all. This is about us. We're not right together.' Stella's heart banged in her chest.

His eyes narrowed, and his nostrils flared. 'We were perfectly all right before you laid eyes on him. Don't try and fool me. I know what's going on here.'

'How dare you? I waited to hear from you for weeks. Not one word. And then I hear you're drinking with old friends in Cambridge, just along the road. You could have telephoned. Anything could have happened. I had to rely on reports from people back at the station simply to know you were alive.'

Her heart pounded in her ears as tears pricked her eyes. 'That's not how you behave when you're in love, Alex, and it's certainly not how you treat people.'

She stopped short, her chest heaving as she struggled for air, and the urge she had in her heart and her entire soul reared up to crush her as the true meaning of being in love hit her with an almighty force. All the doubts ebbed away as a warm glow radiated within her. She was in love with Mac, so much it hurt, and she had to be with him.

'Yes, and ladies don't betray their own kind. You're just as bad as the rest of them. As soon as our backs are turned, you're tempted with money, and silk stockings, and God knows what else.'

Rage coursed through her veins, though there was no point in arguing. 'I'm sorry, Alex. I never meant for it to happen.' She stared into his eyes.

'Oh, dear Lord. You love him, don't you?'

'Yes.'

His eyes glazed over, and he swallowed, his Adam's apple bobbing in his throat just above his tie.

She looked away. 'Alex, I said I'd be there for you, and I still can be, but only as a friend.'

'I don't need more friends; don't you see?' He stubbed out the cigarette, grinding it down forcefully in the ashtray.

'Well, that's up to you, but I can't be anything more, not now.' Stella turned her head to gaze out of the window, following the ripples of fields stretching out across the land, wishing she was crossing them, racing north, racing towards Mac. 'Take me to the station, please. I want to go home.'

He tried to dissuade her, though she refused to listen. Half an hour later, reluctant and sullen, he threw her suitcase into the car. His parents were nowhere to be seen, and he made no excuse for their absence. The journey to the station was quiet. A crestfallen Alex had lost his carefree manner. If it were not for the fact that she knew his age to be twenty-three, she might have mistaken him for a man in his mid-thirties.

When they arrived at the station, he cut the engine. 'Darling, you know I love you.'

'I thought so once, but you have someone else now, and she clearly adores you. If we're honest, there's always been someone else, hasn't there?'

He shifted his gaze.

'Well, there's nothing more to say. Take care of yourself, Alex.'

He grabbed her hands. 'Don't leave me, please, Stella.' His beseeching eyes, bright and glossy, were tinged with pain. 'I don't love her. It's my parents, I can't let them down.'

Yes, that was what led her into this mess in the first place, and as she stared into his desperate eyes, her heart twinged because he was now trapped. 'Alex, I'm sorry. I don't love you. Marry Elizabeth and be happy.'

'But I want you.' He brushed her cheek with his fingers. 'I have to marry Elizabeth, but it's you I want. It's you I need.'

'You can't have both of us.'

His eyes frantically searched hers. 'Well, think about it, we could still be together, and no one need ever know.'

God, he was serious. 'But I'll know, and I won't be your dirty secret.' He lunged forward and kissed her, a hard, suffocating kiss, crushing her chest, taking her by surprise.

She pushed him away as a fire rose in her belly. 'Alex, stop!' Her pulse raced as she shoved him with all her might. 'How dare you?' She stormed out of the car and grabbed her suitcase from the back seat as he looked on.

'It won't last, you know. Everyone knows that Yanks love them and leave them. All too soon he'll be moving on, and you'll be left behind.'

He was wrong. 'Alex, take care of yourself.' She paused, taking one final look at him before leaving.

'Stella, wait, please.'

She saw him get out, but she kept on walking. When she reached the platform, she sank down on the nearest bench, her heart still whooshing in her ears. The wind picked up, and a bracing breeze penetrated her bones, and she shivered. She heard the roar of Alex's car engine and turned to glimpse the flash of ice blue whipping around the corner, out of sight.

She wondered if Mac was flying today. She tried to shake off the bad feeling that swelled inside her. The station bustled with people, and a sea of khaki flanked the platform with bulky kitbags. The war was never far away. She glanced up at the station clock. *Please God, don't let it be late.*

14

An Awakening

Stella leaned her bicycle up against the wall of the Hardwicke Arms. She was meeting Vera for lunch and had been surprised to hear from her so early that morning – more so because she hadn't seemed her usual, effervescent self. Still, it would be something and nothing. She sighed, having heard no word from Mac at all; she had half expected to find him waiting at the station for her, but the platform had been empty except for the guard. Lord, she'd made a mess of everything.

The quaint village pub was dark inside, with a low, beamed ceiling. She spotted Vera sitting at a table by the window, near the open fireplace. Two American airmen leaned against the bar chatting with locals only to pause and exchange glances as she strode by.

'Hello, Vera. It seems busy in here today.'

'I got you a drink, love. So, how was Devon?'

'It was all right.' Stella sipped her port and lemonade, aware of her friend's scrutinising eyes.

'Really? I'd never have guessed.' Vera raised her eyebrows and then continued to light her cigarette.

Stella sighed and looked out of the window. 'It was bloody awful. Let's just say Alex isn't who he seems. Still, I'm glad to be back.' She forced a smile. 'So, what can we have for lunch?'

'Don't get too excited. There's a choice of pickled egg sandwiches or tongue. As the landlord said when I pulled a face, "There's a blooming war on, you know." Stuffy old beggar. I told him, "You could have fooled me".'

Stella laughed, but her friend wasn't laughing at all; in fact, her eyes were serious, and she fiddled nervously with a ring on her finger.

'What's wrong, Vera? Has something happened?' Perhaps she'd broken up with Sam.

Vera took a long drag on her cigarette, then exhaled, watching as a group of GIs strode in through the door. 'Well, the thing is, while you were away, Mac had an accident.'

Stella froze. 'Oh, God. Is he all right?' A wave of fear surged through her and the breath caught in her throat.

'Yes, he'll be okay. Don't worry.' Vera reached across the table and squeezed Stella's hand. 'They had a crash landing and Sam said a fire broke out, and Mac went back inside for his tail gunner.'

Stella sat silently, numb with shock. She opened her mouth to speak, but no words came out, and tears clouded her eyes. 'When did it happen?'

'Saturday afternoon. He's not that bad, I promise you. It's not serious, just a few burns.'

The hairs at the nape of her neck stood on end and an icy prickle spread down her back. On Saturday night, as she'd thought of Mac, that awful, oppressive feeling had

shrouded her. She swallowed. 'Burns are always serious –
don't you remember that night? Where is he now?'

Stella recalled those young men after the crash. The
blackened arm hanging limp from the stretcher, and the
screams and cries of the remaining crew trapped in the
inferno. Cries that the fire deftly smothered. She shivered
and her chin trembled as Mac's image slipped into those
flames.

'He's at the base hospital.'

'I have to see him.' A single teardrop bounced over her
lashes, and she swiped it away with her fingers. 'What about
the other man?'

'He died. He got hit during the mission.'

'Poor Mac.' Stella shook her head. Thank God he was
alive. She plucked the cigarette from the pack in Vera's
outstretched hand, lit it with trembling hands, and took a
drag.

'He's a hero. Sam reckons he'll get a special medal for
this.' Vera flashed a reassuring smile. 'Come on, love, he'll
be all right.'

Stella didn't care for bravery or for medals. She wanted
Mac to be well and in one piece, but he had burns, and she
knew what that entailed. 'Oh God. You've seen them,
afterwards. Those young men.' Tears ran down to her
mouth, and she licked her lips and sniffed, the bitter salt
reminiscent of sea water. No, she couldn't bear to lose him,
so it didn't matter how injured he was. She didn't care as
long as he recovered.

'Come on, Stell. Sam's seen him, and he said it's mainly
his hands.' Vera put her arm around her. 'He's in the best
place, love. You'll see, they'll fix him up, and he'll be back
in no time.'

Stella wiped her tears away, aware she was attracting attention. As she glanced up, the GIs at the bar stared at her, concerned looks on their faces as they muttered between them.

'Don't mind them, they're friends of Sam's from the base.' Vera finished her drink.

Stella felt an icy chill wrap around her. They knew it was serious, she could tell.

Later, when she returned home, she almost trampled Mrs Brown, who was in the hall by the front door unbuttoning her coat.

'I'm glad I caught you. Can I use the telephone please – I have an urgent call to make,' Stella gasped, trying to get her breath back having cycled like fury all the way home from the pub.

'Well, yes, dear. Is this anything to do with that young man of yours? I don't know, the youth of today.' She shook her head. 'Are you all right? You look very flushed.' She put her basket down on the hall table, but Stella breezed straight past without a word and picked up the telephone. It didn't take long to get through to the base, however, the doctor had been reluctant to tell her anything.

Stella found Mrs Brown busy making a pot of tea. What's happened?'

'Mac's in hospital, and the doctor says he can't have visitors as they're moving him to Addenbrooke's. I need to find out when I can see him.' Her eyes misted over, and her lower lip quivered as she fought hard not to cry.

'Oh, now, I'm sure he'll be all right.' Mrs Brown smiled. 'Sit down and we'll have a nice cup of tea and you can tell me all about it, dear.'

Stella gave her the news of Mac and told her all about Alex and how stupid she felt, stopping here and there to blow her nose. 'I told Mac to leave, and he did.' Her face crumpled as her chest heaved and tears flowed. 'I have to see him.' She sniffed and dabbed her eyes with a handkerchief.

'Well, you try telephoning Addenbrooke's tomorrow. Now, drink your tea. I've put half a sugar lump in yours, dear, seeing as you've had a shock. Happen you need it.'

With a sad smile, Mrs Brown left the room, returning a minute later with the photograph of the soldier from the living room. She passed it to Stella. 'I've seen you looking at him, but I suppose you've been too polite to ask. His name was Captain James Allyson. He joined the Grenadier Guards in 1913.' Her face lit up, radiant. 'We were engaged.' She sat down and closed her eyes for a moment. 'And then the war came. Oh, I can see him now as I waved him off at the station. The platform heaved with soldiers, with kitbags and rifles and all us women clutching our hankies. He was so excited to be going – well, they all were in the beginning. He was so handsome and young. Goodness, we both were.' She smiled and chuckled, yet Stella guessed her smile masked something more.

She returned the photograph.

'He had his own company of men, and he was only twenty-one. I still have all the letters he sent. Everyone said it would be over by Christmas that first year, but we didn't realise how bad it would be. It dragged on for four years and in that time boys became men, hardened or destroyed by what they'd gone through. James changed. He was so jumpy and quiet.'

She looked away as her blue eyes glazed over, pressing his face close to her chest as if she could make him a part of her for eternity. 'Oh, how I looked forward to his leave – one time he was due home for a whole week. But then his sister called at our house, something she'd never done before. I still remember how my tummy lurched when I saw her standing there, white as a sheet. I knew before I even opened the door.' Her voice quavered, and she glanced at Stella, her brow furrowed, her eyes red. 'He was killed in France, at the Battle of Arras on the twenty-eighth of March, 1918. We would have been married in July that year. Of course, we wanted to marry sooner, only my parents decided we should wait until the war ended. Then, as it dragged on, father gave in, and we set the date. But it was too late.' She sniffed as she gazed down at the photograph, tracing his outline with her fingertip in a smooth, gentle caress.

Stella blinked fresh tears away. 'I'm so sorry, Mrs B. That's so sad.' It was times like this when words were so inadequate, so futile and yet so necessary.

'I vowed never to marry, and then years later I met my husband. He was a kind soul, and I came to love him in time, but not a day goes by when I don't think of James and what might have been. I had a good marriage, though it was too late for any children by then.'

She'd have made a lovely mum, Stella reflected as she wiped a tear away.

'So, you visit your young man. Don't be afraid and grab the chances life throws you with open arms. Ride through the challenges and you'll come out the other side stronger and happier. That way you'll never miss an opportunity. Pay no attention to the things people say. He's decent, and I'd know if he wasn't. So, when you see him, tell him how you feel. Don't waste a minute of time, it's too precious.'

Mrs Brown returned the picture to its rightful place on the mantelpiece and smiled, brushing her finger softly over his mouth. 'You must follow your heart, and sometimes you must take a leap of faith.'

In Cambridge, a honeyed sun shone through acres of blue as people hurried along pavements and vehicles trundled through the town. As the bus crossed the River Cam, Stella glanced down, mesmerised by the light that danced on the ripples of water. She strolled through the grand gated entrance of the hospital and along the tree-lined drive, stepping into the entrance of the main foyer, which was flanked on either side with sandbags. Inside, Addenbrooke's bustled with people and medical staff, and the clinical smell hit her at once – intense and unsettling. Memories of her father flooded back, and a lump swelled in her throat. She swallowed and took a deep breath, forcing herself to stay calm and carry on. When she reached the ward, it was impossible to pick Mac out from a sea of men and bandages, but a helpful nurse pointed to his bed.

Stella wondered why it was screened off and she hesitated, wild thoughts rushing through her mind as she wondered how badly injured he might be. She swallowed; her palms were moist with sweat and her heart pounded. Gingerly, she pulled the screen aside. Her heart sank as she gazed at him lying there with his eyes screwed shut and beads of sweat shimmering on his brow. He thrashed around as if he was dreaming, turning his head from side to side, and then he muttered something she couldn't quite hear. Bandages covered his hands and lower arms, and he had dressings on the right side of his face and across his chest. He looked so vulnerable – smaller, somehow. Quietly, she sat down in the chair next to him.

'No! Birdie, get outta there,' he called out.

'Mac, it's all right. You're dreaming.' She touched his arm, gently. 'It's me, Stella.'

He stopped muttering and reached across with his other hand, placing it on hers. The bandage was already soiled, and she turned away, trying not to dwell on the state of his hands beneath. His face was rosy, and rivulets of sweat rolled down his temples. A bowl of clean water sat on the bedside cabinet with a cloth, which she soaked and then dabbed his face and brow. His eyes flickered open, and he gazed at her and mumbled something before closing them. Oh, why did she tell him to leave? She'd been such a fool. It was Mac who had needed her, and now more than ever. She longed to hold him, but how could she? He winced, and she saw pain in his contorted face, and her whole being ached. She stroked his shoulder and placed her hand gently on his chest. Somehow, the rise and fall and warmth of it comforted her. When the nurse bustled in and made a point of glancing at her watch, Stella knew it was time to leave.

'He's very restless.'

'Yes, he's in a lot of pain at the moment, and we've had to give him morphine. He's rather groggy right now so I doubt he's making much sense.' She wrote something on the chart and replaced it at the foot of the bed.

'How bad is he?'

'Well, he has burns on his hands which will need surgery. The burns on his chest are more superficial, but he'll need surgery for the face. It's early days. Shall I tell him you came by?'

'Yes, please. Just say that Stella was here. Thank you.'
She leant forward and whispered in his ear. 'I'm going now,
but I'll be back soon, I promise.' She looked at him one last
time and kissed him on the forehead, and he wrapped his
arms around her, pinning her to his chest.

'Stella,' he whispered, and then fell silent, and his arms
relaxed, releasing her.

On her way out, she passed a man in a grey chalk suit,
sitting on the side of a patient's bed. He adjusted his black
horn-rimmed spectacles, and Stella clearly heard him say,
'You boys are all the same. Always taking your goggles and
gloves off when you're flying. Well, not to worry. I'll fix you
up.'

He must have been a doctor, and his accent was unusual.
Was it Australian? Perhaps, she wasn't sure, but he sounded
jolly. His tone was soft, gentle, and reassuring, and Stella
saw how the patient grinned, even though his eyes were
bandaged and he was obviously in a bad way. Suddenly, her
chest grew tight, and she could barely breathe. She hurried
along the corridor, half-running as her heart raced. Outside,
she turned her face up to embrace the fresh air and the
golden touch of the sun, sucking in deep breaths and
gradually her heart slowed and her chest eased. He'd
whispered her name. God, she couldn't bear to think of
Mac in pain like that. When he'd held her, his firm hold had
reassured her, but now he needed the reassurance.

15

The Beauty Shop

Mac cast a gaze at the nurse as she wheeled a trolley laden with piles of crisp, fresh linen out into the ward, its wheels squeaking, protesting beneath the burdening weight. She approached one of the beds, removed the clipboard that hung at the end, and wrote on the chart, then glanced at the mound beneath the covers.

'Not getting up today, Pete? Sister Jamieson's on duty, you know. She'll have your guts for garters so she will.' Her Irish accent, soft and light. An auburn lock of hair escaped her cap, and she tucked it behind her ear.

'I'm supposed to be on sick leave, Bea. Can't a chap have a lie in for once?'

'Sick leave, you say? Ah, for a minute there you had me fooled. I could have sworn I saw you racing that wheelchair up and around this ward last night. Having a whale of a time, you were. And I'm sure it was a man just like you that almost knocked that poor woman off her feet. And I suppose you'll be telling me next it wasn't you who got drunk and fell into the bath while it was still full! Water all over a clean floor and you dripping right through the ward.' Her mouth curved up into a smile.

As he opened his mouth to speak, she cut in again. 'Mr McIndoe has bent over backwards for all of you, but there are limits, you know, and last night you surpassed them.'

Pete's face glowed scarlet. 'Well, it was all just a bit of fun. You know how it is when boys get together.'

'Oh, I do. And just so you know, Sister will be keeping her eyes fixed on all of you today.' Bea raised her eyebrows before bustling away to the next bed. Just then a guy whizzed by, propelling his wheelchair while gripping a pint of beer between his thighs.

'Top of the morning, Bea,' he said, in a mock Irish accent.

Her jaw dropped, and she stood with her hands on her hips, her eyes narrowed. 'Good morning, Mr Evans. It's early to be drinking, don't you think?'

'Well, that's a matter of opinion. What doesn't kill you makes you stronger, the hair of the dog and all that.' He laughed and propelled himself across to the breakfast table where a few of the men sat, helping themselves to tea and toast.

The morning sun bathed the ward in golden light. Fragrant roses, carnations, and tulips flowed from vases placed by every man's bed. Mac wondered who brought the flowers. Blooms of pink, orange, and cream blended with fern and sure did brighten the place up. Nurses busied themselves making beds; crisp, starched white sheets with light green counterpanes on top, tucked in tight with traditional nursing corners and the sheet folded back over the counterpane to lie neatly at the foot of the pillows.

In rows, the beds reflected regimented military bunks, and it was the only order you would find here. Everything else other than medical care seemed to be haphazard, irregular, unruly, and goddamn weird. The United States Army had a saying for such things: SNAFU – situation normal, all fucked up. Mac smiled. And the guys here really knew how to shoot a line.

A bell rang out, and Mac could hardly believe his eyes when one of the guys sailed into the ward on a bicycle. He stopped, dismounted, and pulled a brown paperbag from the basket on the front and shouted out, 'Eccles cakes. Get your Eccles cakes.' He then dipped a hand into the bag and dragged out the cakes one by one and threw them onto the beds.

The doors to the ward swung open, and Mr McIndoe strode in and surveyed the scene like a general scrutinising his troops, then he removed his spectacles and wiped the lenses with his handkerchief before heading to Sister's office. Mac was desperate to know how long he was going to be stuck here. Mr McIndoe had seemed like a great guy when he first met him and had made him feel at ease and in safe hands.

He glanced over at the guy in the next bed, who was having surgery later. He was from Idaho. After a skirmish with a German fighter, the fuel tank in his Spitfire had exploded. God knows how he bailed out. He was a mess. When Mac asked him what he did before the war, he said, 'I was studying at art college. When this is all over, I'm hoping to go back.'

Just like Birdie. Mac looked down. Maybe he was all washed up. The war had in one sense been a blessing in that it had revealed his true passion – flying. He was born to fly; he felt it, and if the US Army Air Force now took away his wings, it would be like restricting the air he breathed. He took a deep breath and slowly exhaled, aware of his heart hammering in his ears.

He recalled his excitement when he'd enlisted. But reality had soon dawned, and the war, which he'd thought to be a just cause, had transcended into a monster that sucked the life right out of you. It stripped away any religious beliefs one layer at a time until all you felt was a hollow in your gut and an ache in your chest that grew heavier, deeper, until it crushed you inwardly and you could barely breathe, hope, or care whether you lived or died. That was where he'd been when he first spotted Stella across a crowded dance hall, and by the time she turned and met his gaze, his heart whispered she was for keeps. He screwed his eyes shut.

His thoughts turned to his crew. A well-oiled machine ripped apart, with Mac as the damaged cog. Service life had become his life and now, separated from the only other home he'd ever known, he was adrift in strange waters. Vera Lynn crooned over the radio – 'We'll Meet Again.'

He'd lain in bed for a week since arriving; not that he could recall much. The nurse told him earlier that he'd had a pretty bad infection, but today he felt stronger. In the early hours, he'd woken in sweat-drenched sheets to find the night nurse hovering over him, her hand on his shoulder asking if he was all right. *Hell no, I'm goddamned burned,* he'd wanted to yell.

'You were shouting out in your sleep. That's the second time tonight.' She'd smiled at him, but it was a pity smile.

The dreams were growing more vivid, and last night he swore he saw Birdie for real. And when he clambered out of bed to check around the ward for signs of his dead gunner, the nurse had scolded him like a child. She insisted it was simply a dream, but he was darn sure he'd seen him standing there in flames. Jesus, he'd smelt the burning flesh like roasted pork, and it drifted all around now, thick, lining his throat. Maybe it was his own flesh. He couldn't shake it off so he closed his eyes as Vera sang of blue skies and dark clouds.

His injuries showed signs of healing, so he'd been told, and at least the pain wasn't so bad now. It was a relief to ditch those stinking pyjamas and put on his service pinks and greens, and he felt a step closer to his former self, but he had to know how bad he looked. The nurse had brushed him off this morning when he'd requested a mirror. What was that all about? She'd applied a light dressing to his cheek and neck. 'It's healing beautifully,' was all she'd said. Her opinion. Everything was a mess. He couldn't fly, he was trapped here, missing the guys, missing Stella. And now he couldn't do anything for himself. This wasn't how he'd imagined it when he enlisted, only back then he hadn't given much thought to dying either.

A friendly voice fractured his reverie. 'G'day, mate. I'm Dickie – a pilot with the Australian Air Force. Welcome to the Beauty Shop.' He took out a battered cigarette case and offered it to Mac.

'Mac. I'm with the Eighth.' He gestured with his bandaged hands, unable to hold a cigarette.

'No worries, mate.' Dickie lit it for him, reached over, and placed it in Mac's mouth. 'Not be long and you'll get those bloody bandages off.' He lit one for himself and removed Mac's so he could flick the ash.

'What did you call this place?'

'Listen, boys, we got ourselves another Yank.' Dickie grinned at him, his once sun-kissed skin from the Australian shores had faded, replaced by scar tissue, but his sparkling, almond eyes held an air of mischief. 'The Beauty Shop, mate – it's where you come to be made up, you know, after you've been fried. Mind you, some of the blokes call it a madhouse.'

He laughed, then drew on his cigarette. 'It's all right. We're a mixed bunch – Pommies, Yanks, Poles, Aussies, Kiwis, Free French, all mashed, burned, or fried for King and country.' He studied Mac for a moment, grinning. 'Could have been worse, you know.' He glanced at Mac's bandaged hands. 'Bloke down the end there, they've got him wrapped up like a mummy. He's well and truly fried, poor bugger, and blind.'

Worse? Yeah, he should be dead, like Birdie. Mac sighed. *Jesus*. He glanced around at everyone as Dickie's voice seemed to fade away. One guy wasn't even in his bed. He was in traction, suspended above it, a mass of bandages stuffed in striped blue and white pyjamas with a thatch of thick brown unruly hair.

Dickie's voice cut in. 'That bloody waster opposite is Lee.'

Mac glanced across at a guy in RAF blues wearing an eye patch, slouched on his bed, reading a copy of *Rafters* magazine.

'And that's Pete over there by the bathroom. He's a laugh.' Dickie drew on his cigarette. His eyelids were bright red and drooped like hoods, and his entire face was a patchwork quilt of scarlet and pale skin, like his hands.

Lee glanced up from his magazine and nodded his head, which he held at an awkward angle, and Mac froze. Lee had a roll of skin like a sausage attached to the bridge of the nose, which hung down across his face and reached inside his shirt. Mac wondered where it ended. The guy couldn't hold his head upright, and it sure looked uncomfortable.

'Watch out, lads, stand by your beds. Dragon approaching twelve o'clock high.' Dickie stood up. 'Take it easy, mate.' He winked.

Sister Jamieson made a beeline for Mac, carrying a brown medical file, walking with a rigid, straight back, her thin lips curving into a faint smile. Her white headdress sat aloft her greying hair, which was scraped away from her sallow face and pinned at the back.

'Good afternoon, Lieutenant. I'm glad to see you looking more comfortable. Mr McIndoe will be along shortly to reassess you. In the meantime, the orderly will take you to the saline bath.' She raised her pencil-thin eyebrows, her brow transcending into multiple furrows.

'Yeah, the nurse said I had to have the baths twice a day. Thanks, Sister.'

She nodded and walked away with her head held high. She reminded him of his old high school teacher – Mrs Stewart, a middle-aged woman with the roar of a lion if you crossed the line, except her bark was worse than her bite. He looked around. *So this was the top place for plastic surgery.* The ward was basic – a primitive wooden hut in the grounds of the hospital. It was drab, just like the RAF bases the Eighth Air Force had requisitioned. Tatty, rusty tin can huts with rustic, shabby furniture left behind by the RAF, sparse and moth-eaten. Still, the Mighty Eighth had moved in and made everything shipshape, discarding old for new.

Bassingbourn had been in pretty good shape to begin with, and Mac's outfit had been lucky. Brick-built buildings and real rooms – no sleeping in Nissen huts. They called it the Country Club, and it sure was a cut above the rest. He wished he was there right now, and he wondered what the guys were doing. The barracks had almost become a home from home and for some, it would be the last home they would ever know. He squeezed his eyes shut as the sharpened edge of realisation nudged him in the guts. Birdie was dead. Whether it had been the fire or the flak, it didn't matter. What mattered was that as the pilot, he was responsible. His heart thudded harder and faster, skipping a beat at times, and the breath caught in his throat. He closed his eyes and waited for it to pass. It usually did.

'Ready for the bath, mate?' Jimmy, the bathroom orderly, stood before him at the foot of the bed with a wheelchair.

'Sure, I got no place else to go.' Mac eased himself into the wheelchair, wincing at the sting in his lower legs, which shook and almost gave way when he first stood up. Jimmy had a rounded, friendly face with a long, pointed nose and Mac guessed he was mid-forties, with short, thinning, dark brown hair. He sighed, feeling suddenly tired. He wanted to be left alone. He wanted Stella. That had ended badly, and he longed to see her now. If only he'd gone back that day, but it had seemed hopeless. He didn't exactly understand things, although he ought to have respected her commitment to a friend, regardless of what he thought of Alex. What if he'd lost her? He guessed he probably had, and his heart clenched.

The saline bathroom lay at the end of the ward. Mac stared, bewildered at the many dials and pipes on the wall. 'The first day you brought me in here, I thought this was a lab.'

Jimmy laughed. 'Don't be daft. It's an ordinary bath, though there's a bit of technical stuff that goes with it. He helped Mac undress. 'It's quite clever, isn't it? But then the Maestro is a genius. He realised quite early on that the pilots who came down in the sea healed quicker than anyone else. Something to do with the salty water.'

'Well, it sure is soothing.' Mac lay back in the water as Jimmy unravelled the bandages on his hands and those on his lower legs. Within minutes, the dressings lifted off painlessly and floated to the surface. Now when he saw his burns, he no longer had to suppress the rush of nausea that lurched in his gut, although as he gazed at his hands, he gritted his teeth – they were the worst. They remained swollen and chubby, fingers like plump scarlet sausages, a little contracted. He tried to straighten them out, but it was hopeless. Small, pale pieces of dead skin floated all around him, translucent in the water, and as he stared, mesmerised, an image of men tumbling from their aircraft sailed into his head and he turned his gaze away. He sucked in a breath as he visualised Stella's hand in his. She wouldn't want these hands to touch her, and she wouldn't want *him*. Like a crisp, fallen bloom, he was caught on the breeze, hurtling this way and that to someplace bleak.

Wilson had said he was lucky. He looked down at his hands again. Jeez, would they ever be normal? He held his right hand up in front of him. The red, fleshy appendage was flecked with charred, black patches extending down to his fingertips, and he hoped to God he wouldn't lose his fingers. A searing pain pierced his palm, and he submerged it once more beneath the warm saline.

'Don't worry, the Maestro will fix you up, you'll see. You're in the best place.'

'Why does everyone call the doc that?'

'Well, he's in charge for a start. Some of the lads call him the Boss, some of them call him Archie.' Jimmy raised his eyebrows at that, and Mac guessed he would *never* do it. 'Some have even called him God.' Jimmy strode over to the door and peered out. 'Fancy a fag?' He produced a pack of John Player's.

'Sure.'

Jimmy lit one and placed it between Mac's lips. 'There you go, chum.' He took one for himself. 'If you hear Sister's footsteps, you let me know. God help me if she catches me smoking.' He winked and turned to check on the water temperature.

'Say, there's a guy out there with a weird nose. What's that all about?'

'Oh, that's a tubed pedicle flap. It's amazing how it's done. If someone needs a new nose, the Maestro takes a piece of skin, a flap, say from the stomach, stitches it into a tube, leaving one end still attached to the stomach for the blood supply and he stitches the other end to the arm. After two or three weeks, when the blood supply is healthy and strong, he removes the end from the stomach and attaches it higher up on the chest. So then the arm's connected to the chest, see?' Jimmy held his arm to his chest, just so, and Mac nodded. 'After another few weeks, it can be removed from the chest and attached to the bridge of the nose, so then the arm is connected to the nose. Then the last stage is modelling it into a new nose. Bloomin marvellous what he can do. New eyelids, lips, ears, entire faces. Modern medicine, eh?'

Mac closed his eyes. It dawned on him that he truly *was* one of the lucky few. He could only imagine what it felt like to lose your entire face. He wondered what he looked like.

Why were there no mirrors here? He sighed. Was he really that bad?

'By the way, you're allowed to smoke as long as you can flick the ash, but once your bandages are back on you'll have to ask one of the lads. They don't mind helping each other out. Everybody mucks in. We're like one big family in here.'

Family. One dead, the rest ripped apart. He'd received a letter that morning from Wilson, letting him know that Danny was okay and they were all back on duty, filling in as spares with other crews. Mac's eyelids suddenly grew heavy and flickered closed, and his entire body relaxed for the first time in a week as he drifted off to sleep.

Later that evening, as Mac sat in bed, all he could think about was Stella. Did she even know where he was? Some of the guys were playing cards at a table in the middle of the ward, and they burst out laughing. They seemed buoyant enough, despite their gruesome injuries. When the young VAD had fed him earlier, he'd felt like a baby, and he hated it, but he realised he'd have to get used to it. He couldn't use his hands at all – not to bathe, feed, dress, or write letters home. *What a way to lose your independence.* It was kind of hard to take. Afterwards, she'd helped him to the bathroom, where she undressed him and pulled on his pyjamas. God, his face had burned. Being unable to undo your own pants was damn frustrating. The nurse looked younger than him, for Pete's sake, and what seemed worse was her calm, quiet manner. She barely uttered a word the entire time, although she told him her name while she tucked a chestnut curl behind her ear – Lily.

He lay back and closed his eyes. No, Stella wouldn't bother with him after this. At the previous hospital, he'd dreamt about her, and he swore her gentle voice had sung in his ears, but he'd woken to loneliness. He clenched his jaw, and a searing pain shot through his right cheek, a timely reminder that everything had changed. He didn't need anyone taking care of him, and he didn't want any pity.

His gaze followed Lily as she attended to the guy opposite. His entire head was bandaged, with slits for a nose, mouth, and eyes, and Mac imagined what lay beneath, conjuring up a legion of ghoulish images. There were a few like him here, and as Dickie had said earlier, they were well and truly mashed, boiled, and fried.

The poor guy in the next bed kept on hollering, 'It's a bloody madhouse in here.' He seemed real distressed.

Sister Jamieson appeared, her face growing more thunderous by the second. She bellowed at a few of the guys, who laughed and yelled at one another while racing around the ward in wheelchairs, gripping their beer glasses snugly between their knees. Beer swilled and slopped, soaking their legs and the clean floor. And poor Lily, ordered to tend to the mess, meekly grabbed a mop and bucket like a scolded child and risked life and limb as she tried to clean up the spillage, dodging wheelchairs and slaps on the bottom as they whizzed past. Her face flushed scarlet to match the cross on her white VAD apron. A group of guys sauntered over to Mac's bed and gathered around him in a cluster, with cries of support as if cheering on champion jockeys.

'Three to one that Jerry wins,' Pete said, taking a swig of beer.

Mac noticed that he too had a tubed pedicle and was growing a new nose. Pete grinned back at him from his heavily scarred face, completely unfazed by the trunk-like attachment. *They're all crazy*, Mac thought. The cheering continued and finally Jerry, now breathing hard with rosy cheeks, was hailed the winner. Pete insisted that all three line up for the awards ceremony as he presented the winner's prize – a scarf with a packet of cigarettes attached to it which he draped around Jerry's neck like a lei garland while Lee handed out more beer.

'Bottoms up.' Pete flicked the radio on and 'Kiss the Boys Goodbye' drifted out into the ward. He turned up the volume, then passed Mac a half-pint glass of beer with a straw.

'Thanks.' Mac took a slurp. 'Man, that's watered down.'

'Course it is, mate, but it's still beer.' Dickie slapped him on the back.

It sure felt good having a real drink, even if it was warm and he couldn't hold it himself. Afterwards, when the excitement fizzled out and the guys retreated, Mac lay back, tired. Maybe it was the beer or the banter, but his heart lifted, and he decided to write to Stella. He sighed, realising he had to see her, even if it was for one last time. *Stella, a beautiful name for a beautiful girl.*

His mother always said that things happened for a reason. *Life's mapped out for you, John.* He could hear her voice now as if it floated in on the sweet, mountain breeze all the way from Montana, and a familiar ache squeezed his chest.

He was exhausted, and he tried to fight the fatigue as he dreaded the dream that drifted in the night shadows. He didn't want to face Birdie tonight. Why hadn't he been able to save him? But he had no control over flak or fighters in the sky. A lump lodged in his throat and as the guys crooned along to the radio, he longed to yell at them to pipe down, but his strength ebbed away as his eyelids finally lowered.

Bliss, tomorrow, Stella. Fatigue draped over him like a blanket, and he pictured Stella at home with him in Montana. The vast plains, the hills, and all that green beneath an endless crystal clear sky. And the only sound for miles was the lulling cattle that roamed the prairies or the screech of the golden eagle, scything through the silence like a fingertip touching water, casting ripples on the surface.

16

Nothing Is Impossible, May 1943

Archie glanced at his watch. It was already quarter to eight. He'd have to make the ward round a priority before beginning his theatre list. As he slammed the door of his glossy black Austin 12, a sharp pain zipped through his hand, which immediately began to throb. He clenched and unclenched it a few times and rubbed it on his way through the grounds, and the fuzziness and pain faded away. It was all right. Or was it? He forced out a long breath. He kept telling himself that, but just lately it had worsened. Perhaps it was something to investigate. There was such a lot to contend with just now, and the lads had to be his priority. It was bound to be fine. He pushed his spectacles up onto his nose.

The spring sunshine warmed his face, the well-tended gardens bloomed with an array of flowers, and a mix of sweet fragrance drifted in the air as he swept by. It was shaping up to be a beaut of a day. He burst through the doors of Ward III and found Sister Jamieson marching along, inspecting the beds and their occupants, her hawk-like eyes sweeping across everything and everyone.

Archie nodded as he caught her gaze. 'Morning, Sister. Any problems today?'

'No, nothing you don't already know about.' Her thin lips curved into a pleasant smile.

'Jolly good. Right, I'll take a look at the new fellow first.' Archie ran both hands through his hair, smoothing it down, picked up a medical file, and began to flick through the pages.

'You'll find him in the saline bath.' Sister stood with her hands clasped together in front of her, waiting. 'The war artist is with him, painting.' She pursed her lips and her brow furrowed. 'And I'm afraid Mac's a little down today, too.'

'Ah, right. Thanks.' He dropped the notes on the desk and headed towards the bathroom, nodding as the boys greeted him along the way. So, Mac had taken a bit of a dive. It was only to be expected. Good to know Freddy had made an early start, although using Mac as his muse might not have been such a great idea. A group of boys sat around the table listening to the radio with faraway looks in their eyes as 'He Wears A Pair Of Silver Wings' swayed out into the ward.

At the bathroom door, Archie took a deep breath before entering. 'Morning, all.' He glanced at Freddy, who sat in the far corner on a stool, with his sketch pad on his knee and a charcoal pencil in his hand. He then settled his gaze on Mac, who didn't bother to look up but carried on staring into the water as if in a trance. Still, it was early days.

The bathroom orderly was busy hosing Mac's face and neck with warm saline. 'Morning, Maestro.' He nodded and grinned.

'Morning, Jimmy.'

The humidity grew steadily, and the tang of salt drifted in the warm, moist air, evoking childhood memories of family days spent by the sea in Dunedin. Archie inhaled deeply, savouring the memory that was equally tinged with sadness as he thought of his brother Jack, still a prisoner of war.

'Now then, Mac. I see you're the latest muse for Freddy here. Who knows, we might even see your portrait hanging in one of London's galleries one day.' Archie squatted down next to the bath. 'I wanted to have a look at your hands. Would you raise the right one for me?'

Mac turned his head away as he did so, and Archie gently took his arm and guided it down to rest on the side of the bath. 'I don't think it's as bad as I first thought. It was a godsend you had your gloves on – they've saved me a lot of work.' He cast a reassuring smile, even though Mac was avoiding eye contact. 'You're a rancher back home as I recall.'

'That's right.' Mac's eyes darkened.

'Ah, tough work. Well, you're going to need your hands if you're working with ropes and cattle.' Archie studied Mac for a moment. He was a decent young man, a long way from home. From the look in his eyes and the edge in his voice, he was lost and floundering, no doubt thinking the worst. Still, he'd been lucky and pulled through a nasty infection. He had a mix of second and third-degree burns to his face, neck, and hands. It could have been a lot worse, and it was only natural for a chap to feel a little down after something like this. He had to find his way again. Spending too long in the dark did a fellow no good at all.

The roaring gush of water topping up the bath filled the silence. 'Can you fix my hands, doc? If I can't use them, I'm finished.' Mac raised his chin, and his voice wavered, his speech slow.

Archie stared long and hard into Mac's eyes, where a faint flicker of light flared. These boys had to deal with horrific injuries while struggling to cling to whatever little glimmer of themselves remained. It was the future outcome that mattered most. Archie had a vision for such things, unlike his patients. Allowing them to see the full extent of their facial disfigurements in the early days was simply too traumatic. A former patient, Geoff Page, flashed in his mind. With similar injuries, he'd recovered and was now flying again, but it had been a long, hard slog. Archie flicked a gaze at Freddy, who continued sketching, his charcoal pencil gripped in his right hand as he made sweeping strokes on paper, his lips pursed.

'It's the fingers, you see. Saving them is one thing, but preventing contractures is another.' Archie recalled the agony Geoff had endured, with his hands strapped to splints which mercilessly straightened his contracted fingers over time. There were always possibilities, and there was always hope.

'Don't worry. The surgery will fix that to an extent, then you'll have to push yourself afterwards and do the therapy to get them working again. It will be hard and painful, but worth it in the long run.' Archie lightly gripped Mac's shoulder, and the muscle tightened beneath his hand. 'As for your face, that will require a skin graft and more surgery in the future, and I'm afraid there will be some scar tissue, though it's likely I can do something to improve that.'

'So, how long will it take? I'm itching to get back to my squadron.' Mac straightened up and met his gaze.

Another one. 'It's hard to say. You're going to need two operations initially, and you'll require further surgery in the future. Rome wasn't built in a day, unfortunately, and I'm afraid you're a work in progress, but we'll get there. As for returning to service, well, it's a little too soon to be thinking along those lines. I can fix you up, although we still won't know for certain how much hand function you'll have. They won't be as good as they were before, but they'll work.'

Archie paused as Mac's gaze returned to the water; his shoulders drooped and his mouth settled in a tight line. It was always the same. They couldn't wait to wage war, and settle a score or two. Of course, Archie realised it was more complex than that. They needed to prove that they weren't hiding behind their injuries, and there were always people who were quick to judge. The old saying – saving face – meant one thing to Archie and quite another to these boys. And then they needed the camaraderie of their brothers. Bonds forged in war, stronger than steel. He sighed. 'I'll do my very best for you, Mac. I'm afraid it's going to take time, however, if you're determined then who knows what you could achieve.'

Mac nodded. 'I'll do whatever it takes.' He slid his hand back beneath the water.

'Don't worry, we'll have you roping steers in no time at all. Well, I'll leave you to your soak. Good to see you again, Mac. Cheerio.' Archie grinned and winked.

'Thanks, doc. I appreciate it.'

Archie blew out a breath as beads of sweat rolled down his back. It was early days, and Mac was grappling with the reality of his situation, rolling through a range of emotions. It was the way of it, and it was normal to grieve for what seemed lost and beyond reach. Mac was clinging on to his former self, and, although he didn't know it, there would be further battles to win if he were to live a full life. Archie realised he would have to push him in the right direction.

Something caught his eye and he stopped. 'Is this yours, Jimmy?' Archie held up a copy of *Bazaar* magazine, which depicted a picture of Lauren Bacall posing with the American Red Cross on the front cover.

'What's that, Maestro?' Jimmy squinted across the room. 'No, that's not mine. You take it.'

Archie sauntered through the ward, his mind reeling with thoughts. These boys couldn't wait to get back in the air. Was one roasting not enough? He pinched his lips together and paused at the office door to speak with Sister, but before he could utter a word, angry shouting erupted in the ward. Pilot Officer Stan Johnson was out of bed, frantically tearing at the dressings on his face while the young VAD looked on, her eyes wide, and a look of utter helplessness on her rosy face. Sister Jamieson dashed out to help, with Archie close on her heels.

'Get me a bloody mirror – now!' Stan yelled, his bandages hanging loosely around his neck, revealing his burned face, devoid of expression – devoid of a nose and eyelids. Swollen, scarlet lips bulged out from his bloated face – even his ears were partially burned away.

'Please, Stan, we don't have mirrors in this ward. The nurse meant nothing by it. She's so young, that's all,' Bea said, trying to calm the man, who was now gasping for breath.

Sister Jamieson brought some portable screens and placed them around the bed to shield him from the curious stares of the other men. 'It looks like the new VAD got a shock when she saw his facial injuries. She may have said something in error,' she said to Archie with wide eyes, wringing her hands.

'May have? She bloody well must have for him to be in this state. Well, I don't want her on this ward. She'll have to go – at once.' Archie's eyes narrowed, and heat spread up his neck and flooded into his face. 'Stupid girl,' he muttered. He heaved in a deep breath; the nauseating odour of burned flesh rushed into his nostrils, and he snorted it out. 'Now then, young chap, what's all this about a mirror? It's far too soon – you haven't given me a chance to show you what we can do yet, and besides, your first surgery is scheduled for this afternoon. Let's get that out of the way first and then you can judge the results for yourself.' Archie sat down on the man's bed and patted his shoulder.

'Look at me. I'm finished.' Stan hung his head, his shoulders drooping.

Sunlight trickled through the window, spilling over the bed and the table. 'You've got some pretty serious injuries, but I promised you when you first arrived that we'd fix you up, and that's what we're going to do.'

Stan sank down on the bed and sighed. 'I'm a mess, Archie, a bloody mess. How in God's name are you going to fix this?' He pointed at his face, his chin trembling.

Archie laid his hand upon Stan's shoulder, and tremors snaked up his arm. 'One step at a time, that's how.' Archie stared into the lad's eyes and nodded. 'Now, Bea will put some fresh dressings on and I'll see you shortly in theatre.' He stood up. 'It takes time, but you'll get there.'

He charged off to Sister's office and closed the door. The blood rushed through his ears. 'Make sure you dismiss that girl. I won't tolerate behaviour like that – it's no good for the boys. What message do you think she's just given him? It's bad enough when their own wives and girlfriends abandon them. We do not abandon them, nor do we judge. What the hell do these girls think war is? It's horrific and bloody brutal, and I want people who won't flinch. Is that understood?' He was aware that almost everyone could hear him, but he didn't care.

'Yes, Mr McIndoe.' Sister Jamieson, usually so composed and unflappable, seemed a little stunned, as a scarlet tinge flooded her cheeks.

Archie was still fuming when he reached his office. He needed girls who could keep their heads at all times. He was trying to show these boys that they still had lives worth living. How could he do that if silly girls were going to look horrified whenever they saw a disfigured face? His staff needed to treat them all normally otherwise his methods would fail, and he was not about to let that happen. No, he would have to recruit some fresh faces. The boys could do without these young, well-meaning types who had no idea how to control their emotions or disguise their feelings.

Archie pursed his lips. For Christ's sake, these lads had almost lost their lives, and many had lost their faces, their boyish looks, and their independence. They were transformed from glorious, revered flyboys to faceless dependents whose stars had dimmed, searching for their identities. Some depression was inevitable, and silly girls acting hysterically around them were bound to propel some of them head-first into the black.

His nurses needed to act the part, and they had to be convincing if they were to show the boys that looks weren't everything. He needed girls who could flatter and make them feel good about themselves no matter what; help them to feel like a man – needed, desired. He glanced down at the copy of *Bazaar*. Lauren Bacall was certainly a stunner, the perfect medicine, although he had little chance of charming a Hollywood actress to East Grinstead. No, but there was another way. He smiled to himself.

Childish laughter and squeals of delight flowed in through the open window. Archie spun his chair around and gazed outside. Two small boys sailed through the hospital gardens ahead of their mother, with their arms outstretched like wings. Gulls squealed as they circled above. A sudden sadness gripped his chest, and he heaved in a breath as the sight evoked childhood memories of New Zealand summers. Memories which elicited feelings long since forgotten.

A family weekend away in Brighton, New Zealand, at the beginning of the Christmas holidays in 1912. Jack, his elder brother, had squelched through the wet sand barefoot, dressed in shorts and a top as he clambered over the rock pools that lay on the reef at low tide. They went there most weekends, to their family holiday cottage. The gulls cried overhead as Archie's feet sank into the wet, gritty sand, warming his wiggling toes. Jack hoisted a crayfish from the green pool on the reef and lowered it into his bucket of seawater. Archie's gaze flicked out to sea, to the giant waves in the distance as the breeze whispered warm, salty air into his face and mouth. That's when he saw it. A huge mountain of black granite that rose from its deep-sea bed as waves lashed and fizzed at its sides, blowing foam onto the granite ledge. *A secret island.*

Squinting at the endless blue above, he gazed in awe at a stretch of white feathered clouds. 'Angel Wings.' A shadow passed over him as a white albatross glided out over the ocean and swooped down to settle on the rock – *his* island.

The bird, relaxed and free, turned and cast him a taunting look, then beat its wings and soared into the blue with grace. The tide had turned, and the water crept closer as waves roared in and ebbed away with a shush, the relentless beating heart of the ocean, another taunt. A burning flared in his chest. 'I'm going to swim out there.' Archie crossed his arms and held his head high as he quickly assessed the distance.

'No, you're not. It's too far, Nookie. You'll never make it.' Jack laughed.

'Who says? It's not too far for me.' His brother ought to know better than to set a challenge. 'Besides, I'm the best swimmer in the family.'

Later, at home, when Archie told his parents of his plan, his mother's face paled. 'You can't swim that far, it's not safe. You're getting too many wild ideas just lately.'

His father sucked on his pipe and chuckled. 'You're only twelve, and it's too far for a shrimp to swim.'

'I have to do it. I promised. It's my New Year's resolution, and I can't break a promise, can I?'

And so the next day at low tide, he stripped down to his bathing trunks and dived in as his family watched nervously from the shore. Archie battled the raging current that prevailed in the Channel and the Pacific rollers further out until, finally, he reached the rock, grabbed the ledge, and hauled himself out, propelled upward on the swelling arms of the ocean. Breathing hard, he waved to his family, who waved back, then he turned his gaze out to sea. The heart of the ocean raged and spat froth at the rock and drenched him, yet Archie was the victor, and his heart swelled as he raised his chin and puffed out his chest. The gulls cheered from above, as he dared to dream of adventures that lay beyond the shimmering horizon.

His determination and sheer iron will had brought success, and that very flicker of determination flared within him still. Never in his wildest dreams could he have imagined that his adventures would eventually lead him here, to East Grinstead. 'There's always a way.' Jack was so often in his thoughts, and he prayed his brother was being treated well by his German captors. Archie blew out a heavy sigh and pinched the bridge of his nose.

Faces, looks, identity. A scene suddenly sprung to life from a childhood book. When Alice first saw Humpty Dumpty sitting on the wall, she remarked, 'The face is what one goes by, generally.' Quite right, first impressions and all that. Of course, Humpty Dumpty had complained how all faces were the same and how he longed to see a face with a mouth at the top and both eyes together on one side. As a young boy, Archie had thought how strange that would be, and he'd laughed. How he'd tried to imagine such a face – and now he barely had to imagine at all.

He pondered the words from the story as various meanings and theories bobbed around in his head. A world where such difference might be tolerated and accepted. Here, in this small town, he was in the throes of accomplishing that very feat. As for the rest of the world, well, even he could see that was going to take time.

17

Just A Little Prick

'Mr Hicks, what are you doing in bed?' Bea said with a hint of disapproval. 'You'll miss breakfast if you don't get a move on.' The linen trolley rattled and squealed until she abandoned it at the foot of the bed.

'I've been trying to move for the last fifteen minutes, nurse. Some bugger's tucked my sheets in too tight again. I can't budge with these ruddy bandages on my hands.'

Mac suppressed a laugh as Bea glared at the men sitting at the breakfast table. They were huddled close, casting sideways glances while attempting to stifle their laughter, sniggering. Bea untucked the blankets and Dave Hicks clambered out of bed. As he made his way to the table, Mac heard him say, 'I'll bloody swing for you lot one of these days. Just you wait.'

An outbreak of hearty laughter erupted, and one of the guys almost choked on a piece of toast, coughing and spluttering as his face turned a deep shade of scarlet. Dave perched on a chair at the table with a smirk and Pete slapped him on the back, poured him a cup of tea, popped in a straw, and pushed it across to him. Next, he took a slice of toast, scraped a thin layer of butter on top, and held it up to

Dave's mouth. Dave took a bite. 'Ta,' he mumbled through the mouthful, the prank already a fading memory.

Mac marvelled at the camaraderie; it was a routine, something they did every day, so well-rehearsed that Dave didn't even need to ask.

Mac cast a gaze at the screens positioned around the bed next to his as voices drifted out.

'Come on, Ginger. Give me one of your famous bed baths.'

'I don't know what you're talking about and keep your voice down or Sister will hear you.'

A VAD nurse with fiery red hair slipped out from behind the screens and marched off to the sluice room.

'Now then, is there anything I can get for you, Mac?' Bea stood at the foot of his bed.

'Can someone write a letter for me?'

'We can indeed. I'll send Lily over to you. Not be long.'

Mac wondered what to say to Stella. His head screamed not to write, while his heart insisted. Maybe he was wasting his time. She wouldn't want him now anyway, and even if she did, she'd soon get tired of looking after him like a child. He'd just write and say he was injured and might be here a while. It was the right thing to do.

Swing music bubbled through the ward. Mac watched as Bea slipped by, wheeling a trolley and disappeared into the sluice room. Then, the linen cupboard door slowly creaked open, and from the inside, Dickie cautiously peered out into the ward, glancing both ways. The coast was clear. He caught Mac's eye, his mouth curved into a wicked smile, and he winked. Mac nodded. *What the hell was he doing?* He didn't have to wait long to find out. No sooner had Dickie walked away, a young VAD emerged from the cupboard, tucked a few loose strands of ash-blonde hair into her white headdress, smoothed her hands down the front of her apron, then marched off into the sluice room. As Dickie passed Mac's bed, he paused.

'What can I say, mate? Can't get enough of me.' He laughed and swaggered off to join the guys at the breakfast table, lighting up a cigarette on the way.

Unbelievable. As Mac pondered over what to say to Stella, the ward doors opened, and a young woman teetered in on high heels, clip-clopping across the polished linoleum floor, casting her icy-blue gaze over each bed. She clutched her purse tightly against the brown tweed suit she wore, and with her free hand, lifted it to her matching tweed hat as if to check it was still in place. Mac watched as she walked by. Her eyes raked over each and every one of them as her face took on a startled, uncertain look and she flicked her tongue across her ruby lips.

'Beth, you came.' George Thomson called out. He lay in the second bed along from Mac and was easily within earshot. 'Sit down, love.' He propped himself up.

The woman paused at the foot of his bed, her lips pursed. The poor guy had been waiting for a visit from his wife for weeks now and by the look on her face, she didn't seem too pleased to be here. Hesitantly, she sat down. Mac turned away, but he could hear their conversation plain enough. There wasn't much room for privacy here.

'I knew you'd come, Beth,' George said. 'I missed you.'

'Yes, well, I had to see for myself.' Beth sniffed.

Her voice was cold and shrill, and an icy trickle slipped through Mac.

'Really, Beth, it's not as bad as it looks.'

'You've lost your leg, George. How much worse could it be?' she snapped. 'How are you ever going to work again? Look at you. You're not the same man I married, lying there like that.'

George patted the bed. 'Come and sit here, love.'

She didn't move.

'Sorry, George, but I can't do this. I can't be stuck at home caring for you like some nursemaid. I want to dance – how are you going to dance now? Life will never be the same. That's all there is to it.' She rose majestically, her face solemn. 'I told you not to join the RAF. I'll send your things on to your mother.'

One of the guys flicked the radio off, severing the music.

'Beth, love. You don't know what you're saying. You've got to give me a chance. It'll work, you'll see. The Maestro is going to fix me up.'

Long faces peered over at George and flicked gazes at one another while George implored his wife to stay and listen. She backed away, her narrow eyes empty as she turned and marched off, her head held high as her clattering footsteps echoed, fracturing the ensuing silence.

How could she abandon him like that? It was cold and cruel. *She couldn't be a nursemaid*, that's what she'd said. If a man's own wife can't do it, what hope did *he* have? Mac swallowed.

George lay sprawled on his bed, his mouth wide open, as tears slipped silently down his cheeks. He was in no position to go after her. One by one, the boys approached him with empathetic gazes, and one patted his shoulder while another lit up a cigarette and passed it to him. Another placed a pint on his bedside table, maybe for later, and returned to his chair. While most ebbed away, two seated themselves at the bottom of the bed, smoking and waiting.

Mac couldn't suck in air fast enough. He had to see what he looked like, but where would he find a mirror? Girls flocked around GIs, but no one wanted to be saddled with a disfigured one. He pictured Stella and a light dimmed inside. His eyes misted over, then he spotted Lily through the haze, who smiled and waved a writing pad up in the air. Inwardly, he groaned.

'Bea said you wanted to write a letter home?' Lily sank down in the chair, waiting with her pen poised.

'Yeah, well, I'm not sure if it's the right thing to do.'

'Oh?' Lily smiled warmly. 'Is it a girl?'

'Yeah, only I figured she's better off without me.' Mac leant back against his pillows and closed his eyes. Cigarette smoke wafted in the air, mingling with the stale, nauseating odour of burned flesh. He sniffed. A faint scent of lavender rose through it all and his heart squeezed.

'Well, I don't know about that, but if it were me, then I'd like to be the one who makes that decision.'

She had a point. He'd pursued Stella like crazy, and it seemed she'd felt something for him. Of course, after what he'd witnessed, he had no right to ask anything of Stella – or to expect it. Besides, he didn't want a nursemaid. A surge of pain tightened in his throat, and he was powerless to grab or punch anything right now. Each time Lily moved, lavender assaulted his senses, and he drank it in, fuelling his hunger to hold Stella in his arms and kiss her lips, and fuelling his rage for craving her love.

'Come on. There's no time like the present. You tell me what to say.' Lily cast a reassuring smile.

His jaw tightened. He was backed into a corner. So let her write the damn letter. What did he have to lose? Mac kept it simple as he dictated the message, and Lily scratched away with her pen. He didn't want Stella to be pressured into visiting and besides, he had nothing to offer her.

'She must be special, this girl.' Lily's gentle voice jolted him from his reverie.

'Yeah.' She sure was and always would be. Tears sprang to his eyes.

'Well, that's the letter finished. I'll see it goes in the next post. I'm sure Stella will be thrilled to hear from you.' Lily smiled and hurried away to the nurse's office.

'I doubt that,' Mac muttered.

Later that evening, Mac waited until the night nurses were busy attending to other patients before slipping out of bed. Dickie had said there was a mirror in the side room, which was empty right now. He slipped in, and all was dark. It hung on the wall opposite the door and snatched the faint glow of light that now streamed in from the corridor. Dickie had already loosened the dressing off so all he had to do was lift it up from the bottom, which was not so easy with bandaged hands, but he managed somehow. His mouth ran dry. The smell of burned flesh was even stronger now, and he almost gagged. He clenched his jaw and stepped closer to the mirror, closing his eyes. The nurses didn't allow mirrors because they didn't want you to see what you had become, and he didn't want to see either, only he *had* to know. He took a deep breath and opened his eyes. Even from the shadows, he could see the mark of war. Laughter from the guys out in the ward fractured the silence, and he jumped.

The right side of his face was red raw; a cluster of weeping blisters lay below his right eye, fanned out across the cheek, and slipped down to his neck. The skin was puckered – rigid and ugly. The Maestro's words rang in his ears. *We'll fix you up*. Words weighted in confidence. How was he going to fix this?

The breath caught in Mac's throat, and his chest heaved. On the normal side, stubble thrived. How strange it didn't grow through the burned flesh. That side of him reeked of death and decay. The blackout curtains masked the night and shielded the moon, and he suddenly had an urge to see the universe above, as if seeking reassurance that there was more to this life than what lay here in this place right now. He parted them slightly and gazed up. A yellow crescent hung in the sapphire night, and he closed his eyes and summoned her image. Ruby lips, green eyes that shimmered like the Pacific, svelte hands that had graced his skin with silk. He took a deep breath, holding her image a little longer in his heart. No, she wouldn't want him now, not like this. Now he had to lock her away in the farthest corner of his mind.

He faced the mirror. 'Birdie died because of me.' His face crumpled, tears flowed, and salt water snaked down his cheeks, soothing. He conjured up the German people caught within the bombers' path who lay beneath mounds of burning rubble. All human beings. He swallowed to drown the guilt, but it fought back and floated to the surface. 'God forgive me.' His shoulders heaved and shook and his voice cracked. Musical notes drifted in through the open door – 'We'll Meet Again.' Mac lowered his head, and his body gave way to the emotion that had bound him for days.' He leaned back against the wall and sank to the floor. After some time, someone placed a hand on his shoulder. 'Don't worry, mate. I've seen far worse.' Dickie smiled as he crouched down in front of him. 'Mac, look at me.' Mac's breaths were short and shallow as he sucked in air and the heat rose in his face. He raised his chin.

'Take deep breaths, nice and steady.' He placed his hands on Mac's shoulders. 'Slow and steady, now. That's it.'

The tightness in Mac's chest gradually eased, and his heart slowed as he took longer, deeper breaths.

'That's better, mate. You'll be all right, you'll see, and when your face is fixed those scars will fade a little. You'll be amazed at what the Maestro can do.' Dickie secured Mac's dressings in place. Next, he took out two cigarettes, lit them and put one in Mac's mouth. 'This is as bad as it gets. You're on the up, now. Trust me, I know.'

Mac stared into his eyes and somehow he believed him. Here, they were one and the same, and there was no explaining to be done. Here, they could believe they were normal.

'Right-oh. Let's get you back before you're missed and I'll grab us a couple of beers.'

Mac followed him to the ward, his head reeling with thoughts, a cigarette dangling from his lips. One side of his face was a mess, and he wasn't going to be able to hide away here forever. How would people react to him? *Jesus.* He heaved out a breath. He should never have had Lily write that damn letter.

Another week passed by and finally it was time for Mac's first operation. He still hadn't received a reply from Stella, which was probably just as well. He didn't want her to see him like this. Dickie tinkled on the piano, flirting with a cute VAD, seemingly teaching her how to play, except it looked like he was showing her more than the piano as he whispered in her ear. She blushed, giggled, and shuffled closer.

They had woken to a wet, misty day, and the smell of rain penetrating dry earth drifted in on the breeze through the open windows. The delicious, sweet, scent carried memories of home, and as Mac waited for surgery, bile rose in his throat. *What if it made no difference?* He thought of his squadron, and he screwed his eyes tightly shut.

Lily had persuaded him to do a jigsaw yesterday. What a joke. She'd sat by him on the bed, trying to figure out which piece went where. 'You tell me which ones will fit, then,' she'd said in that gentle, sweet voice of hers. He couldn't make any of the pieces fit, not with his hands, not now, maybe not ever. And so he gave up and sat staring at the wall, and she'd been real sweet about it, but nothing she said made him feel any better.

He'd suffered the indignity of having his entire left arm shaved earlier by Sister Jamieson. Then he'd jumped as she doused it with ether, a cold, icy spray which made his eyes water as the fumes reached into the back of his throat. Afterwards, Jimmy, the bathroom orderly, shaved his left leg and groin. Now he lay on top of the bed like a mummy, with his hands, lower arms, and his right leg wrapped in sterile dressings and bandages.

'Strewth, mate. I see you got the full works,' Dickie chuckled. 'Hey, how about a drink?'

'Don't think I can, boys. Save me one for later,' Mac said.

'No alcohol for you today, at all,' Sister Jamieson bellowed, stepping forward. 'This man is having an operation, and I'd advise you not to be plying him with beer. Mr McIndoe is most strict about that on surgery days. And it's rather early, don't you think?' Her tone was acid, and she cast Dickie a steely glance.

'Can't break one of the Maestro's commandments, now, boys,' Pete muttered through half-clamped lips.

Sister glared at him, her eyebrows raised, and she walked away.

'She should be in a museum.' Dickie smirked. 'Thou shall not covet beer on ops day.' The guys laughed.

Mac glanced at the clock. It was almost eleven. They'd be coming for him any moment now. His mouth was as dry as the desert, and he was desperate for a sip of water as he licked his lips and swallowed. A letter on his bedside table caught his eye. He didn't recognise the writing, but his heart hopped in his chest as he ripped open the envelope.

'Good news?' Pete asked.

'Not sure.' Mac's eyes flew across the lines, hungry for her words.

Dear Mac,

I was so relieved to hear from you. I was terribly worried when Vera told me about your accident and I'm so sorry to hear that your friend died. You were so brave in rescuing him. I came to see you in Cambridge, but you were sedated and sleeping so I don't suppose you knew I was there. You didn't say much in your letter so I'm hoping that everything is all right.

I'll come and see you just as soon as I can get leave. There's so much I need to say, and we parted on such bad terms. I'm sorry for what I said and for hurting you. Well, I hope they're looking after you there and that you're feeling better. I miss you.

Love,
Stella xx

Mac's eyes fixed onto that second last word: love. Did she love him? His heart leapt, and he read the letter again. So she *did* come to the hospital in Cambridge. He blew out a breath. Even so, she hadn't seen the real him, and while his heart and soul ached to see her, he realised nothing had changed. She was still better off without him. He screwed his eyes shut and swallowed the lump in his throat.

'All ready?' Archie's face appeared serious as he strode towards him in his surgical scrubs, but his eyes twinkled and bore that mischievous look.

'As I'll ever be, doc.'

'I'm afraid you can expect some pain when you wake up, although we'll keep you topped up with morphine for that. It can take a few days for it to settle, then once we know the grafts have taken, you can start doing some therapy.'

'I'll do all the therapy and more if it gets me a one-way ticket back to base.' Mac managed a nervous smile.

'You'll be fine, Mac. Try not to worry. Right, I'm off to get ready. See you soon.'

Mac lay back and closed his eyes. He winced. His hands had been throbbing that morning – a constant reminder of the accident – and a sharp pain zipped through his palm and into his wrist.

'Hey, Mac,' Dickie called over to him. 'I'll walk down to theatre with you.'

'Is that even allowed?'

'Course it is. We do it all the time – take it in turns. Sometimes the Maestro lets us watch – well, those of us who can stand it.' He turned to check the clock. 'Last time I saw an op with a bloke who'd recently had his nose done. He passed out – only went and landed on his conk, didn't he? The Maestro had to re-do it.' Dickie broke down laughing so heartily at the memory that tears rolled down his cheek. 'Besides, there's nothing much going on around here.' He sauntered over to the piano, sat down, struck the keys, and sang – 'Roll Out The Barrel.'

'Yeah, it's a barrel of laughs all right,' Mac muttered, thinking back to jollier times. He took a deep breath. The first time he'd set eyes on Stella had been one of those thunderbolt moments, and he knew she was the girl for him – only she had been with the wrong guy. But now *he* was the wrong guy. The doors to the ward burst open, and Jimmy barged through, whistling and pushing a theatre trolley.

'Ready then?' he asked. 'Hop on.' He turned to the boys in the ward. 'Right then, which one of you lousy lot is doing the theatre run?'

'I'm your man.' Dickie stood up, took a swig from his beer tankard, and charged up through the ward.

'Lord help us.' Jimmy rolled his eyes.

Mac lay down on the trolley while Jimmy dragged the blanket over him. On the way to the operating theatre, Mac offered up a prayer to God. He wondered if Dickie was right. The doc always sounded so confident; maybe he could fix him up. But it would never be enough. What would he say to Stella? Maybe she'd be repulsed, but he'd have to see her one last time just so he could let her go. What did she mean in her letter when she said there was so much to say? It was probably nothing – probably more talk about how sorry she was to hear about the accident. He didn't want her to face life with him like this. The shadows were closing in already, and Bill's face flashed in his mind. A vice clamped his chest, and he swallowed. They passed through the open doors of the theatre to where the anaesthetist was ready and waiting, dressed in surgical scrubs.

'You'll be all right, mate. We'll all be here for you when you get back.' Dickie patted his shoulder and moved out of the way.

Archie's voice filtered across the room, above the spray and splutter of gushing water. His tone was light, and there was something reassuring about it. The doc was a good guy and Dickie had to be right. Archie would fix him up, eventually.

'Ah, we meet again. Now then, Mac, I'm just going to put a needle into your arm.' The anaesthetist, John Hunter, was a tall, burly chap with a kind face and sparkling eyes. There was a rather playful youthfulness to his voice, which held such rise and fall and made him sound as jolly as he looked. 'Now, it's well known that my anaesthesia is more superb than that of other doctors, and I assure you that when you come round, you won't feel sick. Anyone who does can have a free pint on me.' His face crumpled into a warming smile.

'I might hold you to it.' Mac laughed nervously.

'Right then, where were we?' He took hold of Mac's right arm and looked for a vein, tapping the skin until a thin turquoise streak bulged on the surface. 'Now then, just a little prick,' he said in a hushed, velvety voice.

Mac looked away as a sharp sting shot through his arm. He glanced up and noticed the viewing gallery above with several people peering at him. Spectators in an operating theatre. This place sure was a madhouse. A strange, floaty, heavy feeling drifted through him as he began to laugh. No wonder the guys called themselves guinea pigs. Everything was experimental, and now here he was, on display in a zoo, and then... nothing. Mac strained to open his eyes; his eyelids were lead-heavy, and he tried to keep them open, but it was no use. Suddenly, a loud drumming kicked in, and Mac turned his head to the window. As he peeked through half-open eyes, the black-grey edges of his vision cleared. A golden glow flooded the ward as the drumming ceased and droplets streaked down the glass. Blue sky loomed, and the drumming continued in his head as sharp pain hammered his hands as if nails were being driven through them.

Still drowsy from the anaesthetic, he drifted in and out of sleep. The pain in his hands intensified, building up to a crescendo as the nails transcended into red-hot pokers. Finally, he cried out. The nurse said something, but he couldn't make it out, and then she left, and he closed his eyes and drifted through a sea of pain.

18

A Fresh Start

Stella steeled herself as she breezed through the gates of the Queen Victoria Hospital. A helpful nurse directed her to the grounds at the rear, where she saw a group of wooden huts, Ward III being among them. She took a deep breath and checked her reflection in her compact. The Max Factor red had faded on her lips, but her hair was neat. Her cheeks glowed rosy from the warm sun and the walk from the station. What if he didn't want to see her? She'd replayed their argument again and again, and she pictured his face before he'd walked away – before this. Her whole body ached for his strong arms to hold her. Her heart kneaded her chest, and she took a deep breath, opened the door, and sailed into a smog of Dettol disinfectant. As she peered along the length of the ward, she spotted a group of men crowded around the piano. A wolf whistle rang out, slow and shrill, and her cheeks prickled with heat as a shy smile tugged at the corners of her mouth.

A young man in RAF blues whizzed towards her in a wheelchair. 'Hello, looking for me by any chance?'

Surprised and stunned, Stella smiled, noticing his porcelain, taut facial skin and oddly shaped eyes. 'I'm here to see Mac – Lieutenant Mackenzie.' The gaggle of voices died away, and she felt all eyes on her.

'Oh, you mean Tex, our regular cowboy? Over there, sixth bed on the right. Good luck.'

'Thank you.' *Why did he say that?*

'Better watch out, Miss. Hang around here long enough and they'll whip off a piece of you and stick it on one of us.' Those within earshot laughed, and Stella smiled out of politeness more than anything else. What an odd thing to say.

Perhaps Mac wasn't having a good day. Once again she'd come at the wrong time, but would there ever be a right time? She stopped at the foot of his bed and her eyes were drawn to the dressings on his face, and her breath caught in her chest. How badly burned was he? His hands and lower arms were bandaged and elevated on pillows which lay by his sides. His eyes were closed.

'Hello, Mac.'

His eyes flickered open and widened. 'Hey, Stella.'

He seemed surprised to see her and his face creased into a smile and, tentatively, she perched herself on the chair next to his bed.

'I got your letter. Oh Mac, I'm so sorry to hear what happened and, well, I had to come.'

His smile slipped. 'You shouldn't have bothered. It's a long way from Cambridge.' He stared at the ceiling as he spoke.

The coolness in his voice sent a shiver jolting down her spine. She swallowed and gazed around, quick enough to catch curious faces before they swiftly turned away. Why had he written to her if he didn't want to see her? Some of the men were playing a game of cards at a table further down. Cigarette smoke drifted over, and she caught the waft of beer in the air; it was then she spotted pint glasses sitting on tables, some full, some empty. That was something she'd never seen before in a hospital.

'The ward seems nice.'

Mac met her gaze and cast a half-smile, but it lacked warmth and meaning somehow. 'Yeah, real nice. Everything's swell. So, how are you?' His eyes were cold and his words stung.

'I'm all right.'

'And Alex, how's he?'

'I don't know.'

'I take it you went away with him.'

Stella took a deep breath. 'I went to meet his family, yes.' His mouth was set in a tight line as he stared at her. This wasn't going the way she'd hoped. 'Mac, the last time I saw you I said some things I shouldn't have. I'm sorry. I never meant to hurt you.'

He shrugged his shoulders. 'Don't worry about it. Alex is important to you. I get that.'

'Yes, well he is, and he isn't. What I mean is, he's... ' Her words trailed off. Why was it so difficult to explain?

'Stella, when I wrote that letter, or rather, when the nurse wrote the letter for me, I may not have been thinking things through very well. You see, I have no intention of getting in between you and Alex. In fact, you ought to be with him. After all, he can look after you.'

Stella couldn't believe those words had slipped from his mouth. Reliable, dependable Mac, who had pursued her for weeks.

'But I don't love Alex.'

'Well, he sure loves you. Remember, I got the sock in the jaw to prove it. Go back to him. He's bound to have you.'

What was he saying? Stella's skin prickled as goosebumps erupted. He wasn't even looking at her, for goodness' sake, and did he think she was a parcel to pass around? 'Mac, I don't think that's fair. I'm sorry about the accident and about your friend.'

'I don't need pity.' He flicked his gaze at her, his face red, his eyes narrowed. 'Go back to Alex. Go home and live your life. At least you still have a normal life.' He rubbed his brow.

His words left a bitter taste in her mouth. A single tear pearled on her eyelash, and she quickly swiped it away and sniffed. A normal life. Glen Miller's 'American Patrol' swung out and Stella glanced up to see an airman in RAF blues next to the radio. She fixed her gaze on Mac, glancing at his bandaged hands, and swallowed. 'You have a life too.'

'I don't rightly know what I've got, and I won't for some time. The doc says I might never fly again. In fact, I might not be able to do a lot of things.'

She placed her hand on his shoulder but he stiffened, so she drew back and shuffled in her seat. 'I'm sure it's not that bad.'

'What would you know?'

The air rushed out of her chest. 'Well, tell me.'

He pursed his lips. 'I have a mix of second and third-degree burns to my face, neck, hands and legs. I've just had the first round of surgery on my hands so I won't really know anything for a little while. If I'm lucky, I'll still be able to use them, though maybe not as well as before.

'Oh, well I suppose it's bound to take time. It sounds serious.'

Stella fixed her gaze on the man in the bed opposite, who picked up his beer glass with both hands, gripping it to his chest with hands that were more like stumps. He wore a look of intense concentration and a lump swelled in her throat as tears rushed to her eyes, but she blinked them away. She was transfixed until he met her gaze and cast the most radiant smile as if nothing in the world was wrong. Stella smiled back as heat warmed her face and neck. She turned to Mac. 'You knew I was coming today, didn't you? I said I'd be here in my letter.' She shuffled in her seat.

His gaze was intense. 'I didn't get any letter.'

'Oh, I see.' That might explain why he was being so cold. 'Well, I suppose the post is struggling at the moment what with the amount of service mail.' She grinned, nervously biting her lip. 'Oh Mac, I'm so sorry this happened.'

'Wasn't anything anyone could have done, except me.'

'What do you mean?' She stared into his eyes, but he turned away. 'You did everything you could and hurt yourself in the process.' Out of instinct she reached for his arm, gently stroking it. 'Here you are, thousands of miles from home, helping us fight this cruel war and look what it's done,' she said, her voice quavering.

'Hey, come on. It's me that got hurt. Don't feel sorry for me, I can take it.' Mac cast a sad smile, and she could tell he was trying to make light of the situation. 'I'm glad you came. I thought that maybe after you received my letter, well... ' He paused and looked away.

The lost expression on his face moved Stella, and she sensed something different about him. He was distant, but then it was hardly surprising after everything he'd been through. Just then, the man in the next bed groaned, quietly at first, and then, when no one responded, louder. His head was bandaged, with only slits for his eyes, mouth, and nose.

'What does he want?'

'Probably a smoke. The guy misses them like crazy. He's so bandaged up he can't move.'

Stella glanced all around and noticed a packet of cigarettes on his table. She rose and went to his bedside. When she asked him if he wanted to smoke, the reply was a muffled 'yes'. She lit a cigarette and placed it in his mouth. The ward seemed to hush, and she turned to see that all eyes were on her. Stella took the cigarette, flicked the ash into a tray, and gave it back to him. She noticed the chart on the end of his bed, and she picked it up and read his name. 'Hello, Mike. I'm Stella. Very pleased to meet you.'

Mike said something but the plaster muffled his words, and she felt awkward at having to ask him to repeat. She took the cigarette and flicked the ash as Mike exhaled plumes of smoke, and she wondered how badly burned he was beneath the bandages. 'I hope that's all right. If you need anything else, just shout.'

She smiled, stubbing out the cigarette, and turned back to Mac, whose disgruntled expression had softened slightly. Stella had never seen a ward like this before, and some of the men barely looked old enough to be serving. Being here shed light on yet another branch of this horrid war, and her heart ached at their suffering.

One of the boys turned up the volume of the radio as the voice of Anne Shelton flowed like velvet – 'A Nightingale Sang in Berkeley Square.' She looked at Mac, who hadn't complained once so far. The other boys sat in silence, listening with faraway looks on their faces.

'Stella, the last thing I wanted was to pressure you into coming here.' He glanced at her then looked away. 'The last time I saw you, I thought that maybe there was still hope. You chose Alex, though there was always hope. But now, I can't see a future for us. I'm sorry. The fact is you're better off without me.'

'No, don't say that.' She touched his hand, lightly.

'Please don't.' He turned to look at her now, his soft, blue eyes pleading.

'I don't want Alex. I never did. I went because he needed a friend.' A tear rolled down her cheek, and she gritted her teeth, desperate not to cry. 'I didn't come here just because you asked. I came because I care.'

'Damn it, Stella. That's just it. You don't have to care about me. I'm no good for you. I'm no good for anyone. Please, go home.' He screwed his eyes shut and his chest heaved up and down.

'Can't we just talk?'

'Jeez, Stella. You're not listening.' Mac's eyes flashed. 'I've got nothing to offer, I can't fly, and I can't marry you, not now.' His voice broke and trailed off as Stella's entire body shook and tears rolled down her face.

She quickly rummaged through her bag for a handkerchief.

'Great, and now I've upset you, and I can't do anything about that either. Don't you get it? I'm useless. I can't wash, get dressed, feed myself. I can't do a goddam thing. You don't need this.' He took a deep breath and slowly exhaled. 'I'm sorry. You've come a long way, and I sure appreciate it, but please, don't come again. Don't waste your time.'

Stella dabbed her eyes, sniffed, and blew out a breath. She picked up her bag and rose to her feet, aware of the others in the ward watching, listening. 'I hope you get better soon, Mac. I really do.' Another sob hit her in the gut, and she steeled herself. How could she go? But then, how could she stay? He didn't want her there; he didn't want *her*. She pursed her lips. 'Take care of yourself. Goodbye.'

His eyes were on hers, and she melted into blue one last time before leaving as quickly as she could. She had to get outside. Her chest was tight, and she gasped for breath. She burst through the doors and fled out into the grounds, stopping to rest against the wall of the next building, gasping for breath, sobs racking her chest.

'Hello.'

Stella gulped as a man emerged from Ward III. There was something familiar about him.

He adjusted his black spectacles, and his mouth curved up into a kind smile. 'Are you all right?'

'Yes, thank you.' She dabbed her eyes quickly, cringing at being caught in such a state.

'I noticed you were visiting our young American friend, Mac.'

She suddenly realised who he was. She'd seen him at the hospital in Cambridge that day. 'Are you a doctor?'

'I am indeed. Archie McIndoe.' He extended his hand. 'How lovely to meet you.'

His eyes crinkled at the corners and twinkled bright blue, catching the glint of the May sunshine. 'Stella Charlton.' As she shook his hand, his grip was soft yet firm, with a radiance of confidence and ease. Stella suddenly felt a surge in her chest and a sob stifle in her throat. More tears flowed, and she swiped them away and took a deep breath.

'I can see you've had a bit of a shock, my dear. I was just about to return to my office and have some afternoon tea. I'll ask my secretary for two cups.'

He smiled so sweetly and spoke so charmingly that Stella allowed herself to be steered away to goodness knows where by a man she didn't know anything about, except that he was a doctor. 'Thank you, Dr McIndoe.'

'Oh, not at all, and please call me Archie. Everyone does.'

In his office, he gestured to a chair, and Stella sank down. The sweet scent of cut grass drifted in through the open window. The secretary brought in tea and biscuits. 'Now, I couldn't help overhearing while you were sitting with Mac. He's having a bit of rough time at the moment, although it's only to be expected, I'm afraid.'

'He will be all right, won't he?' Stella sipped her tea, her fingers burning against the heat of the china cup.

'Oh yes, absolutely. The trouble is, my dear, these boys think you can put a sticking plaster on everything and they'll be back in the air before they know it. Unfortunately, it's not that simple. It takes time, and that leads to frustration, boredom, and time to dwell.' He raised his eyebrows.

Mac had been dwelling on everything, and now he'd pushed her away. He couldn't have stopped loving her just like that, surely. 'Will he ever fly again?'

'I can't say. It's early days, and I'm afraid it would be unethical to discuss details, Miss Charlton. Oh, it is Miss, I take it?'

'Yes, and please call me Stella.' She smiled.

'Well, Stella, the thing is, these boys need someone to believe in them – someone to help them along with their recovery. The physical injuries are just one side of it. The psychological impact is often far worse and harder to manage. Visitors help, and I was pleased when I saw you earlier. No one else has been here to see Mac as far as I know.'

'Well, I'm afraid he's told me not to come back.' Stella placed her cup down on the desk and gritted her teeth as she fought to hold back fresh tears.

'Oh, I see.' Archie studied her for a moment as if he was thinking. 'Well, that doesn't surprise me. If I were you, I'd pay no attention. Come back another day. If he doesn't want to talk to you, talk to someone else in the ward. He'll soon come around.' Archie smoothed his hair back with his hand. 'We're always looking for willing volunteers here, and there's plenty of things you could do. Don't give up just yet.'

'But the things he said. I've never seen him so angry before.' Stella took a deep breath as her throat ached.

Archie's gaze softened, and he sighed. 'Yes, so often things are said in haste and all that. Of course, he's never been in this position before.'

Stella contemplated the words. Perhaps Mac was struggling and finding it hard to cope.

'If you really like him, then perhaps this is your turn to fight. And prepare yourself for a rough ride. Sometimes people lash out because of their accident, but you know, we always hurt the ones we love. I've seen it all before, although so often it's the other way around.'

'I'm sorry?'

'Oh, nothing. But please think about it. He needs you now more than ever. It's so vital these boys have someone. And Mac has you. Now, he may well be angry when he sees you again, but he'll come around.'

Stella didn't know what to think, and the thought of Mac being even angrier with her was unbearable. She gulped, aware of Archie's intense gaze.

'You know, these boys have had to put up with such a lot, and here they have far worse to cope with. Can you imagine how it feels to be permanently changed in some way? It isn't easy.'

She looked into Archie's knowing eyes. He was right. She'd seen sights today that had shocked her, even though she hadn't shown it. Men with no eyelids, or an empty socket where an eye ought to be, trunks for noses, and stumps for hands. All *she* had to deal with was Mac's anger. If she could tolerate that and his rejection of her, then perhaps she could help him in some way. It was the least she could do.

'I can appreciate that it's difficult for all of them.' She blew out a breath. 'I'll do it as long as you're sure I'm not causing more distress.'

'Oh, I shouldn't think so. Mac will be far worse if you simply disappear, I can assure you.'

19

Divine Intervention

Archie tugged his green surgical mask up over his nose and mouth and plunged his hands into the flow of warm water spewing from the tap. His right hand was stiff and twinged as he scrubbed up, and he huffed out a breath. The antiseptic odour of iodine hung in the air.

'All ready for you, Maestro,' the theatre orderly said.

Archie nodded. 'Thanks, George.'

He'd gone over his plans for this surgery once more last night and hadn't slept well at all, and now, as he plodded into the operating theatre, an uneasiness burgeoned within him with unabated fury. He slipped into his gown, which the nurse held out ready, and flicked his gaze over his patient. Flight Engineer Tom Chandler, a young man of nineteen, lay upon the operating table, anaesthetised.

Archie sucked in a breath as he scrutinised Tom's ruined face. He was the sole survivor of a Lancaster Bomber crash in Italy. His eyelids and scorched facial tissue had been doused in gentian violet. The damn stuff did more harm than good and hardened, making it impossible for a person to blink. Thank God the Air Ministry had listened when he'd hounded them to banish it, although it had been too late for Tom. The news was taking its time to filter through to the field hospitals in Europe and the Mediterranean, and now Archie held the future of Tom's sight within his gloved hands.

He'd studied the boys 'before' pictures and raked over every detail again, double checking before he began. How he'd paced the floor in his office, agonising over the best way to do this surgery. Tom's original features were firmly imprinted on his mind – the symmetrical, round eyes with long lashes, the slim, long nose with a very subtle upturn. Of course, he'd replace that later. Once he grafted new eyelids, the lashes would regrow in time. But as Archie gazed down at him, pain and tingling zipped through his right hand and fingers, and the boy's old image scrambled and faded like wisps of smoke. He would have to start from scratch. His heart thumped against his ribs and his mouth ran dry.

He flicked a gaze at John Hunter. 'Happy with everything?'

John looked up from his seat, at the head of the patient. 'All's well at my end, Archie. Proceed at your leisure.' His mouth curved into a broad grin, and he promptly pulled his mask over his nose.

As Archie gazed at the boy's face, a shadow of doubt flickered within him. The canvas was as blank as his mind, the face so burned, it was featureless. He recalled the portraits of disfigured Great War veterans that hung on the walls of his cousin's office. Painted by the war artists, they'd helped Harold Gillies rebuild the shattered faces of veterans. From a sea of shattered men came hope, forged by art.

'Crank up the old gramophone, George, liven things up a bit.' Music for the soul. It helped him relax, to create, and he needed to muster inspiration from somewhere. 'Oh, and bring that picture closer, will you?'

'Right you are, Maestro.' George grinned as he sifted through a pile of records. Within a few minutes, Beethoven Symphony No. 7 struck up and echoed around the theatre. George dragged a stainless-steel trolley close to the operating table, with a picture of Tom taken before the accident propped up on top.

Pain jolted through Archie's right hand and sparks radiated into his fingers. That was all he needed. The surgical lights scrutinised him with a luminous glow, trapping him in their beam for all to see. Where should he begin? Never before had he felt so lost. He stepped back and pursed his lips tightly as if that would hold it all in and he could swallow it back down. All eyes were upon him, including the steely stare of his theatre sister, Jill Mullins, her grey-blue eyes burrowing into his. He frowned as he clenched and unclenched his right hand. What if he made a mistake? He couldn't go on like this. No, he'd have to get it sorted out before it was too late.

When he'd asked Tom what he hoped to do after the war, the reply had startled him. 'I intend to study medicine.' Well, he certainly needed his sight to do that, but then there were his hands to consider. A bit of work was needed if he wished to become a doctor.

Sister Mullins, anticipating his first move, held up the stainless-steel scalpel like a trophy. Archie grasped it firmly, then hesitated. If the numbness in his hand returned mid-way through, he'd be stuck. His heart hammered and his mouth grew dry. Failure was simply not an option, and he couldn't let this boy down. The operating theatre was his domain – his studio. He inhaled a deep breath. The skin for the eyelids – the graft – would come from the thigh. He glanced long and hard at Tom's picture before him, focusing on the eyes. He would also take a piece of skin from the stomach, a flap for the tubed pedicle, to use for the nose at a later stage.

Poised, scalpel ready to incise, he took a deep breath and prayed to God to help amidst the rendering, moving music of Beethoven. The uplifting strings and flutes flowed like birdsong, heralding a new dawn in his mind, gathering up his thoughts, re-joining the edges to create the image, piece by piece.

He began with an incision as renewed energy flowed through his right arm, guiding his hand as he worked, swift and neat like a tailor crafting a garment. Where his guidance came from in that moment, he did not know, but he was glad of it. When he finished, he blew out a long breath, banishing all the tension from his body. As he admired Tom's bloodied eye patches, Archie suspected that Da Vinci himself could not be more pleased.

He peeled off his surgical gloves and flicked a gaze at John Hunter. 'Thanks, John. I suppose it's my shout later.' He grinned and slapped his colleague on the back.

'Oh, you know me too well, Archie. I'm not one to turn down a free pint.' He chuckled.

'Well, I'm joining a few of the lads at the pub after work, so I'll see you there, say around half past six.'

Archie watched as Jill painted Mercurochrome over Tom's new eyelids, the antiseptic staining the skin red. It was vital to protect the new graft, while it also helped to reduce the scar tissue. Of course, the boys frequently complained about having to put up with red stamps for eyes, yet it was a small price to pay. Lord knows they'd already paid an extortionate fee to warrant being here in the first place.

'Blackie, these boys will be with us forever. I'll never be able to completely retire because I'll be fixing them up for years.' The thought of it weighed heavily on Archie's shoulders, but it was his duty. They deserved the best of help, and nothing was too much trouble.

'That reminds me, I had a word with George Reid about setting up the workshop at the hospital. I managed to persuade him it would be mutually beneficial all round. The idea of the boys manufacturing precision instruments for the RAF makes sense. George's quotas are filled, and the boys get to be useful. He's all for it and thinks it's an excellent venture.'

'Right. Where exactly are we going to set up?'

'He's going to come down and take a look. There's one building that's empty right now, and it might be ideal.' Archie rubbed his right hand and clenched and unclenched it a few times, watching his thick fingers intently as he did so. To think they were capable of doing such delicate surgery had always tickled him. Years ago, Lord Moynihan had been the one to tempt him away from his work in America, with the lure of surgical work here in London. After observing Archie in his operating theatre, he'd said, "You have the hands of a ploughboy, but they behave like an artist's."

Archie sighed. The problem was worsening and now affected both hands, although he worried more for his most valuable asset – his right hand, his scalpel-wielding hand.

He recognised the signs with stiffness in his fingers and a transient numbness, and his heart sank. Even writing was becoming challenging and painful at times.

'Everything all right, Archie?'

'Blasted hands. They've been giving me a spot of bother for months now. The trouble is, it's getting worse, and I think I know what it is.'

Blackie lit a cigarette. 'Arthritis?' Smoke curled into the air.

'No, worse than that. Dupuytren's contracture. I've been having bother for a while now. Stupid really, but at first I put it down to tiredness. Damn war – we're all tired. Unfortunately, it's more than that. I've been ignoring it, only it's getting worse. If I don't have it looked at soon, I'm afraid it might be too late.'

'What do you mean?'

'I could lose my livelihood. A washed-up surgeon – over my dead body!' Archie frowned and poured himself a brandy. 'It means surgery, and whoever does it will have to do a bloody good job. I've got a specialist in mind, a colleague of mine. I might ring him tomorrow.'

He rubbed his brow and sighed, hoping to God he hadn't left things too late otherwise his artist's hands might well be reduced to those of a ploughman.

'On a different note, I wanted to run an idea past you.' He sank down in his chair and took a mouthful of brandy, savouring the warm, fiery flavour in his throat. 'The boys could do with a little cheering up. After the incident in the ward, I don't want any more nurses having hysterical outbursts. We may not be able to control the behaviour of the general public, but we can, at least, try to do so with our own staff.'

'I agree. What did you have in mind?'

'We need girls who can put a brave face on when required – girls who know how to put on a show and who can make a man feel he's still a man.' Archie raised his eyebrows, picked up the copy of *Bazaar* magazine, and pointed at the cover. 'Look at this. Lauren Bacall and the Red Cross. Beauty and medicine. It's all hands to the pump for the war effort.' His face broke into a wide grin as he passed the magazine to Blackie.

'What? Bloody hell. You want me to telephone Lauren Bacall and tell her to get over here?' He chuckled. 'Hollywood comes to East Grinstead. Mind you, we did manage to grab Clark Gable that time for the lads. His talk was hilarious and a great morale boost for the troops.'

'Exactly, man. You've hit the nail on the head. That's precisely what I'm driving at.' Archie laughed. 'Mind you, we haven't a hope of luring Lauren Bacall over here. She'd never fall for it, and I doubt we could afford her fee. But look at the picture. She's smouldering, isn't she?'

He stared at Blackie, searchingly, who smiled and nodded. He could always count on Blackie; they were often on the same wavelength. 'What about ENSA and the girls entertaining the troops here and abroad? There's Vera Lynn and Gracie Fields. The men love their shows.' Archie drained his glass. 'So, that got me thinking. How do you fancy taking a little trip to London's West End?' He smiled, taking delight in Blackie's puzzled expression.

'Why do I have the strangest feeling about this? I suppose this is another of your ploys.' Blackie frowned.

'A ploy? No, no, it's a beaut of an idea. Can't fail. A ploy... heavens, my mother used to say that when I was up to something.' Archie chuckled. Trawling for girls was not exactly something a man of his stature ought to be doing, although it was in aid of a good cause – at least *he* thought so. 'If we can persuade some amiable girls to work here, then they can help the boys – take them out and so forth. Now if that doesn't boost morale, I don't know what will.'

He needed girls who could look them in the eye without feelings of revulsion. The girls would be required to look the part and act the part. Such a pity he couldn't steal Stella away from the WAAF. Watching as she'd tended to the other patient had been very touching indeed; of course, he didn't let her know that he'd seen her. She was just the sort he needed here: loyal, caring, sensible, and beautiful. Mac was a lucky man, even if he didn't realise it just yet. Seeing her that day had made a refreshing change to the women who came instead to ditch their men. Archie only hoped that Stella would come back. Now if she did that, Mac would come to his senses soon enough and snap out of this fog.

'Good morning, Sister. How is everyone?' Archie grinned as he flicked a gaze at the clock on the wall.

'All's well, Mr McIndoe, but I'm afraid our American pilot is struggling. His spirits have plummeted further today, and he's refusing to get out of bed. He hasn't said very much either.'

Archie flicked through the medical notes and stuck his head out of the office door, glancing down the ward. Sure enough, Mac lay sprawled on his bed, simply staring into space by the look of him. He was still grieving, obviously for the death of his friend and no doubt countless others, but also for his own loss. Right now, he had no idea just how much of himself was lost. To him, he was helpless and

alone. Archie sighed, gritted his teeth, and steeled himself
for a showdown. The boy needed a firm hand and a push
in the right direction.

'Morning, Mac. How are you today?' He grinned, and
the bed creaked as he perched on the edge.

'Not bad, doc.' Mac's voice was flat and impassive. He
rolled onto his back and heaved himself up a little.

'It won't do you any good lying in bed all day. You need
to get up, take a short walk outside, sit in the gardens. A
little sunshine will perk you up.' Archie waited for a reply,
but none came. 'I'm going to assess your hands tomorrow,
then we can see how things are. Perhaps next week we
might be able to remove your facial dressings, seeing as the
wounds are healing nicely.'

'Great. Then everyone can see what a freak I am.' Mac
turned away.

He *had* taken a bit of a dive, and he was a different young
man to the one Archie had first met a few weeks ago. It was
almost as if he'd lost all of his fight. 'Mac, I know this is
tough, but I warned you it would take time. Now, I am
going to fix you up, and you will use your hands again. You
won't be helpless for much longer. Right now, you need to
buck yourself up. Like I said before, you're going to have to
do the therapy to help things along, so lying around here
feeling sorry for yourself is no good at all.'

Archie met Mac's gaze and saw fury burning there.
Good. He still had some fight in him. 'It's hard, but you
have to get on with your life, and you need all the help you
can get.' He sighed. 'I met your visitor the other day, Stella.'

Mac's eyes flashed, and his cheek twitched.

'Yes, she's a lovely young woman. I've asked her to come again and help us out a little. We always need capable volunteers.'

'You have?' Mac sighed. 'Oh, gee, you don't understand. I can't see her again. It's killing me.'

'Yes, I can see that.'

'She's better off without me.'

Archie sighed and shook his head. 'How do you know she's better off? It seemed to me she was quite upset when she left.'

'Who wants to be saddled with all this?'

He was lashing out. Another phase he had to pass through before acceptance. 'I think it's only fair to ask the young lady's thoughts first before you end things. At least then she might understand.' He flicked a gaze at Mac, whose eyes had narrowed, his mouth clamped in a tight line.

'Well, anyway, she said she'll come back next week, and she seemed happy about helping out.' Archie stood up. 'Right then. I'll leave you to get dressed and rejoin the living. Cheerio, Mac.'

Archie strode back to the office, and a smug smile tugged at his mouth. Didn't want to see her again? Honestly, who was he trying to fool? He chuckled to himself. *We'll see about that.*

21

A Different Country Club

As Mac sat reading his letter from home, a twinge tugged at his heart. Montana might as well have been a million miles away. His folks had been relieved to hear he was safe and in a hospital. His hands were healing well, and the grafts had taken without a trace of infection. Now he had another mission to complete – therapy. The therapist had given him a small rubber ball to practise with to improve his grip and dexterity. All he had to do was squeeze and crush it tight in each hand as he curled his fingers around it, except it turned out to be a lot tougher than he'd envisaged.

He was glad to be finally free of the thick bandages on his hands; he now had thin dressings secured in place, but at least he could use his hands and was no longer useless. Being able to eat and dress was a great relief, although his hands were stiff and awkward, and he fumbled and struggled with buttons and laces. It had taken him almost ten minutes to tie one shoe earlier. His legs had healed with only mild scars as a reminder. The skin graft to his face had taken well, so the doc said, and he supposed it looked a little better, but it was a permanent disfigurement. The doc said he could do more, though he'd never be able to make him as he was.

The doors to the ward swung open and in waltzed Stella. Mac heaved himself upright on his bed as she strode over towards him, tucking a loose blonde curl behind her ear, her head held high. So, the Maestro was telling the truth. His heart jumped and hammered against his ribs. What was he going to say to her after the last time? He'd been harsh, and man did she look cute today. She wasn't wearing her uniform and that thin, pale blue summer dress skimmed her curves just right, accentuating the sway of her hips as she moved. There was something different about her too – something in her eyes. A fire flickered there that hadn't flared before. When Archie had told him she'd be coming back, Mac had seen red, but now, he shrank a little inside as his previous bitter words hurtled around in his head. He swallowed.

'Hello, Mac. How are you?'

'Not bad, thanks. I didn't know you were coming.' He couldn't suppress the grin that was tugging at the corners of his mouth. 'Take a seat.' He gestured to the chair next to him.

'Thank you.' Stella sat down, crossing her slim smooth legs.

Mac swung around and sat on the edge of the bed. 'Stella, I want to apologise for what I said last time.'

'There's no need, really.' She smiled and glanced around the ward.

Mac dragged a hand through his wavy hair. 'There's every need.' Hell, he wanted to say sorry and take her in his arms, but he couldn't go back now, and his heart ached. Seeing her again had really thrown him off course. This wasn't the way it was supposed to be. *Why did the doc have to ask her to help out here?* It didn't make much sense, and now it was going to crush him having her so close. That sweet lavender scent she wore drifted on the air, so he inhaled deeply, savouring the rush.

'You look much better. It's good to see you up and about.'

He guessed she was a little uncomfortable too, but before he could reply, one of the men called out.

'Hello, nurse.' He winked.

'Don't mind those guys. I guess they're still hung over from last night.' Mac shook his head.

'Why does he think I'm a nurse?'

'Well, they figured you did a great job last time.'

Stella blushed, and her mouth curved up into a radiant smile. 'Well, I did come here to help, after all.'

'Nurse, can you help me with this, please?' A patient held up a piece of paper and waved it around.

'Oh, yes, all right.' Stella glanced at Mac and stood up. 'Duty calls.'

He looked on as she perched on the end of the guy's bed, smiling and chatting away as he passed her a pen and paper. Mac didn't quite know what to make of her. Why did she come if not to see him? Maybe it was to show him what he was missing. Well, mission accomplished. He got up and stormed off outside, bursting through the doors as his heart thudded and a rage stirred inside him. He embraced the rush of fresh air and found a bench to slouch on, turning his gaze to the sky.

The blue siren stretched out like one vast ocean, streaked and feathered with wispy clouds, so tranquil, until the veil slipped, revealing acres of black which dragged swarms of bandits and cannon fire overhead as aircraft rained down. The sky was soiled with death and maiming. His breathing quickened, beads of sweat formed on his brow, and he snapped his eyes shut as he fought to banish the bad memories.

When he returned to the ward, he heard sobs coming from the sluice room; the door was ajar. He hovered there for a moment when a voice spoke.

'It's not right. He can't touch me like that. If my father hears about this, he'll go mad.'

Mac recognised the voice. It was the new VAD nurse. She was just some kid – only seventeen, she'd said.

'The trouble is, there are no boundaries here. Mr McIndoe has done away with all that. This ward isn't like any other, and it's that way for a reason. Dry your eyes and I'll do my best to keep you out of his way for today. And whatever happens, you mustn't say a word to Mr McIndoe. It won't do any good. These boys are war heroes and we all have to do our bit for the war.' Bea's voice.

He sauntered over to his bed to find Stella leaning against the piano with a few of the guys for company. He sat down, and flicked through his copy of *Stars and Stripes*, but he couldn't concentrate, and he looked up to see Bea shepherding the VAD out of the sluice. It was obvious what that was about. There was more than one guy here with wandering hands. He gazed over at Stella.

'What do you want me to play next, Stella? Name a tune, anything you like,' Dickie said.

'I don't know. Let's think. How about Vera Lynn's "White Cliffs"?'

'Bonzer.' Dickie struck a chord. 'Everyone ready? Here we go, and you all have to sing.'

Mac had never heard Stella sing before. He glanced over as they all huddled around the piano. Dickie shuffled across on the stool, and Stella sat next to him, real close. Mac clenched his teeth, and a hot poker stabbed him in the chest. Dickie sure had an eye for the ladies. Mac flicked a steely glance at him. As they sang, Stella's voice rose above the others, soft and pure, and Mac lay back on his bed as melodic words flowed from her lips like rippled satin, his skin tingling with every note. He closed his eyes as the longing to hold her grew, and he rubbed his temples as if he could massage it away, all the while willing her to turn round – except she didn't. She was intent on helping out, all right, and ignoring him in the process. It was probably just as well. If he were allowed to fly again, it wouldn't make any sense to be involved with a girl, but his heart ached as he watched her. She wasn't just some girl. He was in love with her, and inside he was breaking. He wanted her so badly, only she'd been hurt enough.

At that moment, the ward doors creaked open, and Archie appeared and strode into Sister's office. After a few minutes, he reappeared and headed over to Mac.

'Hey, doc.'

'How are you today?' Archie pulled up a chair. 'The hands are looking superb, Sister says. Healing well. I'll take a look tomorrow when the dressings are next removed. How's the pain?'

'It's getting better.'

Archie glanced at the group by the piano. 'I see your visitor is helping out. If only she could leave the WAAF and come here.' Archie paused, watching them wistfully, and then slapped Mac on the back. 'She's doing a grand job.'

'Yeah, real swell.' Mac sighed heavily.

'Oh well, I did ask her to help us out. I didn't think you'd mind too much.' Archie flicked a gaze at the others as music flowed from the radio and his eyes bubbled with mischief.

Man, he could really shoot a line. 'Doc, you could at least *try* to be subtle.'

'I don't know what you mean. Besides, subtle isn't my style, not when you want results.' Archie raised his eyebrows and winked.

'I told you how it is. Nothing's changed.' Mac glanced over his shoulder. She was dancing now with Dickie, and he huffed out a breath and lowered his gaze to the floor.

'Hasn't it? That's a shame. I think she's good for you.' Archie sat down in the chair.

There was a definite jovial tone to his voice, and Mac swore he was enjoying this.

'Right, let's see what you can do with this.' He passed him the small, exercise ball, which Mac held in each hand in turn. His grip was almost back to normal on the right, and somewhat reduced on the left, but there was evidence of improvement over the last week, Mac was sure of it. He winced as he squeezed the ball, and he opened and closed his fingers and then demonstrated the pincer grip. The more he worked, the more his hands ached and throbbed, but he gritted his teeth and continued.

'Okay, now squeeze my hands.' Archie held them out for Mac to grip. 'Steady on,' he chuckled, his face turning puce. 'You've got some strength there. Well, I'm impressed, and I can tell you now I wasn't sure you would do this well, so, good work. Keep practising with the ball and stretching out the fingers. Excellent improvement. The more therapy you do, the better the results.'

'Thanks, Maestro, will do. I'll squeeze the heck out of this thing if it gets me back in the air.' He glanced at Stella. Still dancing, and laughing. The way Dickie held her so close sent a torrent of rage coursing through his veins. His hand on her back had better not slip any lower.

Archie's face creased into a faint smile. 'Have you told Stella your plans?'

'Not in so many words. Trust me, doc, she's better off without me. If anything happens, well, I couldn't forgive myself.' Mac looked over his shoulder and finally caught her eye. She flashed that warm, sweet smile of hers and the blood fizzed through his veins.

Archie pursed his lips. 'Well, there's not much keeping you here for now, but I don't want to send you back to your base just yet. I'll need to see you in another week, and you might need one more operation. Will you agree to a short stay at Dutton Homestall? The place belongs to a good friend of mine who allows us to use it as a convalescent home. It might be a refreshing change and a rest for you. Besides, it'll do you good to escape for a while.'

'Sure, if you think so doc.' Mac nodded. So Archie thought he might have a chance to get back in the air? At least he could get away from here. He glanced at Stella.

'I wouldn't worry about Dickie. He's not her type.' Archie was about to walk away, and he hesitated. 'Just one more thing. A friend is throwing a party for us in town – it's next month, the end of July. Everyone who's well enough can go.'

'Sure, sounds great.'

Archie's eyes twinkled as he grinned. 'And feel free to bring a certain pretty blonde along.' He turned and walked away with a shrug of his shoulders.

For all his charm, his dancing eyes and his boyish grin, Archie held a commanding presence, and there was no doubt of who was in charge here. And British humour was one thing, but his New Zealand style was something else. Mac could see what he was trying to do, except he was wasting his time. The trouble was, she sure was the prettiest girl he'd ever seen. How was he going to get her out of his head?

Dutton Homestall resided between East Grinstead and the Ashdown Forest in twenty-eight acres of grounds. Blackie had offered to drive Mac as there were a couple of airmen staying there who he wished to see. As they turned into the drive, Mac whistled in surprise. Mature trees flanked the road and just around the next corner, the drive gave way to gravel bordered by neatly manicured lawns, and the house sprung into view.

'It's a grand sight, a Tudor mansion,' Blackie said. 'Belonged to Lord Tommy Dewar, the whisky distiller from Scotland, and when he died his nephew inherited the place. They mainly stay in London, but this was their weekend retreat until war broke out. All right for some, eh?' Blackie raised his eyebrows.

'What a place! Man, this sure beats the ward. I'm starting to feel like I'm on vacation.'

'Wait until you see inside. Actually, you'll meet a few faces you know. Now, the rules are simple. Treat the place with respect. No returning late at night *wasted*, as you Americans say, and no foul language inside the house. All bad behaviour is reported back, and the Maestro will come down on you like a tonne of bricks. Other than that, you're free to do as you please.' Blackie clambered out of the car.

Mac turned his face up to endless blue, soaking up the sun's rays which pricked his scars. The nurse had finally removed his facial dressings yesterday. He'd dreaded it, and had felt naked at first, yet strangely free. It was the first step to the rest of his life, and he had to embrace it.

The sweet scent of fresh-cut grass hung heavy in the air, drifting in the warm breeze. Mac grabbed his bag from the back of the car and almost dropped it as a sharp pain radiated through his hand, but he adjusted his grip and followed Blackie inside.

'G'day, Mac. I see they've finally kicked you out.' Dickie slapped him on the back.

'It looks that way.'

'I'll leave you boys to it. Enjoy yourself.'

'Yeah, sure will, and thanks again for the ride.' Mac gazed around. The hall was dark with oak panelling, though refreshingly cool with a stone-flagged floor. Dickie gave him the grand tour, including the dorm where a number of beds lay in regimented rows, the bathrooms, and the dining room where they all gathered for meals. As they passed another room, Mac spotted a group of guys standing by a bar while another played the piano. The stale odour of cigarette smoke was thick and mingled with beer.

'Just the other month the Boss arranged for Clark Gable to drop by. He stayed here as well, imagine that? Apparently, he gave a lecture about his own plastic surgery on his ears, without which he'd never have had a Hollywood career. The boys said it was hilarious, a riot.'

Dickie looked vibrant, and his face glowed. The change had obviously been beneficial for him. 'Just one other thing you should know.' He took out a cigarette and gestured with the pack. 'We're not the only ones staying here. The place is brimming with bats. It's all right during the day when the furry buggers are sleeping, but at night, watch out. I don't know where they come from, but they whizz along these corridors with more flying prowess than a fighter pilot. They scare the shit out of some of the lads.' He grinned. 'Honestly, I swear they'd rather face Jerry.'

Later, alone in the bathroom, Mac stepped closer to the mirror on the wall and studied his face. The skin on his right cheek looked smoother. The doc had done a great job, though the joins were ugly. Archie said the redness would fade in time, but Mac's gaze sailed over the patchwork of scars and varying skin tones and he wasn't convinced. A flap of skin from the underside of his arm now thrived, stretched taut across his cheek. Maybe some Montana sun would fix him up – if he ever made it back.

He swallowed. The mirror revealed his alter ego. His skin grew clammy, and his chest tightened. As he focused on the abnormal side, he barely recognised the person staring back – and he didn't like him much either. That guy had pushed Stella away. He gazed into the dark, narrow eyes of the monster who consumed him, while dreading the future and a lifetime of horrific stares and pointing fingers. Some of the guys had far worse injuries than him, and he knew he'd been lucky, but it wasn't enough.

Birdie's death would be on his conscience forever, ingrained into his soul, worn in his scars. Fear rooted and grew faster than anything he knew and right now it was paralysing. A lump swelled in his throat. The number of times the scene had unfolded in his mind – maybe if he'd altered course at the right moment that cannon fire would have missed. He rubbed his jaw and longed to drown out the thoughts, the images. He had to fly again, to absolve himself. It was the only way. He clenched his fist as best he could and gritted his teeth as a searing, burning pain jabbed his hand. *Damn it all.*

That wasn't him in the glass, and this wasn't happening. He turned away, stomped back to his bed and sank down, holding his head in his hands. His chest heaved and tears slid silently down his face. A familiar odour rushed into his nostrils and stirred the threat of nausea in his stomach. Would it ever leave? Day after day, night after night, the stench of charred, roasted pork had leached out into the air they all breathed, ingraining its festering, rank mark. A weight constricted his chest, and he gasped, sucking in ragged breaths.

Stella. He might not be able to make it with her, but he damn well couldn't make it without her.

21

Red Badge Of Courage, June 1943

'Hello. I'm here at Mr McIndoe's invitation – Miss Charlton.' Stella smiled. It was refreshingly cool in the oak-panelled hall of Dutton Homestall. She snapped her compact shut, her lipstick applied. The magazines called it the red badge of courage, and right now she had to agree. On dark days, it was necessary to paint on a smile.

'Oh yes, Miss Charlton. We've been expecting you.' The VAD nurse stepped out from behind the desk in the hall. 'Everyone's out on the terrace. Come this way.'

Stella assumed Mac would be here too, and she sucked in a deep breath and released it slowly as she wondered how much more of this she could take. So far around Mac, she'd managed to keep up a pretence while her crushed heart and soul ached for his love, and she didn't know how much more she could take. It was madness coming all this way on what would appear to be a fool's errand, but then she *had* been helping out, and it gave her such a boost to see the boys and to be able to help them. Her reward was seeing their faces light up with a smile – or, in some cases, their eyes – and it had nursed her bruised heart these past weeks.

Mac hadn't given her any indication of wanting her back and being so close to him and yet so far apart was bloody frustrating. Golden light and voices tumbled in through an open doorway ahead, and Stella forced a smile despite the heaviness in her heart. Nerves simmered, and she clutched her stomach as if she could pin them down before stepping outside to a sea of servicemen and civilians, milling around on the terrace.

'Stella, you made it.' Archie strode over to greet her, his eyes twinkling as his face creased into a broad grin. He had a pint glass in his hand. Tables laden with plates of sandwiches and cakes adorned the terrace. 'Come and meet some of the boys and I'll get you a drink.' He took her arm and steered her towards a group of young airmen. 'Gentlemen, this is the young lady I've been telling you about. Stella. She's been an asset to our merry ward.'

As they greeted her one by one, her eyes picked out the USAAF uniform directly in front of her and her heart leapt as she was reminded of the first time she and Mac had met. He stood with his back to her, tall and broad and the smooth tone of his voice sent a tingle coursing through her veins.

'It's jolly nice to meet you, Stella.' A young RAF officer held out his hand, jerking her back into the present.

Mac spun around, and the breath caught in her throat. It was the burned side of his face that appeared first, and for a second she thought it must be someone else until he faced her fully and she saw him as if for the very first time. The skin stretched taut across his right cheek, coloured like red wine, bleeding into paler skin below his eye, puckering around the outer edge, crinkling now as he smiled. She held in a breath, and she knew she was staring, but she couldn't speak. A faint pink tinge crept into his left cheek, and his smile faded. His beautiful face... yet Archie was right – it could have been so much worse. Entranced by Mac's deep blue eyes, she failed to take the RAF officer's proffered hand.

'Stella, I didn't know you were coming today.' Mac took a step towards her. He was as handsome as ever, and she longed to reach out and touch him, except he wouldn't like that. Just as words formed in her mind, a hand took her arm gently.

'Stella, Dickie tells me you have a beautiful singing voice. Come and sing for us. I'm afraid we've been let down today as our singer has cancelled. I had no idea we had a songbird in our midst.' As Archie led her away, she glanced over her shoulder at Mac, and he grinned back. Her heart swelled. It was something, at least.

'I'm not that good a singer, Archie, really I'm not.'

'Oh, she's a natural, Maestro. Just wait till you hear. Come on, Stella. You'll be ace.' Dickie beamed, holding a sheet of music in his hand. 'We're just through here.'

She followed him through French doors to where the piano stood, then she turned and gazed out at a sea of expectant faces on the terrace as a crowd gathered, prompted by Archie. Among them stood Mac, his intense eyes upon her. Stella tore her gaze away and took a deep breath. 'I can't do it.' She swallowed; her palms were moist with sweat.

Dickie placed his hands on her shoulders and looked her in the eye. 'Come on, you'll be great, I promise. Just pretend there's nobody there. It's just you and me.' He nodded, a reassuring smile etched on his lips, then he thrust a crystal glass in her hand. 'Dutch courage.' He chuckled. 'Go on then, down the hatch.' He ran a hand through his cropped, sandy blond hair with its side parting.

Stella took a sip. It was fiery and coated her tongue in malt, and she wrinkled up her nose and blew out a breath. 'I never drink whisky.' She coughed, and Dickie laughed.

He began playing the keys. 'Recognise it?'

She nodded.

'Know the words?'

'Doesn't everyone?'

He launched into the music, and Stella began to sing 'A Nightingale Sang in Berkeley Square.' Her voice trembled at first, the notes quivered, and she clenched her fists by her sides as a flash of warmth spread upward from her neck. The chatter died away, and all eyes were upon her, scrutinising. She glanced down at the floor for a second as her heart raced and she told herself there was no one there, and as she raised her chin, she found her focus – Mac. She gazed into his eyes, losing herself in their sapphire depths, as his mouth curved upward into that heart-stopping half-smile as if he believed in her, and the words flowed from her lips, sweet and melodic. When the song ended, and the piano music ceased, people applauded, and the jovial hubbub of voices erupted once again.

'Stella, that was beautiful. Thank you for stepping in,' Archie said. 'Isn't she wonderful?'

Mac stepped forward. 'She sure is.'

'Ah, Dickie, can I have a word?' Archie steered Dickie away, leaving Stella transfixed by Mac's twinkling eyes, alone.

'You were a knockout.' Mac rubbed the back of his neck. 'I had no idea you could sing. You're full of surprises.'

A gentle breeze of cedar wood flowed towards her, and she drank it in. 'Well, I don't make a habit of it, especially not in public.' She grinned and looked around. She longed to tell him that he was still handsome, that his scars made no difference to her, only she wasn't sure how he'd react.

'Say, would you like to take a walk?' He scraped a hand through his hair.

'All right.' She followed Mac out into the garden, and he led her around to the side of the house where a bench seat nestled beneath the shade of oak trees. As they sat, she noticed how he left a space between them, and her heart sank.

Mac took out a packet of Lucky Strikes and offered it to her.

'Thanks.' She plucked one and leaned in close for a light, and his hand cupped hers, sending a tingle streaking up her arm to her chest. 'You're looking well.'

'I'm okay. The doc's work is almost done.'

'That's good. Do you think they'll send you home?'

'I doubt it. I'm going back, Stella. I wanted you to know.'

The air rushed out of her lungs. 'You mean you're going to fly?'

'Yeah, if they'll have me. I just have to pass the medical.' He spoke as if it was a mere formality.

'Mac, you can't. They won't pass you.' Her heartbeat pounded in her ears. He wasn't fit to fly bombers. She swallowed as she pictured him in the cockpit of a B-17 in a turbulent sky swarming with the Luftwaffe, and a swell of nausea surged in her gut. She turned away towards the shimmering horizon as tears clouded her vision.

'The doc says I might make it. I need more tests, and then there's the therapy, but so far so good.'

Why was he doing this? He could take a desk job. Be safe. She couldn't bear losing him, even though he wasn't hers to lose. A tear bobbed on her eyelash before slipping down her cheek, and she gritted her teeth.

'I just wanted you to know, after all, we were... well, I didn't want you finding out from somebody else.'

Was that all? He just had to tell her his good news as if she'd never been anyone special at all? When had he become so cold? She bit her lip as her shoulders shook and she tried in vain to swallow down the sob. The flying was one thing, but his coolness towards her hurt more than anything and she squeezed her eyes shut.

'Hey, come on, honey.' Mac placed his hand on her shoulder.

She turned to face him. 'I can't believe you're doing this. What about everything you said? What about me?'

Mac shook his head and bit his lip. 'This is exactly what I wanted to avoid. Stella, you know how I feel, but I can't risk hurting you, or worse.'

'Never coming back?' she choked. 'Is that what you mean?' She swiped tears away with the back of her hand. 'You said you loved me, and then you pushed me away.'

'Oh, come on, honey. Please don't be like that.'

'Like what exactly? Like someone who happens to care a lot about you? Well, more fool me.' She rose, grabbed her bag, and drew in a deep breath. 'I'm glad you've recovered so well, truly I am, but I think you're making a mistake. Still, it's your life. Bye, Mac.'

His eyes flashed and she spun on her heels and fled, tears stinging her eyes as she marched off down the drive.

'Stella, wait.'

She didn't turn around. If he wanted to follow her, that was up to him. She was in the middle of nowhere, although there was an inn just along the lane – she'd noticed it when she arrived. Perhaps she could telephone for a taxi to take her to the station. At the end of the drive, she stopped and leaned against the wall, catching her breath, flicking a gaze back along the winding drive and her heart sank. Clearly he didn't think she was worth running after.

From her bag, she pulled a handkerchief, dried her eyes, and took some deep breaths. She'd failed. It was obvious Mac had made his mind up weeks ago. He wanted to fly and had cast her aside. Alex's words echoed in her head. *He'll love you and leave you.*

A low guttural cry slipped from her throat, and an iron fist closed around her heart, and she couldn't bear to think of never being in his arms again, of slipping her hand in his, of tasting his lips. No, she had to get away, so she dried her eyes and strode off towards the inn, her head held high as she squinted into the sun.

22

A Shot In The Dark

'Mac. Stella not with you?' Archie drew on his cigarette.

'Well, she was, until about five minutes ago. She took off.'

Archie exhaled a cloud of smoke. 'Took off? Where?'

'I don't know.' He looked down at his feet.

'And you let her leave, just like that? A gentleman always escorts a lady home. Does she even know where she's going?'

Mac hadn't thought of that. *Jeez, how stupid could he be?* He gazed up at Archie. 'I guess I said the wrong thing.' He blew out a breath. 'I told her my plans, and she got upset.'

'Ah, yes, well it's only to be expected. You know, Mac, as much as we might try to control situations, it's not always possible, and sometimes we have to take a leap of faith. You said before that you were protecting Stella, but I wonder if you might be running away. Perhaps it's time to run to her, don't you think?' Archie's face creased into a soft smile and he returned to the house.

Mac swallowed, and he sprung up. Archie was right. He'd allowed her to run off, and she didn't have a clue where she was going. Mac broke into a light run and headed down the drive, only there was no sign of her. He stopped at the end, panting. Man, he was a little out of shape from all this lying around. Which way would she have gone? She wouldn't have turned left because that road ran for miles and there was nothing down there. No, she'd have gone right, the way she came in. He picked up the pace again, and after a couple of minutes, he rounded a bend in the road just in time to glimpse a flash of blue sailing around the next corner. The late afternoon sun burned and a gentle warm breeze drifted towards him, mingled with the intoxicating aroma of wild spring onions. His scars prickled beneath the heat.

'Stella.' He broke into a run, and when he whipped around the next bend, she was right in front of him. 'Stella, wait.' Mac drew up by her side, out of breath as he wiped beads of sweat from his brow. 'You walk mighty fast.'

She glanced at him with narrowed eyes and carried on walking, then he caught her hand and pulled her back. 'Hey, wait up. I'm sorry. I've been a jerk.' He gazed into her misty, red eyes, and an ache surged in his chest. 'Come here, honey.' He pulled her towards him, only she drew back. 'Hey, I never meant to hurt you.'

'Well, you did.' Her eyes hardened. 'Telling me who to marry. Pushing me away after chasing me for weeks. Who are you to tell me what to do?' Her eyes flashed and temper lashed her cheeks scarlet. She pulled away, her hand slipping out of his grip, and strode off.

The distance between them widened and Mac's chest tightened. He'd done that. *What a jackass.* She was mighty cut up about the things he'd said, but that could mean only one thing, surely. 'Well, here goes nothing, doc,' he muttered as he gritted his teeth and sprinted after her. 'Stella! Wait up.'

She turned to face him, a wariness lingering in her sunflower eyes. 'What do you want, Mac? Am I going the wrong way? Is that it?' Her voice was ice-cold.

'Yeah, you're damn right you are.' He moved towards her, slipped his arm around her waist, and pulled her close, his lips on hers. She stiffened in his arms and beat her hands against his chest, though after a few seconds, she softened and kissed him back. 'Now you're headed in the right direction.' He smiled, and she rested her head against his chest, gripping him tighter than she'd ever done before. 'God, I love you, Stella.'

She lifted her face, and fresh tears glistened on her eyelashes. 'Do you really? Because if you did, you wouldn't have pushed me away or said all those things.'

'I'm sorry. I did it to protect you, but I can see I was wrong.'

'If you truly wanted to protect me, you'd be asking for a desk job.'

'Ah, gee, honey. It's not that simple. I came here to do my duty, and that's what I have to do.'

'You've done it. Don't you see?'

She had a point. He had – only he wasn't through. How could he make her understand? After everything that had happened, and all the friends he'd lost, he was terrified at the thought of flying through hell once more, and of never holding her in his arms again. He sighed. 'I'm sorry. It's hard to explain, but I have to do this. I owe it to those that are lost and to myself. I was trying to protect you because I knew you'd be hurt if I went back, and, well, if anything were to happen, then I wanted to spare you that.' He looked away as he thrust his hands in his pockets.

She stood by the side of the road, her eyes boring into him. 'Is that the only reason?'

Gee, she didn't miss a thing. He sighed and looked down at his feet as he kicked some loose stone chippings, which skittered along the lane in a cloud of dust. 'Well, I guess for a while I thought you'd be better off with someone else rather than being saddled with me.' He looked into her eyes and held his hands up. 'What you see is what you get, and frankly, I hate it.'

Stella moved towards him and reached up to cup his right cheek. He stiffened for a few seconds, despite savouring the warmth flowing from her touch, soothing his skin, reaching into his soul. But he was damaged goods, and he didn't want to see pity or disgust on her face; when he dared to gaze, however, he saw that usual smile of hers that fired up those sunflower eyes.

'Oh, Mac. All those weeks when I could have helped you. Time wasted.' Her eyes misted over. 'You're still the same man to me, handsome, even with the scars. You're beautiful, inside and out.'

He reached up and covered her hand with his. She hadn't flinched once and he couldn't believe how he'd got it so wrong. 'I'm sorry for hurting you, only you deserve to be happy, to have a whole life.'

'Mac, you make me happy, the happiest I've ever been, and it's you that makes me whole.' Her eyes swam like the ocean, and he raised her hand to his lips and kissed her fingertips.

'Back in the hospital, I was lost for a while. The thought of you and of flying again kept me going – that and the other guys, of course. They've been swell. I'm still finding my feet, and there's no one I'd rather do that with than you. But I have to fly if they'll let me.' He moved towards her and held her face in his hands. 'I'm so in love with you, and I'm lost without you. Do you think we can start over?'

Her lower lip trembled, and she blew out a breath. 'Yes, as long as you promise that from now on, you'll tell me if something's worrying you. Don't push me away.'

He planted a soft kiss on her lips. 'I promise.' He folded her in his arms and held her tight, unmoving, his chin brushing the top of her head as he drank in a haze of lavender. 'Hey, are you hungry? They do great food at the inn. Why don't we call in and get you something to eat?'

She nodded and took his outstretched hand.

The Maypole was dark and refreshingly cool, with aged oak beams stretched across the ceiling. The aroma of food wafted in the air, and Stella's stomach rumbled. Ale mingled with tobacco and cast a cosy, heady scent into the atmosphere, and then Mac's protective hand was on her arm, steering her towards a table in the corner. The hum of voices thrummed like the distant growl of an engine.

'What would you like to drink?'

'Oh, a port and lemon please.' She couldn't take her eyes off him – the way he sauntered over to the bar, and leaned in as he chatted to the landlord. The velvet drawl of his voice set her nerve endings ablaze, and when he turned to gaze at her and flashed that smile of his, she could barely breathe. Mac loved her and needed her as she needed him. But a dark cloud lingered. He said he hated his looks. That was why he'd told her to leave. He must have been struggling all this time – alone – and, like Alex, Mac was wedged in a dark corner. Was he even fit enough to fly? She closed her eyes for a second.

Later, after they had eaten, Stella sighed and settled back in her chair, stifling a yawn. 'That was good. I'm so tired, I could probably fall asleep standing up on the train.' She sipped her drink, hoping to refresh herself, but it began to have the opposite effect.

'It's a long slog from Cambridge.' He traced the side of her hand with his finger, and as she met his gaze, sparks flickered in the blue. 'Maybe you should have stayed over.'

She had considered it, except she only had two days leave. 'It makes sense, and I'm dreading the journey home tonight, especially in the blackout.'

'I'll have a word – Jack's a decent guy. He's sure to have a room going spare.'

'First name terms already?' She grinned.

'Well, you know how it is.' He shrugged and cast her a coy smile.

Stella felt her eyelids grow heavy, and she fought to prise them open. The thrum of voices faded as she drifted, then Mac bumped her hip with his as he sat down and pressed cold metal into the palm of her hand.

'Hey, sleepyhead. There's your key.'

'Oh Mac, thank you. How much is it?'

'Oh, forget about it. I've settled up.' He smiled warmly and put his arm around her. 'I can't have my girl paying the bills.' He drained his beer. 'As much as it pains me to say it, I think I'm getting used to warm beer.'

Stella laughed, her mind hanging on his words – *my girl.*

Later, he led her by the hand up the steep, creaky wooden staircase at the rear of the inn. On the landing, they found room two, and he unlocked the door and stepped to one side, gesturing to Stella to go first. She put her things down on the double bed and looked around. The room was sparse with a mahogany bedside table and a tall brass lamp.

Mac checked his watch. 'Well, it's half past seven. I guess I'd better head back and leave you to rest.' He walked over to where she stood by the window and slid his arms around her waist. 'You're so beautiful, did I tell you that already?' He rested his brow against hers.

She raised her chin as his mouth met hers, his warm breath tinged with beer. His kiss was firm, and he threaded his fingers through her hair, and she tingled all over as her heart thumped faster. He pulled her even closer, his hands beating nerve endings into a frenzy as he caressed her back.

'Oh Stella, honey. God, I want you.' He broke away and gazed at her, his eyes searching hers as slowly, he unfastened her dress. She wanted him, and she knew she shouldn't, yet her heart and her body ached for him. Reaching up, she undid his jacket, unbuttoned his shirt, and placed her palm flat against his firm chest, caressing his muscular physique. He led her towards the bed. She reached up and ran her hands through his hair as he kissed her again, moving down to the swell of her breast, his tongue grazing her skin.

Wasn't this what she wanted? Other girls had done it, but not her. Not yet. She didn't know what to do or what to expect, and she suddenly felt exposed, confused and afraid. He pulled her gently back onto the bed and Stella lay there as his hand cupped her breast. She gasped as he kissed her, savouring the taste of his warm lips. When he'd told her to marry Alex, his words had cut deep and now, just as they might have a chance, he was going to be flying missions again. The thought was unbearable, and she couldn't think straight.

'Oh, Stella.' He was almost on top of her, one leg hooked over hers, pressing against her thigh as he covered her neck in kisses.

'Mac, I can't.'

'You know I love you, don't you?'

'I know, it's just too soon.'

He stopped and looked at her with a serious expression. 'Is this your first time?'

She nodded, her cheeks burning. Nervously, she bit her lower lip and shrank inside. He sighed and buttoned up the dress, his fingers fumbling a little, but she left him to it, noting the flash of frustration in his eyes.

'I'm sorry. I guess I got carried away.' He lay beside her and wrapped his arms around her. With his finger, he traced a line from her temple to her jaw, cupping her chin. 'I don't want to force you into anything, baby.' He kissed her, soft and tender, and lay back, drawing her into his arms.

'I'm sorry.' Tears pricked her eyes.

'No need to be. I shouldn't have, only I've missed you so bad.' His lips brushed her cheek.

Outside, the setting sun cast a pink glow against the blue. She gazed up at Mac. His eyes had closed, and he twitched as he drifted off to sleep. Was he allowed to stay out all night? 'Mac,' she whispered in his ear.

'Huh?' He rolled onto his side, gave her a gentle squeeze as he tenderly brushed her cheek with his lips, and then he was still, quite still, other than the sound of his breathing. She lay watching him while he drifted and slid her arm around his waist, revelling in the firmness of his body pressed up against hers. Placing her hand on his chest, she tingled as the muscles rippled beneath with each rhythmic breath. Never before had she been so close to a man – so intimate – and her gaze slipped across his face, eager to learn every fine detail of his new skin. Her chest tightened as she ruminated over all the anguish and pain Mac had endured alone.

Stella wished it could be like this always, but all too soon the dark thoughts descended like birds of prey, picking through her mind. She couldn't bear it if she lost him, and she drank in his familiar scent of cedar wood with greed as a cloud of unease crept over her.

RAF Bourn languished beneath a slate-grey sky. Stella cycled through the light mist, thinking of the night she had spent with Mac. He'd woken her in the early hours with such an anguished cry and then clambered out of bed and scoured the room. Finally, he lay back down, clammy, with sweat glistening on his skin, and Stella could only imagine what dark shapes haunted his mind.

The grim start to the day didn't improve when she arrived at work, and she sensed the cloud from the moment she stepped into the office.

'Oh, Stell, it's awful. Three of our Lancasters didn't make it back from last night's raid. The boys reckon there were no survivors.' Vera's red eyes glistened.

Twenty-one men missing. Stella gazed around at the sea of misty eyes, and a lump rose in her throat. Somehow it felt as if everything slowed down. One of the girls was visibly distraught and was led away to the CO's office.

'What's wrong with her?' Of course, it didn't take a genius to work it out.

'Oh, her fiancé was one of them.'

Stella swallowed. How simple it was, here one minute and gone the next, just like snatching a breath, and all the while the world turns and people move on, just as she was about to right now.

At lunchtime, she headed to the mess hall with Vera, and three of the tables remained as they had been earlier that morning – laid out for breakfast, twenty-one place settings pristine, waiting for crew to return. Stella's heart ached. It was surreal to think they were gone. The war just kept on rolling, and it was never-ending. How long would it be before it finally caught up with Mac? She blew out a long breath.

After lunch, Stella decided to go and see how Jean was. She hadn't been in the canteen earlier, and when she asked around, it seemed that no one had seen her at all. Outside, rain fell like bullets, soaking everything and everyone in seconds as black, ominous clouds amassed against pewter. Stella draped her raincoat over her head yet still the drops slipped down the back of her neck and splashed her legs, dappling her stockings muddy brown.

The supplies hut loomed, but the door was closed, which was strange, because Jean would usually be surrounded by chutes, packing away. Suddenly, the rain ceased, as if someone had flicked a switch, and the sun peeked out from her shroud to cast her glow across the land.

Tentatively, Stella opened the door and stepped inside. The hut was dim and humid with the smell of a garden shed in summer, of baked timber and something she couldn't quite place. Rows of shelves were stacked with parachutes, neat and orderly, and as she stole past a tall shelving system on her left, something caught her eye up ahead. She blinked. Her eyes fixed on the black leather regulation shoes and she froze. Shoes that were three feet up in the air.

An icy chill slithered down her spine as her gaze zipped up from the shoes to the legs, and she heard the eerie, piercing cry, so shrill it echoed. Her eyes darted all around but she was alone, and only then did she realise it was coming from her.

'Jean!' she cried. 'Oh Jesus, what have you done?'

Instinctively, she grabbed Jean's legs and tried to hoist her up, to take the strain of the rope off her neck, yet it was hopeless. Jean's wide, dark eyes fixed on hers, lifeless, peering from a blue-grey face. Stella dashed outside and spotted some ground crew by one of the hangars. She yelled and waved her arms in the air. Two of the men sprinted over, and when they saw what had happened, they swung into action. One of them held Jean's body while the other swiftly cut the rope, and they laid her gently down on the dusty, wooden floor. One of them brushed his hand over her eyes, closing them. She looked so young and fragile.

'She's so grey.' Stella stared, transfixed by Jean's lifeless face, wondering how anyone could do such a thing. She must have been in turmoil.

'I'll tell the CO, Charlie,' the first man said. 'It's too late to do anything for her, poor soul.'

'Are you all right, miss? You've had a nasty shock.' Charlie's voice brimmed with concern. He took out a handkerchief and handed it to her.

Stella sank to the floor of the hut, trembling. Such a waste of life. It was too much to bear, and she released a choking sob, her shoulders heaved, and her body shook as tears spilled down her cheeks. She saw Jean, but her tears flowed for others who flashed in her mind – and for Mac. Years of pent-up fear, frustration, and worry poured out amidst the dust on the floor until she could cry no more.

She longed for Mac's strong arms around her, holding her against his firm body, his warmth flowing through into hers. She sat hunched on the floor, as if in a trance, rocking back and forth, her arms hugging her knees to her chest. She was barely aware of the girl who draped a blanket about her shoulders, and who, with the help of the CO, took her by the arms and hauled her to her feet, leading her away to the office. And then a whiff of whisky emanating from a steaming mug of tea placed in her grip jolted her back to reality. She turned her gaze to the window.

Outside, the last of the ominous clouds blew over, revealing acres of blue in their wake. All was silent, and birdsong returned, shrill and sweet, and the larks and swallows soared and swooped once more.

23

A Lone Raider, July 1943

Archie made a fist with his right hand, then relaxed it, repeating the action twice more before sinking into the chair at his desk. In one week's time, he would be having surgery in London, under the care of his colleague and friend Rainsford Mowlem. He'd tried and failed not to dwell on it, but the stakes were too high. He should have sought help much earlier before his hands became quite so problematic. What if the condition was too advanced? That could potentially make the surgery even more difficult or impossible, and his hands really were his livelihood.

Right now, he was trying to put everything in order before he took time off. After his operation, he had the party to look forward to. The Chesters had been huge supporters of the Guinea Pig Club since its inception, and they often opened their home to the lads.

He had something else to organise too before he left and he needed Blackie's help. George Reid had agreed to set up the workshop in the empty hut in the hospital grounds, and he wished to organise training for the boys. Manufacturing aircraft precision instruments for the RAF would suit the majority of them, so George thought. The lads needed to be active, to have a purpose, and George had it within his grasp to grant them just that. The sweetener for the boys equated to money. In addition to their RAF pay, George had agreed to remunerate them for their work.

'So who's going to supervise them?' Blackie asked.

'They're sending us one of their head technicians and four female workers to get us started. They have various assembly jobs, though they're relatively straightforward enough. George said the boys can learn each task in a few hours.'

Blackie seemed doubtful. It was a big step, but Archie had complete faith. 'If some of them can fly a Spitfire or a bomber, I'm damn well sure they can assemble the instruments they've been flying with. Besides, it's going to be excellent therapy for improving hand function and morale and they won't even realise it.' Archie knew Blackie could manage, nevertheless, he hated having to take time off in case there were any problems.

At least he'd completed the surgery on Mac's hands. The boy was as determined as hell to return to his squadron, and it looked as if it might be possible. He'd been incredibly lucky. Archie rubbed his brow. What if he'd left things too late? Visions of an early retirement formed in his mind, and he huffed out a breath.

Rainsford was a specialist in this type of hand surgery, but even so, Archie couldn't disguise his nervousness. 'There's really no need to worry. I've done this operation before, many times.' He met Archie's gaze, and his intense dark eyes flickered.

'Yes, I know, but not on *this* hand, and I trust you'll take extra care. It's the only thing between the bankruptcy courts and me.' Archie sank down in the leather wing chair in Rainsford's office.

Rainsford chuckled. Archie trusted him to do his best, but was it going to be enough? He could kick himself. What a fool to keep putting this off, particularly since his own self-diagnosis had been spot on. He was determined not to lose everything he'd worked so hard for. He always told his patients the truth, and his own words echoed in his head. 'We'll fix you up.' Yes, he always said that, and it was true, although how much a man could be fixed varied widely, depending on his injuries. He hoped to God that his hand could be fixed.

This was how his boys must have felt when meeting him for the very first time, clinging to his words as if they were a lifeline, desperately clawing at each syllable to save them and make everything right once more. To make them well enough so they could fly again. Flying was their life, just as plastic surgery was his. *Oh, how the tide had turned.* Archie swallowed.

Tomorrow was the day of reckoning. The seventh of July – the day his career was to be saved or ruined. He was in a precarious position and unused to placing himself in the hands of another. His fate rested with Rainsford, and as reality quickly sunk in, the loss of power and control was unsettling, and he was like a cornered animal, trapped with nowhere to run. Now it was his time to learn to trust another; to lean on a colleague; to take a leap of faith.

Friday 9th July 1943

The air raid siren whined over East Grinstead, its eerie, echoing wail resonating throughout the town. Mac checked his watch. Five o'clock. He glanced at Pete as the nurses halted in their tracks and Bea ran to the window. *Stella.* She'd left about an hour ago, saying that a walk to the station would do her good. His stomach turned ice-cold, and he swallowed.

'They're running to the shelters.' Bea's voice was edged with anguish.

'Keep calm, nurse.' Sister Jamieson stood like a rod of iron, her thin lips pursed.

'Probably a false alarm again.' Pete cast a glance at Mac. 'Don't look so worried. It's always a bloody false alarm.' He looked at the cards in his hand, then placed them down on the table. 'Full house, boys,' he proudly proclaimed, a smug grin forming on his lips.

'Oh, you've gotta be kidding me, not again.' Mac flung his cards onto the table, and they splayed out. He glanced over at Bea and an icy chill gripped his shoulders. False alarm or not, he wouldn't be happy until he knew Stella was home – safe. The sirens persisted. A few minutes later, a low distant rumble filtered in, creeping nearer, growing mightier. The boys rushed to the windows and looked out as the rumble transcended into a thundering drone.

'That's not one of ours.' Pete pointed to the dark outline of a large aircraft.

'Hell no. It's a Jerry.' A lone Dornier circled low above the small town, a black and white cross on its fuselage. 'And I think its bomb bay doors are open.' Seconds later, dark shapes plummeted from its belly. Tremors from the explosion rumbled beneath them, and the glass rattled in the window frames.

'Mother of Mary, that's in the town centre! There'll be people shopping.' Bea turned to face Sister Smith, her eyes wide, lifting her hand to her mouth. 'The Friday matinee's on at the Whitehall. They'll wipe them out.' She was trembling, and her face paled as she spoke.

'Nurse, pull yourself together. You may be needed later.' Sister Jamieson seemed to falter too as she watched from the window, wringing her hands tightly, her mouth gaping. The Dornier circled around as plumes of black, thick smoke billowed with fury into the sky. No doubt the pilot had scored a direct hit.

'The bastard's coming round again. Jesus Christ, I bet they're firing at people in the streets.' Pete glanced at Mac.

A surge of adrenaline pumped through Mac's veins and his heart raced. 'Stella.'

'She'll be fine, Mac. She's probably caught the train by now.' Pete didn't look convinced.

'That's what I'm worried about. That's the station over there.' Mac sucked in a breath.

Whatever damage the Dornier had done was now over as it turned and headed out towards the Channel. Mac rushed to his bed and grabbed his tunic jacket. He recalled all the missions he'd flown, all the bombs they'd dropped, and wondered how many innocent people had fallen. A lump rose in his throat.

'Wait up, Mac. I'm coming with you,' Pete said.

The sirens caught her off-guard. Her heart pounded against her ribcage and the breath hitched in her throat. She'd much rather be with Mac until the all-clear, but she didn't have time to turn back now. In London Road, a small trickle of people, mainly children, filed out of the Whitehall Cinema. Others hurried off up the road and Stella followed behind, assuming they were headed for the nearest shelter. An ARP warden rushed towards them, his face beetroot red beneath his black tin hat, his breathing hard.

'Come along, now. Hurry up, love. Off to the shelter with you.' He pointed up the road, the way everyone was headed, and Stella nodded and carried on.

The droning sound of an aircraft cut in and grew steadily louder. At the end of the road, out of nowhere, there was a flash of khaki as someone lunged at her and a man's voice yelled, 'Get down!' Dragged to the ground, Stella twisted her ankle and cried out. She wasn't sure whether the soldier now lying partially over her was American or Canadian, but he didn't sound British. His tunic jacket brushed her mouth, and a mix of stale cigarettes and cologne drifted beneath her nose. The drone of the engines grew into a roar, and the thrum juddered through Stella's body. She froze. It wasn't one of theirs, and an icy prickle crept up the back of her legs as she turned her face to the sky. The dark shape loomed low. Her mouth gaped as bombs fell from its belly and the soldier stared into her eyes.

'Keep your head down, ma'am.' His eyes bulged from his reddened face, and his weight pressed down on her chest, squashing her lungs, and she snatched breaths. She stiffened and steadied herself for the impact. An ear-splitting crump roared all around, and the ground shook beneath her as debris fell about them, some of which showered her, and something sharp hit her head, grazing her skin. Her stomach churned. The soldier raised his head briefly, then tightened his grip on her and positioned himself over her chest and face, shielding her further. More crashes thundered, more ear-splitting booms and she tasted dust and grime and the acrid smell of smoke wafted in the air. A dark shadow slithered across them as the aircraft sailed overhead. The soldier sprang to his feet, and Stella heaved in a deep breath as her lungs sighed with relief.

'I don't think he's leaving us just yet. He's coming about again. Stay down, ma'am.' He crouched low.

Stella raised her chin as the aircraft made a sweeping turn in the distance. Several people stood in the street, their faces turned upward, and a young boy crossed the road, his clothes grey with dust, his eyes filled with fear, locking onto hers. As the aircraft approached once more, it flew low enough for her to glimpse the gunner aiming his machine gun at the people in the street.

'Dear, God, no.' Her body trembled as her teeth chattered and her saviour gripped her tight.

'It's okay. He's done his worst now.'

His voice was all she could hear before her ears popped and the siren cut in along with the screams and cries of people, and the mighty roar and crackle of fire. The soldier helped her sit up. Her knees were bloodied patches, her stockings ripped. Her uniform was grey with dust, and something wet trickled down her cheek. She raised a hand to it and glanced at her fingertips, now streaked crimson.

'Best not do that, ma'am. Here you go.' He took a handkerchief and pressed it to her temple. 'Hold it there and keep the pressure on.' He smiled warmly. 'What's your name?'

Her teeth chattered so much she could hardly get the words out. 'Stella,' she managed at last.

'Well, Stella. I'm Dan. Let's see if we can get you on your feet.' He put his arms around her and helped her up to stand, but as soon as she put any weight on her foot, a searing pain shot through her ankle, and she cried out.

'Do you mind if I take a look?' He crouched down on the ground, with one hand on her injured foot.

She nodded. His brown hair was flecked with grey dust, which also crested his long eyelashes.

'Well, it's a little swollen and bruised I'd say, although I don't think it's broken. Wait here. I'll go and get help.' He pulled off his tunic jacket and wrapped it around her shoulders before he left.

A coppery tang swirled in her mouth and she ran her tongue over her lips and swallowed. As she waited, she realised she was just around the corner from what she imagined to be a horrendous sight, where the bombs had fallen. The cinema. Oh, Lord, she hoped everyone had got out. The people in the street. The boy. *No. Oh dear God, no.* She turned to look and saw a small body lying on the opposite side of the road, unmoving, the breeze ruffling his white blonde hair. A sob escaped from her mouth, and tears sprung to her eyes and slipped down her face. What about the hospital and Mac? *Oh please, let them be all right.*

The minutes ticked by and she began to wonder if Dan was ever coming back, and bile rose in her throat as she wrestled with the urge to be sick. Her head was muzzy and hundreds of white dots floated in front of her eyes. She lay the jacket on the ground and gently lay down on her side as she took deep breaths.

Next thing she knew, a warm hand was shaking her by the arm, and she opened her eyes.

'Stella, are you okay?'

Her heart skipped a beat as Mac crouched down beside her.

'It's okay, honey. You're gonna be fine.' He took her hand in his, lightly squeezing it. 'We'll get you to the hospital.'

Thank goodness her teeth had ceased chattering. She wanted to speak, and tried to open her mouth, yet the words wouldn't come, but at least Mac was here, and he was safe. He'd take care of her now. Her eyelids lowered.

'Stella, stay awake. You listen to me now. Don't go to sleep.'

Her eyelids fluttered and she strained to lift them, peering out of narrow slits, but she couldn't hold them any longer, just as a mother would never be able to hold the little boy with the white blonde hair any longer. Her heart contracted as she slipped into darkness.

Someone stroked her hand, then a finger brushed her brow. Voices reached her through the darkness. A sudden clang, a trolley rattled, and she jumped.

'I think she's coming around. Stella?'

Mac's voice. Warm, soft like velvet. She turned her head and winced as a sharp pain fired through her left temple, making her head throb. She moved her legs; a pain jolted through her right ankle, and she groaned. Her eyelids fluttered half-open, and a fuzzy face slowly came into focus.

'Mac.' Her mouth was dry, gritty and tasted of dust. She licked her lips.

'Hey, you had me worried back there.' He leaned in and kissed her cheek.

'You're all right. Thank, God,' she muttered, her eyes closing.

'Yeah, it was just the town that got hit. You had a lucky escape.' He stroked her cheek with his finger. 'You've got a sprained ankle and concussion. Something must have hit you on the head.'

That explained why her head was banging. 'Where am I?'

'At the Queen Victoria Hospital. I think we're stuck with you for now. You need to rest.'

'Thanks, you certainly have a way with words.' She wrenched an eye open. He was grinning at her, but his eyes were dark, his face pale and drawn. 'What time is it?'

'It's late, almost eleven o'clock.'

Goodness, the last time she'd looked it was just past five o'clock. She must have blacked out. Her body trembled, and her teeth began to chatter again. 'You're tired, Mac. Go and get some rest.'

'I'm never leaving you again. Jeez, I could have lost you today.' He gripped her hand in his.

She rested her head back as she tried to recall what had happened. The German pilot had flown quite low on the second pass, and she'd seen the outline of the gunner. 'Those people, all those people on the road. 'He... he murdered them.'

'Shh, don't talk, honey. The doc said you have to rest.'

She released a sob. 'I saw them. They had nowhere to run.'

The boy. Just a little boy and he'd crumpled before her eyes as the bullets rained down. She shielded her eyes with her hand as she sobbed, and Mac drew her into his arms and held her close. Her chest ached as the boy's face flashed in her mind, his open mouth and his innocent, wide eyes.

This was what they were fighting. Men who could be so ruthless and inhumane. They had to be stopped. She swallowed and raised her chin, meeting Mac's gaze. His eyes had seen men cut down too, and he relived those moments with every breath, yet he was determined to do all he could to fight the tyranny that threatened them.

It was either them or us, and she squeezed her eyes shut.

24

The Crux Of The Matter

Archie stared at his bandaged hand, which was elevated on a pillow at his side. The pain was intensifying, building up like a wave, and a restlessness crept into his bones as he longed to get up and do something – anything – except lie there. He had to occupy his mind, but instead the path ahead plagued him with thoughts he'd rather not deal with, and the darkness closed in, planting seeds of doubt. Rainsford had assured him the surgery had been a success and had ordered him to rest.

He pursed his lips as he pictured the stack of medical files and letters he'd be returning to, not to mention the problems. There were always challenges and things going wrong and equipment and supplies they needed and had to fight to procure. Then there were the complaints. He winced as a sudden sharp pain jolted through his hand, and he prayed that he wasn't finished. His pulse hammered in his throat, and he sucked in a breath. The view from the other side wasn't very good at all. As bleakness consumed him, he had no doubt his boys experienced that and more besides.

Just then, a nurse dashed into the room, dragging a portable telephone on a trolley behind her. 'Mr McIndoe, there's a call for you from a Sister Mullins at East Grinstead. She says it's urgent.'

Archie felt the hairs on the back of his neck bristle. What was so wrong they were telephoning him here? He picked up the receiver. 'Hello, Jill?'

'Archie, I just wanted to let you know. The town's been hit – bombs fell on the Whitehall just after five tonight. It's absolute carnage, and as you can imagine, it was packed. There were quite a few children in there.'

Archie could hardly believe it and rather hoped he'd misheard as a host of thoughts sailed through his mind. 'What about the boys?'

'They're all accounted for. The hospital wasn't hit.'

'Thank goodness for that. Well, keep me posted. On second thoughts, I'll come down. I can't do much stuck up here.' He balled his good hand into a fist. It had to happen when he wasn't there. Damn Jerry.

'Archie, no. You have to rest. It's all under control. We've brought in extra staff and all the medical teams are here to deal with the casualties.'

'How many so far?' He sensed from her tone and her words that the situation was grave.

'We're not sure. First reports state about fifty dead and more than a hundred injured.'

Those numbers were bound to rise as they sifted through the rubble. 'What the devil happened, Jill?'

'A single German bomber flew over the town and saw an opportunity to ditch his bombs. And if that wasn't bad enough, he came back round for another go and fired at people on the streets.'

Archie slammed his fist down on the bed. 'The bastards. What a time to be stuck here.'

'There's nothing you can do.'

Archie paused. 'Well, thanks for letting me know, Jill.' He replaced the receiver. The blood surged through his entire body, and his heart pounded. His hand ached and throbbed as he lifted it from the pillow. He had to do something. *Damn hands. Damn bloody war.* He was in his pyjamas in a hospital bed, for God's sake, with a hand he couldn't use. Feeling useless was one thing, but feeling sorry for yourself was something else. He needed to take action. Bugger the instructions.

Using his left hand to support himself, he sat upright and swung his legs out of bed. He reached for his clothes. In wartime, you pulled together, regardless of the circumstances.

When the night nurse spotted Archie fully dressed, carrying his bag along the corridor, her face fell, eyes wide with surprise. 'Mr McIndoe, it's the middle of the night!'

He halted in his tracks and cast a smile in spite of the hammering pain rolling and crashing through his hand. 'I'll telephone Rainsford in the morning and explain.'

'But Mr McIndoe, you were given strict instructions.'

'East Grinstead has been bombed, and it's rather a grave situation. My hospital is overrun with dead and wounded and I must return.' The poor girl took a step back, as her mouth gaped. He began to walk away, then turned to add, 'Thank you for everything, nurse. I'll be sure to tell Rainsford that you did your best to stop me absconding. Goodbye.' He forced a smile.

His hand throbbed and burned, and in truth, he didn't feel like going anywhere. He held the bandaged appendage across his chest in an attempt to keep it elevated, but he could only do so much. Driving might prove a little tricky, of course, but he was going to do it anyway.

Rainsford's words rang in his ears as he defied all medical advice. *That hand was worse than I'd realised. The Dupuytren's tissue that causes the contraction was far more extensive and progressive. I'd say I've operated in the nick of time. Any later and that hand of yours would have been rendered useless.*

He'd frowned, almost as if scolding a naughty child, and a frown didn't sit well with Rainsford's naturally friendly face, but Archie deserved it. He certainly had been stubborn, and he should have done something about it much sooner. After all the advice he regularly dished out... well, he ought to have known better. Archie realised he'd had a close call. Too close, although there was no time to worry about it now.

The drive back proved to be a challenge, especially during the blackout, and changing gear was a difficult business, so when Archie arrived back in the wee small hours, relief washed over him. Ward III was quiet, and the night nurse said the boys were all accounted for. Her eyes flicked over Archie's arm, and she raised her hand to her chest.

'Oh, Mr McIndoe. You've hurt your hand.'

'Oh, no, it's just a minor procedure I've had done. It's nothing, really.' He didn't wish to cause a scene, and he didn't want to answer any awkward questions.

Taking pity on him, she insisted on fitting a sling, which brought some relief from the pain. It was then she told him about Mac and Stella. His heart began to race, and he marched off to see them. He'd encouraged the girl to come back and help out, and basically do whatever it took to change Mac's mind. He was partially responsible for Stella's presence here – the girl could have lost her life.

Adrenaline rushed through his body as he passed various walking wounded and more seriously injured people along the way. Nurses hurried this way and that, while porters swept by pushing patients on trolleys, as people from the town wept openly in corridors or stared into space as they waited for news. He was useless in the midst of a crisis. He pursed his lips, thrust his good hand into his pocket, and sighed. War had finally come to their door.

Once he reached the ward and asked about Stella, a nurse took him aside. 'One of your boys is with her, Mr McIndoe. He won't budge, and Matron's not happy about it at all. We've had to put screens around the bed.' She raised her eyebrows. 'There are other female patients to consider.'

Archie sighed. 'Leave it to me, nurse.' He pulled the screen aside and slipped through. 'Hello, Mac,' he said in a hushed voice. He cast a glance at Stella, who was sleeping. He noted the dressing wrapped around her head. 'Can I have a word outside?'

Mac rose and followed him out of the ward and into the corridor. 'Hey, doc. What's happened to you?'

'Oh, the sling? It's nothing. I've just had surgery on my hand for something that's been brewing a while.' He glanced at Mac. His face was drawn and pale, his eyes red and bloodshot. 'I'm sorry you've been caught up in this. I gather you brought Stella in?'

'Yeah. When the bombs hit, I knew she was on her way to the station. I had to find her.' He dragged a hand through his hair and cleared his throat.

'Yes, well I'm glad you did, and I'm relieved she's all right apart from a concussion and some bumps and bruises.

They'll probably keep her here for a few days. Now, as much as I hate to say this, I'm afraid the nurses need you to leave. Why don't you come back to the ward and get some rest? She's not going anywhere, and you can come back first thing tomorrow.'

'I don't know, doc.' Mac slipped his hand into his pocket and heaved out a sigh.

'She's in good hands, and you need some rest, otherwise you'll not be much use to her in the morning. Come on.'

Mac turned to gaze back at the ward. 'Well, I guess she'll sleep now.'

'You know, she's a remarkable, strong young woman, and she cares about you a great deal. That's rare and precious to find, and you might want to keep hold of her – if you love her of course.'

Mac grinned. 'I do, and I will. You could say I took that leap of faith you were talking about.' His face fell. 'My entire world was almost blown apart tonight. I could have lost her, and if that had happened, I'd never have forgiven myself.'

'I can understand that.' Archie studied him for a moment. The boy had already endured his fair share of grief. 'You know, we can't save everyone, Mac. Life's a strange old business, and things often happen beyond our control. In war, it's even worse, but then you know that. The natural reaction is to feel responsible sometimes, yet the truth is, we aren't.'

He gazed at Mac and anguish flashed in the boy's eyes, no doubt a pain burning for more than Stella. 'We all have to move on and keep moving forward. Perhaps this is your time for a new chapter – with Stella.'

Mac looked away, a distant look in his eyes. 'I know you're right, it's just so difficult sometimes.' He sighed. 'I made a mess of everything, but after everything you said at Dutton the other day, well, I think we've made it up now.'

'Good, I'm glad to hear it.' Archie slapped Mac on the back.

'Hey, don't think I didn't know what you were up to, pushing us together. You're quite the matchmaker.'

'I'm a man of many talents, yes indeed. Right now it looks as if I'm joining your ranks. With my arm in this sling, I'm fit for nothing at all.'

'Well, you've helped me, doc, and I'm mighty glad to see you, and I think you'll find your presence has been missed. Besides, you'll be okay. You just need to give it time.' Mac grinned.

'Is that so?'

'Well, that's what you're always saying.' Mac looked down at his feet. 'Gee, I don't know what I would have done if you hadn't told me to go after her. I could have lost her, but then at least she wouldn't be here, like this.'

'You can't think like that. Sadly, war has a way of rooting us out. Besides, I've seen the way you look at her. I simply gave you the push you needed. You're well suited.'

'Well, I guess you're right, just as you were right about my hands. You said I'd get there and I have.' Mac gestured to Archie's hand. 'Looks like it's the same for you. You'll be back doing surgery before you know it.'

'Yes, no doubt. I'd better make the most of my recuperation period while I can.' Archie chuckled, though a darkness had etched out a hollow inside him, and he couldn't help wondering if Mac was right. He glanced into Mac's eyes and saw a flash of steel there. After tonight, he'd be more determined than ever to get back in the air and give Germany hell.

After walking back to the ward with Mac, Archie decided to have a wander through the hospital. It was in full swing as nursing staff and doctors bustled around. Every single operating theatre was in use. The deluge of admissions showed signs of slowing down, according to one doctor, although Archie learned there was a burgeoning queue for surgery. If only he'd dealt with his own medical emergency much sooner, he'd be helping out here tonight. He clenched his jaw.

The entire hospital staff had risen to the challenge admirably, and Archie could only stand and look on – a middle-aged man in a grey chalk suit, fit to burst with pride at the smooth operation and yet overshadowed by a growing darkness that threatened to swallow him whole. The scene before him hinted at an alternative future, a different path, and it was one which left a bitter taste. He squeezed his eyes shut. No, his course was set, and no matter what it took, he had to stand firm. Plastic surgery was his life and people depended on him, and he wasn't about to let anyone down, least of all himself. A knot grew and tightened in his gut.

How stupid and frivolous he'd been with his own prized asset. He'd been treading a tightrope for months. Now he had to swallow his own advice, words he regularly dished out to his boys, words that rang like bells in his head. Time was a healer, and patience a necessary virtue.

Archie stood surveying the scene in London Road. The Whitehall Cinema showed some damage at the front, but the foyer was a scene of utter devastation. Gold plush lay amidst twisted metal girders and masonry, still smouldering and dusty in the early morning light.

Patches of dark, dried blood spotted, streaked, and smeared the rubble, road, and pavements reddish-brown, no doubt where the bastards had cut them down with their blasted machine guns. He pictured the scene yesterday, and his stomach tightened.

ARP Wardens picked through the ruins along with police and Canadian troops, who had been drafted in to help from a nearby base, their grimy faces streaked with fatigue and sadness. Two fire trucks stood in the road and firemen aimed hoses at the building next to the Whitehall Cinema, dousing the smouldering rubble within. The fire had raged all through the night, one of the onlookers explained. Dirty grey-black trails sailed upward into a sterile blue sky, and acrid smoke drifted in the air.

Archie glanced at one of the wardens who stood amidst the rubble. His face was dubbed with black streaks, as were his hands, and his shoulders drooped.

'Any more survivors?'

The man took out a handkerchief and wiped some of the dust and black from his face. 'Not looking likely, I'm afraid. Brought the last beggar out in the early hours. Just digging through the rubble for the rest, but I don't give it much hope.' He shook his head.

Hope was such a strong word, and without it, there was nothing. Locals stood in the road alongside shopkeepers, a scene of white faces and hollow, dark eyes staring intently as if willing the rescuers to find more survivors. They all clung to hope, the final lifeline for anyone who remained buried beneath the carnage. Archie took one last look around and huffed out a breath. Perhaps the time for a miracle had passed. The Reverend from St. Swithun's Church swept past, chin held high, sombre-faced, dressed in his black cassock, his hands clutching the Holy Bible, pressed to his heart.

25

The Aftermath

A dark cloud hung over the ward. Latest figures revealed one hundred and three people lay dead while more than two hundred lay seriously injured. Mac had spent the last few days by Stella's bedside. She had a concussion and dizziness, but other than that she was fine.

Bea kept bursting into tears. She flicked out a crisp white sheet, which billowed up in the air like a sail, and waited for Lily to grab the other side before tucking it in. Mac listened as Bea poured out her heart. Her best friend had been killed, along with her younger sister when the Whitehall was hit. Bea had gone along to support Sarah's mother last night, who had to identify the bodies. Two daughters killed in an instant in that decisive moment when a Luftwaffe pilot jettisoned his bombs. Rather than destroy military targets, he'd opted for helpless, innocent civilians and children. There were plenty of open spaces around, and he had to choose this town.

'You should have seen it. Utter devastation, everywhere. It's a miracle anyone came out alive. Dead people lay in the middle of London Road, sprawled out, all dirty and bloodied. After we'd been to the garage, I stood and watched as they brought more people out of the Whitehall. And the children, limp like rag dolls, with dusty, bloodied faces and I thought – this can't be happening.' Her face crumpled as she sobbed into her hanky.

'Come on, Bea,' Pete said in a gentle voice. 'There's nothing you could have done. Those swine. Christ knows why the pilot didn't just dump the bombs in the Channel. That's what we do.'

'Yeah, except he had other ideas,' Mac said.

She sniffed and dried her eyes. 'I expect there's barely a soul in this town who didn't lose someone or knows someone who did. I know we're close to London, but up until now we've been lucky.'

'Here, get this down you.' Pete offered her a nip of whisky.

'Lord help us. Where did you have that hidden? Sister Jamieson will have your guts for garters. Beer's one thing, but spirits.' She glanced around the ward, but Sister was nowhere to be seen. Taking the glass, she downed the whisky in a single gulp. Her eyes widened, and she coughed.

'There you are, you see. That's the spirit.' Pete smiled. It was a warm, heartfelt smile, one that seemed to linger as they both gazed at each other. He offered her a clean handkerchief, and as she took it, their hands brushed.

'Thanks, Pete.' She dabbed her eyes before moving on to the next bed.

Mac strode across to the window and gazed out at the town, watching as smouldering black smoke rose and swirled up into the blue. To think that Stella had been caught up in that.

'So, Pete, what's the deal with you and Nurse Bea?'

'I don't have the faintest idea what you're talking about.' Pete cleared his throat, and a faint pink tinge coloured his cheeks.

'Well, are you asking her to the dance or not?' Mac took out a packet of John Player's and offered him a cigarette before taking one for himself.

Pete gazed wistfully at Bea. She was standing on the other side of the ward, and their eyes met. Her mouth curved up into a sweet smile. 'I may just do that.'

After four days in the hospital, Stella was discharged, and Mac called a cab and went with her to the station. 'I hate leaving you, honey. I wish I could take you home.' He folded her in his arms as the train steamed into view. He didn't want to leave her.

'I'll be fine, honestly. If only these dizzy spells would clear up.' She smiled.

'Yeah, well I'll call you tonight just to make sure you get home safe.' He pressed his lips to hers and pulled her close. 'I'll miss you.' He grabbed her bag and held open the door as she climbed up into the carriage, passing it to her.

'I'll miss you too.' She stood by the open window as Mac took her hand in his. The guard blew his whistle, and the train began to snort out of the station.

'Look after yourself, Mac.' She reached out quick and kissed him.

'Love you, honey. Take care.'

He walked briskly along the platform, holding her hand for as long as he could until the steam engine stole her away in a haze of swirling smoke, tearing her hand from his, surrendering him to a chasm of desolation. As he turned away and ambled back towards the town, he sighed and lowered his gaze. The last thing he wanted to be right now was sociable.

Mac lay on top of his bed, waiting for Bea to remove the dressings from his hands. The last operation had been successful, and the skin grafts had taken well.

'You were so lucky. They're so much better than when you first arrived. At least, everything works.' She grinned, putting the forceps down into the kidney dish on the dressing trolley. 'So, are you looking forward to the party?'

'Sure am.' He could hardly wait to be with Stella again. She was staying overnight, and he wondered if he could persuade her to go away for the weekend. His eyes lingered over the back of his hands, now a patchwork quilt of scars. 'How long does it take for scars to fade?'

'Oh, everyone's different. Time, give it time – it's a healer, you know.' She said it with a distant look in her eyes, and somehow Mac didn't believe her. She bustled away with her trolley, wheels screeching as metal instruments rattled in kidney dishes.

'Mac, I'm off to the Rose and Crown with Doug. Fancy a pint?' Pete shut the book he'd been reading with a thump.

'Sure.' Mac held his hands up in front of him. His fingers were straight, and a warmth radiated throughout his body. Squeezing the life of that small therapy ball had paid off. The Maestro had done a swell job, real neat. Off-key piano notes fractured the silence. The guys laughed, and one of them threw a piece of apple at the unsuspecting pianist, which bounced off the back of his head.

The walk into town was a sombre affair as they strolled along, golden sunlight streaming through the trees, dappling the pavement. They passed people on the street and were met by faces filled with despair or blank stares with an occasional half-smile.

'I reckon Bea's right. There's probably not a single soul untouched by the bombing.' Pete sighed, running a hand through his thick, brown hair.

Mac's stomach tightened. It had filled him with a rage worse than any fire. 'Yeah, I reckon he had a score to settle.' Jesus, it was the lowest thing. What kind of man did that? He sighed. Maybe one who had lost his own family in Germany.

The combined bomber offensive saw the RAF flying missions at night while USAAF flew daily. Operation Gomorrah began in June, and the Brits and the Americans had battered Hamburg day and night for an entire week. Tens of thousands had been reported dead and half a city levelled. It was one hell of a way to win a war. Mac pictured the scene from the air above – fires, smoke, and total devastation. Thousands of tonnes of bombs unleashed on the unsuspecting city. The heat from the flames would have been intense enough to melt anyone near and burn them up in an instant. A shiver zipped through him, and his mouth ran dry. The enemy would never cease, and he'd seen how far they were prepared to go. The consequences of not fighting were too great, and he had to push his conscience aside and close down mentally for the journey that lay ahead. His father always said war was dirty. There was no victory without suffering.

As they headed towards the Rose and Crown, they passed a jeweller's, and something in the window caught Mac's eye. 'You guys go on ahead. I'll catch you up.' He paused before opening the door and took a deep breath as he glanced at his hand. Maybe he should have worn gloves.

Too late now. His body stiffened, and he swallowed. The doc always said to look people in the eye. The shop bell tinkled above the door as he strode in and a middle-aged man buttoned up the jacket of his navy flannel suit as he stepped forward. 'Can I help you, sir?' His face creased into a warm smile as he looked Mac in the eye.

Mac smiled, and the tension ebbed away. 'Yeah, can you show me that locket, please?' He pointed to a gold heart-shaped pendant.

'Ah, yes.' The assistant brought out the tray. 'An excellent choice, sir. Solid gold, eighteen carats.' He placed the red velvet tray on top of the glass counter.

Mac gazed at the heart and pictured Stella wearing it. When the assistant handed it to him, he opened it up. It wasn't large, but it would still hold a portrait image. She'd love it. 'I'll take it, thanks.' He turned his gaze to the window. 'Actually, there's something else that caught my eye.'

'Oh, of course. Perhaps if sir could point it out please?' He stepped out from behind the counter and followed Mac to the window.

Fifteen minutes later, Mac re-emerged with two small, black velvet boxes. The price should have shocked him, but since his hospital stay, he'd saved a considerable sum. Besides, it was for Stella, so it was money well spent. He hoped he could persuade her to go away for the weekend. Pete had given him the details of a swell guest house and he'd already booked separate rooms. He smiled, still unable to believe she was finally his girl.

He caught up with the guys who were up ahead, having a smoke.

'You took your time. Buying up the store?' Pete laughed.

'Sorry, fellas, I spotted a little something else while I was there.'

'Yes, we all know you Yanks are overpaid.' Pete chuckled, slapping Mac on the back.

'Yeah, well they had to give us a sweetener for coming over here and flying these damn fool crazy missions. I don't know about you, but I need a drink.' Mac placed his hand in his tunic pocket, brushed it over the smallest box, and smiled. He'd surprise her with that one at the party.

'Here we are, lads.' Pete looked up at the sign on the front. 'The watering hole at last.'

Mac swung the door open, and a haze of food, beer, and cigarette smoke drifted out into the air and coaxed them inside.

Pete led the way to the bar. 'Hello, landlord. Three pints of your best bitter please,' he requested, smiling at the burly balding barman with a ruddy face. 'Oh, and er, can I have a straw with that please?'

The young barmaid smiled as she glanced at all three of them; her eyes lowered from Mac's as she perused his face and he promptly turned away from the bar. He didn't want people gawping, and he didn't want to be different. He heaved out a breath, figuring they had to look at least once. At least he still had all his fingers and thumbs, and they worked. Doug hadn't been so lucky. He almost escaped the flames, but stopped to rescue his injured radio operator before bailing out. Now he had to learn to use hands without fingers, although he still had thumbs. As the landlord placed their drinks on the bar, Pete popped the straw into a pint and Doug reached out with both hands, childlike, to gather up the glass.

'Enjoy your pints, lads. If you want any food, just let me know.' The landlord smiled at Doug, who hugged his pint glass to his chest with a strained look of concentration etched on his face.

'Thanks,' Doug said. They found a table next to the window, which overlooked the main street. The pub was quiet with only several people, but as Mac looked around, he couldn't help noticing they were attracting attention, although none of it hostile. Locals nodded and smiled. Ill at ease, Mac stared down at his glass and sipped his beer, convinced that all eyes were on him. Heat flashed up his neck and into his face. Before the accident, people had looked at him in the usual way, or girls stared in a flirtatious way. Now, he was different. An oddity. They all were, and they stood out from the crowd. Even now when he looked in the mirror to shave or caught sight of his reflection in a shop window, his heart sank, and he wondered if he'd ever adapt to being different. Bea had said time was a healer. He sucked in a breath and raised his chin.

Doug sipped his beer through the straw. 'Thank God my nose worked out okay.' He was relieved to be rid of his dangling pedicle. His face was a mass of scar tissue with new droopy eyelids revealing hooded eyes, and he had to raise his chin to see properly.

Pete glanced at it. 'Yes, you lucky bastard. Mine took two attempts. The first one dropped off and narrowly missed a drowning in my mug of tea.'

Mac and Doug glanced at one another and roared with laughter.

'It wasn't funny at the time, I can assure you, and Archie wasn't happy about it either. I've been plagued with rotten luck.'

Mac flicked a gaze at Pete's hands. Although not as severely burned as Doug's, he'd lost three fingers, and he always wore his tan leather gloves when out in public, even on a warm, summer's day.

A middle-aged couple sat close by and cast sour sideways glances at them. The woman whispered something to the man and he peered round, but when he caught Mac's eye, he quickly turned away. There was a screech as the woman scraped her chair back, and the couple brushed past Mac as they headed to the door.

'It shouldn't be allowed, not in public,' the woman said, an edge to her voice.

Mac could barely believe what he'd heard. *Were they that hideous?* His heart began to race, and he felt a flutter in his chest as anger surged. He sprang up, taking care to retain his composure.

'Excuse me, ma'am. There's something you should know.' Aware of the anger in his voice, he took a deep breath and clenched his hand into a fist as he fought to remain calm. 'We put our lives on the line to save people like you from Hitler's bombs and were burned in the process. Do you have any idea what it's like up there? At the very least you could show these boys a little respect, and if you can't bring yourself to bestow a little Christianity, then it might be best if you said nothing at all. Have a good day.'

Mac sank down on his chair and drained the last of his beer while his friends looked on with stunned expressions. The woman's cheeks flushed scarlet, and they scuttled out of the pub without another word.

'Well, that told them, old boy.' Pete laughed, taking out a silver cigarette case and offering it around.

Mac looked up. 'Landlord's coming about, eleven o'clock high.'

'Here, lads, get those down you.' He placed a tray on the table with three more pints.

They all stared in surprise, and Mac was taken aback by his generosity. 'Gee, thanks. We sure appreciate it, don't we boys?' He glanced at Pete and Doug, who nodded and muttered their thanks as they reached across the table to grab a glass each.

'Never mind what that woman said. Take no notice. I don't know who they are, but they're not from around here. The majority of us in this town are indebted to you lads, we are, so if anyone bothers you again, you tell me and I'll sort the devils out.' With that, the landlord smiled, tucked the tray under his arm, and returned to the bar.

Later that evening, Mac lay in bed amidst the snores and the occasional groans, and the night nurse with her pen scratching line after line in the notes while sat at the wooden desk in the middle of the ward, her lamp casting a golden narrow beam across the paper. He thought about the woman in the pub earlier. Revulsion had lain in her eyes. Jesus, that was a kick in the guts. It was dirty, it was low, and it was... The memory reared like a siren as the image flashed in his mind, and Mac clamped his eyes shut and pursed his lips. He was nine when a few of the older kids from school had dared him to call at Mr Bowers' place. He lived in an old ramshackle of a house on the edge of town. People said he was a veteran of the Great War, and when he finally returned from the fighting, he broke off his engagement and became a recluse. The boys swore he was some kind of ghoul.

Mac followed the dirt track up to his house as the sun beat down, baking the ground to a dry crust. He could almost taste the dust, and just as he reached up to rap at the door, it swung open with an eerie groan, and he saw him for the first time. Oh yeah, he really saw him. Then he understood. Whenever he'd seen him before, the old guy had looked different – not disfigured, just odd, with a face like porcelain that didn't move except for his eyes. In that moment, Mac realised he'd been going around town for years wearing a mask.

'Get outta here, damn fool kids,' the man hissed. He spat into the dirt right at Mac's feet. Frothy spit soaked into the earth's crust, leaving a dark stain, and Mac turned and fled. The boys laughed and jeered at the old man every time they saw him, and it was not until now that he realised the guy probably hadn't been old at all. He must have only been in his thirties or forties maybe. It seemed he'd had good reason to withdraw from the community and hide away. Gargoyle – that's what the boys called him.

Tears flooded his eyes, and the breath hitched in his throat. He swallowed. He had become Old Man Bowers, just like most of the guys here. He realised he had to accept it, and he had to atone. God says to love thy neighbour, well, he could do that. He sighed. Reality cut deep. One minute you're in demand as a serviceman, and the next you're disfigured and cast out; an abomination. Stella sailed into his mind and infused him with a honeyed glow. She always brought the light.

26

Moving Forward

Mac sat in the late afternoon sun waiting for Stella, agonising over the best way to ask her about spending the weekend with him. Maybe she would be offended. A group of Canadian soldiers lugging their bulging kitbags across the platform interrupted his thoughts. They must have had a furlough this weekend. A shrill whistle sang out, and a scarlet train swung around the bend and steamed into East Grinstead Station. The brakes squealed as it came to a halt and exhaled a plume of steam. The drift of burning coal and oil hung in the air as he strode across the platform.

Carriage doors swung open and for a minute, the platform was a sea of colour as people milled around. After all the doors had closed, the guard blew his whistle. Mac's heart thumped as his eyes darted left and right, and then as the smog of steam and smoke cleared, he saw her, standing near the end, her suitcase on the ground. She flashed that shy smile she had as he strode towards her and his heart lifted. He folded her in his arms, pressing his lips to hers right there as people all around looked on.

'I've missed you.' Dark shadows lurked beneath her eyes, and a faint yellow-brown bruise coloured her temple. Mac put his arm around her and drew her to his side. He'd never let anything hurt her again. On the way to the guest house, they walked through the park, stopping beneath an aged oak tree, where, unable to resist, he drew her close, and she giggled only to be silenced by his lips on hers. 'Stella, I was wondering if you'd come away with me this weekend to Hastings. I've always fancied seeing where old King Harold met his fate.'

She laughed. 'Actually the Abbey's inland at Battle.'

Mac rubbed his jaw. 'Right, well, maybe we could go *inland* and see it?' He said it in a mocking tone, flashing a grin. 'Pete told me about a sweet little guest house and before you say anything, we'll have separate rooms, of course.'

Stella gazed at him, nervously biting her lip. 'Mac, I'm not sure. My mother would faint if she found out.'

'But how's she gonna know?'

'Hastings does sound lovely. When?'

'Tomorrow morning. We can catch the ten o'clock train.'

'We're off to the party tonight, and I told Mrs Brown I'd be back on Saturday.'

'So, call her and tell her you won't, honey.' He grasped her hand, holding it firm, and picked up her bag.

'I'll take that.' She reached for the bag, but he shooed her hand away.

'I can handle it just fine.' He flashed a reassuring smile. 'So, how about it?'

Her face was blank.

'Hastings.'

'Oh, all right then.' She gazed up at him from beneath long lashes.

'Gee, I sure am the luckiest guy around.' He beamed, kissing her quickly on the lips, enjoying the smile that swept across her face like a breeze. 'Come on, let's get you settled in at that guest house. It's only a short walk.' He wouldn't tell her that he'd already booked the rooms in Battle.

'Where's the party tonight?'

'Oh, it's at the home of Mr and Mrs Chester. They're the doc's friends, and they live nearby. Most of the boys are going.'

'Sounds smashing. I hope they know what they're letting themselves in for,' she said, laughing.

After checking in at the guest house, Mac carried Stella's case upstairs and placed it on the single bed. He strode across to the window. 'Hey, you got tombstones for company.' He sank into the chair, removed his crush cap, and unfastened his tunic jacket. 'Sure is warm.' He glanced at Stella. She seemed a little quiet, and he hoped his presence in her room wasn't making her too uncomfortable. 'It's not a bad room.'

'No, it's nice.' She gazed out of the window. 'Thanks for meeting me. I hope your hands aren't sore after carrying my bag.' She cast a half-smile and then opened her tunic jacket.

She suited blue. It brought out the colour of her green eyes. 'I'm okay, quit worrying about me.' He reached for her hand and pulled her towards him, easing her down on his lap. 'How about you let me do all the worrying?' Over the past couple of months, he'd watched as she'd blossomed from a shy, young girl into a strong, beautiful woman, yet sometimes he saw a shadow of insecurity and he longed to scoop her up and take her away from all this. He leaned in to kiss her, slipping his arm around her waist, resting his hand on her shapely thigh. She gasped, and a mini electric current zipped right through him, and when she threaded her fingers through his hair, his skin tingled. Time to rein it in. He broke away, placing a final peck on her nose.

'Well, I guess I'd better leave you to unpack. I'll pick you up about seven o'clock tonight.'

'You don't have to go right now, do you?'

He flicked a gaze at her. The afternoon light framed her silhouette with a golden glow. God, she was beautiful. 'I'm afraid I do because I don't trust myself.' He smiled and paused as they looked at one another, unspeaking, a rosy glow suffusing her cheeks.

'Oh, Mac, your cap,' she rushed over to him.

'Thanks.' He drew her close and kissed her lips as he closed his eyes, lost in a dreamy haze, sensing her warm, slender body moulded to his. 'Sorry, I couldn't resist.'

'I'm glad you did.'

'Well, I really am going this time. See you at seven.' He took her hand and pressed it to his lips as he dreamt of a time when he wouldn't have to say goodbye.

At seven o'clock prompt, Mac knocked on her door, and when it swung open, he whistled.

'Wow, honey, you're an absolute knockout.'

Her hair curled softly about her shoulders, spilling onto her navy-blue evening dress with a matching wrap. His gaze slipped over her defined waist, and he couldn't help noticing the way her dress draped over her hips and accentuated her hourglass figure. He smiled when he saw how her cheeks blushed scarlet. She really had no idea how beautiful she was.

'Say, have you seen a cute little WAAF around here? I left her a couple of hours ago.' He smirked. 'Didn't I see you in a movie?'

'Mac.' She laughed, and a wide grin tugged at the corners of her mouth.

'There's just a little something missing.' He pulled a small velvet box from his tunic pocket and flipped it open.

Stella gasped. 'Oh, Mac. It's beautiful. You shouldn't have.'

He smiled and took the gold heart-shaped locket and placed it around her neck. 'There, perfect.'

She gazed in the mirror admiringly, and as Mac dipped his head and brushed her neck with a silken kiss, she tingled.

The Chesters had a grand country home. Smart, manicured lawns stretched up towards the house, and as they strolled along the tree-lined drive, the heady floral scent of rhododendrons rose to greet them. The front door was open wide, and voices drifted out, bubbling over musical notes into the sweet, evening air. Mac steered Stella inside, and they stepped into a spacious hall with a black and white tiled floor.

Piano music flowed from another room, and Mac spotted familiar faces among the crowd. The musk of cigarette smoke blended with beer and flowed through the house. A group of guys chatting burst out laughing, all except for one. He had no lips to smile with, and his face remained expressionless, but his shoulders heaved up and down, and his body shook. Yeah, he was laughing all right.

'Ah, another one of Mr McIndoe's fellows, I presume.' A tall, middle-aged man smoking a cigar descended the sweeping oak staircase. He buttoned up his navy suit jacket and held out his hand, 'Alistair Chester. Welcome.'

Mac shook his hand. 'Thank you for the invitation, sir. You have a beautiful home.'

'It's very kind of you to say so. Well, enjoy your evening.' Mr Chester smiled at Stella. 'There's a bar in the dining room, just over there.' He pointed the way, and Mac glimpsed a waiter in a white jacket standing behind a real bar, pouring a drink for a lady in a black cocktail dress.

'Look, Archie's here.' Stella pointed at a group of men who stood in the middle of the room, chatting.

'Oh, yeah. That's John Hunter with him, one of the anaesthetists. The guys call him the gasworks.'

Stella grinned. Archie's jolly laugh pierced through the hubbub of voices and true to form, the Maestro was holding court, with guests hanging on his every word. Mac glimpsed Pete, Doug, and Dickie, who were chatting to some very glamorous-looking girls.

Stella glanced around. 'How generous of them to open their home like this.'

Mac plucked two drinks from a waiter's silver tray as he sauntered by. They stood for a few minutes, sipping punch while they listened to the piano music drifting in from the next room.

'I love classical music,' Mac said.

'So do I.' Stella smiled. 'That's something we have in common.'

'I bet we have a whole heap of stuff in common.'

'How can you tell?'

'I just know.'

She gazed intently into his eyes. The pianist ceased to play and a minute later, 'In The Mood' swung out, casting an air of energy throughout the house, and people leapt up to dance. A disfigured young airman asked a svelte brunette in a red floral dress if she would like to dance. She took his outstretched hand as he twirled her around. Archie danced with Mrs Chester and Mac caught sight of Pete twirling Bea around the floor and smiled to himself. He knew she was sweet on him.

'Shall we?' Mac put his glass down and held out his hand.

'I thought you'd never ask.'

He drew Stella close and gazed dreamily into her eyes, which tonight burned bright with an intensity he'd never seen before. She seemed different all of a sudden – more assured. Her blonde hair glinted beneath the grand crystal chandelier. The other people, sights, and sounds faded into the background. Damn, there was no denying it. He loved her, body and soul, and although he longed to marry her, the last thing he wanted was for her to be left alone, maybe with his child. He nuzzled the top of her head as she rested against his chest.

As musical notes melted away, Archie strode over flashing a wide grin. 'It's lovely to see you again, my dear. How are you?'

'I'm absolutely fine, thank you. Fully recovered.'

'Well, that's a relief, because I've got a favour to ask.' He raised his eyebrows and glanced at Mac. 'Didn't I say she was a fighter?'

'You sure did, doc.'

'Stella, would you sing for us? You have such a beautiful voice, and it's such a shame to waste it.'

She smiled and a rosy glow tinted her cheeks. 'Just the one, then.'

'Splendid. Come this way.'

They followed Archie into the drawing room, and he introduced Stella to the pianist. She opted to sing 'The

White Cliffs of Dover,' watching as Mac ambled across the room to chat with a couple of the guys from the ward. As Stella sang the first words, a hush descended, and people looked up, while others moved closer to listen, but Stella kept her eyes on Mac. His heart swelled, and the hairs at the nape of his neck bristled. When the song ended, she bowed while everyone applauded, but her most enthusiastic supporter was Archie, who smiled so broadly his cheeks must have ached.

'Doesn't she have a beautiful voice, Mac?' Archie slapped him on the back.

'She sure does.'

'Well done, my dear. Have you ever thought of singing professionally?'

'Oh, I don't think I'm that good.'

'Nonsense. You're a natural. It's worth considering, if you're ever at a loss. Perhaps once this war's over.'

'Are you propositioning my girl, doc? She isn't going to have time for that anyway, not with what I've got planned.' Mac cast a knowing smile, and he took Stella's arm and led her outside into the garden. Alone at last. The late evening sky grew scarlet, with a streak of peacock-green, as the light remained while the setting sun clung to this side of heaven.

'It's a beautiful night.' Stella turned her face to where a star glittered all alone.

'It sure is from where I'm standing.' He smiled coyly, losing himself in emerald green. He took a deep breath. 'Stella, there's something I have to say. I'm having another operation next week, and that might be all I need for some time.'

'What do you mean?'

'Well, after that the doc says he can discharge me, so they'll be sending me back to my squadron.' Her face fell, and he drew her to him and wrapped his arms around her. 'You know I have to do this.'

'I know.' Her voice was thin and high. 'Only I can't bear the thought of it.' She squeezed her arms around him.

'At least I'll be near you again, and we can see each other as often as we can. It's been killing me being so far away.' His lips brushed the top of her head, and she began to tremble. Was she crying? 'Hey, honey. Look at me.' He cupped her chin with his hand, and slowly she turned her face to his. Her misted eyes glinted with the last vestiges of light.

'Please, Mac. Don't ask them to take you back. Do something else. Anything except flying.'

He stiffened. 'If I don't do this, I'll regret it for the rest of my life.'

Her face reddened, and she stepped away from him and wrapped her arms around herself, her ruby lips settled into a tight line.

If only he could make her understand. His chest tightened as he slipped his hand into his jacket pocket and grasped the small velvet box. 'I can't explain it. I don't want to do it. I *have* to do it because it's my duty. It's the only way to make sure we win this war.'

'But why *you*? You could be safe.'

He heaved out a breath and gazed up into the sky as if he could pluck an answer from among the sailing clouds. Safe.

'Were you safe caught up in the bombing? You sheltered just around the corner from a direct hit.' Red drained to soft pink as her eyes widened. 'You were nearly killed, Stella. No one's safe anymore, and it's up to us to do something about it.'

He closed his eyes for a few seconds and Bill's face slipped into view, wearing that grin of his that stretched from ear to ear when he heard the news he was a father. His words sang. *I have a son.* A son he would never see. Jesus. A savage pain squeezed Mac's chest, catching his breath, and he uncurled his fingers from velvet and dragged his hand from his pocket. He couldn't do that to her. This was hard enough, and it was crushing her. He couldn't make promises. Not yet. He folded her in his arms and nuzzled her hair. Piano music drifted out through the open windows, velvety notes. 'Clair de Lune,' he murmured. And it would have been so perfect. 'I love you so much, and I always will.'

Stella sniffed. 'I'm scared. I do understand, really.'

He cradled her against him. She didn't have to explain. They were all scared. How could you not be when everything was so uncertain?

'I love you, Mac.'

Four silken syllables, heaven-sent. He closed his eyes. 'You're my girl, always will be.'

27

Battle, Conflict & Love

'I can't wait to get there. It's been a while since I spent time by the ocean.' Mac laughed. 'Although I've sure flown over it plenty.'

Flying. An icy prickle crept across her back, and she shivered. The party had been perfect yesterday until he mentioned returning to Bassingbourn. The way his eyes had flashed when she begged him not to do it surprised her. An empty hollow grew inside her as she realised that a desk job for someone like Mac would be soul-destroying.

'Which train is it?' Mac's voice broke her from her reverie.

'Sorry? Oh, we'll have to check,' Stella said, a little flustered. 'I thought you had this all worked out?'

'I figured I could leave that to you, what with me being a foreigner in a strange land.' His face creased into a broad smile, his blue eyes twinkling.

The train was just drawing into the station. With tickets hastily purchased at the ticket office, they dashed across the platform. On board it was heaving, and a large number of Canadian servicemen spilled out of overflowing carriages and lined the narrow corridor. The guard ushered Stella and

Mac through the sea of khaki, squeezing past men and kitbags, into a compartment near the rear where there were two free seats. Stella wedged herself between a vicar and a middle-aged woman travelling with a little girl. Opposite, two Canadian officers sat slouched, one of whom was asleep. Mac stowed their bags in the overhead luggage rack before sitting next to them, away from the window.

Stella cast a sideways glance at the woman next to her, who was reading *Life* magazine with a picture of Clark Gable on the cover. Hollywood glamour had arrived in England, what with Gable now serving as a gunner with the Eighth Air Force. There was no escaping the war. She turned her gaze to the window as the Ashdown Forest flashed by. Half an hour later, they huffed into Battle.

Mac hailed a taxi outside to take them to the guest house. Hastings and the surrounding area had taken a pasting since the war began, with the Luftwaffe bombers jettisoning bombs on their return home. More recently, two hotels had been reduced to rubble in a bombing raid, killing and injuring some Canadian troops stationed there, along with many civilians. Stella recalled reading the news in the paper while visiting Mac in the hospital.

The guest house lay within the gaze of the abbey and had a country cottage feel. After checking in, they found their rooms, and Mac followed Stella into hers.

'What a lovely view,' she said, gazing out of the window at the church. To her right, she could just see the abbey. 'Such a pity we can't see it properly. I had no idea it was being used as a military hospital.'

Mac laughed and drew her close, brushing his lips across the top of her head. 'You couldn't be any more perfect if you tried.'

Stella's cheeks glowed, and her heart quickened as she drank in his woody scent. She loved being in his arms, loved his touch, his smell, everything about him. Mac pressed his lips to hers, and she softened in his arms, kissing him back, her breath mingling with his. His hands moved down her back, coming round to skim upwards over her hips and then up towards her breasts. Stella gasped as he slipped his tongue into her mouth, and he pulled her even closer to him, his desire for her all too evident. He kissed her neck, drifting down to her chest before stopping himself.

'We can't do this, not yet, not here.' He dragged a hand through his hair and huffed out a sigh.

'No, I suppose not.' A heaviness caught her chest, and she turned away.

'Jeez, Stella, it's not that I don't want to. The truth is, I'm dying to, you know, it's just I wouldn't want you to think I was taking advantage.' He glanced down at the floor as a faint red glow coloured his face. 'Why don't you get freshened up and we'll go out for something to eat?' He headed to the door. 'Come and get me when you're ready, honey.'

Hmm, she was ready now. Talk about a hasty retreat. She sank down on the bed, then fell backwards, and lay staring at the ceiling. *For heaven's sake, what's it going to take? So much for being oversexed!* She sighed. An image of Jean flashed in her mind. Poor girl. A life snuffed out before barely having a chance to live it. Stella had an overwhelming urge to grasp life and live each day as if it might be the last, whereas Mac seemed to be holding back, although she understood why. She sighed and began to unpack.

Later that evening after an excellent meal in a local pub, they strolled along High Street, arm in arm. It was half past nine and still light, the sun dipping down in the west, the horizon nibbling at it piece by piece. Mac hadn't said much in the pub and Stella had noticed some people staring, although nothing was said, but he was clearly uncomfortable. A shadow had passed over his face, then when he looked into her eyes he cast that half-smile and chased it away. People were bound to stare, it was only natural, and they had to get used to seeing the scars, just as Mac had to.

They slipped past Battle Abbey, the custodian of the town, and wandered into the churchyard where they found a seat and sat down. He draped his arm around her shoulders as she snuggled up to him. She loved the softness of his tunic, the clean smell of him, the press of his warm, firm thigh against hers. The sky was awash with colour and in the distance, black specks buzzed as the sound of Merlin engines filtered in. The dark shapes grew and merged into a squadron of Spitfires, probably heading back to their base.

'Your guys.' Mac watched until black faded into the twilight sky.

'You wish you were up there, don't you?'

'The only place I want to be is here, with you.' He leaned in and kissed her. 'Since the first time I saw you, I knew you were the girl for me.'

'You did?' A smile tugged at her mouth.

'I sure did.'

Stella's neck warmed. 'How did you know? I mean, when you saw me at the dance, I could have been anyone, a spy perhaps.' She laughed.

'You, a spy? Man, that's cute.' She thumped his leg. 'Hey!' He turned to face her, taking her head in his hands, his face serious. 'I just knew. It was a hunch, and something whacked me hard out of the blue, and I couldn't take my eyes off you. I knew you had another guy, but it didn't matter, not when you looked into my eyes that first time. And if I'm honest, that's when I knew for sure, and I wanted to hold you in my arms and never let you go.'

'Which you did as I literally ran into you.'

'Yeah, you were heaven-sent all right.' Mac pressed his lips to hers. 'I love you so much I can't bear to be without you.' He pulled her to her feet, and she nestled against his chest as he wrapped his arms around her, enveloping her in safety, a place she longed to remain forever.

The next day after breakfast, they took a taxi to Hastings. Mac gaped as they passed mountains of rubble strewn amidst rows of Georgian and Victorian buildings. Ugly barbed wire blocked off the beach, and the pier, closed since the war began, seemed desolate now that a twenty-five-foot section of it had been demolished – all part of the coastal defences in case of an invasion.

They went to the Cutter Inn for lunch and afterwards they strolled along to the beach, the fresh, briny breath of the ocean warm on their faces. They found a seat, and Mac slipped his arm around Stella, drawing her to his side as they gazed out to sea. All along the seafront, a stream of khaki and RAF blue marched along in twos and threes, their faces upturned to the sun. The ocean glinted like diamonds and a Royal Navy destroyer bearing the White Ensign at the stern danced close to the shimmering horizon. Mac flicked a gaze at the anti-aircraft gun which overlooked the beachhead.

An older couple walked by, gawping at him, and Mac squirmed and turned his head away. 'Jeez, could they make it any more obvious? Haven't they seen injured people before? God, I hate this.'

Stella caught his hand and held it tight. He blew out a breath and looked into her eyes as anger thundered through his veins. She smiled. Man, that smile – so pure, brimming with promise. She deserved the best and yet she'd settled for him. The thunder calmed as he drew her towards him, his eyes fixed on hers. She gave him strength and courage when he needed it most. It lay in her touch and flickered in her eyes, and she dazzled him each time she smiled.

As she rested her head on his shoulder, a droning noise filtered in and a dark speck sailed into focus from across the sea, growing, sputtering, and belching out black smoke.

Stella looked up. 'Oh, Lord, it's a Spitfire.'

Mac grabbed her arm. 'Move, now!' He half dragged her, forcing her to run with him to the other side of the road. 'Come on.' When they reached the other side, he spun round. The Spitfire had descended and the pilot made a sweeping turn as he lined up for his approach.

'He's gonna land her on the beach. Jeez, he's got no landing gear.'

Stella looked on, her heart hammering her ribs and it seemed as if everything went silent. The breath caught in her throat as the Spitfire belly landed with a dull thud, and slid along a stretch of beach, spraying a dust storm of sand in its wake.

'Wait here.' Mac sprinted across the road, followed by several Canadian servicemen and together, they breached the barriers and ran towards the aircraft. Stella froze to the spot, her heart racing as her gaze followed Mac.

A crowd of people drew near to watch, and she followed, crossing the road, oblivious to the oncoming cars, most of which had stopped as the drivers got out to watch the unfolding drama. The Spitfire slumped in the sand, the canopy still closed. Thick black smoke swirled and puffed upward, forming a blanket of cloud above and around the crash site, shrouding her view. She picked out the shapes of men moving around and saw someone climb onto the port wing and prise open the Perspex hood. The breeze blew and cleared the scene long enough for her to glimpse Mac crouched on the wing with one of the Canadians. Between the two of them, they hoisted the pilot from his seat, dragging him clear of the cockpit and lowering him down into waiting arms.

'Watch out for the mines,' a soldier yelled.

Stella couldn't see Mac any more as scores of people moved and blocked her view, all vying to see as black smoke swirled upward, thick, choking, the acrid smell flooding her nostrils. All seemed still – until the explosion. She jumped at the deafening roar, and a river of adrenaline surged through her body as bright orange flames lashed out through the black. Her knees buckled, and she sank to the ground, numb as people charged in all directions. She snatched at breaths as pain gripped her chest. Open-mouthed, she stared at the beach. Several men shook their heads.

'Please, God, no.' Tears welled in her eyes and the blood whooshed through her ears. 'Mac,' she whispered, staring straight ahead at the palls of smoke. Seconds sailed into minutes and as she gazed into the road, she swore the small boy lay there with fear glazed in his eyes. She began to tremble.

'Honey, are you all right?' Mac crouched down next to her, and she fell into his arms, sobbing. He stroked her hair, and whispered soothing shushes in her ear, and for a few seconds, she could hardly believe he was safe.

'I couldn't see you. You vanished. I thought... ' She broke off, her words drowned out by sobs.

Mac held her close. 'It's all right; I'm here in one piece. Shh, don't cry, honey.' He reached into his pocket and pulled out a handkerchief. 'Here you go, dry your eyes and I'll take you back to the guest house.' His face was smeared with grime, and the acrid smell of smoke clung to his uniform, his hands ingrained with dirt and grease. 'The pilot's pretty beat up, but he'll live.'

'All thanks to you.' She sniffed.

'The damn canopy was jammed. Poor guy couldn't get out.'

'But you could have been... ' She stopped herself and swallowed. He was a hero, and the relief she felt overwhelmed her. He took her hand and pulled her to her feet.

When they reached the guest house, Mac led her straight to her room. 'Maybe you should have a rest, you're in shock. I'll get you some tea.'

'Don't leave me. I don't want to be alone.' She looked at him, misty-eyed. 'Please Mac, just hold me.'

He held her gaze, pushed the door shut behind him, and reached for her outstretched hand. He led her to the bed and lay down, shuffling across to make room for her. She turned to face him as he cradled her in his arms.

'I thought I'd lost you, and I couldn't bear it.' She gazed into his eyes as he stroked the hair away from her face and dabbed the fresh tears from her cheek. He leaned in and pressed his lips to hers, soft and gentle, and Stella gave way to the passion that had been building inside her like a volcano. He kissed her neck and moved down to unbutton her shirt, kissing her chest.

Stella gasped. 'Make love to me.'

He raised his eyes to hers. 'Are you sure?'

She pulled him to her, kissing him more passionately than ever, exploring the softness of his mouth with her tongue. With his lips still on hers, he unfastened his shirt, his fingers fumbling with buttons. He stood up, unbuckled his belt, and dropped his trousers to the floor. Taking Stella by the hand, he pulled her up towards him, planting a soft kiss on her brow. She slipped her hands inside his shirt and eased it slowly over his shoulders, the sleeves skimming his arms before it swished to the floor. As she gazed into his eyes, a fierce intensity burned there, and he pressed his lips to hers, firm, with fresh hunger.

Unhurriedly, he traced his finger across the swell of her breasts, then eased her shirt off. He unzipped her skirt and moved closer, stretching his arms around her back to release her bra. He gasped.

'You're so beautiful.' He kissed her breast before scooping her up in his arms and laying her softly on the bed. Her heart pounded faster as the blood surged through her body. Thank heavens she was wearing the cream satin underwear and not those awful regulation woollen knickers.

Never before had she been so exposed and yet uninhibited, about to do what suddenly seemed so natural. It was an urge that had swelled like a high tide and was poised to crash. As she caressed Mac's chest, she marvelled at the muscular contours and slid her hand down across his ribs and in towards his navel. He gasped, and his warm breath caressed her neck as he kissed her ear, sending a shiver through her entire body. He slid his hand down her

her cheek, and then his mouth was on hers, a long, lingering kiss before he rolled onto his back, cradling her in his arms.

'I love you,' he said, catching his breath.

'I love you too.' She felt a slight chill and pulled the blanket over them as they lay watching the sunset through the window. Hues of salmon pink and lilac infused the sky. 'I never expected it to be like that.' She felt a lump in her throat, feeling so in love and loved.

'Like what, honey?'

'Perfect.'

Later that night, Stella was unable to sleep, and she lay listening to crumps in the distance, along with the ack-ack bursting into the darkness as aircraft droned into the night. The south-east coast was getting a pasting. Naked, she rose and tiptoed to the window. Startled by another crump, a fiery glow rose in the distance, illuminating the horizon, and then Mac was behind her, his firm body warm against hers, his arms slipping around her, and she leaned into his muscular chest. 'I wonder where it's happening tonight.' She stroked his leg, marvelling at the sparse covering of wiry hairs across his muscular thigh.

'Looks like it's on the coast. Could be Hastings, although I reckon it's a little further east. Jerry getting rid of the surplus before they fly home.' He kissed the top of her head.

'Mac, I can't bear to think of you flying again.' She hugged him tight.

'Whoa there, you're crushing the life outta me, woman.' He laughed, cupping her chin with his hand as he brushed his lips over hers. 'I love you more than anyone else in the world, but I came here with a job to do. And now I've got you to come home to, you can be sure I'll do whatever it takes.'

'Promise me you'll come back.'

'Stella, I hope I will, but you know I can't promise anything.'

'I need you to. Please.' She laid her head on his chest, which rippled on the wave of his deep sigh.

'I promise I'll do my best. I'd do anything for you, you know that.' He brushed her head with his lips.

Anything except take a desk job. A numbness crawled into the hollow of her stomach. If only they could stay like this, or just have another day or two together. She clutched at time greedily, of course, time waited for no one and invariably ran out. She closed her eyes, drinking in the smell of him, his warmth on her skin, imprinting every inch of his being in her memory to cherish later. But it would never be enough. She wrapped her arms around him, breathing him in as an unsettling darkness grew inside her.

'Wait right there, honey.' Mac prised himself away, strode over to his jacket and pulled something from the pocket.

As he sauntered back, wearing nothing but his shorts, warmth flooded her entire body. She flicked a glance at the jewellery box in his hand, and her heart raced. He led her to the bed and sat down beside her.

'Stella, I've loved you from the very first moment I saw you across that crowded dance hall, and I've been waiting, hoping ever since.' He stroked her face with his right hand, then cupped her chin, brushing her lips with his. 'I love you so much it hurts, and I never want to be parted from you again.' He got down on bended knee and took her left hand in his. 'Stella Charlton, would you do me the honour of becoming my wife?' He flipped the box open.

The breath hitched in Stella's throat at the diamond that captured the incandescence of the moonlight. 'Oh, Mac.' Tears welled in her eyes. 'Yes, yes I will.'

Mac plucked the gold ring from its velvet perch, and as he slipped it on her finger, a bond like a silken ribbon wrapped itself around them, binding them together at last.

'My mother will think I'm mad – we hardly know one another.'

Mac's smile faded, and he held her hands. 'I know you. You're the gal that walks through my dreams. It's your face I see each night before I fall asleep and each morning when I wake. And when I'm flying, you're right there with me through the clouds, across the Channel, following the glint of the Loire River all the way and back again. You're in here.' He patted his heart.

A single tear pearled on Stella's lower eyelashes, wet, tickling, and bounced onto her cheek. Mac gently brushed it away.

'I can't make it without you. I can't do any of this without you, honey.' His dark blue eyes bore into her soul, and his brow furrowed, each ripple carrying the burden and grief of war.

A vice clamped her heart, and she swallowed as she lifted her hand to cup his cheek. 'You don't have to. I'll be with you every step of the way.'

As Mac drifted off to sleep, the sounds all around became acutely sharp. The whoosh of a passing car, voices followed by laughter. Footsteps tip-tapped along the corridor, then a bang as a door slammed. Outside the wind blew the trees, and the leaves cackled back, but he didn't mind. He was flying. The old Curtiss Jenny was light and lithe in his hands, soaring over the prairie beneath the burning sun. Soaring into a fog, dark and thick, slipping into the freezing cockpit of the *Texas Rose*. A familiar voice buzzed in his ear and then a suffocating heat consumed him, and he gasped just as a hand reached out and pulled him close, and he danced with the girl with blonde hair and green eyes. With a start, he woke to find Stella's hand upon his chest, smoothing out his metal dog tags, her lips formed to speak as she shushed him, her eyes on his, soothing. His breathing was rapid and shallow, and his gaze darted all around, but no one else was there. He focused on her sunflower eyes and sucked in slow, deep breaths as his breathing steadied.

'You cried out,' she whispered.

Beads of sweat formed on his brow. He sat up and planted his feet on the cool, wooden floorboards. Stella padded across to the window and heaved up the sash. A cool breeze flowed and wrapped itself around him. Mac sniffed – the familiar perfume of the Beauty Shop, roasted flesh, would it ever leave?

Stella got a handkerchief and wiped his brow. God, what must she be thinking? 'Thanks,' he muttered, taking hold of her hand and pulling her towards him. He buried his head against her chest as she wrapped her arms around him and he caught the floral scent of her skin and drank it in. The night held the memories, releasing them in pieces like ghosts. An icy chill draped across his shoulders, and he lay back, his head sinking into the pillows, pulling Stella down beside him.

He closed his eyes as she rested her head on his chest. It was moments such as these when he wondered what he was doing going back to the 91st, risking everything he had. He kissed the top of her head. 'I love you, Stella, more than anything.'

'More than flying?'

He gave her a squeeze. 'I reckon that's a whole different kind of love, but yeah, more than flying.'

She snuggled into him without another word. His body was heavy and ached for peace, though as much as he tried, he couldn't sleep. His heart sank at the thought of leaving her again. Service life kept you all bound up in rules and duty and snatching snippets of happiness like this wasn't much, but it was priceless.

28

An Uncertain Farewell

Archie propped the door wide open as a group of lads jostled by with three of the new recruits as chaperones. 'Off to the pub, boys?' He grinned as they strolled along, linking arms with beautiful girls who seemed to have eyes only for them. The air thrummed with energy, like Spitfires raring for the off.

'How did you guess, Maestro? Care to join us?' an airman asked.

'I'd love to, but I'm afraid there's work to be done. Another time, lads.' Archie smiled. No doubt the girls would boost their confidence a treat. He'd told Blackie it was a cracking idea, even if it had appeared to be a little mad. Trawling the West End. Goodness knows what people must have thought. There had been some raised eyebrows, whisperings, and disapproving looks. He smirked. Two older men chatting up young women.

Of course, Blackie had faltered about the quest and quite rightly so. But, as Archie had explained, it was all in aid of a good cause. Besides, the lads would feel more comfortable on the arm of beautiful girls rather than nurses.

He glanced around and spotted Mac slouched on his bed, squeezing the devil out of a therapy ball. 'Morning, Mac. How are you?'

'Couldn't be better, doc.'

'And how's Stella?'

'Swell. I asked her to marry me.' He flashed a broad grin.

'And?' Archie's eyes widened.

'She said yes, of course.' Mac laughed.

'Well done. Congratulations. So, when's the big day?'

'Oh we haven't talked about it yet, but we will just as soon as I get out of here.'

Archie slapped him on the back. Another success story. Some of the boys had dates, one or two others were going to be married. Obviously whatever he was doing here was working. A warm glow spread inside him. 'Well, I expect an invitation.'

'Really? You'd come?'

'Try stopping me.' A smile tugged at his mouth. 'Well, I'd best have a look at you if you're in a hurry to escape.' Although the last operation had been a success and Mac had more hand function than before, a degree of stiffness persisted in the fingers. If only the results had been a little better. Of course, he'd known Mac was never going to have perfect hands, though he'd hoped for a slightly better result than this. He heaved out a sigh, then pursed his lips.

His own surgery had been a success, thankfully. He'd been lucky. He examined Mac's face; the new skin graft had taken well. He'd used a piece of undamaged skin from the underside of the other arm this time. 'The face is looking far better, healing very well, and we've managed to remove most of the thicker scar tissue.'

'Will I still be badly scarred?'

'Oh yes, but it's a damn sight better than it was.'

Mac's smile faded and his brow furrowed as he dragged a hand through his hair.

'I'm pleased with it. Excellent progress.' Archie patted Mac's shoulder and nodded. 'Keep applying the cream. It helps the skin to heal and reduces the scarring a little.' Archie scanned the medical notes. 'Let's take a look.' He took Mac's outstretched hands and examined them in detail. 'Grip my hands, as hard as you can.'

Mac gripped them, a look of concentration on his face.

'Steady on! I see you've been working hard. By Jove, you must be squeezing the heck out of that ball.' Archie chuckled. 'Now, you'll remember that I mentioned the need for further surgery. The good news is, I don't think that we have to do anything right now, although in time you'll require more work on those hands.'

'Thanks, doc.' Mac grinned, his eyes crinkling at the edges. 'I guess I can abandon those damn splints too.'

'Oh, yes. They've done their job. Well then, there doesn't seem to be much keeping you here. I don't suppose you'd care to reconsider?' Archie studied him, his eyebrows raised.

'Reconsider? Oh, you mean, will I change my mind?'

'Well, you could have a successful and rewarding career down here on earth, and I hear that even the Mighty Eighth is short of good fellows to keep everything running smoothly. Why don't you give it some more thought?' Of course, Archie realised it was hopeless. A flyer didn't want to do anything else, and wings burned in the boy's heart.

'I hear what you're saying, Maestro, only the thing is, I owe it to my crew to get back on the horse, and I never finished my tour.' Intensity flared in Mac's eyes.

'The problem is, Mac, that no matter what you do, your hands will never be as dexterous as before. You might think you can manage one of those heavy bombers you boys fly, but once you're up, there's no going back. All you can do is get on with it and when the going gets tough, well, I can't vouch for what comes next.'

Richard Hillary slipped into his mind, drawing with him an icy chill. Archie wasn't confident that Mac was up to flying those heavy bombers, in truth, and all he could do was hope that the MO made the right decision.

'I understand. I won't take any risks, doc. I'll make sure I can handle the ship before they pack me off on a mission. Besides, I'll have a co-pilot, and eight crew.'

Archie studied him for a moment. He often pondered over the act of fixing these boys up, only to send them back to war. Richard Hillary had been unfortunate and had persevered to the point of despair. It didn't help that the Allied Forces kept the pressure up, demanding the return of their men as soon as possible, if they were fit enough. Yes, good men were in short supply these days. A hollowness crept into Archie's stomach. 'Mac, just make me one promise. Don't struggle or suffer in silence. Any problems, no matter how small, telephone me right away. Is it a deal?'

'Sure, doc. It's a deal.'

Archie slapped him on the back. 'Right, well I'll write to your commanding officer. You'll need to see the MO, of course, and pass a medical, and then it's in their hands, but I wish you the best of luck. Let's see now, if you stay on until tomorrow, you'll be able to catch the morning train to London and then change for Cambridge. I'll telephone the base so they know to expect you.' Archie reached out to shake Mac's hand.

'Thanks, Archie. I appreciate everything you've done for me and Stella.'

'Yes, well, just take care of yourself, and that young lady of yours. And if you have any further problems at all while you're still in England, remember, my door's always open. You only need to ask.'

Archie stood up to leave and paused. 'Keep in touch, Mac. Drop me a line here and there and let me know how you're getting on, and remember, keep the gloves on, always.' He pointed skyward, flashing a smile.

Leaving another patient, sending him back to a normal life, would ordinarily offer him such satisfaction. But now, in the midst of war, such farewells provided a mere taste of that and quickly soured. It felt hopeless in a sense, especially knowing they were never fully healed, least of all mentally. He had no doubt the American military would welcome Mac with open arms.

Archie strode into the meeting room in the town hall in East Grinstead and marched past occupied seats, glancing left and right at the people who filled them. The hubbub of voices gradually faded. It was a full house, and he smiled to himself. Mr Donaldson, the local councillor, stood beaming.

'Good evening, Mr McIndoe.'

'Hello. Excellent turnout. Well, I'd best get started.' Archie spun around to face the crowd of locals, flicking his gaze briefly at the clock that hung on the wall above the open fireplace. *Six thirty*. The drift of cigarette smoke filled the stale, humid air. He coughed to clear his throat.

'Hello. I recognise some faces among you here tonight, but for those who don't know me, I'm Archie McIndoe. I run the plastic surgery unit here at the local hospital, and I care for many servicemen who have been severely burned and disfigured.'

A couple of people who had been chatting in the back row suddenly ceased and looked up. Good, he had their attention too. Beads of sweat formed at the nape of his neck and above his top lip, and he flicked his tongue over it and savoured the tang of salt. He glanced at the half-open window as a slight breeze whispered a breath of fresh air, and he inhaled it greedily.

'A man disfigured in battle fights that battle for the rest of his life. Now, the treatment these boys require is often complex and takes place over many months and years. The majority of them are not sick, which means they're often frustrated and left with nothing to do between surgical procedures. This is where I hope you will come in.'

Men, women, and children in the audience gazed at him with wide eyes, some open-mouthed, and some with raised eyebrows, clearly puzzled.

An elderly woman raised her hand and rose from her seat. 'But what is it that you want us to do?'

'I'm glad you asked. Well, firstly, we always need willing volunteers to come into the ward and read or write letters for the boys. Many of them don't receive visitors so it's good for them to see people from the outside world.'

Faces in the audience nodded and smiled. He had their full attention, and they were clearly considering his request.

'What I aim to do is to show these boys how to live again. That may sound odd, but you must realise that the scars from their injuries are more than skin deep. They need to know that they can come out among you without being met with rejection, jibes, and stares. I believe people should be judged on their character and their actions, not on appearances or their social status. All I ask is that you look them in the eye and say hello. That's it. And if you feel like striking up a conversation, by all means, only don't ignore them. Even a smile speaks volumes. And while at first glance you may feel they look peculiar and different, remember, they're still the same person inside, and they need your support.'

'Are they all British?' a man asked.

'No, they're a mix from the Allied Forces. Some are British, some are French, Belgian, Australian, American, and so on.' Archie pushed his spectacles higher up on his nose.

'My uncle lives in America,' a young boy with curly red hair called out, only to be admonished by the woman he was with, presumably his mother. 'Well, he does,' he protested. A muffled wave of laughter erupted around the room.

Archie suppressed a chuckle. 'You've all heard about the "friendly invasion" and now that our American friends have joined us, households around the country have been asked to take GIs into their homes for tea and suchlike. This is just the same, the only difference is that these lads are burned and disfigured. They've sacrificed so much, and they really are lucky to be alive, however, they'll be even luckier if you make them welcome and put them at their ease. It's such a small step for you, but if you're willing to take it, you'll be moving mountains for them, and they'll appreciate your support. Think of it as doing your bit for the war effort.' Archie looked around the room at each of them, nodding his head as he did so, planting seeds, and he noted the reaction on their faces and in their eyes as he connected with them.

'One last note. If anyone would like to volunteer to be a visitor, then you can either sign up here tonight or contact the ward directly and leave your details with Sister. With your help, we can embrace a plan of holistic care and help these boys to live full lives once again.'

As Archie made his way to the local pub, a radiant glow flowed through him. He was forever breaching barriers, tonight being no exception. Educating the locals was working a treat, and this evening's talk had been a useful mission. Aside from being a plastic surgeon, running around after a large number of airmen, and giving talks in the community, there was a fair amount of wining and dining to take care of; after all, he needed people on side should the need arise. Whatever was required for the ward and the boys, he liked to ensure he had the means to procure it. Nothing was too much trouble. Why shouldn't people be useful? If certain things were within their power, then it ought to be put to good use. The number of favours he'd requested were stacking up and he smiled to himself, well aware of his sheer audacity.

The pub was crowded and Archie strode into a smog of tobacco.

'Over here, Maestro.' Dickie waved. He was sitting at the piano, as usual. 'Tom, get a pint for the Maestro.'

'Ah, Archie. Just the chap.' John Hunter slapped him on the back.

'You made it, John. Well, let's see if we can't drink this rabble of youth under the table. What do you say?'

'You're on. They don't stand a chance, poor buggers.'
He chuckled, his laugh deep and jovial, eyes twinkling.

29

The Country Club

Bassingbourn bustled beneath a bright August sun in a cloudless sky. Mac arrived at Station 121 in the afternoon just as a group of Flying Fortresses were droning their way home. The sound of the Wright Cyclone engines was soothing somehow, and he turned his face skyward as one thundered overhead, the thrum of the engines coursing through his soul. The ground crew waited out on the grass by the watchtower, their faces lifted to the sky, lips pursed. Yeah, he remembered that feeling. His stomach tightened as he turned away and headed over to the officers' mess. Once he found his room, he dumped his kit on the bed. He reached into his pocket and pulled out the small card Bea had pressed into his hand when he was discharged. He glanced at it and grinned.

To whom it may concern. If there are any further problems, please send on the bits c/o The Queen Victoria Hospital, East Grinstead.

When he reached the Colonel's office, he hesitated while he straightened his tie and puffed out a breath before knocking.

'Enter.'

Mac marched into the room and saluted.

'At ease, Mac. It's good to see you. Take a seat.' Colonel
Edwards greeted him with a firm handshake. No hesitation.
'Thank you, it's good to be back, sir.' Mac glanced at the
silver-framed picture on the mahogany desk that depicted a
woman and a small child, smiling.

The Colonel opened his cigarette case and offered it to
him. The ashtray was already piled high with cigarette stubs,
the air thick with a mist of smoke.

'Thanks.' Mac took out his own silver lighter and lit up.

'You're looking well. Those Brits sure looked after you
down there. How was it?'

'It was okay, sir. They took good care of me, and as you
can see, I'm in one piece and ready for action.'

The Colonel cocked his head to one side, his dark brown
eyes searching. He drew on his cigarette, exhaling smoke
rings. 'Well, I'm glad to hear it. We always need good men.
Experienced men. We've had a lot of rookies lately, so darn
cocky like you wouldn't believe.' He smiled. 'You've got a
medical scheduled for tomorrow at ten o'clock. If you pass
that, then I'll get the ball rolling here.'

He took a long drag on his cigarette, his brow furrowed,
and a heavier, serious expression crept into his face. 'Mac, I
wanted to be the first to tell you. All of your original crew,
except for Wilson, are listed as missing in action. We had a
tough mission three weeks back – lost a few ships that day
as a matter of fact.' He rose from his chair and strode across
to the window, gazing out over the airfield. 'It was a bad
run all right.'

Mac shook his head, numb with shock. God, the boys,
gone, just like that. Another knock, more like a kick in the
gut. Jeez, he was too late. He swallowed hard, and a lump
lodged in his throat. 'But Wilson's still around?'

'Yeah. He was having time out at the Flak House when it happened.' Colonel Edwards sighed as he picked up a couple of glasses from a table by the window and set them down on his desk with a clink. He slid open a drawer and lifted out a bottle of Scotch. 'For times like these.' He tipped a generous measure into two glasses. 'I'm sorry you came back to bad news. There's still hope – several guys counted eight chutes.' He frowned. 'I know you weren't expecting it, but hell, you know what this is.'

Mac drained the Scotch in one gulp. 'Yes, sir.'

'It really is good to see you.' The Colonel smiled warmly. 'They fixed you up pretty good, Mac. Could have been a whole lot worse. Well, that's about all for now. I'll leave you to settle in, and I'll see you tomorrow after your medical. If the MO passes you, I'll be glad to have you back.'

Once outside, Mac puffed out a breath. Life here just rolled on and on, regardless of who didn't return. Numbness filtered into his bones, and he pictured Stella's face as she'd pleaded with him not to fly. The truth was, he didn't want to fly bombing missions or dodge the Luftwaffe's cannon shells any more than the next man, except it was his duty, and it hung around his neck like a dead weight. The only way to shake it off was to fly. The only place to be was here, with his brothers who he could depend on.

The next morning, Mac sat waiting outside the medical officer's room at a quarter to ten. At five minutes to, Colonel Majors opened the door and beckoned him inside. Majors had been there from the beginning. He was older than most – Mac guessed he'd be around fifty – and his hair was black, except for a strip of grey running through the middle like a centre parting. The guys called him 'Badger.'

'Take a seat, Lieutenant. It's good to see you looking so well, and keen, by the look of you.' Majors cast his narrow brown eyes over him, scrutinising the handiwork of Archie McIndoe. 'You remember I saw to you when you first had the accident?'

'Yes, sir.' Did he have to bring it up? All Mac wanted to do now was put it in a box and lock it away.

'Excellent job, I see.' Majors scrutinised Mac's face. Hold out your hands.'

Mac shuffled forward in his chair and placed his hands out in front of him. Majors took hold of them, turned them over, and back again. 'Okay, now grip mine.'

Mac steeled himself. This was his one chance, and he didn't want to fail.

'Okay, that's enough!' Majors said, almost shouting. He rubbed his hand, which was bright red from the force. 'Well, I don't think we have any problems there at all.' He opened a medical file and began flicking through the notes and then looked up. 'The doctor sent these on from the Queen Victoria. They sure are efficient, these Brits'. He put his spectacles on to read. 'It says here that you had three successful surgical grafts. Seems to me you've been very lucky. It could have been a lot worse. Damn lucky to have saved all your fingers too.' He picked up his stethoscope. 'I'll just have a listen to your chest.' After a series of sighs and gestures, he sat down at his desk. 'Everything seems to be in order.'

'That's it? You're passing me fit?'

'That's right. If you can squeeze the hell out of me, then you'd better go give Hitler a piece of that instead. You're back on duty as of now.' Majors scrawled something down in the records and looked up with a warm smile. 'Take care of yourself, son. I wish you the best of luck.'

'Thank you, sir. I sure appreciate it.' Mac grinned so wide his cheeks tightened as if they might burst. Now he had to give the CO the good news.

Colonel Edwards looked up from a stack of papers, his face grave, his eyes glossy. 'Mac. Take a seat.' He ran a hand through his hair. 'So, what's the verdict?'

'Passed fit to fly, sir.'

'Well, now that's music to my ears.' He put his pen down on top of the letter that lay on his desk. 'Okay. I have a crew who recently lost their pilot. They've been out of action for over a week, and they're going stir crazy here on the base. I want you to take over. They're experienced, and I think you'll make a darn good team.' He drew on his cigarette before dropping it in the ashtray. 'I'm pairing you up with Wilson. He's due back today. And one more thing. Those boys need someone like you to keep them together. They could do with a guiding hand.'

Mac grinned. At least he wasn't being assigned a bunch of rookies. As for Wilson, he knew what to expect there.

'So, any questions?'

'No, sir, only, when do I get to meet them?'

'I'll ask Lieutenant Valentine to meet you at the Officers' Club at twelve hundred. He'll introduce you to the others and take you out to see the aircraft. You'll need to do a few training flights as a crew before we can return you to duty. Now, any problems at all, let me know.'

'Yes, sir, and thank you.' Mac saluted before leaving.

There were several guys in the Officers' Club. Tired, pained eyes peered out over glasses of bourbon or whisky or whatever the hell it was they were drinking. It was a battle-weary look, and one that harboured every mission flown and every tragedy witnessed. One of the guys turned around. His face was lightly bronzed, and his blue eyes twinkled.

'I'm looking for Lieutenant Valentine,' Mac asked.

'That's me. You must be our new pilot.' Val smiled, holding out his hand.

Mac met it with a firm handshake. 'John Mackenzie, but call me Mac.'

'It's good to meet you. Dale Valentine. Call me Val.'

Val's gaze lingered over Mac's scars and unease swept into his veins; he lowered his head as he recalled Archie's words. *Brush over it, and remember, any embarrassment comes from you, so look them in the eye. People are never sure what to say at first so you have to make the first move.* Mac stared into Val's eyes as he stretched up tall.

'Say, Mac, how about we take a ride out to see the ship? Then I'll round up the guys.' Val cracked a smile.

Mac gave a sharp nod. 'Lead the way.' He was glad of Val's friendly, easy-going personality. He rubbed the back of his neck. Perhaps things would work out. Even so, he wished he didn't feel like the new kid again.

Val drove out to the far side of the airfield to where their Fortress stood. Two ground crew busied around doing maintenance work. 'There she is. *Hell's Fury.* Been real reliable, all things considered.'

Mac walked around her, then he climbed up through the nose hatch. Being out here, close to the crash site, brought a rush of ragged memories flooding back, and he clenched his jaw and swallowed them down along with a waft of oil and aircraft. As he flicked a gaze over the pilot's seat and the instrument panel, and his hand touched the sun-warmed metal, his stomach turned to ice and his palms grew damp.

'I heard you boys were grounded.'

'Yeah, I don't think they knew what to do with us. They were about to use some of the guys as spares, but then you came along.' Val rubbed his jaw, casting a sceptical look.

'Okay, I've seen enough. Oh, one thing. The ship needs her own distinctive look. I saw Slater earlier – he's about the best there is for nose art.'

Val grinned, and his face relaxed as he jumped back into the jeep. 'Sure thing, Mac.'

Later, Mac took a walk along the perimeter track out to his old spot by the farm. In the adjoining field, land girls formed a wave of khaki in dungarees of yellow-brown topped off with bright headscarves, as they dug in harmony. He swallowed. So much bad had been aired out here. All the prayers he'd whispered had sailed into the wind, and yet he'd never returned to the base any lighter. His gaze flicked across a field of straw; its golden ears swayed and whispered in the breeze. He pursed his lips. A bird of prey cried out above, and he lifted his face to the sky, shielding his eyes from the sun's glare. Black wings fanned out in the blue as the sun's fingertips caressed his skin and his scars burned in the heat.

The *Texas Rose* and all but one of his old crew were gone. He recalled their faces and heard their voices. He had to block them out. Thank God he had Stella. He loved her body and soul, but was he doing the right thing in marrying her? The truth was, he was damned either way. At least she was happy. Yet a dark shadow hung over him.

All this time, he'd been desperate to resume his tour of duty, craving service life, yet the reality was he was starting afresh. He realised it was a different camaraderie he craved, one where he was surrounded by his brothers from the ward. He had stepped away from an existence of familiar normality and acceptance and had ventured into new territory. At least Stella was close by.

He glanced at his hands and clenched them a few times. His fingers were stiff and ached. Maybe he'd been overdoing things. He offered up a silent prayer and asked God for help. All he had to do was make sure he stayed in one piece. He heaved out a breath and steeled himself for all that lay ahead.

30

Peenemunde, August 1943

'Charlie. What are you doing back here?' Stella's heart lurched. He was supposed to be with Alex up in Lincoln. Did that mean Alex was here too? He cast her a nervous smile and as she ambled towards him, he slipped a hand into his tunic pocket and dragged out a pale blue envelope. She faltered. Alex used stationery just like that; in fact, all of the letters he'd ever sent her were in envelopes exactly like that.

'Hello. Might I have a word?' Charlie's voice was soft, with a nervous edge.

The hair at the nape of her neck bristled. 'Yes, of course.' What did he want with her? Probably the messenger on behalf of Alex, no doubt. Lord, he was still plotting how to keep her in his life. She opened the door to the staff room, and Charlie followed her in. She glanced at him, raising her chin. 'Well, what is it, Charlie? I know this isn't a social call. You're here because of Alex, aren't you?' She stared at him, long and hard, narrowing her eyes.

'Yes, I'm afraid I am.' He glanced at his feet, his brow furrowed.

Stella huffed out a breath and her heart gathered pace. 'How many times do I have to tell him? It's over, finished.

I ended things for good reason.' Her head pounded, and heat flared in her face. 'For goodness' sake, he's supposed to be getting married.'

Charlie took a step towards her, still grasping that slip of blue. 'I'm afraid he's not getting married anymore.'

Oh, so he'd sent the messenger to do his dirty work. That was low, even for Alex. 'Well, you can tell him from me that I don't want to know. He treated me appallingly, and he deserves everything he gets.' Her chest heaved as the torrent of words gushed out of her.

'Please, Stella. Just listen for a minute. Sit down.' His tone was curt and took her by surprise.

She met his gaze, and his eyes flashed with pain and the breath caught in her throat. She didn't want to sit, though he was sitting now so, reluctantly, she sank down beside him.

'Stella, Alex isn't getting married, and he didn't send me here today, not exactly.'

She swallowed. Her mind hurled words around, scrabbling for some kind of logic, and when she looked into his eyes, she stiffened.

'I'm so sorry. Alex went down with his crew over Germany a couple of weeks ago. No chutes were seen.' He reached out and placed his hand lightly on hers. 'Peenemunde. We lost a number of aircraft.'

Stella froze, staring, transfixed, at Charlie. All of Bourn's aircraft made it back that night. Grief flashed in his eyes as numbness crept into her soul. Alex couldn't be dead. He had to be safe.

Charlie's eyes were brown, the colour of hazelnuts. She swallowed. As he continued to speak, she saw his lips move, but all she could hear was 'no chutes' echoing around in her head. Her eyes swam with tears until she couldn't focus and then silently they fell, and Charlie's voice filtered through.

'I'm sorry. I know you'd had a falling out. Alex didn't elaborate, although I could see he felt rotten about it. Whatever it was about, he regretted it. He told me that much.'

A sob escaped Stella's lips and took her by surprise. Her chest heaved and another came, even though she tried to stop it. She shouldn't be feeling like this – like her world had come crashing down around her. She'd been so angry, but she never wanted this. 'Oh, Alex.' Her jaw trembled as she cried and Charlie squeezed her hand, then pressed the blue envelope into her palm. She gazed down. It was addressed to her. Alex's writing.

'If anything happened, he wanted me to give you this. I think it explains things.' He glanced at the clock on the wall. 'I'm so sorry. It's been a terrible time. Alex's death hit everyone hard. Well, I'm afraid I must get back, or they'll think I'm AWOL.' He cast an apologetic smile as he rose and headed for the door. 'Look after yourself, Stella.'

She continued to stare at the envelope. A part of her didn't want to read his words while a part of her was hungry for them. Carefully, she tore it open and unfolded the letter within.

My darling Stella,

If you're reading this, then it is because I have gone. Please don't grieve for me. I loved you, truly I did, in spite of everything. I'm so sorry for hurting you and making such a mess of things. There was only ever one girl for me, and it was you. It was just a pity I couldn't see clearly enough at the time. What I did was unforgivable. I was weak, and I hurt you. Please try to forgive me, my darling. Marry your American if that's what you want and know that I am happy for you. I wish you a long and happy life, for you truly deserve it.

I shall leave you now, and know that I am safe and among friends. Perhaps one day we might meet again. I'd like that very much. God bless.

With all my love,

Alex. xxx

Stella's chest lurched and heaved as she sobbed, and she drew her legs up and curled into a foetal position on the chair, the letter in her hand, scrunched against her chest. Pain seared through her, severing her breaths. She screwed her eyes shut and summoned his face. Yes, she'd loved him, more like a brother at the end, but she'd loved him, and now she was breaking.

After a while, she blew out a breath and was silent. She glanced at the clock on the wall. Six o'clock. She'd been there over an hour. She gathered her things and wandered outside, clambered on her bicycle, and headed for home. The sun was bright in a milky blue sky, and the birds chorused with joy. Everything carried on as normal, except nothing was normal and she wanted to shout and scream and tell them to stop singing because Alex was dead, and she sobbed into the warm breeze as she cycled home.

Mac headed out to RAF Bourn. He glanced at his watch – ten past six. 'Damn.' A cyclist sailed around the bend up ahead, wobbling around all over the place like a pilot struggling to stay in formation. *Stella.* She cycled towards him in her grey-blue uniform as the wind gently teased her blonde hair from beneath her peaked cap, and stray curls oscillated in the breeze. He slammed the brakes on and skidded to a halt, sprang out of the jeep, and stood in the middle of the road with his hands on his hips.

He beamed as he eased his crush cap back with his forefinger, his face creasing into a broad grin. She was a picture all right, only she wasn't slowing down fast enough on that damn cycle of hers. The brakes squealed, and he put his arms out, managing to grab her and the cycle and bring them to a halt and she fell against his chest, sobbing.

'Hey, what's happened?' He held her tight. 'It's ok, honey. I've got you.' Eventually, she ceased and sniffed and raised her face up to his. Her reddened eyes glistened. He pressed his lips to her brow, then rested his head against hers. 'What's happened?'

'It's Alex. He's dead.' She broke down again and buried her face against him.

He held her tight. *Jeez, he was gone.* Mac wouldn't wish that on anyone, even Alex.

'How did you find out?'

She pulled away from him and dragged a handkerchief from her pocket, dabbing her eyes. 'His friend turned up at the base and handed me a letter.'

Mac pursed his lips. A letter of regret, no doubt, making her feel a whole lot worse. 'What does it say?'

She took a deep breath and blew it out slowly. 'He apologised for everything.' Her lower lip trembled, and she caught her breath. 'I can't believe he's gone.'

Mac's stomach tightened. He hated seeing her upset, especially over him. 'I'm sorry.' He was, but a part of him couldn't help wondering if Alex still held a piece of her heart. He sighed. 'Come on. I'll take you home.'

Stella looked into his eyes, dabbing her nose with a hanky, a dazed expression on her face. He took the cycle from her, crammed it into the back of the jeep, and sprung into the driver's seat.

'I don't think you should be riding that thing. It's lethal. I'll get it fixed for you.'

Stella never uttered a word, and an air of uncertainty slipped between them as he drove silently to Lilac Cottage, drawing up outside five minutes later. He walked her to the front door, his arm around her, pressing her to his side. The door swung open well before they reached it.

'Oh, how lovely to see you again, young man.' Mrs Brown glanced at Stella and her smile faded. 'Oh, dear, whatever's wrong?'

'She's had a shock, ma'am. Sad news about Alex.'

The older woman's eyes met his as she stepped back and ushered them inside, into the living room, and then said something about making tea. That seemed to be the magic drink here. Everything was solved with tea. Pity they couldn't soak the entire German army with the damn stuff.

Stella sat on the sofa, and he crouched down in front of her. 'Hey, I'll go get your bicycle and leave it outside for you, okay?' She stared at him, her eyes glossy, wide. He dashed outside and hauled the cycle out of the jeep. He stood there for a moment longer, rubbing his jaw as alarm bells rang in his head. It sure had been a rough day. He considered his own bad news about his old crew; something he now couldn't share with her. He blew out a long breath.

Back inside, Mrs Brown had given Stella a cup of tea, and she took Mac aside.

'She hasn't said a word. Did she tell you anything?'

'Well, she said he'd gone. I just assumed he went down on a mission. Then she clammed up.'

'I've never seen her like this before. I suppose she's in shock.'

'Yeah, probably, ma'am.' Stella began to cry, and he sat beside her and took her in his arms. 'Come on, honey. It'll be all right. Wasn't anything you could've done.'

'I could have helped him, should have.' She stifled a sob. 'I told you when we met that things were difficult. I was worried about what he might do.'

Mac didn't know what she was driving at. Come to think of it, she never had explained things, and he'd never asked her as he'd been so wrapped up in his own problems. 'What do you mean?'

'He was a mess. In front of everyone else he put on an act, but inside he was crumbling, piece by piece. Ever since he lost his friends, and then his cousin. I don't think he could cope.'

'That's not why this happened. Stella, he must have been shot down. There's nothing you could have done. It happens.' Now he saw where this was heading, and he swallowed.

'I abandoned him. Don't you see? He asked me to promise not to leave him. He needed me, and I wasn't there. I did this.'

'Oh, sweetheart, you weren't to know, and it's not your fault. Please don't cry.' He wiped her tears away with his thumbs. The voice from the grave had certainly stirred things up.

'I let him down.'

Mac shut his eyes for a second and sighed.

'I made you promise.' She sat up, pulling away from him.

'Hey, I'm not about to let you down. And you didn't let Alex down so quit saying that.' Her face was red, her eyes wide and glazed. 'What exactly did the letter say?'

'It doesn't matter.' She got up and walked over to the window. 'Mac, if you don't mind, I'd like an early night.'

Her cold, detached voice hit him in the chest. 'Okay, if that's what you want.' He stared at her back as she wrapped her arms around herself. She never turned around. He moved towards her and lightly placed his hand on her shoulder, her muscle tensing beneath his touch. 'Maybe I'll see you tomorrow or the next day.' He paused. Hell, he couldn't leave it like that. He wrapped his arms around her and brushed the top of her head with his lips. 'I love you. See you soon, honey.'

As he reached the jeep, he turned to look back at the window where she stood, hugging herself, her eyes in a trance. No smile, no wave. Nothing. He didn't know what to do or how to reach her, and he could only hope that she would snap out of it soon.

31

Painting Beautiful Souls,
September 1943

The setting sun cast the last vestiges of golden light through the open window, illuminating the painting which glistened beneath its touch, the oils still wet. Archie stepped closer, careful not to tread on the squeezed-out tubes of paint that lay abandoned on the bare, wooden floor.

Freddy's studio was strewn with canvasses, some stacked against the walls, while others hung around the room. The smell of linseed oil and the mix of turpentine and oil paints hung in the air and intensified the closer he stepped to the canvas. It was a familiar odour that reminded him of home, of his artist mother, Mabel and his elder brother, Jack, and his chest tightened as he drank it in fervently.

Freddy stepped back as he studied the image before him, his lips pursed tight, his forehead furrowed, a streak of black smeared across his cheek. The palette rested in the crook of his left arm while he held a cigarette casually between the second and third fingers of his left hand. In his right hand, he raised the brush and made some fine, sweeping strokes to the canvas, adding detail and definition to his subject's face. Archie stood, transfixed, with the same, intense fascination he'd had as a child while watching his mother paint. He recognised hues of burned umber and yellow ochre as Freddy mixed colours to add to the complexion. The look of intensity etched on his face suggested that he was far from satisfied with his work and a pensive wave rolled in the air. Archie edged away.

Freddy had asked him to drop by and take the first glance at the painting when he ran into him yesterday at the hospital. As Archie gazed around, his eyes were drawn to a particular oil painting on the wall. It depicted an RAF crew standing in front of their Lancaster Bomber on a grassed airfield. The crew gazed into the distance with brooding eyes. Seven young men, all unsmiling, dressed in their flying clothes, and the breath hitched in Archie's throat as he imagined what they'd been thinking at that precise moment. One of the men wore a defeated expression, almost as if he knew what lay ahead – or was perhaps thinking of a previous mission – and Archie's skin prickled as the hairs bristled at the nape of his neck.

'Freddy, when did you paint this one?'

'Hang on a mo.' Freddy added some fine brush strokes to the canvas, and then spun around. 'Ah, that was RAF Binbrook. I did a short stint there, last year.' He dipped his brush into a clear glass jar and sloshed it around, and the water swirled into murky brown almost instantly. He then sauntered over to join Archie.

'Yes, I remember that day most vividly. They had their minds on the mission ahead and were rather rattled at having to pose for me. However, orders are orders, and so they posed, and grumbled, while I attempted a quick sketch.' He drew on his cigarette and savoured it for a moment as if recalling that very day, that precise moment, and then released a vapour of white into the air.

'Yes, the bombardier had to endure a little good-humoured ribbing from a couple of the lads. He'd recently become a father.' He hesitated. 'They never returned from that mission.' Freddy gazed at the painting for a few moments longer and heaved out a heavy sigh, his eyes dark and serious. 'Right then, come and have a look at this. Time waits for no man.'

'Don't I know it?' Archie strode across to the latest creation. The man in the saline bath – one of his own patients to be precise. 'Ah, yes. Excellent, Freddy. It's very humbling.' Archie scrutinised the scene. 'You've illustrated the nurse superbly, tending to her patient. She's almost angelic. And the airman looks relaxed, just as he should be in the tub.'

His eyes lingered on the nurse wearing her white surgical mask. A thick lock of black hair had escaped from her headdress and cupped her cheek. She was slim, the curve of her hip defined as she leaned over the enamel bath wearing black rubber gloves, delving into the water with a pair of forceps to remove a dressing from the man's leg. The man lay outstretched, his arms resting on the side of the bath, the burns to both legs clearly evident – red and raw. The angle of his head was dipped as he looked down at his injuries, and the definition of his shoulders, the trapezius and deltoid muscles, was illustrated to perfection. Freddy had captured the mix of emotion perfectly in the man's posture and in his burned face, although the face was not exactly clear – obviously an artistic decision.

As Archie drank in the emotion of the scene before him, goosebumps erupted on his forearms. The subject in the painting was someone he'd come to know very well, and there had been so many thoughts hurtling through the young pilot's mind back then.

As Archie studied the scene further, he also saw disillusionment and sadness; after all, airman's burn was often life-changing, and the scars penetrated deep beyond the skin. The longer he mused, the more he thought how this represented something more conflicting, perhaps. It evoked beauty in so many ways. The nurse was beautiful, evident despite the fact her face was half covered with a mask. The scene of a caring nature carried beauty and tenderness within it, and then there was the man himself.

'Just needs a few more finishing touches.' Freddy put the palette down and stood back, drawing his hand up to his tousled, mousy brown hair, smoothing it back from his forehead.

Archie glanced at the young artist. Freddy had never flinched or recoiled in horror at the sight of any disfigured man. He merely sat sketching, analysing every detail, every contour, absorbing every inch of maiming as if it was all in a day's work, but Archie recognised his impartiality and the intensity that flashed in his eyes. The act of a real artist, discovering and revealing beauty in all its guises.

'It's marvellous.' Archie grinned as he gazed admiringly at the scene before him, his chin held high. Art was open to interpretation, which was always subjective, and he had been interpreting the effects of burns on real patients for years. 'It's such a powerful, symbolic image. Truly compelling, Freddy. The Air Ministry ought to be happy with it.'

'Ah, well I had a good muse that day.' He grinned, a streak of black almost vanishing into a fold by his mouth as it creased at the corners and curved upward. His shirt was awash with colour, mirroring his palette.

Freddy had painted Mac as he'd seen him that day, his head down, focusing on all the bad, slipping into that dark place they all found themselves when they first arrived on Archie's ward. Of course, his young lady had been a refreshing change from the usual sort. She had courage and determination, and she'd made him see sense and helped him to embrace life fully, after a little innovative meddling. It was the only way. Archie sighed, and his gaze returned to the ill-fated Lancaster crew on the wall, their futures now erased.

Outside, the Ashdown Forest brimmed with life, and pink bell heather and yellow gorse blossomed, carpeting the forest floor. From a treetop perch, the rise and fall of the elusive male nightjar's churring song chorused all around this flourishing corner of Sussex, untouched by war.

32

Acceptance

'Hey, Mac. You still seeing that girl?' Wilson slid his side window shut and dragged off his earphones.

'Yeah, sure am. As it happens, we just got engaged.'

'Why didn't you say so earlier, buddy?' Wilson slapped him on the back. 'Congratulations. So when's the big day?'

'Oh, we haven't set a date, but you'll be the first to know.' Mac hoped they still would. He hadn't seen or heard from Stella for a few days now, although he'd tried calling a couple of times, yet no one had answered.

'Come on. Let's get outta here. The drinks are on me, but first I gotta show you something.'

The aches and numbness had increased in his hands over the past few days, and it troubled him. He'd managed that morning's training flight, however, how would it be over enemy territory? Riding through flak, prop wash, and dodging fighters was bound to throw up a whole new set of challenges. Knowing what to do was one thing, but could he handle it? He pressed his lips together as he dragged a hand through his sweat-drenched hair, ruffling it a little.

After they'd changed and dumped their kit, Mac followed Wilson over to the barracks where his former crew had bunked. The bunks were all taken by new guys and a whole new set of personal effects littered each bedside, with posters and photographs plastered across the walls, except for one wall. The memorial. Mac swallowed as Wilson wandered down to the end of the room, and there, in the middle of the wall, near the top, he pointed to words that had been painted on in red.

'Virg wrote that while you were up in the hospital.' Wilson removed his cap.

Mac stepped closer. 'James T Bird, Arizona, 17.ᵗʰ April 1943.' A lump formed in his throat and his stomach tightened. He gazed at the name a little longer, picturing the young man, who would have made a great artist someday. 'Blue skies, Birdie.'

'Amen.'

Stella poured the tea. 'Thanks for coming round, Vera.'

'It's all right. Sam's flying today and besides, I feel as if I haven't seen you in ages. These bloomin' shifts. We're always working opposite one another.' She sipped her tea. 'So, come on then. What's wrong?'

Vera had intuition like radar. Stella sighed. 'Charlie turned up at the base a few days ago.' Her chest tightened, and she gritted her teeth as she choked back the tears. 'Alex is missing. His Lancaster went down over Germany – no chutes.'

'Oh, Stell. I'm so sorry, love.' Vera threw her arms around her. 'I can't believe it.'

Stella drew away and looked down into her cup at the swirling vortex of tea. 'I shouldn't have left him. He needed help.' Her thoughts turned to Elizabeth. Was she distraught?' 'Charlie gave me a letter. Alex said he was to deliver it if anything happened.'

Vera raised her eyebrows. 'Where is it?'

Stella pulled it from her pocket and passed it over. Vera read it to herself. Then she folded it, handed it back, and sniffed. 'I know I said he was no good for you, but he was all right. I'd never have wished this on him in a million years.'

Stella's chin trembled, and she swallowed the lump in her throat. 'It's my fault. I should have helped him. Oh, God, I can't bear it.' She held her head in her hands and sobbed.

Vera wrapped her arm around her. 'There, it's always better to cry it out. Now, listen to me. None of this is your fault. You couldn't have stopped that happening. Look at how many crews we've lost. When they set out, they never know who'll make it back. It's bad luck.'

'I can't do it, Vera.'

'Do what?'

'Marry him.'

Vera puffed out a breath. 'You love him, don't you?'

'Yes.'

'Well then. What are you harping on about? Time's not going to wait for you. And don't let guilt stop you. Alex has given you his blessing in that letter.'

'Mac said he needs me. That's just what Alex said, and now he's dead. Don't you see?'

Vera shook her head.

'If anything happened to Mac, I'd never forgive myself. I can't do that to him. I can't.' Her chest heaved. 'I'm bad luck. What about Alice Turner? Every man that asked her out went missing on a mission. In the end, no one would look at her. They all said she was a jinx.'

Vera sighed, her mouth opened, one eyebrow hitched up. 'Stella, you're not making any sense, and that was a load of old codswallop.'

Stella sniffed, glanced at Vera, and shrugged.

'Well then.' Vera shook her head again. 'Silly girl. It's simple. You love him, and he loves you. Take this chance, love. You might not get another as good or as worthy. Don't waste it, not for a second. He needs you, and you need him. Take what you can for as long as you can. That's all any of us can do.'

Stella dried her eyes and sniffed. 'Mac was here, the day Charlie gave me the letter, and I asked him to leave, and he hasn't been back since. It's not like him to stay away.'

'Oh, Stella.' Vera flashed a warm grin and shook her head. 'What are we to do with you? It's just as well he loves you.'

Stella flicked a gaze at the picture of Mrs Brown's former fiancé on the mantelpiece and a pain seized her heart. She clenched her jaw. 'I need to see him, make things right.' She checked her watch. 'It's just gone three o'clock. I have to go.'

'What? But I've only just got here.'

Stella ran out to get her shoes with Vera on her tail. 'I have to get to the base.'

Vera rolled her eyes.

'Are you coming?'

'Me? Don't be daft. I walked here. You can give me all the details tomorrow.'

Stella went around the side of the cottage and grabbed her bicycle. The day was fresh, the air lukewarm. She raised her face skyward as she cycled. Lead-grey clouds hung like a dense blanket and she hoped it wouldn't rain. An olive-green jeep zipped past her and vanished around the bend in the road, and a squeal of rubber screeched out. She braked, only the cycle barely slowed and, spying the gentle hill ahead, she waited, and as she climbed, the cycle gradually slowed to a halt, by which time the American jeep drew up alongside. She glanced over and smiled.

'Mac, I didn't see you until the last minute and I couldn't slow down.'

He shook his head and jumped out. 'What did I say? I don't want you riding this death trap, at least until I get one of the guys to check it out.' He swaggered over, put one hand on the cycle and slipped the other around her waist and put his lips on hers. 'Now, let's get this heap in the back. I sure missed you, honey. Where were you off to anyway?'

'To see you.'

His mouth curved up into a half-smile. 'Well, that's a coincidence because I was on my way to see you.' He helped her into the jeep. 'Come on. Let's go someplace where we can be alone.'

Mac drove a little further along the road and turned off right into a farm.

'What are we doing here?'

'They won't mind. Farmer's kind of used to me by now. I come here all the time after a mission. Come on, let's take a walk.'

They strolled hand in hand through the field that bordered Mac's base, where Flying Fortresses basked on their hardstands in the late afternoon sun. 'Mac, I'm sorry about the other day.'

He sighed and pulled her towards him. 'No need. I understand.' He wrapped his arms around her. 'I know you're hurting, but it's going to get better. You just need to give it time.'

He brushed her lips with his and the blood quickened through her body. She slipped her arms around his waist, as he drew her close, exploring her mouth with his tongue. 'Say, put me down, woman. We don't want to go giving the farmer here any ideas, now.' He cast her a mischievous look, and she playfully thumped his arm. 'Hey, what was that for?' He laughed.

She dipped her hand into her pocket and withdrew the letter from Alex, holding it out.

Mac's smile slipped. He unfolded the notepaper, and she watched as his eyes darted across the lines. When he'd finished, he looked up and sighed. He handed it back, and Stella slipped it into her pocket. 'I'm glad you let me read it. Sure makes things a little clearer.'

Stella glanced at him and saw sadness in his eyes. 'I did love him, though in the end, I realised it was more like a brotherly love. I just wanted to be there for him, and I feel as if I've let him down.' She turned away to gaze out across the open farmland. *Poor Alex.* She hated thinking of how he'd died.

'You didn't let him down. He knew that.' Mac wrapped his arms around her, and she clung to him, burying her head against his chest. The whiff of manure drifted on the breeze so she buried deeper, hunting for soap and cedar wood, his warmth soaking into her skin.

She glanced up at him. 'I know he was grieving, but he knew about us and the way things ended, well, I can't help wondering if... '

'If he shouldn't have been flying that night. I know, honey, except it doesn't work like that, and if you keep thinking that way, you'll drive yourself mad. It's tough, but you have to move on.'

She gazed at a horse grazing in the next field as it snorted in short bursts. Mac was right, though her heart remained bruised. 'Life's rotten at times. Why does it have to be so hard?'

'Life is what we make it, and man makes war. That's just how it is. Yeah, man makes many mistakes, that's for sure.' He took her hand in his. 'Remember, after this is over, I'm taking you home with me. You need to get away from all this and go somewhere new, where you can make fresh memories with me.'

His words wrapped around her like his strong, warm arms and she harnessed comfort from them. He was right. Her heart lay with his now, and perhaps they could be as one in Montana.

'Mac, take a seat.' Colonel Edwards leant back in his chair. A stack of papers leaned precariously close to the edge of his desk and his pipe rested in an ashtray, the drift of tobacco smoke swirling into the room. 'I have some good news for you. The United States Air Force is making you a captain, so, congratulations. Secondly, I'm putting you and your crew back up there. There's a milk run in a few days so you can test the water. Do you think you're ready?' Colonel Edwards looked at him with his hawk eyes, dark and searching.

'Yes, sir. And thank you.' Mac's stomach quivered.

'Okay, good. There's a big one coming up soon, and I'm going to need you to fly lead.'

Mac swallowed. 'Yes, sir.'

The Colonel sucked on his pipe as he rose and strode across to the window, gazing out across the airfield. 'You know, Mac, there are all kinds of people in this crazy, twisted world of ours. You're a good man, a leader, level-headed – either that or you're one crazy son of a bitch when you could have walked away from all this.' He smiled, and his eyes twinkled. 'Well, that's all. Good luck, captain. See you at the briefing.'

Mac's face creased into a smile. 'Thank you, sir.' Yeah, he was right about one thing. He must be crazy. He thought about Stella and how she'd opened up to him earlier, drawing him closer than ever before. He was never going to let her go again. It was time to put that request in.

33

Emden, 2nd October, 1943

'Bombardier to pilot, we'll be at the IP in one minute.' Val's voice.

'Okay, she's all yours, Val.' Mac gazed out at the armada of bombers around them. They were flying lead today, sandwiched in the middle layer of the combat box formation. The group had crossed the Channel, cutting inland across the Netherlands, heading straight towards the seaside town of Emden, riding on shock waves, juddering and bouncing as flak exploded all around them. The engines shook with an almighty fury, shaking Mac like a horseback rider with no seat. He felt uneasy, strangely disconnected from this ship, former bonds lost in the flak, swallowed by the flames of hell through which they flew, and a part of him was drifting.

'Can't see a damn thing down there.' Val's strained voice sliced through his reverie.

'Nine-tenths cloud. They got it wrong again.' Mac shook his head. Plumes of thick black smoke billowed upward just ahead of them. 'First wave must have dropped their bombs.'

'Okay, I see a landmark,' Val's voice over the interphone.

Val's eye would be fused to the bombsight, his finger hovering over that button, poised, ready to unleash hell. Mac's mouth ran dry, and his hands were like slippery eels inside his gloves.

'That's it. Bombs away.' Val's voice edged with relief and excitement to match *Hell's Fury* as she lifted, now thousands of pounds lighter. 'Bomb bay doors closing.'

Mac peered through a break in the cloud as plumes of smoke rose and swirled. Emden was burning. The image of Stella amidst the fire and the rubble crept into his mind. 'God forgive us,' he muttered to himself. He tightened his jaw. 'Let's take her home, boys.'

He put *Hell's Fury* into a sharp turn, banking left. Images raced through his mind of collapsed buildings, with people buried beneath, as it had been that day in East Grinstead. The people. *Oh Jesus, people, and children.* That wasn't some aircraft or munitions factory; it was individuals and lives. It was enforced retaliation, something he had to live with, somehow. He swallowed hard as his heart hammered against his ribs. He had to block it out. There was no time to dwell, and no time for mistakes.

'Where're the fighters?' Emmett's voice.

'Fuck knows. Keep watching. They're coming, I can feel it.' Carleton's voice.

'There ain't no one out there but us.' Ivan's voice from the tail.

The returning formation had so far only been hit by flak. A couple of Forts bore jagged tail sections and fuselages riddled with holes. As they approached the coast, they punched their way through a heavier barrage of anti-aircraft fire and Mac bounced around in his seat as the ship lunged a couple of times, but he held her steady. He glanced at the

Fort on his port side. Their number two engine trailed thick black smoke and then fiery sparks erupted. She'd be slowing up some, running on three for the rest of the way. His mind and his heart raced for home; raced to escape the hell of the sky. Then he could wash up, ditch the baggage, and go see his girl. Warmth flickered in his chest. Stella made everything glow.

They left the flak behind as they flew out across the shimmering waters of the Channel. Here, the cloud was breaking, and sunlight streamed through, sparkling silver upon the calm ripples below. It was almost over, and, thankfully, it had been a milk run. Mac felt a flicker of relief, yet he couldn't shake the darkness that pinned him down and threatened to haul him in. The world had gone crazy. And it wasn't only the bombings. There was talk of the Germans clearing entire communities by other means; rounding up Jews like cattle and taking them to camps. People were saying all kinds of stuff right now. He wondered if the Luftwaffe pilots felt the same way as he did. Just because you're doing your duty doesn't mean to say you agree with it all. No. It didn't matter how wrong it all was, he was simply one cog in that wheel of war – necessary, yet expendable. And if they didn't fight, Hitler would march in, and unleash an even greater hell.

He sighed, spotting the English coast up ahead. Norfolk beckoned and then beyond, Cambridge.

After landing, they got coffee and sandwiches from the Red Cross girls. No matter what time of day it was, they were always there to greet the boys with a honeyed smile on a perfect made-up face. Smart hair, ruby lips, crisp uniform.

'It does a man good to see a beautiful girl,' Wilson said.

'Sure does.' Mac wasn't looking, he was thinking of Stella.

Colonel Edwards scraped back his chair, shot Mac a steely glance, and strode across to the window. He sighed. 'Did you know that ninety percent of all marriages during the First World War failed?'

'No, sir, I did not know that.'

'Well, you can guess why. Dangerous times do the wildest things to a man's mind and a woman's at that. Live for the day and all that crap, not thinking about all the tomorrows. Take it from me. Have all the girls or friendships you want while you're here, only leave out the love stuff.' He flicked a glance at Mac, his eyes narrowed.

Mac was not about to be put off or dismissed. 'Colonel, with all due respect, this isn't a fleeting friendship or a chance encounter. I've been serious about my girl for months. I intend to marry her or die trying, sir.'

The Colonel ran his hand through his dark brown hair, glancing at Mac with a look of exasperation. 'I don't doubt that, I really don't.' He stared at the papers on his desk waiting for his attention. 'See this stack here?' He picked up a dozen or so pages from the pile and waved them in front of him. 'All letters to loved ones, wives, mothers, fathers, telling them their boys won't be coming home, ever. It's not right, but it's war and it's one damned mean bastard! You hear what I'm saying?' His face reddened.

Mac bowed his head, sighed, then looked the Colonel in the eye. 'Yes, sir, I do. But I have to do this, sir.'

Colonel Edwards sighed. 'Okay, Mac. I can see you're hell bent on this so I'll sort out the paperwork, and I'll need to meet Miss Charlton. You understand, it's protocol.' He shook his head. 'Well, I guess there's nothing left to say, except congratulations.'

As the days sailed by, Mac flew a couple more missions, both milk runs, but his hands ached worse than ever. Handling the aircraft controls was awkward, and he'd noticed his lack of strength while holding the control wheel. If he had to pull up from a dive, he didn't know if he'd manage it. That took a whole lot of strength, zapping your arms and your hands.

After Stella's meeting with Colonel Edwards, the Colonel collared Mac afterwards in the officer's club and congratulated him again in front of the guys. There were slaps on the back, and the drinks flowed all evening as they celebrated. Mac's heart lifted. He was so lucky, yet a tiny corner of his mind housed a snippet of darkness that had stitched its claim and no matter how hard he fought, he couldn't tear it out, and he couldn't rest easy. He ought to be waiting until the end of the war, whenever that would be, for her sake, but he guessed that band of gold on her finger was irrelevant if the worst should happen. She'd be destroyed either way.

The next day, when he turned up at Stella's place, no one answered the door. He peered through the living room window and saw her stretched out on the sofa. He tried the front door and found it was open, so he let himself in. As he paused in the living room doorway, she did not stir. Her eyes were closed, and her chest rose and fell rhythmically. Was she asleep? He crept over, crouched down beside her, and planted a kiss on her lips. She jumped.

'Mac! You scared the life out of me. You could have been anyone.'

'Oh, so you'd kiss anyone like that?' He cast a half-smile, crouching down next to her.

'You know what I mean.' She gave him a light shove.

He pressed his lips to hers. 'You're my girl now.' He gazed into those sunflower eyes, mesmerised for a second by flecks of gold floating amidst the green. 'Tired?'

'A little. I'm not suited to night shift, that's all.'

'Oh, honey, just wait until this war's over. You can come to Montana and take care of me. There'll be cooking and cleaning and socks to darn.'

'John Mackenzie, is that why you want to marry me?' She raised an eyebrow.

He drew her close. 'No, it's not.' He pressed his lips to hers, and she softened and kissed him back. 'I'm marrying you because we're meant to be together. You and I are soul mates, destinies entwined for eternity.' He squeezed her and kissed the tip of her nose. 'Besides, I've seen your sewing skills and I reckon I can do a whole lot better.'

She thumped him lightly on the arm, and he chuckled.

'What? You're marrying a lowly rancher, and there's always socks to darn, and sweaters and pants.' He winked as she reached out and caressed his cheek with her fingertips. 'I think Colonel Edwards has taken a shine to you. Singing your praises after your visit.'

'Oh, really? Well, perhaps I should marry him instead. He was very nice to me.' She crossed her arms and raised her chin, defiantly.

'Sorry, honey. He's already taken. Say, what do you mean? You're only supposed to have eyes for me.' He leaned in and grabbed her waist and she crumpled over in a cloud of laughter as he tickled her sides.

'Mac, stop.' She giggled, and her face flushed scarlet as she fought his hands away, finally grabbing hold of them. 'So, when can we set a date for the wedding?'

'We just have to wait for the service paperwork to be authorised. The colonel said it's just protocol, so, nothing's stopping us.'

'Just my mam.'

'Maybe you could call her now?' Mac pulled her up to her feet. 'No time like the present.'

Stella placed the receiver down in its cradle and heaved out a breath. Mac squeezed her hand. 'That was rough.' Her mother had cried, shouted, and cried again upon hearing the news about Alex and then of her daughter's engagement to an American. 'I think she's in shock.'

'Give her time, honey. She'll come around.'

'She's not happy. I could tell by her voice.'

Mac kissed her brow.

'And she cried when I said we'd be getting married here.'

'Well, this is your home for now. Besides, she can come here, maybe spend some time with you before we get married.' He folded her in his arms. 'It'll work out, you'll see.'

'Open it, honey.' Mac sat down at the kitchen table, staring intently into her eyes, a boyish grin toying with his mouth as he pushed the brown paper parcel across to her.

Tentatively, Stella snipped the string with scissors and unwrapped it. Her eyes bulged with surprise. 'Oh, Mac. Where did you get it?' She lifted the bundle of white silk carefully as if it were a newborn and delivered it into Mrs Brown's arms.

'You can thank Uncle Sam. One of the guys had to bail out the other day so it's kind of convenient, wouldn't you say?'

'I can't believe it.' She slid her hand across the fabric, caressing the silk, and she imagined herself wearing it, while the image of a man bailing out of an aircraft tinged the moment with darkness. 'Oh, Mrs B. Do you think we might be able to make a dress?'

'Oh, yes, dear. I know we can. It's such a lot of silk too.' Mrs Brown ran her hands over yards of white, her mouth curving up into a smile, her face filled with awe until the kettle whistled and she sprang into action and resumed making the tea.

'And don't worry about a cake.' Mac grinned.

Stella cast him a puzzled glance.

'Let's just say I called in a favour at the base. One of the guys is taking care of it.'

'Oh, Mac. A real cake?'

He cast her a puzzled glance this time. 'Yeah, a real cake. What other type is there?'

Mrs Brown smiled broadly. 'Oh, that's so generous. It's going to be a wonderful reception.'

'It's going to be cold.' Stella glanced at Mrs. Brown. 'I hadn't thought about it until now. I'll freeze in a dress.'

'Oh, I've got it all worked out, dear. Don't you fret. We'll find or make a lovely white wrap for you. Now then, sit down at the table, you two and we'll have tea.'

The date was set, November 14th, 1943.

34

Bremen, 8ᵗʰ October, 1943

As Mac and his crew slipped over Great Yarmouth and out across the Channel, he gazed at Stella's picture above the instrument panel. Things would be different after the war, and hopefully, she'd be happy to live in Montana. The breath hitched in his throat as he remembered the St Christopher, and with gloved fingers, he reached for his neck and found it nestled beneath his dog tags.

Bombers flanked him above, below, and all around. Further out over the sheet-metal grey water, the gunners tested their weapons, the staccato sound juddering up through the body of the ship, flowing into the cockpit. Acrid smoke from the nose guns below drifted up to greet him. Mac pictured the trail of red on the briefing map that bled into the heart of Bremen, a place they already knew and were all too aware of the reception that awaited them. Earlier, the Colonel's clipped tone and his pensive face had conveyed the tension aptly.

They had taken off at twelve hundred hours and sailed into a filthy grey sky. The air had been chilled on the ground, and was even colder at twenty thousand feet. A few of the fingers on his right hand were growing numb already, although that had nothing to do with the cold. That morning, he'd struggled to dress, his fingers fumbling with buttons as his hands trembled, and he knew it was more than fatigue. The problem had grown steadily worse since his return, and it wasn't so much the pain that troubled him as the transient numbness, which made his hands weak and clumsy. He blew out a breath. They had to make it through.

Slater had done a swell job with the nose art, and *Hell's Fury* now had her own persona and proudly displayed her nose art of a busty redhead in a blue dress, with a trail of fire blazing behind her as she prodded a parody of Hitler with her pitchfork.

'Well, we'll set the shipyards ablaze, all right.' Wilson's eyes were dark, but something more flashed there, and Mac guessed it probably bothered him just as it bothered the other guys. His heart weighed triple, but at least they were hitting industrial targets today.

'Bombardier to pilot. Permission to arm the bombs?' Val's voice.

'Pilot here. Granted.' Mac stamped his feet. A couple of hours in and they were throbbing from the icy air. The P-47 fighter support zipped around them, but they would have to turn around pretty soon as they didn't have enough fuel to make target and back again. The enemy fighters were just biding their time. He glanced at the unnamed Fortress on his port side, and the waist gunner flashed him a thumbs up. There was something to be said for safety in numbers and here, packed into a tight, defensive combat box, a tiny orb glowed inside of him, but it wasn't quite warm enough to thaw the ice.

All too soon, their escort turned for home and Mac's heart sank. 'There they go.'

'So long, little friends.' Ivan's voice from the tail.

They had followed the coastline past the Netherlands and further on towards Germany, and now they turned sharp south for Bremen, following the murky loose coils of the Weser River. The anti-aircraft fire had kicked in as soon as they reached the coastline at Bremerhaven. Mac glanced out of the window at the swatch of green fields through a break in the cloud. Black puffs hung in the air, and the ship shook with the explosions, jolting him in his seat.

'Weather don't seem too good over here either,' Wilson said.

'No. Look at those clouds.' Mac peered at the gathering of grey-black cumulus that was creeping in around them. He gritted his teeth.

'Fighters, twelve o'clock high.' Walt's voice from the top turret.

Machine-gun fire vibrated through the ship, mixing with the thrum of the engines, and Mac's entire body trembled in his seat, his insides shaking, his head bursting.

'Jesus Christ, a Fort's just exploded down in the low formation.' Wilson stared, wide-eyed, breathing heavily.

Mac swallowed. He didn't want to look, but he glanced down at the fireball as pieces of aircraft plummeted into the black smoky haze. Another Fort dropped away from the formation. Jeez, they were falling like flies. The fighters had bided their time, just as he'd predicted. Their cannon fire was intense, accurate, and relentless. There was a dull clunk and *Hell's Fury* shook. An icy draught hurtled across the back of Mac's neck and Wilson turned to look.

'Flak's hit the port side and left a gaping hole.' Wilson wiped sweat from his brow.

Great, as if they weren't cold enough already. Now they were going to freeze. Mac sweated, and his back was soaked from fighting to keep the ship in formation. His hands ached and throbbed and even his face was sore where sweat pooled around the edges of his oxygen mask, which dug into his right cheek. They had to make it. They had to. He glanced at Stella's picture and swallowed. She was expecting him home for dinner at seven.

'Fighters, twelve o'clock high.' Walt's voice from the top turret.

'Christ, they got Taylor's ship. It's a flamer. She's going down.' Val's voice.

Mac steeled himself as black forms up ahead zoomed towards them, transforming into yellow-nosed Messerschmitt Bf 109s, cutting through the formation in a bid to break them up. Gunners from the surrounding ships shot lead out across the sky as fast as they could to fend them off.

They were almost over the target. Mac glanced down. There was some cloud and a whole lot of smoke, but there were breaks through which glows of red flashed.

'Pilot to bombardier. How's that target looking, Val?'

'Almost there. I see it. Bombs gone.'

Mac gazed around at the Forts as they dropped their ladder of bombs and out of the corner of his eye, two Focke-Wulf 190s flashed towards them. 'Fighters, eleven o'clock high.' He took control of the ship and made a wide sweeping turn for home. Another ship dropped out of formation and headed down into hell.

'We sure did set off some fireworks down there today,' Wilson said.

'Radio to pilot. Get us home.' Red's voice. 'Jeez, I always wanted to join the Navy, see the world, only I get sea sick. Someone said join the Air Force. Goddam fools never said anything about this.'

The ship shook and bucked her way through the shelling and jolted Mac in his seat.

'Jesus Christ! A piece of Nazi flak just missed my head.' Red's voice, filled with anguish.

'Pilot to radio operator. You okay, Red?'

'Yeah. Just got a gale force icy blast blowing through my office.'

'Fighter, nine o'clock high.' Emmett's voice from the waist.

Mac turned to look and saw the yellow nose first, then the arc of tracer fire headed towards it, no doubt coming from the waist. The Messerschmitt dived beneath them and resurfaced on the other side, firing continuously, then he zipped up ahead, banked, and came at them head-on. Cannon fire hit the Plexiglas nose, and there was a loud thud as the ship shuddered, jolting Mac forward. His heart drilled against his ribcage.

Wilson looked out at the starboard wing. 'Number three engine's on fire.'

Mac glanced at the plume of black smoke. 'Extinguishers. Feather the prop.'

'It ain't working.' Flames of orange flared from the engine, licking the wing.

'We'll have to dive. Red, get me a C wave.' Mac waited for the radio frequency. 'Group, it's Captain Mackenzie. We're dropping out of formation. Wingman, you're lead plane now. Okay, here we go. Hang on, guys.'

Mac put *Hell's Fury* into a dive, pointing her nose towards the ground, descending at an alarming rate. Seconds seemed like minutes, but as they watched, the flames gradually died, leaving a trail of grey-black smoke streaming from the engine.

'Wilson, help me pull her up!' Mac yelled, breathing hard. His hands were throbbing so bad they were almost numb, and he didn't know how much longer he could hold on. The control wheel shuddered violently, sapping his strength even more, and he gritted his teeth so hard his jaw ached.

'Pull her up, goddammit!' he yelled, flicking a glance at Wilson and then at the ground below, which hurtled towards them with trees and buildings blossoming large, fast, too fast. Just as he was certain they were going to crash, the nose lifted towards the horizon, and she gradually levelled out at six thousand feet. Mac was breathing so hard his chest grew tight and ached, and as he relaxed his grip on the control wheel, his hands hurt even more. He needed to rest up. 'Wilson. Take over for me.'

Wilson glanced at him, looking on as Mac clenched and unclenched his hands. He nodded and took the wheel.

Flying at this height, they had a bird's eye view of the German countryside, but they were also a prime target for the buzzing fighters and the anti-aircraft gunners. 'Better start climbing, get us out of here.' Mac reached for his water canteen and took a drink. Nausea swirled in his gut, and he puffed out a breath, but man, that land was an unbelievable green.

They began to climb. 'Pilot to nose. Damage report.'

'Bombardier to pilot. We're okay.' Val's voice. 'The Plexiglas is all busted, cracked to hell.'

'Okay, Val.' They'd been lucky. They were headed towards the coast, and the ocean was in sight, but first they had to wade through the flak at Bremerhaven, and flying at a lower altitude posed a far greater risk. A lone Messerschmitt Bf 109 spotted *Hell's Fury* and darted across for a better look. Its pilot whipped all around the ship, careful to keep his distance as if he was inspecting her before darting up ahead.

'He's coming back round. Twelve o'clock high.' Walt's voice.

The German fighter swung his yellow nose around in a wide turn and came back for another pass, spitting sparks of cannon fire from his gun ports. *Jesus, he was going for the nose.* Machine-gun fire hailed from around the ship and tracer fire shot out from the nose. The ship shuddered and tremors snaked up through Mac's feet and flowed through the control wheel into his arms and body as the fighter slid beneath their wing.

'Navigator to pilot. The Plexiglas has gone and Val's hit.' Jim's voice.

'Pilot here. Is it bad?'

'Can't tell. It's the shoulder. I'll do the best I can.'

The Messerschmitt dived below their belly and darted away just as the ship lurched and number four engine belched out smoke.

'I got him. Take that, you bastard.' Ivan's voice from the tail.

The Messerschmitt nosedived towards the ground as thick smoke belched out, and then a blossoming plume of white sailed through the black.

'He's bailed.' Ivan's voice, tinged with disappointment.

Mac hit the extinguisher button and kept his gaze on the propeller until it ceased to spin. The wing was peppered with holes, and several chunks had been gouged out.

'Val's hit pretty bad, and it's blowing an icy gale in here.' A brief pause. 'Blood's soaked right through his flight suit.' Jim's voice.

'Okay. Do what you can. Get him in the radio room.' Damn. It was all falling apart, and as Mac gazed through the side window, Fortresses from their group sailed on by. They couldn't keep up, and shortly they'd be all alone.

'Pilot here. Everyone check in.'

One by one, they checked in. Only Val had been hit. *Hell's Fury* had slowed more, and the fuel gauge wasn't looking too healthy either. The chances of them making it across the Channel looked slim. Wilson transferred fuel from both damaged engines to the remaining two. If they were going to make it, they would need every last drop.

'Listen up, everyone, we're flying on two engines, and we haven't even crossed the Channel. Fuel's getting low so get your chutes on and be ready to bail.' Mac's voice was solemn. Wilson glanced at him before grabbing his chute.

More Fortresses sailed on by, and Mac's heart sank. His hands were half useless, and he was fighting himself just to keep on going. Wilson was going to have to pull his weight. There was a chance they could make it, although it was tight. He didn't know what to do for the best, but ditching in the Channel was not an option, especially at this time of year. They wouldn't stand a chance in those freezing waters. The ship lurched again, and the control wheel shook and shuddered.

'Christ, what now?' Wilson looked to Mac for guidance. 'Oil pressure's dropping on number two. I don't fancy our chances of making it home from here, do you?'

Mac glanced at him. 'I'm prepared to give it a damn good try if you are.' Wilson looked real uncertain. Several ships had gone down, damaged. A number of guys had bailed out and were probably being rounded up by the Germans right now. *Goddamn it, he was going home.* They rocked and rolled on waves of flak as they followed the German coastline and headed towards the Netherlands.

'Christ, red flak.' Carleton's voice. 'That was fucking close!'

Mac said a silent prayer and his father's words whispered in his head. *Bring her home safe, son. Sing her home.* A warm glow burst in his chest, and he smiled.

Shells exploded behind them, and the force rocked the sky and the Fort as they bounced and bucked along for a few seconds more before sailing into calm, leaving Germany behind. No more Forts passed them by. They were alone. Mac checked his watch. Already five thirty, the time they were scheduled to be back at the base. Of course, there were always some stragglers, and some who wouldn't be returning at all. He prayed they weren't one of them. The guys would be sweating it out at the airfield, and the Colonel would be up on the tower, his eyes glued to his binoculars, waiting, counting, hoping.

He glanced at Stella's picture. All that time she'd worried about him, about this, and she'd been right to worry. A burst of machine-gun fire hit them like a hail storm. A chorus of voices broke out at once over the interphone.

'Bandits! Twelve o'clock high.' Walt's voice. Machine-gun fire hailed from his top turret and Mac stiffened as two

Messerschmitts headed directly for them, closing in fast, veering off left and right just at the last moment.

Wilson ducked out of instinct then shook his head. 'Christ. Crazy bastards!'

The ship shuddered and bucked again, and Mac tasted a mix of cordite and rubber beneath his oxygen mask.

'Jesus, sweet Jesus, I'm hit!' Red's voice.

'Navigator to pilot. Red's hit in the leg. It looks bad.'

Mac glanced at Wilson. 'Do what you can, Jim. Where are those fighters?'

Wilson craned his neck to search the sky. 'They're coming about for another pass.'

'Bandits, six o'clock high.' Ivan's voice.

The fighters flashed past them, peppering both sides of *Hell's Fury* with cannon fire. Something punched Mac's arm near the shoulder and he was knocked sideways as a burning ache radiated through his arm and the side of his chest, winding him and he gasped.

'Christ.' Wilson stared wide-eyed at a hole in the fuselage where an icy wind roared through like a hurricane.

'That was lucky. You okay?' Mac glanced over at him as his heart drummed.

'Yeah. You?'

'Fine. Let's fly this ship home.' That piece of Nazi shell must have torn his flight suit. Yeah, they'd been lucky. The icy wind pierced his left shoulder and burrowed into the side of his chest. Mac glanced at the fist-sized hole in the fuselage. Man, that was close. His heart hammered, and he gasped for breath.

'Fighters have flown. Hit and run.' Walt's voice.

They left the Netherlands coastline and soared out across the Channel. He wasn't bailing now. He focused on Stella and those eyes, his guiding light.

'Pilot to crew. You can come off oxygen now. We're at ten thousand feet. Navigator, how're the casualties?'

'Val's pretty bad, but he's steady. He's had morphine. And Jim's real sleepy. I've put a tourniquet on the leg and dressed the wound, but it's soaked through again. I can't do much else.'

'Mac, can you take her for a while? I just need to use the pee tube.' Wilson flicked an awkward glance at him.

Mac nodded and took the control wheel. Great. Trust him to need a piss at the wrong time. He glanced at the instrument panel. The oil pressure was stable; fuel had dropped a little more, but it looked as though they'd have enough to get back. It was going to be real close. He glanced at the murky waters below. The sun hovered on the horizon, a ball of fire with streaks of orange caressing the sapphire sky as night waited to fall.

'Pilot to navigator. Jim, I need you to be on hand to help us home. You'd better come on up here.' His head hurt and his vision suddenly blurred. He strained his eyes to focus and sucked in a breath, and a sharp jab pierced his side.

Wilson returned and sank down in his seat. 'Hey, Mac, you okay? You don't look so good.'

Mac closed his eyes, just for a minute. He needed to focus. 'I'm okay.' His voice came out slow and slurred. He puffed out a breath as his heart galloped.

'I'll plot the course.' Jim placed his hand on Mac's shoulder, and the light pressure radiated like fire and he cried out.

'Jim, take a look at him. I think he's hit.' Wilson took the controls.

Jim hovered over Mac, scrutinising his left arm. 'Oh yeah. He's hit all right. In the arm. Shit. I'll go get the medical kit.'

'I'm hit? Where?' Mac pulled at his flight suit, his fingers sweeping his arm until he reached frayed cloth and a hole. He pulled his hand away and peered at glistening gloved fingertips. Damn. Stella was going to kill him now for sure. His heart swelled. He didn't mind what she did as long as he got to see her again. 'Can't be that bad, there's barely any blood.'

'Just relax. There's quite a pool beneath your seat, as it goes.' Jim grabbed a dressing pack, some sulphur powder, and morphine.

'I don't want any morphine. Wilson might need my help to land.'

'But you're in pain.'

'I'm always in pain. Makes no difference to me.' He was, and right now his hands ached and throbbed. Maybe that was why he couldn't feel much pain in his arm. His eyes flicked over the gauges. The oil pressure was running a little low on number one engine. All the other Forts would be back by now, and the officers on the tower roof would be going in search of hot coffee while the ground crew hung their heads, collected their bicycles, and rode away with faces that said all was lost.

The night sky deepened, the fire eclipsed. He glanced at his watch. Half past six. He closed his eyes. It was eleven thirty in Montana. Dad would be out on the ranch, maybe breaking in a new horse. Mom would be making lunch for everyone like she did every day. His eyes flickered open and latched on to something dark grey, looming in the distance. 'Is that land?' Mac struggled to focus, his vision blurring.

'Yeah, that's the Suffolk coastline. Almost home,' Jim said.

'Home. Yeah.' Stella would be waiting. His eyelids grew heavier and heavier until he couldn't hold them up any longer. Then someone was shaking him vigorously, a hand gripping his good shoulder.

'Mac, come on! Stay awake. I might need you.' Wilson's voice. 'Like now. Shit! Number one engine's smoking. Oil pressure's falling. Mac, come on. Feather the prop.'

Mac's eyes flickered open. He looked at the gauge. The pressure was low. He pressed the feather button, and the strain of leaning forward sent a searing pain ricocheting through his shoulder. He glanced at the dressing that now sat there. It was dark red.

'We're almost home. We've just cut in across the coast, and we're making a south-westerly heading to the base. ETA around ten minutes.' Jim's voice.

Mac took a breath. It hurt. His chest was tight, and his breaths shallow, almost as if he couldn't suck in enough air. 'Landing gear.'

'I've got it.' Wilson glanced across at him. 'Jim, give him some oxygen for Christ's sake. He's grey.'

Grey? Jeez, he sure felt weak.

'Crap. The hydraulics must be shot out. It's not coming down. Co-pilot to flight engineer. I need you to check out the landing gear.'

Mac slouched in his seat, staring into the darkness. Jim slipped the mask over his face, and he sucked in pure oxygen, cold, refreshing, even with the nauseating stench of rubber. His eyes grew wide, his gaze latching on to the sickle moon high over King's College, and as he reached over to touch the control wheel, hard metal vibrated through his hand. What a Fort. Still breathing, still pushing on.

'Landing gear's trashed.' Walt's voice. The manual crank ain't working either.

A firm hand gripped Mac's good shoulder. 'Mac, we're gonna have to belly land. I need your help.'

Yeah, Wilson had never done it before. 'First time for everything,' Mac said.

'You're gonna have to take her down, Mac. I can't do it.' Wilson's face filled with fear.

Mac had heard all about his disastrous emergency landing a short while ago, and from the look in his eyes, he was freaking out. 'Co-pilot to crew. Get in the radio room and prepare for crash landing.'

Mac glanced at Wilson, whose eyes flashed with uncertainty. 'Take her down, line her up for me, and then I'll try, but you'd better be ready. You can do this.'

As Wilson brought the aircraft lower, treetops thrashed her belly, and there, in the distance, a faint strip of lights glowed like fireflies along the runway. Peace sailed over Mac like an unknown presence as if old friends now rested soothing hands on his shoulders, allaying all fear. The ship's engine thrummed and flowed through his feet, travelling to his heart where whispers concurred and forged a connection. His father's voice. *Make her sing.* He was finally one with his aircraft.

As they descended further, treetops slapped the undercarriage, and suddenly, the last engine spluttered.

As darkness approached, Stella couldn't settle. An uneasiness had drifted over her, and a nagging voice screamed in her head. She couldn't explain it. There was no logic. Quickly, she grabbed her jacket and her cycle and headed off to the base in the dusky night.

When she reached the entrance, the guard politely informed her that she was not allowed in, however, she refused to budge and breathlessly begged him to telephone Colonel Edwards. That did the trick because he lifted the barrier and waved her through.

'Wait here please, ma'am. Someone will come down shortly.' He nodded, unsmiling, and ambled across to the guard post.

Stella waited, her face turned up to the sky as the drone of an aircraft grew close. It was a different sound. This one was wounded. She'd seen a few return earlier. Some had been riddled with holes, their skin peeling and jagged, while others had chunks gouged from tails and wings. One had no nose left. They were so shot up it was a miracle they'd managed to make it home at all, then she remembered Mac's words. *They're not called Flying Fortresses for nothing.* Her heart raced, and nausea surged inside her.

No. Something was wrong. A dark cruciform emerged from the night sky, descending, and the breath hitched in her throat.

'Okay, Mac. Have you got her?' Wilson kept his hands on the control wheel, ready. 'Walt, fire the flares.'

Mac grabbed the wheel. He widened his eyes, struggling to focus, his vision blurring. 'Just got to keep her straight and level, keep the nose up.' They whipped the last of the trees as they came down a little too fast, and as *Hell's Fury* touched down with a thud, they bounced back up before landing with a hard, determined crunch and slid along at speed.

'Brakes.' He must have been holding his breath as now his lips tingled, his chest ached and burned, and his head was floating, but they were down, thank God. Now all they had to do was stop. From the corner of his eye, wispy black smoke spiralled up.

'We can't burn.' His voice was slow and slurred. The *Texas Rose* drifted into his mind, with Birdie, standing in the waist grinning at him like a Cheshire cat. They had to make it. He wouldn't leave Stella. He shook his head, but it was no use. He gasped for air; he was floating, spinning, and he slumped over the control wheel, dissolving into the black.

35

Realisation & Integrity

In the distance, someone was calling his name. Mac's eyes flickered open. Everything was silent. Where was he? That smell, something clean, sterile, in place of oil, cordite, and rubber. He glanced left. The outline of a bed. Did he land?

'Hello again, Mac.' A familiar voice.

Mac glanced up as Badger, the MO, hovered over him, his outline still a little fuzzy. 'Where am I?'

'You're in the field hospital. You got hit on the mission yesterday. Don't you remember?'

'Oh, yeah, my arm.'

'Well, that and you had a collapsed lung, but you'll be back to working order soon enough.'

'Can't get enough of the place, doc.' Yesterday. He must have been out for hours.

'Do you think you're up to visitors? I have a concerned young lady waiting to see you.'

Stella came to his side. 'Oh, Mac.' She grasped his hand and gently touched his brow.

He opened his eyes and strained to focus. 'Sorry, honey. We're a little late. Don't think I can have that dinner after all.' He closed his eyes, squeezing her hand in his. She wasn't going anywhere. Pain slithered between his ribs on his left side, and his left arm felt weird. His mind was filled with a foggy haze and iodine hung in the air. The last thing he remembered was skimming those trees as they roared overhead.

Silken skin brushed his brow, his cheek. He loved her touch, and a faint sweet lavender breeze drifted towards him. He was home. 'I'm glad you're here.' He tried to hitch his mouth into a smile. He curled his right hand and a sharp pain burrowed inside of it. He glanced down and saw he was attached to an IV.

'I knew something was wrong yesterday. Oh, Mac. You were so brave, and you even managed to land the aircraft.'

'I did?' He could barely remember. Oh, Jeez, the guys. 'What about the others?'

'Oh, they're all going to be fine, thanks to you. Red's sitting up in bed at the end there and Val's okay, although he'll be on sick leave for a while, the doctor said.'

Thank, God. 'Am I in one piece? What about my hands?'

'The doctor said you're as tough as leather. They don't make them like you, Mac. And yes, you're in one piece. Whole.' She squeezed his hand and smiled, her eyes watery.

He'd done it. He'd brought his crew home, safe and he'd survived, and the girl he loved stood by his side. With Stella he could do anything, be anything. He was going to live a whole life – just as soon as he could wake up fully. Jeez, the doc must have pumped him full of morphine. His eyes flickered shut again.

'You had me so worried. I didn't know what to think when I saw you land. My heart was in my mouth.'

He hitched one eye open. 'What? You were here?' She must have been terrified.

'Yes, With Colonel Edwards. I must say, he was rather concerned too.' Stella's voice choked.

'Stella, is my arm really okay? It feels kinda numb. They're not holding anything back, are they?' With his good hand, he reached across and ran it up and down his injured arm. He puffed out a breath.

She sighed, leaned down, and brushed her lips on his. 'No, darling. They're not.'

'Hmm. I like the sound of that.' He gazed up at her, those large green eyes swimming in red. A tear bobbed on her eyelash and hovered before spilling down her cheek. He pulled her hand to his lips and kissed her fingertips. 'Hey, come on, you.'

'I'm sorry. It's just when they carried you out of the aircraft, you were so grey. I thought I'd lost you.' Her chin trembled, and she dipped her hand into her coat pocket, dragged out a handkerchief, and dabbed her eyes.

'I told you I'd be back.' He squeezed her hand. 'When we were struggling up there, you hauled us back. I kept on looking at your pretty picture up there by the instrument panel, and I prayed.' Mac's eyes grew misty, and his chest ached – only partly due to the injury.

Stella sniffed, and her mouth curved up into a brave smile.

'I'm so tired. It feels as if I've lived a hundred years already.' He yawned, his eyes closed once more, and a single crystal droplet emerged from the corner of his eye and streaked across his cheek.

'You rest, darling. I'll come back later.' Stella brushed her lips across his, and he put his arm around her, drawing her close.

Stella stepped out into the fresh morning air and inhaled. Autumn leaves of cherry, gold, and copper danced in the breeze, scuttling wherever it blew as the overhead trees cackled. She yawned. A wave gripped her chest, and she pursed her lips as tears stung her eyes. Mac almost died. They could have all died. She stifled a yawn and grabbed her cycle, her lead-like limbs protesting at the prospect of a long ride home.

'Stella?'

She spun around to face Mac's co-pilot. 'Hello.'

'Are you off home?'

'Yes. I've left him to rest.'

'Here, I'll give you a ride.' Wilson took the bicycle from her hands and crammed it in the jeep. He smiled, his kind chestnut eyes framed by dark circles.

'Oh, thanks. I'm exhausted.' She dabbed her eyes.

'He'll be all right. Tough as old boots.' Wilson winked.

That's what the doctor had said. She smiled. 'Well, I'm so glad you managed to land the aircraft.'

'That was mainly all due to Mac. He's a mighty fine pilot. One of the best.'

She thought back to the conversation she'd overheard last night. The doctor mentioned something about nerve damage to Mac's arm. She clambered into the jeep and heaved out a breath. What treatment would he need for that? Perhaps he'd be grounded for a while until it resolved. Her stomach lifted. She closed her eyes against the bright morning sun with its determined glint through the trees as the jeep hurtled along the country lane.

Mac gazed out of the window as white clouds sailed by in a flawless sky. So, the numbness in his arm wasn't just something that was going to resolve itself in time. Nerve damage. That's what the doc had called it. He shook his head and lay back, his head sinking into the pillows. Swell.

'Hey, Mac. How's it going?' Red positioned his wheelchair at the bottom of the bed.

'Hey, Red. I'll be okay. How's the leg?'

'Doc says I should be up and about in a week or so. Can't walk on it for a few days so I asked the nurse to get me a chair. The hell I'm staying in bed all day.'

'Yeah, I don't blame you. I think I might go stir crazy if I'm stuck here too long.'

'You heard about Val?'

Mac shook his head.

'They're shipping him home. Would you believe that cannon shell almost shattered his arm? He's had surgery, but they told him he'd probably need another op. Bad luck, huh?' Red wheeled himself around to the side of the bed.

Mac's cheek twitched. 'It sure is. I'm glad he's going to be okay. You too, Red. You both got lucky up there.' At least they'd made it home, almost in one piece. He sure hoped Val would make a full recovery.

Red glanced at the floor and hunched his shoulders. 'We were lucky to make it home, and that was down to you, Mac, and Wilson.' Red nodded to him. 'We lost some Forts, and the guys said most of the ones that made it back were all badly shot up, including ours.

'How many did the 91st lose?'

'We lost one, but the group took thirty losses.' Red's eyes glazed over. 'The 91st had several more casualties as well as us.'

Jeez, three hundred men missing.

'Oh, gee, here she comes. Nursey.' Red rolled his eyes as Mac suppressed a laugh.

'There you are. What did I tell you about not overdoing things? And here you are again, pestering Captain Mackenzie. Back to bed for you, quick march. You know what the doctor said.'

'Yes, ma'am.' Red saluted, spun around, and wheeled away.

Mac chuckled until a sharp pain in his chest silenced him, and he winced. Poor Val. He was one hell of a bombardier, and he'd be mad at having to miss out on the war. On the upside, at least he got to go home and keep out of harm's way, as Stella would say.

What was he going to do now if he couldn't fly? Instructing was out of the question. Hell, what was left? He dragged a hand through his hair and his chest pulled. Breathing in was still a little sore, and he pinched his lips. A collapsed lung. Mac shook his head and looked down at his scarred hands. Another mission, another injury, another hospital. How much was enough? And it wasn't just him. What about Stella? Hadn't she been through enough already? And then there was his crew. This time, they'd made it. His hands still ached, and he clenched them a few times. He hadn't been able to pull out of that dive. Wilson had pumped more effort into that mission than ever before and without him, they never would have made it.

The doc was right. He had to call it a day. He couldn't push himself and endanger a crew in the process. All this, everything he'd done, had been in support of his duty, to avenge the deaths of his friends, and to ensure he could hold his head up and state boldly how he'd served his country in the war. It was his pride. Just as his pride interfered each time he dared to stare at his reflection. It didn't matter what he looked like on the outside. It was done now. What mattered was how he lived his life and what choices he made from now on. Appearances don't make a man. A man has to forge his own way.

If he wanted to redeem himself in some way, then he'd done it. He clamped his eyes shut as Bill's face flashed in his mind, then Birdie's, and all the other guys he'd seen come and go while he'd been stationed here. So many faces who'd never see their homes again. His eyes grew misty and a fresh pain seared across his chest as he whipped a tear away.

It was going to be tough, but he knew he'd never fly one of those big birds again. His heart swelled with a mix of emotions and his ears buzzed with the silence. All the things he loved and hated lay in that ship, played out at high altitude. The smell of cordite scorching your nose, the vibration that buzzed through your entire body, and the sharp, icy cold that penetrated your bones. He sure was going to miss it. Flying was so natural to him, and the sky was his second home. It was one of the best feelings he'd ever known – forming up on a bomber's wing, glancing across that divide in the air to see the pilot alongside you give you the nod. Gunners waving back and mighty Fortresses all around like stepping stones in a never-ending ocean.

A new light dawned, one with honeyed undertones, and he'd be a fool to pass up on that. Archie's voice rang in his ears and the breath caught in his throat. *Whatever happens, Mac, don't struggle on. Promise me you'll call. Don't leave it too late.* He huffed out a heavy sigh. It was an omen, for sure. He gazed at the ceiling as an ache pinched his throat. Being part of a crew had really meant something and bonds had been forged that would never be broken.

In a few weeks he was getting married. He sure hoped he'd be fit by then. After everything, there was no way on earth he was going to postpone this wedding.

36

Bourn, October 30th, 1943

The china on the dresser rattled and clinked as the vibration grew and buzzed beneath her feet. Stella placed her cup on the table and slipped out into the garden, turning her face towards the sky. The acrid smell of next door's chimney smoke hung in the air, and across the fields, several B-17s climbed into the clouds. A warm haze filled her, despite the bracing morning breeze. Mac wouldn't be joining them ever again. Her chest tightened at the image of him being stretchered off his ship, an image she hadn't been able to shift from her mind. She pressed her palm to her heart as tears rushed her eyes.

He was being discharged today, and because he was on sick leave, the Colonel had given him permission to stay with them. Mrs Brown had been so sweet about it, although she had voiced concern about the morality of the situation, but as the wedding was so close, she'd agreed. Separate rooms, of course. Stella smiled to herself. Hopefully her mother wouldn't disapprove when she arrived.

Yesterday, he'd told her his news. His flying days with the Mighty Eighth were over, though the Colonel, he said, wanted to speak with him about another appointment. She could tell that Mac was trying to be buoyant about it, but his dark, dull eyes and his downcast face whispered a different story. The darkness had snatched a little piece of him away. She knew he was going to miss it all so terribly, and he was trying to be brave. Oh, but he *was* brave, and now they could finally be together. The B-17s faded into the distance, eclipsed by grey clouds.

'Stella, dear. There you are. Our guest has arrived.' Mrs Brown beamed and squeezed past her as she headed out into the garden with a bowl of grain for the hens. Mac appeared in the doorway, his left arm in a sling and that sweet smile on his lips.

'Oh, Mac. You're early.' She dashed across and wrapped her arms around him.

'Hi, beautiful. Whoa, steady now, I'm still a little sore.'

She turned her face to his, and he kissed her. 'I'm so glad you're here. Now I can take care of you.'

'Hmm, I like the sound of that.' He rested his brow on hers and grinned, his eyes a blur.

'Have you realised we're getting married in two weeks?'

'Yeah.'

His voice was so relaxed, and Stella hitched an eyebrow. 'Well, come and sit down and I'll make you a cup of coffee.'

'Oh yeah, look in my bag in the hall there. I brought my own supplies.'

'You did?'

'Well, I couldn't impose what with the ration and all.'

He thought of everything and she smiled to herself. Mac sat down at the kitchen table and removed his crush cap. While she made coffee, the hairs on the back of her neck bristled and she spun around. 'Why are you looking at me like that? You've got that wicked gleam in your eye, Captain Mackenzie.'

'Oh, I was just thinking of how well you'll fit in back home. Why, I ought to write to Mom and let her know she can finally put her feet up.'

Stella smiled. Goodness, Montana. It was so far away, and her tummy somersaulted. She sank down on the chair next to him and rested her hand on his knee. 'Do you think they'll like me?'

He cupped her chin. 'Oh, honey, they're going to love you. Mom's excited already. They can't wait to meet you. And Jack can't wait to have a sister.' He pressed his lips to hers. Mac always made everything brighter somehow, and inside she beamed.

Mrs Charlton arrived two days before the wedding, bringing with her a whirlwind of emotion, smiles, and laughter one minute and sobbing the next. Stella was quite overcome by it all and beginning to feel rather drained.

'Mam, this is Mac.' Stella held her breath for a moment.

'It's a pleasure to meet you, ma'am.' Mac held out his hand.

Mrs Charlton considered it and then stepped closer and hugged him. 'Well, if you're marrying my daughter you'd best call me Mam, or is it *Mom*?' She laughed, and Stella exhaled as the tension flowed from her body.

Later, when Mac suggested a walk, Stella agreed. She wanted to spend as much time with him as possible; besides, in two days she would be back on duty. The day was dry, cool yet not chilled. Aside from the occasional evergreen, most trees had bared their souls, their leaves of autumnal colours scattering in the wind.

'I love the fall.' Mac thrust his foot into a pile of dry yellow and red leaves, sending them soaring. They wandered up to the church and sat down on a seat in the grounds, where he wrapped his arm around her, drawing her close to his side. 'Hey, this was our first date. You remember?'

'Yes.' She sighed. 'Mac, I've been thinking. I feel awful about moving to America and leaving Mam on her own.'

He kissed the top of her head. 'I know, but you heard what she said. She was pretty adamant she wants to stay here.'

'Would she be able to come to America?'

'Can't see why not. She can stay with us, and we'll look after her.'

Stella smiled and slipped her arm around his waist. 'What if you stayed here?'

'Well, if it comes down to it, I will, only the US Army will send me home when it's time, and who knows how long it'll take to get my discharge, and then I have to make my way back again.' He turned to her. 'I want you with me, Stella, always.'

He pressed his lips to hers and the bond that bound them squeezed her heart. She couldn't be parted from him.

That evening, they were left alone as Mrs Brown and her mother had gone to the church to see to the preparations. Stella brought Mac a cup of coffee and placed it down on the table next to the sofa. He slipped his arm out of the sling, reached for her hand, and pulled her down to him and kissed her.

'What was that for?'

'To say I love you and thanks for looking after me so well.' He kissed her again, this time more urgent, his tongue seeking hers. Stella gasped and then he was on top of her, pressing his lips to her neck, gliding to her chest. 'Oh, God I missed you. Being laid up in the hospital was driving me crazy. I want you.'

'I want you too, but we can't. Not here.'

He stopped and looked into her eyes. 'Two days to go and then I'll have you all to myself.' He raised his eyebrows.

'Mac, honestly. Drink your coffee before it gets cold.' She sat up and cast him one of her stern looks while she watched him reach for his cup with his injured arm. He managed to grasp it, although his hand shook so he transferred it into his right hand. Still, it was an improvement, but it was going to take time.

The next morning, as Stella walked past Mac's door, it was ajar, and she caught sight of him staring at his reflection in the mirror, his mouth a tight line, his eyes sad. She held her breath for a moment, instinctively aware of his thoughts. He would never escape the bad memories. How could he when he wore the scars each day? A vulnerability crept into his face when they were out in public, and he would grip her hand tight, but she was blessed to stand proud by his side, to love and support him. Yes, acceptance would take time.

'Mac?' She opened the door and peered round.

'Hey, morning.' He strode over and took her in his arms.

'I see you're not wearing the sling.'

'No. The doc insisted that I do, only I wanted to have a little time out.'

'How does it feel, your arm?'

'Well, right now, around you, it feels pretty good.' He grinned.

She raised her chin and reached up to cup both sides of his face. 'I can hardly believe we're getting married tomorrow.' She gazed into his blue eyes. 'I love you so much and I always will, John Mackenzie.'

He pressed his brow to hers. 'I like it when you say my proper name.'

'I like it too. I suppose that's what your parents call you so I thought I'd better get used to it.'

'Say, where's your mom?' Light flashed in his eyes.

'She's just gone out with Mrs B. Why?'

'This is the last time we'll be together before we're married. I won't see you until tomorrow.' He gestured to the bed, and his mouth curved up into a broad grin.

'Mac, we can't.'

'Sure we can. We're all alone, and tomorrow you'll be my wife.'

He strode across to the door and pushed it shut.

Stella posed in front of the dressing table mirror, her hands caressing the silk she wore, slipping over the fitted crossover bodice, the long, flowing skirt that skimmed her hips, while her eyes lingered over the elegant, flowing train. Her gaze sailed up to her neck as she relived Mac's soft kisses from earlier that morning – kisses that had glided all the way to her breast, then lower still. Her cheeks glowed warm, and she smiled as her heart swelled in her chest. She drew in a large breath and slowly exhaled. Mrs Brown had created something exquisite out of a parachute, and she was privileged to wear it, and she swore never to part with it. This dress had saved one life and was about to help two more begin a new journey together.

'Stella, are you all right?' Her mother's voice through the bedroom door.

'Yes. You can come in now.' She turned to face them, and her mother beamed, then her chin trembled as tears slipped down her cheeks.

'Oh, no, please don't cry. I was doing so well not to.' Tears sprang to Stella's eyes and she fanned her face with her hand as she blew out a breath.

'Oh, you look beautiful, love.' Mrs Charlton hugged her, her voice high. 'Mac's a very lucky man to have you. I hope he knows that.' She sniffed.

'Oh, I think he does, Mam. You do like him, don't you? I mean, I know you had your heart set on Alex.'

Her mother took hold of Stella's hands. 'Stella, I only ever wanted you to be happy and well looked after, and I think Mac's quite capable of taking care of you. It's funny, but when I see the two of you together, and the way he looks at you, well, I can't imagine a better husband.' She hugged her tight.

'Well now, ladies, I think we'd better get a move on. This wedding's tomorrow, and we need to make sure this dress is fit for purpose.' Mrs Brown blew her nose.

'Who's seeing to the flowers?' Mrs Charlton finished doing up the last button on Stella's dress.

'Oh, yes. Mrs Thompson from up the road and some of the other ladies from the WI have had a rally round, and they're taking flowers to the church today. You can come along this afternoon if you like and help with the arrangements.' Mrs. Brown crouched down on the floor and arranged the train of the dress. 'There we are. Not too short, not too long. Didn't I say it would be perfect?' She beamed up at Stella, her rosy cheeks flushing scarlet.

'You did, Mrs B. You've been amazing. How can I ever thank you enough?'

'Oh, well, your young man has kept us in spam and coffee for some time now.' She laughed. 'Knowing you're happy is more than enough for me.'

'Are we going to have a little drink this evening before the big day?' Mrs Charlton surprised Stella with her suggestion, especially as she never drank.

'Well, I've got Vera coming over. Her chap's off to the pub with Mac tonight. They're having a drink with some friends,' Stella said.

'Well, that's settled then. We'll put the radio on, I'll prepare some food, and we'll have a small celebration. Can I ask Mrs Thompson over, and a few of the other ladies?' Mrs Brown heaved herself up, puffed out a breath, and smoothed down her skirt.

'Of course. That would be lovely.' Stella turned to the mirror, admiring the dress. Mac would be back soon. He'd gone to see the Colonel about something and then he was coming for his things as he was booked in at the Hardwicke Arms for the night. He'd been a little preoccupied over the last couple of days, although that was understandable. Such a lot had happened. But yesterday afternoon, around three o'clock, when everything that could rattled and shook when those Flying Fortresses roared overhead, she'd watched him. He'd looked up from the newspaper, and gazed out of the window, holding his breath, and she'd glimpsed the intense look of yearning that flared in his eyes.

37

Whole Again

Stella gazed up at the silent bells of the Church of St Helena and St Mary as the chilled November breeze nipped her cheeks. Family and friends from RAF Bourn and from Mac's base at Bassingbourn filed into the church to take their seats. Mr Thompson opened the door as Stella stepped out of the sleek black Austin Princess, accompanied by her Uncle Bill.

'Thank you, Mr Thompson.' Stella smiled at the elderly man. He was a friend and neighbour of Mrs Brown and had generously offered to drive her to the church today.

'Stella, I thought you'd never get here.' Vera emerged from the church, holding up her long, pink dress so as not to trip over it. 'You're cutting it fine.'

'Is everyone here?'

'Everyone who needs to be, love.' Vera winked. 'Don't you worry. My Sam's been keeping an eye on him.'

Stella's heart leapt. The big day was finally here, and her man was waiting just a short walk away. She swallowed.

'Ready, Stella?' Uncle Bill held out his arm, his mouth curved up into a smile. 'Your dad would be right proud of you, lass.'

A lump rose in her throat as tears rushed to her eyes. She blew out a breath as Vera arranged the train of her dress. 'Thanks for being here, Uncle Bill.' She placed her hand on his arm and gazed down at her bouquet of pink carnations and fern as she caught the scent of their subtle sweet perfume on the breeze.

'Right then, all perfect. Ready?' Vera rose and ran her hands down her waist and hips, smoothing out her dress.

Stella glanced at her uncle, smiled, and nodded. She took a step forward, and Vera filtered in behind her, carrying a posy of pink carnations. They paused at the entrance, and Stella glanced down the red carpeted aisle to where Mac waited at the altar, his back to her, his wavy black hair gleaming. Seeing him there released a flight of doves from inside her soul and the breath caught in her throat. Beside him stood Wilson, his best man. Mrs Brown was seated at the organ, hands poised over the keys, staring directly at her, waiting for her cue. Stella nodded.

The wedding march rang out, and Stella glided down the aisle, past rows of polished mahogany pews, clutching her uncle's arm for support. Fresh carnations, gypsophila, and hydrangeas adorned vases placed on the altar and around the church. An icy breeze flowed around her, and Stella shivered, glad of the fur stole Mrs Brown had given her that morning. She'd said it was for 'something borrowed.'

The congregation rose. Mac's side of the church was fit to burst, with so many of his friends from the base. She spotted Colonel Edwards sat among them. Nestled near the back was Archie, along with Blackie, Pete, and Bea. She recognised them all instantly and smiled as she passed by. Archie grinned, his blue eyes sparkled, and he winked.

Her stomach rocked and fluttered. That was bound to be nerves. Everyone suffered from nerves before their wedding, didn't they? Her mother had called it the 'jitters.' She was almost there, and everyone paled into insignificance as Mac spun around and their eyes met. Heat flared in her cheeks as he gaped, his open mouth breaking into a broad smile. His uniform was immaculate, and she flicked her gaze over his medals which sat proudly over his left breast, the Purple Heart now complemented by the oak leaf cluster, the most recent addition. Uncle Bill turned and lifted her veil back and kissed her cheek. He took her hand and placed it in Mac's and a tingle like an electric current fizzed through her soul.

'You look so beautiful.' Mac squeezed her hand affectionately.

They both turned to face Reverend Peters, who smiled and glanced at Mrs Brown. The organ music ceased, and a low hustle filled the church – a mix of the wind outside and the people inside, shuffling on pews. The vicar began, and Mac wore a dazzling smile the entire time.

As the ceremony came to a close and Mac slipped the gold band onto her finger, Stella's heart swelled. He gazed lovingly into her eyes. 'About time, Mrs Mackenzie.'

Her stomach soared. She was the luckiest girl in the world, and her gaze lingered for a moment on the medals. Medals that came from fighting a war and from almost dying for your country. Blinking back tears, she linked her arm in his, and they went into the vestry to sign the register. As she scribed her married name in fresh ink, her eyes drank in every new letter formed – letters that bound them together for eternity.

'Well, Mrs Mackenzie. Are you ready to go greet our guests?' Mac held out his hand and winked and her stomach flipped.

The congregation rose and waited as the happy couple made their way slowly down the aisle, arm in arm. Outside the church, Mac's friends had lined up either side of the oak doors to form a guard of honour, with swords raised.

Mrs Brown had arranged for a photographer to take some pictures and there was a lot of fuss made about who needed to stand where and arranging her dress and so on. After several minutes, Stella began to shiver and her teeth chattered uncontrollably as her entire body chilled in the icy wind.

'How about you kiss the bride, Mac? We've come a long way to see this.'

'Archie!' Mac laughed and turned to Stella. 'Better do as the doc says, honey.'

She lifted her chin as he pressed his lips to hers, and a cheer erupted as cameras clicked furiously around them. The taste of him sent her heart soaring.

The trees shook, casting leaves of red and burned ochre into the wind, which scattered among them all like confetti. A few threw small handfuls of rice and Stella giggled when some of it slipped down the back of Mac's tunic jacket and slithered down his neck.

Mrs Brown and the ladies from the WI had done a marvellous job of transforming the village hall, and bunting bearing both the American and British flag hung all around the room, while vases of flowers adorned tables. The musty odour would soon be eclipsed by rising tobacco smoke, no doubt. As Stella strode across to the top table, she gazed admiringly at the feast. 'Oh, Mac. The cake's beautiful.' She admired the white iced two-tiered cake, complete with a miniature bride and groom decoration on top. 'And real fruit.' She grinned.

'Yeah, it sure is something.' He grinned back.

Once Wilson had delivered his best man's speech, it was time to hear from the groom. Mac scraped his chair back and stood up tall.

'Well, I'm not one for speeches, but I'd like to thank you all for helping us celebrate our special day.' He cast a gaze at Stella and smiled. 'Almost a year ago, I saw a beautiful girl across a smoky dance hall in Meldreth, and something smacked me hard in the chest. At that moment, I knew she was the girl for me. But what she didn't know was that she came along just when I needed to believe in something – or someone. And then when I was injured, rather than run for the hills, she decided that maybe I was worth sticking around for.' As the guests laughed, Mac glanced at Archie and nodded. 'And as for the doc there, why he even tried to poach her for his own staff, only the RAF weren't having any of it.'

Archie laughed and raised his glass as people turned to look at him. 'It's all true, of course. I'm well known for poaching staff and people.' He chuckled, and everyone laughed.

'So today I stand here because my beautiful wife and Archie refused to give up on me, and boy can they push and nag a guy.' More laughter rippled around the hall. 'I reckon I'm the luckiest guy in the world, so please raise your glasses in a toast to the bride.'

Everyone stood up and chorused, 'The bride.'

'And if I can just add, Archie, when you first saw me and said you'd fix me up, I didn't quite believe it, but you did.'

His voice faltered for a moment, and Stella reached out and took his hand in hers. He took a deep breath. 'And for that, I'll be forever in your debt, and I'll never forget what you did for me. Please, everyone, raise your glasses to Archie, the Maestro. A great surgeon, an even greater friend, and the perfect matchmaker.'

'Oh, now, I don't know about that.' Archie chuckled. 'You'd better check with the bride first.' Another wave of laughter.

'The Maestro,' everyone chorused.

'Here's to you, Archie.' Mac raised his glass as Archie grinned and nodded.

Mac gazed into Stella's eyes and brushed her lips with his while the guests smiled and cheered. She was the happiest woman on earth. Mac always said they were meant to be, and he was right.

The first notes of 'Moonlight Serenade' swayed out into the room, and Mac held out his hand. 'They're playing our song. Excuse me, ma'am. May I have this dance?'

Stella rose, and as he led her to the dance floor, he slipped his arm around her waist and placed his hand on the small of her back, firm and warm, his touch electric.

'Say, haven't I seen you before?' His blue eyes sparkled as he smiled, the skin crinkling at the corners, and his face lit up her world.

'Oh, Mac. You remembered this was playing when you first asked me to dance.' Tears pricked her eyes.

'Well, Mrs Mackenzie, how does it feel to be a married woman?'

'Perfect, and what about you?'

'A married woman?'

Stella laughed as he drew her close. One by one their guests joined them, filling the dance floor. 'You're mad.' She nestled her cheek against his tunic and drank in cedar wood.

'You'd better believe it, honey. And that's why you love me.' He planted a kiss on her lips. 'I have a little surprise for you, wife.' He smirked. 'How do you fancy two days at a top-class London hotel with all the trimmings?'

'Oh, that sounds perfect.' As the closing bars played, he held her against him and kissed her.

A little later, Stella passed Archie and overheard him talking about his work to a rather captive audience. Some of Mac's crew were huddled around, along with her mother and some of the WI ladies while Archie talked about tubed pedicles, describing them like elephant's trunks. She smiled to herself.

'Hey, Mac, Stella. We wanted you to be the first to know. Bea has agreed to marry me.' Pete beamed as he wrapped his arm around Bea's shoulders.

'Well, how about that? Congratulations.' Mac shook his hand and slapped him on the back, and he suddenly realised he was holding skin, rather than leather. Pete had finally ditched the gloves. He leaned in and kissed Bea on the cheek. 'That's swell news. I'm pleased for you both.'

'Well, that's not all. I'm staying on with the RAF. They're giving me a desk job.

'So much good news,' Archie said. 'Must be something in the water right now.' He smiled and shook Mac's hand. 'Congratulations. I knew you could do it.'

'Well, I almost didn't, and I have you to thank for that.'

'Oh, I didn't do anything at all. The credit is all Stella's.' Archie grinned and winked at her.

As Stella gazed at Archie's kind, genuine face, words failed her. There he stood, such an ingenious man, next to her husband – a man he had quite literally saved. And then there was Pete and all the others she'd met on Ward III. She understood why some of the men called Archie God, and when he turned to her and held out his hand and said goodbye, she smiled and hugged him. 'Thank you, for everything,' she whispered, as tears filled her eyes.

'Not at all, my dear. All in a day's work.' He chuckled. 'Just make sure you *live* life.' He pushed his spectacles up on his nose as his face broke into a huge grin.

'Mrs Mackenzie, how about you and I get a little fresh air.' Mac steered Stella away from their guests and led her outside. The air had chilled even more, and wafts of smoke drifted like smog from neighbouring chimneys.

Stella gazed admiringly at her new husband. He was so smart and handsome. 'I love you.'

He brushed a loose curl from her face. 'I love you too, honey, now and always.'

She moved towards him, raised her chin and gently caressed his face, both sides, comparing one to the other, smooth against roughened, reddened scar tissue. 'I love who you are, Mac. You're beautiful, inside and out.'

He kissed her brow. 'As long as I have you by my side, the world's my oyster.'

'It's funny, I never thought we'd see this day, and now here we are. It's a miracle really, isn't it?'

He cupped her chin and looked deep into her eyes. 'I was lost for a while, but you guided me back to where I needed to be. You showed me who I am and who I could be. You're the only woman for me, Stella. You're all I need. Without you, I'm nothing.'

'As Archie says, what good is a face if the man is not whole?' Stella smiled.

Mac was now whole, the circle complete. She linked his arm and a radiant warmth filled her inside and glowed so bright her cheeks warmed. A formation of Flying Fortresses droned from the east, and within minutes several dark cruciform shapes gracefully roared over their heads. Mac glanced up, his lips moving. He was counting them back.

'Nine.' He turned to her and kissed her gently, his breath warm, with a tinge of whisky. 'All back.'

'How did you know how many had flown today?'

'I counted them out this morning.'

She sighed. 'You miss it.' Stella tried to mask the sadness in her voice.

Mac held her face in his hands. 'You know, the truth is, I missed you more. And there's no place I'd rather be than grounded, here with you.'

Stella's heart drummed to the tune of love. 'You'll fly again, I know it.'

'I know, and I'm taking you with me, remember? Across the prairies, just like I said.' He slipped his arms around her waist and drew her close. 'You're my girl, now and forever.'

She smiled, leaning into his chest, drinking in undertones of cedar wood, with a hint of a prairie future and reminiscent notes of aircraft and war. Two white doves fluttered overhead, circling in the tranquil, sterile blue sky before swooping down to roost in the old oak tree across the road.

Epilogue

April 1990

The years slip by, though memories remain. While their form grows fuzzy, their outline blurred, they remain deeply rooted, roots that will thrive until the end.

Decades pass. Each Remembrance Day, they gather together at an old airfield, somewhere in England. They fly in from all across the United States, and a coach delivers them to Bassingbourn, the former home of the 91st Bomb Group. Sometimes it is sunny, more often it is raining, yet always a breeze blows through as faces and voices sail back to greet them, whispers carried on the wind.

They gather in the grounds by the memorial, seated in chairs in rows, facing the padre who reads the service. Wreaths are laid as old friends are remembered. A soldier plays the Last Post, blowing notes up to the heavens.

Later, they amble across the old airfield and pause for a few moments out on the perimeter track, sucking in the wind that blows in their faces where spirits soar. Memories resurface, blossoming with the breeze, and they pour over the procession of Flying Fortresses all biting to soar as one by one they hurtle down the track into the wind, screaming as they sail into the blue. Nostalgia swells and flows like the tide as they inhale reminiscent wafts of rubber, oil, cordite, and high octane fuel. Memories as vivid as ghosts.

John Mackenzie wanders a little further out, looking towards a corner of the field where once he landed his Flying Fortress, where once an old friend died, and he gazes across the entire site, drinking in the scene as he recalls those who returned and those who did not. A heaviness settles in his chest, an ache he has always carried, one which his wife lightens, although here today it is an oppressive burden once more as old wounds reopen. He catches his wife's eye and smiles.

Age has worked miracles, and his scarred cheek has sagged and settled into the worn skin which bears fresh, deeper lines. He wears age like a mask and here, at his old haunt, the breeze whispers familiar words in his ears. 'Time's a healer.' He sees the face of the nurse who spoke them and smiles to himself.

Red Swanson walks slowly with a cane, the old leg injury prodding him daily with memories of air battle. Val stands tall, taking in the old place as he gazes around, the left arm of his jacket empty, hanging by his side.

As they gather to examine the stretch of old concrete, Mike Wilson taps it with his foot, ruminating over how it's stood the test of time just as they have done, and they laugh. Before they leave, they turn their faces to the sun, squinting into the golden light to glimpse one last memory of those mighty cruciform shapes as they plough through the sky with their thunderous roar. For a fleeting moment, silence falls, sadness caresses their eyes and lips as they scan the sky and see, and as they turn their heads away, the sky is empty.

They move more slowly now, and the wives gather in a cluster and chat and smile while they leave their men to their brotherhood. This is, after all, *their* day. Some of the men have brought along their grandchildren, and they begin to tell stories, drawing the younger ones close, their innocent eyes wide and eager.

When Mac leaves this place, he will take Stella to East Grinstead and revisit the Beauty Shop at the old hospital in the town that did not stare. The hut that was Ward III still stands. His friend and surgeon, Archibald McIndoe, is no longer among them, having passed in 1960, but his memory lives on in all that he achieved and established. There is talk of a memorial to him and the men. Afterwards, they will stay with Pete and Bea for a few days before they fly home to Montana and their family.

Mac joins Stella, takes her hand, and brushes her lips with his. She is still the light, and he is hers, and like two fireflies they hover here at the beacon of Bassingbourn, the place where it all began.

Author's Note

This story is a blend of fact and fiction based on the actual story of the Guinea Pig Club. Sir Archibald McIndoe was indeed a real person, a plastic surgeon appointed by the RAF to run one of the four main burns units in the UK. The British government and the armed forces were planning in advance for war, and so when war was declared in September 1939, Archibald had a team in place, and they were ready to receive the first casualties of the war.

When a group of servicemen decided to form a drinking club in July 1941, they had no idea of the scale of their creation. The club would later be renamed the Guinea Pig Club, and the servicemen treated at East Grinstead, under the care of Archibald McIndoe, became known as "guinea pigs". The fee for membership was incredibly high, and one had to have been fried, mashed, or boiled as a direct result of the war in the air. It is a price many of us would not care to pay and yet, having heard some of the veterans speak about McIndoe and their own treatment, they say they would not change a thing.

What is so remarkable about this story is the sheer scale and power of the club, which is a registered charity, and the innovative approach taken by McIndoe. The two combined created an impressive force that aided and shaped the lives of hundreds of men. These men were not simply treated by a doctor, they were cared for and guided by a philanthropist.

Annual reunions have been held each year, and during these reunions, Archibald McIndoe would re-assess each man if required to see if and when any further treatment was necessary. He quite literally took these men under his wing, and while his methods at the time were viewed negatively by some, they worked, and he helped 'his boys' physically, psychologically and socially. He truly had such great affection for all of them.

While the American pilot in this story was treated at East Grinstead, in reality, this would most likely not have occurred, as the Eighth Air Force would have arranged to care for him appropriately, however, I am confident that Archie would have offered to help, had he known about such a man.

The Guinea Pig Club originally had 649 members, and these men came from Britain, America and all across the Commonwealth and Europe, including France, Belgium, Poland, Canada, Australia and New Zealand. They were the brave few who flew small fighter aircraft during the Battle of Britain and beyond, and they were the brave men who flew and crewed bomber aircraft. They all gave their thanks to their Maestro, Archibald McIndoe.

Today, there are seventeen remaining members. There is a memorial to this pioneering plastic surgeon, and it stands proudly in the town that did not stare, East Grinstead. In November 2016 a new memorial is to be revealed at the National Arboretum, in tribute to those brave men of The Guinea Pig Club. As long as there are people willing to read and write such accounts, we will never forget those who gave their today for our tomorrow.

The RAF pilots in Fighter Command faced appalling odds of survival, and 3,690 pilots were killed during the Second World War. For those serving with Bomber Command, the odds were formidable. 55,573 men were killed between 1939-1945. A total of 350,000 American men served with the Eighth Air Force in England. Of this number, 210,000 men flew combat missions and 26,000 men were killed.

> *In memory of Sir Archibald McIndoe (1900-1960), an outstanding plastic surgeon, son, brother, husband, father, and human being. He saw what others did not and pioneered great change. His memory and work live on today.*

Acknowledgements

My journey in writing this book has been long and emotional, and one which will remain lodged in my heart for many reasons. I would like to thank Dr A. C. Saunders, a member of The Guinea Pig Club, for his help and advice and for relaying his own, harrowing account of the accident that would see him inaugurated into this infamous club in 1945. Mrs Igraine Hamilton was most gracious in agreeing to help and provided much insight into life on Ward III, where she worked as a volunteer from 1940-1941, prior to joining the Women's Auxiliary Air Force.

Mr R Marchant is the Secretary of the Guinea Pig Club and a Trustee as well as the Guinea Pig Club Advisor at the East Grinstead Museum. His advice has been invaluable, and it was particularly insightful to speak with someone who worked alongside Archibald McIndoe. Simon Kerr, a Trustee at the East Grinstead Museum, the late Ilene Younghusband, a former WAAF & author, and the late Ron Brown, a former flight engineer with Bomber Command gave their time, information and advice for which I am forever grateful.

The photographer, Mr A Akrill, has been incredibly generous in allowing me permission to use some of his B-17 Flying Fortress images for marketing purposes. I am indebted to my many author friends who gave their generous time, and advice, and whose support is truly appreciated. My thanks also go to my amazing editor, Katherine Trail, who had a keen interest in the story and whose insights and encouragement gave me the confidence to write the book. Finally, to my family – thank you for being patient and supportive while writing drew me away. I am truly grateful and blessed.

32528364R00236

Printed in Great Britain
by Amazon